CHITTER CHATTER©

A HIP HOP INFLUNCED NOVEL

———————

CRESHIE WRITES®

Thank you . . .

To my heavenly father, for making all things possible. I thank him for guiding me from dark times to bright sunny days. Special thanks to my kids for not arguing and fighting while I write. Thank you to the father of my children for temporarily taking over the role of cooking and cleaning while I pursue my heart's dream. Thank you to my King who cheered and supported my dreams from the start. He kept me grounded when my emotions flew high. To all my family, friends and Sistahs: La Boogs, Nikki, Nukie, Monica, and Tia for reading every chapter as they were written morning, noon, and night. Although, I stalked them for feedback, they never complained out loud. Thanks to my brothers Charlie and Johnnie who were willingly to read a page, a paragraph or a sentence to be interrogated for feedback. They never once spoke of discomfort as they supported my dream. A special thank you to my heavenly mothers who still watch over me to this day like they had when they walked the earth. Thank you to Great, my beloved grandmother who taught all her lessons visually. Great lived up to her nickname given to her by my daughter. She was a great friend, a great mother and a great grandmother at all times and because she was great she wanted me to be great. She led by example so I strive to be great at all things I put my heart into. Thank you to my heavenly angels, Ms. Smith, EJ, Donnelly, and my Cindy Boo; they are my inspiration and motivation for my accomplishment. They were such strong powerful people that their presence is still felt while their bodies are gone. The inspirational songs produced by various artists like Ace Hood, Alicia Keys, Amerie, ASAP Rocky, Ashanti, Biggie, BBD, Bow Wow, Bobby Brown, Brandy, Chris Brown, Ciara, Destiny's Child, Diddy, DMX, Drake, The Dream, Elle Varner, Emeli Sande, Fabolous, Faith Evans, Future, J.Cole, Jadakiss, Jagged Edge, Jasmine Sullivan, Jay Z, Justin Timberlake, K.Michelle, Kanye West, Kelly Rowland, Kendrick Lamar, Kirk Franklin, Koffee Brown, L.O.X, Lil Kim, Lil Wayne, LL Cool J, Lloyd, Ludacris, Mariah, Mary J., Mase, Meek Millz, Miguel, Monica, Nelly, New Edition, Nicki Minaj, Ray J., Remy Ma, Rick Ross, Robin Thicke, Snoop Lion, Style P., SWV, T.I, TLC, Trey Songz, Tyga, Usher, Wale, Wiz Khalifa, Xscape, 2 Chainz, 50 Cent, Thank you for your sharing your talents of storytelling true facts through lyrics riddem and rhymes. Your riddem and rhymes lyrics were with me through every step taken in my life. I greatly appreciate the soul art of Hip Hop that you produce.

About the Author

Creshie is a native of El Barrio, Spanish Harlem. She was raised by her Grandmother along with four siblings and two cousins. She began her family early, she has two children. By day she is an accountant for a food mogul. She earned both her Associates and Bachelor degrees in Accounting at Monroe College. Creshie has also love to write love letters, poems and story stories for her closest friends and family's enjoyment. Her brother, Donnell pressured her to do more with her writing talent. When he passed on to being a heavenly angel, she felt like she owed it to her brother to give her writing dream a heart filled shot. After working fifty hours a week, having five surgeries and two close encounters with death, the self published book is finish. She hopes you enjoy the read.

CHITTER CHATTER©

"Yeah, I been in and out the bank bitch, while you asshole niggers been on the same shit."

Mr. Carter
Lil Wayne ft. Jay Z
Tha Carter III

"Lunch wit da accountant, dis shit is blowin mine." Crystal's chitachatter

Chitachatter (Chitter Chatter) *is the ultimate form free of expression. It's things swimming around in your head but never floats anywhere. It can be bias chaotic conversations between yourself. It might be a song playing. A melody you haven't heard in years. Lyrics, mentally returns you to a day the sounds represents. Perhaps, a persisting replaying tunes ringing between your ears. The repetition of musical buzzing, have you murmuring the jingle. It happens to everyone. Stop twisting up your face; it's one hundred percent true. If anyone says otherwise, they're lying. How many times have you heard people say "Something was telling me..." , "I got this song in my head and I just can't get it out." or been asked to guess the name of a song off of a humming clue. It's the biosphere where words can't be characterized. Words can't be accused of being politically incorrect by passing the need to bandage up any battered feelings. Facts, hearsay and opinions have a tendency to bruise. Chitachatter transpires inside your head and is assumed to stay there.*

"Once a week, I gotta put up wit dis shit, but I gotta be **Au courant**[1] *when it came to my chips. My money is my mother, my father, my sister, my brother, my lover and my friend. Basically my money is my whole universe. Thank God I got plenty chips, so I won't ever be lonely."*

Crystal often has a casual word-hiccup. Using words from distant countries, pronounces her travel sophistication. Ironically, her perfect enunciation of hood lingo told where she was from, not where she has been.

"I hate hearin how many chips I toss around or many I should've kept. These meetins always make me feel like she is tryin to criticize me or sommin. Yes, it's necessary to get a damn manni peddi everyday. A girl like me gotta have her nails and feet lookin good at all times, it's called

---

[1] **Au courant** *is being up to date with matters, in French.*

personal maintenance. It's my fuckin money. What's it to her? Why does she care? I only spent 5 **Hun-dough**[2] in personal maintenance last month? Not bad. It was up to 12, at one point. I'm slackin. I best to find a youngin quick to make me step my game up. Damn, she got me cuttin back on personal maintenance, wit no recognition. From da gate, she's been talkin to hear her own voice. Imma do whatever, whenever wit my shit. Shit, it's mine, so I spend it; I'm out here gettin it, why not? She bests to stop talkin out da side of her neck to me. She must've forgotten who is payin her black ass. I'll fire her ass in a heartbeat. She better start talkin like she wants her job today. All this shit 'bout what I been spendin my fuckin chips on. I've been payin her ass luv luv. I don't hear nuttin 'bout that. Just like I be puttin up wit her shit, she be puttin up wit mine shit too. It can't be easy. When I'm tight, I spread it. I make all employees ready to quit, if they don't manage to get their self fired first. Shit, I couldn't do it. Imagine me workin for somebody? Never dat! It aint all bad for her. I be throwin her perks and shit, after all, she do be tryin to work hard or hard at work lookin like she workin hard. She owes big time, doe. Gettin and keepin her monstrous lookin son of hers in private school, on the Upper east side, wasn't no walk in da park. "The education for gifted and talented" I was at Westbrook I aint see one gifted or talented kid up in there, ya heard! The talent is how they dig up in ya pockets and ya gotta be gifted wit deep pockets like me to even look at the school. Ya already know off the title, what it is? A school designed for da rich. A high price, bullshit school when all ya get is what cha pay for, da damn name. And ya know da rich kids is gettin a costly public school education, if dat. Not worth my fuckin chips, but it was a hook up for her ungrateful ass. I had to pull major strings to get his scary ass up in there, puttin my name on line and shit. Through da whole process of forcin him on da school, I met him 1 time, and dat was 1 too many times, for me. I never wanna see dat lil' baked potato shaped head kid again. As for myself, his looks make me queasy. I hate kids, period. Even if they are cute they are still intolerable."

---

[2] **Hun-dough** is a hundred dollars.

Crystal's chitachatter drives on a roads paved of chips, toward acceptance, but curves on a street of boisterous gloating. The guardrail of seniority overturns her destination. Accelerated steps on others flesh, fabricates heels of taller beauty. Crystal's acquired beauty tailgates to her hollow insides. Majority of the once a week lunch meetings begin and end with Crystal's fine tunes of ranting and raving but today Crystal just sits across from Lisa Scott, her accountant. Her tongue appears to be bind by restraints. The *François Trimestre* restaurant has soft candle lit for light. The walls are covered in French art. The right side of the wall in the dining area has double French door leading to the outside dining area. Today is a freak day in the middle of winter. Spring isn't set to arrive for another two more months but the sunshine is bright like a summer day. The sweet warm rays of the sun heats the soul. The French double doors are open today and a savory stream of fresh flowers blows in tickling the nose with hopes of spring's arrival. The oval tables are dressed in French white silk fabric. The table is formally set French style with the golden silverware and gold trim white bowls, glasses and plates. In front of each chair is a dinner plate, on top of the dinner plate sits a soup bowl. In the center of the soup bowl is a French fan made out of a cloth dinner napkin. To the right of the dinner plate tower is the golden silverware. Above the golden silverware on the right are a sherry glass, white wine glass, red wine glass, and a water goblet glass. The happiness of the French can now be appreciated knowing they have three glasses of wine with their meals. On the left side of the dinner plate tower is a gold trimmed salad plate accompanied with a golden salad fork and a golden dinner fork. As the meal is enjoyed the many gold trimmed plates and golden silverware disappear by the end of the meal the table is cleared. Crystal chooses this restaurant once a week to meet with Lisa. She claims to Lisa she misses the French kiss of the air from her childhood. Crystal's tongue likes to lead Lisa's thought into believing she was raised in Paris. Crystal is a self proclaimed frequent flyer but she has visited France twice in her lifetime. *François Trimestre* captures a piece of France and brings the essence overseas to New York in Manhattan's SoHo area. Crystal's mind journeys to foreign lands, blue skies, transparent water, without leaving her chair. Crystal sails on Lisa's waves of words into her own chitachatter. Through Crystal's eyes she envisions her pleasures. The delights of many desirable men laid out on a beach, invades Crystal's vision. Throbbing manhood's ready, willing and able, fascinates Crystal's imagination. Men laid out the long way, standing tall clouds Crystal's subconscious.

"I need a few good men ready for ya girl. Better skillz then 96 percent of them so-called porno superstars. Shit, if Kim Kardashian can become famous and make mills off of a whack home video, my sexy ass can't double dat. I'm not gonna even touch the subject of a vixen stealin my title and I've seen her work. I know at least ten niccas that would pick my mouth skills over hers hands down!"

Lisa is a modest woman. She composes her professionalism, in spite of Crystal blatant disrespect. She begins with an itemized recap of excessive prior monthly spending. She ends explaining preferred stock percentiles in depth to Crystal. In the middle of the presentation, she offers sound advice, not as Crystal's paid Accountant but out of genuine concern. Crystal's personal maintenance has a price tag of an additional hundred fifty dollars, a service fee, to the original cost of one hundred seventy five dollars for feet and nails cosmetic service. Lisa insists Crystal go to a salon to eliminate house call fees. Lisa wouldn't bring up the topic of the three thousand dollar custom twin designer raincoats for Crystal's two toy Yorkies. Thank god, Crystal doesn't have a current boy toy. Then Lisa would be discussing lavish trips and generous gift giving. One would think she is casting for Robin Leach. Crystal lifestyle of the rich bought her fame. Lisa has Crystal's best interest at heart. This ridiculous sending can land Crystal in the poor house. Lisa looks over to Crystal for understanding validation. Crystal doesn't turn to face Lisa. The left side of Crystal's body is facing Lisa. Crystal is holding her diamond shape head up with the back of her left hand. Her legs crossed outside the table. Crystal's cold vanilla false Caucasian pigment shot chills in Lisa's direction. Lisa gawk at her posture. Crystal reposition her elbow on the table, as if, Lisa's stares rubs her the wrong way. Lisa's voice remains monotone. Lisa's dignity sores above Crystal's plane. Lisa is honorable for inhaling her frustration and not exhaling turbulence on Crystal. Crystal browses the restaurant. Her hooded mud brown eyes hustles the fellow patron's body shapes, facial features, hair, make-up, nails, outfits and anything else she can find to look down on to boost her spirits up. She drifts to fool's paradise and cruise to reality at will. She is professionally trained on blocking Lisa out. Lisa's research, illustrations, and analyzes of the future state of Crystal's finances had no meaning to Crystal's attention. Crystal could have the decency or just a crumb size common courtesy to at least listen to the collaboration of Lisa's hard work. Lisa looks over at Crystal. Crystal has a vacant expression occupying her cold vanilla false Caucasian face and distances in her hooded mud brown eyes. Three ladies, across the room, sitting and dining together has captivated Crystal's concentration. From their looks they had to be around the same age as Crystal, late thirties to early forties but if you ask Crystal she'll say they look about mid fifties, early sixty. Crystal added age to people to subtract from her own age.

"Yuck, yellow clean piss complexion and veins poppin out from under her skin lookin like MTA's multi-color train map, especially around da eyes and mouth. She looks plain 'ole awful. Pissie minute long hair got some white-ish mixed wit a little yellow-ish blond-ish color. A kitchen dye, I'll betcha. Dat kitchen dye blend wit her skin, 'jus ugly. And she got da nerve to be rockin black painted on eyebrows and inch long eyelashes. Da lashes on her eyes is longer than da damn hair on her little round head. Her tities sittin on da table like elbows. Da one to da left of her, even more fucked up. 2 more shades darker and she'll have dat **blurple**[3] *glow, dat street vendor, African blurple glow. Can ya believe her? Still sportin a wave fro? Maybe she was goin for dat mix bred look, but failed, aint a curl or twist up in dat bird's nest. Lips so big, she should be makin a good livin on them ashy knee caps she showin with no shame. I can spot*

---

[3] **Blurple** *is a blend of the colors blue and purple.*

imperfection from a mile away. I saved da best laughs for last. Yeah, this one had a work-down job on her grill, but how? By da looks of, their hair, outfits and shoes they damn sure aint got no chips, much less a penny. I wanna know how they gonna pay for their meal? Dis restaurant is suppose to be **a' la carte**[4]. And when was da last time they ate a real meal? I hope one of dem don't choke 'cus they bustin that food down with no breathers. Damn they really are scoffing dat shit down? This is a French restaurant not a damn super ball party in your living room. "Hood rats found their way to a high end restaurant" movie trailer. **Puthum**[5] on da poster in the train, where the rats live. They gotta know how to get there, if not follow the line under pissie's eyes to find your way. Da made face one, is stuck in eighties, dis aint footloose and you damn sure aint no eighties baby. Where ya find shinny zebra printed spandex at? Bargain table zebra printed high heels, really? Her damn loose short sleeved shirt, is strugglin, like hell, to stay on her body. Not like it was covering anything 'cus it was see-through, da damn bra too. I could see her hard nipples from here. Imma complain to Management. I don't wanna see hard nipples while I'm fucking eatin. Straight up **insalubres** [6]. Some woman can't accept their damn age. If ya fifty, be fifty. Act, dress and talk like ya fifty, for ya grandkid's sake. Ya gonna make their lives a living hell. Nobody wanna hear how fat ya grandmother's ass is. She done fixed dat damn shirt 20 times in da last 5 minutes. She straighten da shirt up, and it slide to da left. She straighten da shirt back up and in 4 seconds it would slide to da right. Yeah, four seconds exactly I counted. Might as well take da shit off. Da whole damn restaurant already know what's under the fuckin shirt. These chicks are downright atrocious. I wouldn't be caught dead in their company. It's bad enough I'm sitting with this fuckin hermit right here."

---

[4] **A' la carte** is Britain term for ordering each item of a meal separately. Each item is also billed in the same fashion.
[6] **Puthum** translate to "put them"

[6] **Insalubres** English translation from French is unsanitary

Crystal rolls her hooded mud brown eyes at the thought of Lisa. Crystal's eyes scrutinize the three ladies interaction with each other, from a distant. They appear to be truly enjoying each other's company, laughing, talking, and little child like taps to one another. It was obvious; a deep bond is shared between the ladies. A sun shining bond strongly built through rainy days. The sexy silky chocolate fudge woman with coily soft curly hair heavy one top, thin in the middle and light on the bottom frame sits with her two other women. The luminous skinned woman with the ultra light blonde baby curls is sitting side by side with the sexy silk chocolate fudge woman. On the other side of the oval table sat a voluminous woman with tasty cappuccino curves covered in zebra print spandex and on her feet are matching zebra printed six inch pumps.

"Bullshit, dat friendship shit aint real. Ya can't fool me. Hussies be actin like everything is all good to ya face. But behind ya back hussies holdin court, convicting ya of fallacious charges wit no evidences, that's how "friends do ya". Ya end up pleading to a jury ya never even meet."

Watching the ladies connection with each other caused a network of unfamiliar emotion in Crystal's insides. Crystal contemplates having a humane relationship. Her companions are two toy Yorkie dogs. Her only form of accompanied recreation is dog walks around her home.

"Put me on trial. I to wanna be fake, smile in hussies faces and talk about dem behind their back. I wanna be **esprit de corps** [7] *too."*

Crystal stumbles into a trance. She materializes herself to be at the ladies' table, sitting amidst the ladies. She saw herself laughing and joking among the ladies. She sits alongside Miss slippery shirt. She aids the shirt back over her left shoulder. Overcome by temptation she finger fuck Miss slippery shirt's hair. Her fingers will determine and measure

---

[7] **Esprit de corps:** *A unique bond among a group of people*

the quality of the golden blond weave. Crystal concludes the hair looks and feels just like straw, just as suspected from her seat.

"I know damn well having friends is a far fetch fantasy, for ya girl. My big ole' stacks of chips are a barrier wit a sign hangin on it screamin "KEEP OUT". Biggie never lied, when he said, "more money, more problems". So what I'm boxed in by my chips, they will never for-snake me, guaranteed. When dealing with people you take a gamble. Only with my chips will I always win."

"Crystal!" Lisa sternly murmured through her soft southern milk chocolate lips. Lisa's slightly heighten tone is ignored. Crystal didn't budge a muscle.

"Fuck her, who she gettin loud wit? Why she keep forgettin where her chips fall from. Surprisingly, she even noticed I wasn't paying attention to her dull ass. If ya add a lil color to her damn wardrobe maybe I could fake listen? Her wardrobe is the same damn business suit in different shades of black, from light ashy to dark ashy. Lookin at her homely hermit ass, make me wanna buy her sommin. But her looks is one thang money couldn't fix, trust I've tried. Under privilege can't be covered up wit expensive clothes and not still show. Once she start bumpin dem gums, her eyes widen behind the Prada glasses. Cheetah printed frame I bought. If I had to look at her ass once a week, I had to have sommin' to look at. I remember the first day I hired her; I had a long hard talk about proper exterior. Any woman rubbin elbows witcha girl had to have the basics in order. Eyebrows, hair, and nails must be done. I nearly threw-up when I spotted dirt up under her nails, at the first meetin. I refuse to cut her slack 'cause she was just startin out. Ya gotta put some things first in ya life. For every woman, worldwide, appearance should be first. Ya whole world can be crumbling around ya. But if ya appearance is up, nobody would ever know. Lookin at these three train rats over there I can see they also missed the appearance lesson wit Lisa's common ass."

A small giggle escapes from Crystal's chitachatter laughter. "CRYSTAL!" Lisa squealed through her soft southern milk chocolate lips.

Crystal slightly tilts her diamond shaped head toward Lisa's direction, in announce. Lisa calling her name has disturbed her. Chitachatter is more entertaining to Crystal than Lisa's rhetoric. Crystal appears to be staring at Lisa's soft southern milk chocolate lips awaiting words to flow but Lisa has paused pending Crystal's response. Silence sat between them.

"I'm done wit dis bitch. It's time to dismiss her boring ass. Dats her last time today acting like she's getting loud or sommin. She best to act like she knows I'm da boss. She'll be full of regrets and jobless."

"Crystal, are you listening? You finally have a suitable offer for your grandfather's empire. The empire you've been desperately wanting to sale. Remember? The buyer agrees to all terms." Lisa's enthusiastic approach bounced with every word out her soft southern milk chocolate lips.

Lisa has been unloading Crystal's inherited assets to the highest bidder for years. This is her last sale. She is eager to close the deal with the buyers. The buyers are a two party team of brothers. Lisa truly didn't appreciate how the brothers drooled over her. Obeying Crystal's outrages demands, Lisa wore a hot red fitting blazer, accompanied by a black and white striped fitting mini skirt, to the meeting. The stripes on the shirt are perfectly symbolic to how she felt in the ensemble. She often felt like a Crystal's prisoner, now she had the stripes to match. The price Lisa has to pay for the outfit was hearing Crystal's endless bragging about buying it for her. Crystal's consist bragging snagged at Lisa especially since she hated the outfit. Too flashy, too tight just too much for Lisa's style. Southern woman have a dress code.

"No changes to the business? Everybody gets to keep their jobs?" Crystal asks through her pale pink painted bottom lip and her thin upper lip.

Lisa is baffled, speechless. She was fired for making this amendment to contract. A change to business operation or employment after acquisition is prohibited as per Lisa. The burden of employed pioneers being jobless after generations of labor calluses wasn't Crystal's concern. Lisa voiced her relations to the blue collar families and stood behind her strong views. Lisa pushed the amendment forward on the contract. Lisa put her views ahead of her job. Now, Crystal attentively inquires about the job security of the company pioneer employees. Formally Crystal could care less. Maybe in the future, she'll state it was her idea, followed by an acceptance peach. "I did it for the kids, Crystal loves the kids." Crystal swaps seats with her purse, now she is sitting side by side with Lisa. She invades Lisa's personal space. Lisa moves over, to make room for Crystal, nearly falling out her chair.

"I gotta make sure I'm hearing her right. Is it time to cash out?" Crystal's chitachatter

The sound of millions of coins falling echoed in Crystal's diamond shaped head. Slot machine's sirens glow behind her empire hooded mud brown eyes. With the last piece of property, stamped with family name, sold the family name will expire. The final sale will sever her affiliation, along with the family name itself, is Crystal thoughts. Crystal currently owned her grandfather's empire a bitter sweet inheritance from her mother's passing on. Ownership reminds Crystal of her mother. Crystal inherited many assets, stocks and a mansion in Virginia. What she didn't inherit along with the money was with the ancestors' priceless morals. The mansion she sold for three million dollars. After auctioning off the appliances, dishwasher, dryer, refrigerator, stoves and washer Crystal's appetite for money was still hungry. She then clearance off all the furniture out the mansion but still needed to feed. She even bargained off the chandeliers and light fixtures as a meal to her bank account. The mansion was stripped domestically. If it had any value, Crystal sold it all. All the money she gained didn't add up to having a mother. She would say she'll give it all back just to see my mother one more time, but who would she tell. Better yet who would believe her?

"How much is the offer?" Crystal's thin upper lip questions Lisa. Crystal's greed stares at Lisa, awaiting a response. Crystal is growing impatient for the answer. Lisa looks up from the pile of papers work in her hands, which she fumbled through from time to time.

"12.5 million, Will be what you'll receive after fees within 10 years." Lisa leans back in her chair. Lisa spares Crystal the details; she knows Crystal interest rests in the bottom dollar. Lisa braced herself for the usual tantrum performance, Crystal is infamous for.

"Is the equipment separate?" Crystal's thin upper lip asks.

"Yes, Crystal, just like you stated in the contract."

Lisa strongly advises Crystal the offer wasn't a lot of money. Crystal could capitalize if she maintains dominions of the empire. Tire production is a lucrative industry. But distance from the family name is Crystal's claimed focus. Lisa suggests changing the name of the empire. Crystal would find another shameless excuse of why selling the empire is commendable on her part. She didn't want to make money on the family's name, but in all actuality she was, by selling the empire. Crystal threatened Lisa with her job for pointing out facts to Crystal. Lisa wasn't allowed to enlightening Crystal on the facts of any matter.

"Fine, where's the pen?" Crystal reached her right hand out.

Lisa quickly rummaged through her brown saddleback leather briefcase. Lisa wasn't prepared for Crystal to sign without a loud embarrassing display of childish behavior. In fact the whole restaurant was peeking over their shoulder for the foresight of Crystal's weekly performances. Lisa hands over the pen to Crystal. Crystal's signature is relief to Lisa's soul. Lisa thanks the heavens. No afternoon show of embarrassment from Crystal today makes Lisa more than anxious to part with Crystal on these terms. Lisa feverishly flips the pages as Crystal signed page after page. When all the pages were signed Lisa let out a soulful sigh. Finally, an ongoing process that could've been resolved in a matter of months screeched two years finally now it's being brought to a close. Crystal swaps seats with her purse again. Crystal returns to her original seat across the table from Lisa.

"I'm glad this shit is over." Crystal leaned back on her chair letting out a sigh from her thin upper lip and signaled for the waiter all in one movement. Lisa slides her left butt cheek back on to chair.

"So, we're done here?" Crystal had a way of speaking at Lisa not really to her in a distinguished superior tone through her thin upper lip.

"Yes, we are finish, I'll call you when the first check is released, and it's going to take few days. I'll call you." Lisa responds.

Lisa emphasizes on giving Crystal the call if she didn't Crystal will start stalking Lisa. Lisa gathers her southern dark brown trench coat and briefcase and headed towards the exit with the belt of her jacket trailing behind her. Lisa hurried and got out of Crystal's area. In second Crystal's rudeness would advance, and Lisa would've been fired today for the thousandth time within ten years. Crystal is full of air. When the wind blow Lisa is by Crystal's side. Crystal fire Lisa and a day later come on her knees with her money in her hand to hire her back. That's how Lisa got her son in private school, on Crystal's dime. And he'll be there until he graduates from high school. Lisa is all she has, whether Crystal admits it to herself or not. When Crystal's sick, who nurse her cold vanilla false Caucasian skin back to healthy pigment? I'll tell you who, Lisa. To be quite frankly, Lisa is her only friend and family. You would think she'd treat Lisa a hell of a lot better. Crystal reaches down in her, white and gold, Ferragamo handbag that sits in the chair that separated her from Lisa, laughing at Lisa's belt dragging on the floor. She pulls out her Gucci sunglass case, using the camera on her iPhone to check her mask of make-up. Checking up on her million dollar face, making sure everything is still in position. She is sure it's fine. She eats with poise.

"The art of eatin with poise take talent. You pull the food off the fork with your teeth, so your lipstick doesn't smudge. Sommin Lisa never practiced."
Crystal's chitachatter

"Yes Ms. Moore, what can I get you?" the waiter stands beside Crystal's right side.

"What can you get from me?" Crystal's thin upper lip mimics the waiter with her distinguished superior tone.

"You can't get me nothing but the fuckin' check. You cleared the table 9 and half minutes ago. How long am I supposed to sit here, waiting on a fuckin' waiter, huh?" Crystal's words shot from her thin upper lip shoving the waiter around.

Crystal verbally assaults the waiter. The waiter didn't take offense. He was use to the assaults, she dined here once a week and by luck he always end up as Crystal's waiter.

"Immigrants can't give good help nowhere, dis days, I swear"

Crystal wants to leave before the three ladies leave the restaurant. She didn't want them to see her sitting at the table by herself. She would never dine alone. No real woman dines alone is Crystal's beliefs. Crystal's thought are too late. The three woman stands and the waiter walk over to the ladies with their jackets on hangers.

"Look at these three cheap jackets, here. Those jackets looks like homeless men donated them. Da bald, da blurple and da tacky are still cacklin. Ain't nuffin dat damn funny! Squawkin for a forty-five minutes I know ya face

gotta hurt from holding that fake smile like that. Here they go, all animated, and shit. Give it a break, fake as hell and I know counterfeit when I see it. I've been around enough chips to know real from fake."

The three woman walked pass Crystal's table. The luminous white chocolate skinned woman, with the ultra light blonde baby curls double takes at Crystal.

"I don't know what dis bald headed pale bitch is starin at? She best to keep movin with her friends, before I throw water on her face and wash away her eyebrows."

The luminous white chocolate skinned woman turns her head around again toward Crystal. Then her body followed. She starts taking steps towards Crystal. Crystal immediately jumps up behind the table.

"Come get ya face washed, glow worm."

"Crystal Moore?" The luminous white chocolate skinned woman questions with a puzzled look glowing on her face.

The luminous white chocolate skinned woman tilts her body to the right, as if the angle gave her a better view of Crystal. Her slow quick steps bring her body closer toward Crystal.

"Why her face is looking like Bow Wow's on 106 and park when Ciara's futuristic videos come on? Awkwardly stiff. Fix your face, Hun. You know who I am, stop fronting?" The luminous white chocolate skinned woman's chitachatter.

"Who is dis bald headed chick? Damn she gotta get a hat. See this da dumb shit? I just can't handle. I recognize the face, but from where? Just by lookin at dis glow worm, I know she isn't someone I would rub elbows wit but how she knows my name?" Crystal's chitachatter

Crystal's diamond shape head aligned straight up. She is facing toward the luminous white chocolate skinned woman afoot. Crystal's hooded mud brown eyes drop down to the woman's shoes and slowly inches back to light skinned woman's face.

*"Ya can tell a hellava lot about a woman from her shoes. Ya rockin cheap shoes on ya tootsies. Ya don't care 'bout ya tootsies. Ya have to treat ya feet good. Its da body part dat gets the most use. Dem **Jim swingers** [8]on her feet, definitely no name. No name aint in my **ordre du jour** [9].Da brightness of dat dress is hurtin my eyes. I knew I took out my shades for a reason I should've put dem on. Oh boy, do I need them right now. It's the end of winter, spring aint here yet. Why she running around lookin like a pink tie dye Easter egg with dat bald head and MTA lines. Dat dress is right off a summer Target commercial, for sure. I can't stay focus. Dat yellow hair and face, wit dat hot pink dress is givin me a headache. Baldie where I know ya from? I gotta figure it out. So I can dismiss her bright cheap lookin ass outta my sight. She's fuckin up my vision."*

The luminous white chocolate skinned woman leans back away from Crystal, with her arms out, wiggling her fingers. The woman is suggesting Crystal to come in closer for a hug. Still nothing is coming to Crystal's mind.

*"Dis chick is trippin, I don't hug the broke, it's **insalubres** [10].She's gonna get dat cheap pink dye on my Dolce Gabbana white lace dress, off the Vogue cover. Limited edition, only 3 in the world, and I got one. I just got it outta da cleaners, dat pink is gonna ruin it. Baldie what is your name? C'mon Crystal think. Who is dis chick? I gotta get away from her. She's fuckin up my outfit. Just standin next to Baldie, I'm startin to feel broke."*

---

[8] **Jim swingers** *are very cheap men shoes.*
[9] **Ordre du jour:** *Agenda*
[10] **Insalubres :** *unsanitary*

"Madison PJ's?" The luminous white chocolate skinned woman speaks as she tilts her head to the right side, with her lips twisted up in the air. Using the tone people use when catching another person in a lie.

The word "Madison" sends chills down Crystal's cold vanilla false Caucasian spine, in that moment; the name and face collided in Crystal's mind and a queasy feeling in her stomach started. I'll tell you how to get to Madison Projects. All projects are one in the same. It's a place where everybody knows your name. It's a place where all are living and surviving the same name game. It's where our trouble is all the same. Govern mental tools built to help but only keep us under the belt. The best stagnation ever felt. Part of the unemployment rate, check late sitting in front of an empty plate. To eat you have to make your own fate. Deemed society rejects. Oh, Madison projects, I'll tell you how to get there. Try walking the straight and narrow but the crooked arrow is in the bone marrow. Roll out of bed. Hit the head. Mr. Coffee is dead. Gloomy days blow clouds out our face. In the race moving at our own pace. Tom cats and felines keep up the lies. Come and play everything is A-OK. Stomach is on the gate. Can't live like this without an expiration date. Govern mental doom from the slate but hate doesn't choose your fate. But watch your back because hate travels in packs. The reliance of the black can't be covered. Stand strong overcome the long haul. All projects are one in the same. Madison projects, oh I'll tell you how to get there but you can find it anywhere. It's the place of the experimental people. It's the place where the youth is temperamental to be the sequel. Rise above the devil in the hole. Above is light. Climb up the pole. Gain the personal moon glow. Go where flowers grow. Wiser to the "know" and now it show. Walk through the garden of "hello's" "thank yous" "your welcomes" and "how you do's". Life is sweet but low. Money is always slow. I can tell you where to go but you already know. Rewind, fast forward but remain in the same place. At night we say our grace. All classed as society rejects. Some proves them wrong and eject. Crystal eject from Madison Projects. She has disassociated herself from Madison

Projects in body and mind. In Crystal's opinion Madison Projects is the creator of a dark place filled with despair.

"Rhonda Wilson?" Crystal's puzzled reply slither out her thin upper lip distinguished superior tone.

"Oh hell to da no, I know dis bitch. I thought I left dis rodents in da dark. How they found their way down to Soho. Dis supposes to be a damn upscale restaurant. But now I know they be servicing rodents, I won't be back." Crystal's chitachatter

Crystal is scanning the room for the waiter, and on cue, the waiter arrives. Crystal's swivels in her purse, snatching out a hundred dollar bill out and hands it over to the waiter. Within milliseconds, her Burberry light jacket was on her back. Her uneasily demeanor was transparent even Ray Charles could see it. The luminous white chocolate skinned woman made Crystal uncomfortable. Crystal's hands tremble. Madison projects are a parts of Crystal's life she has buried deep into memory, but looking at Rhonda's face, memories crashed into sight. The forgotten period of life was going through Crystal's mind like a cartoon flip book. Crystal takes a step forward toward the door. Crystal's movement is interrupted by Rhonda's sudden step in front of Crystal's foot. Rhonda's movement, blocks Crystal's path. Rhonda turns around to the two women awaiting her at the exit, and beckon for them to come over. She turns back to Crystal, exhibiting a silly child like grin. Rhonda is truly amused at Crystal's discomfort.

"I know you remember Tay Tay and Chyenne? Rhonda asks. Tay's fully legal name is Taynasha.

"Hey girl" Tay released the dry words from her heart shaped lips, because she knew Chyenne wouldn't part her sexy silk chocolate fudge lips to say a word to Crystal.

"If I was you I'd take precaution, before I step to meet a fly girl, you know, cause in some portion, you'll think she's the best thing in the world. She's so fly, she'll drive you right out of your mind. Steal your heart when your blind. Beware she's scheming. She'll make you think you're dreaming. You'll fall in love and you'll be screaming demon. Poison. Ooooh yeah, never trust a big butt and a smile." Bell Biv DeVoe must know Crystal's poisonous ass personally, everything she touch turns to shit, literally." Tay's chitachatter

Tay's chitachatter reiterate riddim, rhythms and perfectly selected words, from her inter radio, to harmonize her reactions.

"Yes, I do, How ya'll doing?" the words fought to get pass Crystal's clenched teeth and escaped her thin upper lip. She imitates a greeting.

Crystal's reluctance to remise into her past has been defected. Pictures of the Madison projects are no longer quick passing images. Whole scenes begin to invade Crystal's vision. Crystal is more than anxious to exit at this point.

"How I'm doing? Savaging for the pieces of my fucking life, you broke apart. BITCH. Crystal Moore, don't remember me. Do you remember your bulldozer used to reconstruct my being? Huh, BITCH? Da pain you cause will last me a lifetime but you don't remember me." Chyenne's chitachatter

Chyenne's chitachatter is the concierge at heartbreak hotel. All rooms reserved to testimonial despair. No vacancy for evolution to check in.

"Hey girl, where ya been? Long times don't see. How's life been treating ya?" Rhonda shot question after question at Crystal.

Rhonda didn't give Crystal the chance to answer one question before she shot another question at her. Rhonda hadn't seen Crystal in years. Rhonda enjoys agitating Crystal's uncomfortable spot. Crystal's cold vanilla false Caucasian pigment is flushed with red annoyance. Rhonda notices Crystal's dispatch for the exit in her hooded mud brown eyes. Suddenly Rhonda wraps her arms around Crystal's body tuning up her **chi chi**[11]. She kissed Crystal on the right cheek, giving her a chummy greeting to seal the deal. Crystal strong arm herself to give an air kiss to the left side of Rhonda's chi chi face. Chyenne and Tay just stands on the sideline watching Rhonda at work.

*"Damn, she stinks. Besides da alcohol separating from her cheap perfume, da stench of da hood is steaming from her pores. Get da hell off me! Imma have to take my dress back to the fuckin cleaners to take da smell out, damn. This glow worm got broke, pink and the odor of a fuckin skunk all on me. **Je n'ai jamais**[12] !" Crystal's chitachatter*

"Achoo" Crystal sneezes.

"God bless you, Ya catching a cold?" Rhonda expresses her chi chi concern.

"Thank you, allergies." Crystal mumbles through her thin upper lip.

"Yeah, I'm allergic to bald, blurple and tacky rats from da hood. Move outta my way glow worm, so I can get da hell outta here. Talkin to ya'll counterfeit rats don't make no sense, ya'll ain't 'bout no dollars. I gotta go." Crystal's chitachatter

Rhonda's chi chi is at a hundred degrees. Chyenne keeps her distance from Crystal. Chyenne lacks the ability to be chi chi on demand. Chyenne dislike this woman and everybody knows it. Chyenne waves in Crystal's direction with her hand never leaving her right side, strictly out of politeness. Chyenne didn't want to deal with her friends questioning her advancement of restoration later on.

---

[11] **Chi chi** is being phony.
[12] **Je n'ai jamais:** 'i have never'.

"I would love nothing more than to get all caught up with the blast from the past but, I'm late for an important meeting, I gotta go." Crystal glances at the glass face of a David Yurman gold and diamond watch, on her left wrist as the words spill from her thin upper lip in her distinguished superior tone. Crystal politely brush pass Rhonda making her way to the exit.

"Hold up, let me get ya number, Tay 40th b-day bash is coming, it's this weekend, come kick it witcha girls for da past." Rhonda has her phone in hand. She awaits Crystal's thin upper lip to spit out the numbers.

"2-0-3-4-7-6-0-4-4-0" Crystal's thin upper lip is spitting the numbers in the air like an auction host. The last two numbers she spat over her right shoulder back in Rhonda direction as she raced toward the exit.

"Look at this Bishop type bitch with no juice. She can move forward or backward, but in only one direction. Because she move diagonally, and never straight up she will always remain on a square which she started the game on." Rhonda's chitachatter is talking about Crystal.

"Front NOW!" Crystal squawked into her phone, at her driver before her right foot landed outside the restaurant.

Crystal sits in the back of Lexus RX 350, out of breath and rattled. *"Shit, I didn't get my change from da fuckin immigrate, runnin from dem rats. Being all nosy, sniffin around like rodents do. Where I been? I've been where you haven't been. Shit, maybe I'll show up to their lil house party for some quick laughs at their expense. Show them what royalty looks like. Saw Chyenne bitter ass, still harboring feelins. Get over it." Crystal's chitachatter*

The three woman stands in awe watching Crystal practically break her neck to get to the exit. Chyenne transferred her attention along with her annoyance from Crystal to Rhonda.

"How dare you invite that bitch? I don't want her nowhere around me. Did you forget what she did to me?" The distress and pain made Chyenne voice fluttered in volume.

Chyenne is questioning Rhonda's motives as they too head toward the exit of the restaurant.

"Chyenne grow up." Rhonda responds.

"She's been down and out. She's been wrote about. She's been talked about, constantly. She's been up and down. She's been pushed around, but they held her down NYC. She has no regrets. She accepts the past. All these things, they help to make her. She's been lost and found and still around. There's a reason for everything. You know I've been holdin on. Try to make me weak but I still stay strong. Put my life all up in these songs jus so you can feel me. So take me as I am or have nothing at all." Mary j is swing from the mirror of Chyenne's heart. She went thru a time years ago and we get it. We were there we felt and seen it all. But at what point do you just let it go?" Tay's chitachatter

"You can always remember what you've experience, as a life lesson. But you have to find it in heart to just let go of the past. Harboring old feelings will only consume you and swallow you whole, Chyenne." Tay chimed in quickly, trying to water the fire before it grew.

Tay is having a nice day. Rhonda and Chyenne scream-fest wasn't in the cards for today.

"That bitch ruined my fucking life; it took me five years just to remember who I was. My shit is still under reconstruction, due to unfinished repairs. The shit that vindictive bitch did to me could never be forgotten, I hate dat bitch wit a passion. I should've whipped her ass, four times up in dis bitch today." Chyenne spat.

The crackling of Chyenne's voice threatens to let the bottle up feelings, pour out from her eyes. Chyenne still hasn't fully resolved some issues created from the mayhem Crystal caused in her life. Tay pretended not to notice the microscopic tear that escapes from Chyenne's glassy eyes. As the last few words springs from Chyenne's heart and exits her lips. The grudge she clutched was real and very dangerous. Stopping right outside the restaurant's door, Chyenne scrambled through her purse. Her hand emerged from her purse with a cigarette and a lighter. Her hands quaver as she lit the cigarette. She inhales deep and long on the cigarette. The first pull of the cigarette relaxed her soul. All the wrong in Chyenne's past life circled around Crystal. All sides of wrong to come in Chyenne's life will be squared up to Crystal.

"You content 'cus you got ya revenge on dat bitch, I never got da opportunity to serve dat bitch." Chyenne continues to resale her chafed heart.

"Revenge, not quite. If you wanna get at a bird, just pluck their feathers. Fuck patches! I don't know how Chyenne let her presence make her fall to pieces." Rhonda's chitachatter

Rhonda's chitachatter is referring to the incident from her youthful years. Rhonda had put hair removal in Crystal's shampoo. Crystal's hair fell out in spots. Children can be cruel. Boys and girls circled around Crystal taunting and teasing the missing hair spots earning her the nick name, Patches, while passing around her glue gum jerry curl wig. The nickname stuck to Crystal, well into her high school years. Before Crystal had her chips to stand on, her hair was her platform of superiority. Rhonda took offence to Crystal's many down grading remakes about girls with short hair not only because she liked wearing her hair short but the fact that Crystal always thought she was better than everybody. Rhonda sort revenge by poisoning Crystal's shampoo.

Chyenne continues to list her current anger toward Crystal to Rhonda. Chyenne summoned her past humiliation to Rhonda and Tay frontal lobe. Chyenne decided long ago to keep her forgiveness for someone who deserves it. Crystal could never be worthy of forgiveness. Chyenne's mind traveled over twenty years back. The sores still fresh like they were cuts from yesterday. She has learned to live with the torment Crystal infected her life with. She cuddles the idea that, one day Crystal would get what was coming to her. Someone will teach Crystal, she can't meddle in people's lives and get away with it, forever. One day she will have to pay the price. Chyenne just hope Crystal could pay the price ten times, no money accepted.

"Chyenne for the love of hip hop you gotta let go. Okay ya were battered 20 years ago. How long does it take for these wounds to heal?" Rhonda's chitachatter

Tay rolls her eyes with annoyance. Running into Crystal is bringing down the vibe. Tay is in birthday shopping mood, not Chyenne's pity party mood or Rhonda's verbal reality picture painting mood.

"That conniving bitch should have gotten her ass whipped back then and again today." Chyenne's chitachatter

Chyenne's thoughts are able to be viewed on her face. Her lips are all boxed up. She steams her cigarette like a mad Russian. It's clear, she wants to fight.

"I know it's gonna be challenging to put ya game face on if she show up at da party, but please for me, don't whip her ass up in there, renting out the 40/40 club is costly. I don't wanna get kicked out before time." Tay pouts out her bottom lip as she plea to Chyenne. The lip pouting is added, as a playful gesture. She hopes the gesture will make Chyenne smile.

"Imma try my best to behave it's a big place. Imma keep my distance from dat bitch but I can't control my hands once I've been drinking." the conviction in Chyenne's voice was as strong as hurricane sandy's wind.

Chyenne meant every word. She had envisions several ways to leave Crystal breathless. Rhonda and Tay eyes meet. The panic and terror posted on the two women's faces. Chyenne drunk and inflamed is hazardous to everyone around. Everyone's health would be in jeopardy. Chyenne becomes violent under the influence.

"Stop with all the negative vibes. Let's shop for my birthday dinner outfit. You all know I gotta look stupendous. I've invited Mr. Bryson Mitchell." Redness floods Tay's cheek as the name of this man slithers from her heart shaped lips.

Mr. Bryson Mitchell is Tay's California love from the city of sex. Mr. Bryson Mitchell's occupation is a tattoo artist; from L.A. Mr. Bryson Mitchell, the lean muscular dark chocolate mean money making machine. His resume of tattoo artistry is on the skin of regular people getting notice, due to his ink designs to the spotlight skin of top celebrities. Chyenne, Rhonda and Tay along with other **Sistahs**[13] met Mr. Bryson Mitchell while they were in L.A. They vacationed together once a year. Tay connected acquaints with Mr. Bryson Mitchell was far different than the other Sistahs. In the tattoo parlor all eyes were on Mr. Bryson Mitchell but his sexual eyes were on Tay's cappuccino voluminous curves. Mr. Bryson Mitchell had his mind made up. Mr. Bryson Mitchell liked Tay and he wanted her. Mr. Bryson Mitchell designed the Sistah's skin with the word "SISTAH". For four of the Sistahs this was their first tattoo. Their bond branded in blood and skin. This tattoo made number two for Chyenne. Mr. Bryson Mitchell had the ambition of a rider. Mr. Bryson Mitchell made it all about Tay. Mr. Bryson Mitchell had the thug passion in his eyes with the words to make any woman feel like a sweet

---

[13] **Sistahs** *are not bind by blood. They are siblings born to the same circumstances. Holding each other's hands in the darkest of times and guiding one another to light.*

lady and the body of a Greek God dipped in deep dark chocolate. Mr. Bryson Mitchell and Tay bumped and grinded to slow jams most of the vacation. Mr. Bryson Mitchell's dance moves was how he put his mack down on Tay. Tay is turned out on the "how do you want it" style and technique. When they weren't doing the humpy dance, Mr. Bryson Mitchell gave a tour of the state. Mr. Bryson Mitchell took the Sistahs to the wild west of the Watts and to the Compton's America's most wanted. The Sistah's toured the diamonds shining Diego to the Long Beach Chucks. They stopped in "Only god can judge me" Inglewood. They pass through trading war stories of Oakland to "Sack Town" Cali. They then enjoyed the sight of "I'm not mad at you" Hollywood. They ran the streets of the Bay to Rosecrans from Pasadena Sacramento until check out time. Everywhere they toured Mr. Bryson Mitchell was known to everybody, his artistry gets around. He built a professional name for himself. Mr. Bryson Mitchell had been in the game of tattoo art for ten years. Mr. Bryson Mitchell's untouchable unique artistry skills are recognized all over. Tay entangles her left arm with Rhonda's right arm. She performs the same gesture with her right arm with Chyenne's left arm. They gallop down the New York City street arm to arm like they did when they was younger on their way to school. She was saving the "Mr. Bryson Mitchell" information but had to be delivered early, thanks to an unexpected bump in with Crystal. Tay couldn't watch the smell of Crystal's evil that has been awaken in Chyenne to be released and linger and ruin a sunny Wednesday afternoon of shopping.

"Hhmmm, Mr. Bryson is sommin I'm interested in hearing about. Cat got ya tongue Tay. Spill it, girl." Rhonda inquires. Sex talk consumes Rhonda's conversation. She eagerly awaits Tay's response.

"Who ya kidding, ya favorite topic is **smooth skin**[14] doesn't really make a different who it is." Tay partakes in a little joke at Rhonda's expense.

---

[14] **Smooth skin** *For all you who don't know what smooth skin is, Imma learns you, right now. Smooth skin is when a man's penis is at its highest level of arousal. The precious rod is hard like frozen wood. The stiff muscle is covered with ultra smooth skin like a baby's ass.*

Rhonda rolls her eyes toward Tay's in responses to her comment. Rhonda wasn't appreciative of the pop shot. Rhonda's chitachatter flashes pictures, of the past in her vision. She sees herself and Brooklyn running around Harlem's Madison Projects. Brooklyn is the fifth element to the Sistahhood. Hustling niccas with their **koowie**[15] as bate. Some niccas got to see the koowie and some niccas never would. Dangling the koowie was a fun game Rhonda had mastered in her teenage years. She missed playing the game. Seeing Crystal made Rhonda's chitachatter travel to the past. She kinda missed Crystal. She hadn't seen Crystal in years. Crystal looked cosmetically lighter in weight in Rhonda's opinion. Rhonda's eyes couldn't pin point the difference in Crystal's face but there was a change. Rhonda's chitachatter questions, *"What Crystal changed on her face? Did Crystal have plastic appearance?"*

"Well since I know if I don't tell you now you won't leave me alone. Mr. Bryson Mitchell has some business here, so he'll be in New York for my birthday, so I invited him to my party, I'm sooo exited to see him. You all know we haven't seen each other since last year, but we maintained contact via social media and thru da phone. Phone calls that last for hours. I've been feeling like I'm in high school all over again. Ya know that teenage love. Debating who's gonna hang up first. We even sex Skye from time to time." Tay is tripping over her smile.

Tay reveals her secret relationship to Chyenne in the public with Rhonda around. Tay didn't want to have to explain her actions or feelings to Chyenne. Rhonda had prior knowledge of the electronic relationship. Announcing her yearlong electronic relationship to Chyenne was like salvation to Tay's mind. For a person like Tay, talking comes naturally. Being careful of the word she spill from her heart shaped lips in front of Chyenne was challenging. Now Tay's mind is free as well as her heart shaped lips. As Tay holds the door open to the boutique, the grin

---

There you have it the official meaning of smooth skin.
[15] **Koowie** *is the essences of a woman, a woman's intimate area, woman's vagina.*

plastered on her face like the cat from Alice in wonderland. Chyenne battled her voice box not to say one damn thing, she even silenced her chitachatter.

"Today is all about Tay, Today is all about Tay, Today is all about Tay."
Chyenne's chitachatter

Chyenne didn't want to destroy the mood with foul comment about Tay's foolish behavior. Tay is a grown ass woman with four children, by two different men, Chyenne was not judging her, she was just saying. Tay's hopeless naive romantic outlook on life was frustrating and exhausting to Chyenne. She takes the Sistah's relationship with the opposite sex personal.

"A whole year wit no smooth skin, sorry girl I wouldn't be able to do" Rhonda tease Tay.

Rhonda's sex drive confirms her words. She wouldn't be able to last a day, much less a whole year without a shot of smooth skin.

"I love my man, with all honesty but I know he's cheatin' on me. I look him in his eye but all he tells me is lies to keep near. I'll never leave him down though. I might mess around 'cause I need some affection. Oh soo I creep, yeah. Just keep it on the down low said nobody is suppose to know. So I creep yeah. 'cause he doesn't know. what I do. no attention goes to show. Soo I creep." T-boz said it all. When this hit dropped I cut and dyed my hair just like hers. I've stayed with the color, 'til this day. I gotta have a lil friend on the side. My koowie is my fucking problem. My koowie has a mind of its own, but I put my lil friend on ice, I gotta be tight and right for my baby, Mr. Bryson Mitchell." Tay's chitachatter*

Chyenne rubs Rhonda back in attempt to calm her mind from the thought. She knows that Rhonda with no sex equals a mean and nasty bitch on roller blades. Chyenne follows behind Rhonda into the boutique. Rhonda is a sex addict, even more, since the L.A. trip. More than usual is hard to comprehend, in Rhonda's case, but all so true. Rhonda's only daughter Paris left Rhonda all alone. This makes Paris second year at Clark University, in Atlanta, Georgia. With Paris away, Rhonda has been living like a teenager. Having sex like a mad rabbit, hanging out late, and clubbing on an every night basis. The thought of no sex had Rhonda on the verge of a seizure, especially, after all the action she's been getting in the last two years.

"After the whole thing in L.A., where he was taking us girls to exciting places, expensive spas and showered Tay with elaborate gifts, Boy, was I surprise it was all on Tay's dime. Tay received her monthly credit card statement when we came back home. There were many charges on it, summing up to a thirty one hundred dollars balance, all thanks to Bryson's ass. Yeah, Yeah I know once Tay called his ass up, the balance was taken care of. But I still remember it was his doing. He sent her the money via western union, but the fact remains he used her shit without her permission and she had just met his ass. Where they do that at? I guess in L.A apparently. He pulled a Crystal's move, doing shit without think 'bout the consequences. His "it's already taken care of" attitude just doesn't sit right with me. Tay's naive heart gave him another chance after that. Shit, not me. I would've been part of Mr. Bryson Mitchell's past." Chyenne's chitachatter

Chyenne bit down on her lip, too stop from letting her chitachatter loose in the air. Mr. Bryson Mitchell was a topic she didn't care to discuss. Mr. Bryson Mitchell swept Tay off her feet, along with the rest of the girls, except Chyenne. Crystal has changed Chyenne to a noisome skeptic of everyone and everything.

"My favorite customers and most loved Sistahs. Hello Sistahs, how can I help ya out today?" The soft spoken words came with a greeting kiss to the Sistah's cheeks. Angie delivered the greeting to each Sistah, one after another sealed with genuine Sistah love.

Angie is a distance Sistah. She wasn't weaved together like the original five Sistahs but family, none the less. Angie is the owner of this cute little boutique in the SoHo, on Spring Street. A down low spot where you can get something snappy in a heartbeat, add the right accessories and have all eyes on you, strutting your stuff looking like a million dollars when you only spend a hundred.

"I need a birthday outfit dat would make a man have smooth skin off a glimpse." Tay declared to Angie, as she outlines her voluminous frame with her hands.

Tay was talking to Angie's reflection in the mirror. Tay is a mirror magnet. She loves looking at her body. She is five feet tall but always stood five feet six inches because she wears heels everywhere. She dumps the garbage in heels. It wouldn't surprise anyone if she slept in heels. Her cappuccino complexion complemented her honey brown almond shape eyes. Her natural pouted lips always sparkled with lip-gloss. Her voluminous fame mimics the infamous buff body. Her voluminous bottom is so big, many people thought she had work done to it but the voluminous bottom was all hers naturally. Her chest appears to have an infant sleeping on her body, with the baby's ass up on her chest area. Yeah, her breasts are store bought but she made it look natural. Her body shape mixed with her fashion taste kinda duplicates a stripper's style. Her waist length honey blond weave, with the Chinese cut bangs; half an inch long curled eyelashes and nails are just accessories, in which she groomed regularly. She would definitely correct anyone who confused her to be a stripper; she is a "Model" and please don't forget it. Chyenne and Rhonda took their normal position on the white armless sofa designed for waiting guest, like themselves. Tay dragged them here at least once a month but everyone knows she visits Angie's about once a week. The Sistah tends to their families during the week. The weekend is Sistah time, but they talk to one another on a daily basis.

"I don't have a "smooth skin" section, but I got some new cat suits in this morning, interested?" Angie spoke over her shoulder to Tay, as she head to the back to get the new spandex merchandise, which is the right fit for Tay.

"...and possibly bend you over, look back and watch me. Smack that, all on the floor. Smack that, give me some more. Smack that, 'til you get sore. Smack that, oh ooh. Oh, hell yeah. I need some more of Bryson loving right now. Akon out here just giving away bedroom pointers to men, I'm glad Bryson was listening." Tay's chitachatter*

"Oh hell yeah, I'm interested in anything tight with no pocket on this ass!" Tay pokes her ass out and gave it a nice firm pat to match the verse in her chitachatter.

Chyenne and Rhonda let out a loud chuckle. Tay is known to ignite spontaneous laughter. Tay's naive attitude brings out her silly behavior.

"Rhonda where's ya sister? You better tell her I don't wanna hear any of her bullshit. She's missing da shopping trip today but if she miss da party, imma be forced to take my shoes off and whip her ass."

Tay's treat wasn't to be taken seriously. Tay's ability to part with a shoe is more than unlikely to happen. Chyenne and Rhonda let out chuckles even louder, than moments ago. Tay was a lot of things but a fighter wasn't one of them. Tay's threats were absolutely in vein. Tay's question is referring to Samantha. Samantha is Rhonda's biological sister but Sammy is the name she'll answer to. Tay is inquiring about Sammy's whereabouts. Angie enters to store area displaying a leather black cat suit with low cut to the waist line in the front and low cut down the back on a hanger. Tay's eyes flutter like lights on a Christmas tree. Before a word could come out of Angie's mouth, Tay snatches the garment from the hanger and headed straight to the fitting room, as the hanger was still dangling from Angie's left hand. Before Rhonda could respond to Tay's question, Chyenne grow impatience waiting on Rhonda's response to Tay's question. Chyenne verbally cleared her throat, to rush Rhonda for the answer. The sound from Chyenne's mouth is the cue, Rhonda was taking too long to answer Tay's question, in Chyenne's opinion.

"Where's ya sister at, anyway?" Chyenne repeats Tay's question. Sammy is Chyenne's only ally against Crystal. Sammy would share Chyenne's hatred toward Crystal trifling ass, is Chyenne thought.

"Sammy is caught up in court today. She's representing Teddy at 9 am and at 2 pm she's readdressing Brooklyn's case. Their custody battles are crazy. Hopefully the kids will come out this battle with no mental bruises." Rhonda informs.

Teddy is the younger brother of Rhonda and Sammy.

"Whatcha all think? I'm loving it! Maybe I'll get a ring outta Mr. Bryson Mitchell wit dis outfit right here." Tay eyes herself in the three sided mirror.

"DAMN, I look good enough to eat." She didn't need Chyenne and Rhonda comments of approval. Tay is satisfied.

Tay had hundreds of various leggings, she thought because she purchased leggings at the boutique they were equivalent to jeans, slack or any forms of pants. So, the fitting cat suit was right up her alley.

"Yeah, it's really complements ya ass and tities." Rhonda's acknowledgement of Tay's beauty was all Tay was looking to hear. Rhonda agree with the mirror, Tay do look like a magazine's cover super model in the outfit.

"Where to next?" Chyenne investigates as she examines her waist watch.

Chyenne's alarming question made Rhonda suddenly steal her attention from Tay eye-balling herself in the mirror to eyeing Chyenne. Rhonda had no qualms reminding Chyenne it is Tay's birthday and wants no nonsense this afternoon. Rhonda knew seeing Crystal really had Chyenne get all up tight, but it's not about her today. As her Sistahs, they too had to survive Crystal's mayhem to Chyenne's life, but were now over the whole thing. Its clear Chyenne still harbors salty feelings toward Crystal.

"Don't start ya shit, girl! Why ya still mad? First of all, dat shit happen years ago. Second of all, you have two beautiful children. Third of all, you got a marvelous man that adores you. You have what Tay has been prowling the earth for, true love." Rhonda's chitachatter refers to Chyenne.

Rhonda is giving Chyenne the look you give your kid when your kid is cutting up and is about to get popped. Tay quickly changes her clothes and paid Angie almost as fast as Crystal flew out the restaurant. Crystal looked foolish run out like she did. Crystal never personally crossed Rhonda but what she did to Chyenne really pierced vascular organs, of anybody who heard the story. Rhonda was just tired of hearing the story.

"We going to get shoes from Bloomingdales, and then Rhonda gonna drop me off at Jasmine's to get hair, nails, eyelashes and eyebrows done. Jasmine is hooking me up for my Birthday, and Jasmine is off Thursday and Friday I gotta go today. I'm not gonna have time Saturday morning, even if I make her squeeze me in. I gotta make sure the caterers got their shit together; arrange car service for the drunks that comes outta the party. Saturday nite we gonna parrrr-tay."

Giving Chyenne the afternoon's agenda was to put Tay at ease. She didn't want to deal with Chyenne's child like etiquette. Plus, Chyenne's trust issue still wasn't rectified after two years of therapy. Chyenne is always precautious thinking everyone is up to something deceitful, thanks to Crystal.

"It's only two." Tay's words rolls of her tongue like an innocent child.

Tay holds up her index finger and middle finger playfully. Tay was trying to get Chyenne to loosen up, a bit. Boy, did the sight of Crystal fuck up Chyenne's mentality. A two second hello has reverse years of triumph for Chyenne. Rhonda picked Tay and Chyenne up in her midnight blue X5, BMW to take them to lunch at the restaurant. The ladies climbed back into their assigned seats. As soon as key turns in the ignition, music blared out filling the car's air erasing away any train of thought anyone might of have. Miguel bellows the lyrics to Adorn, directly into the ladies ears.

"Yeah these lips. Can't wait to taste your skin, baby. Whoa, and these eyes, yeah. Can't wait to see your grin, ooh ooh baby, just let my love. Just let my love Adorn you. Please baby, yeah." *Shit, now Bryson is running thru my mind. Miguel words are guilty for the wetness in my underwear. He is proof. It's not what you say; it's how you say it."* *Tay's chitachatter*

This lovely song shouldn't be played at maximum volume. This here is top of the line smooth skin music. It's an early Wednesday afternoon and New York City streets are quiet, it was a serene feeling. Once Rhonda turned down the radio's volume she was able to hear the agitation in Chyenne's face. Chyenne is quick to complain about almost losing her hearing in ear drums.

"Why do ya car does that every fucking time? When we got outta da fuckin car there wasn't any fuckin music playing!" The boisterous venom being discharged was unnecessary but Chyenne's actions today can be classified as totally unnecessary.

"DAMN, Chyenne don't chew my fuckin' head off. Like I told you earlier, Benny has da fucking car programmed, like he has everything in my whole damn life programmed. Last week I had to call him to turn off da fuckin stereo, at my own fuckin house. Sorry to inconvenience you, Chyenne." Offering empathy to Chyenne's irritation, Rhonda start off shouting then her voice settled in to a monotone.

Benny is Sammy's son, Rhonda's nephew. Rhonda pierced her lip, trying to keep her true words from flowing freely from her lips. Rhonda was ready to read, edit and rewrite Chyenne's snotty attitude.

"Buckle up ladies, Tay we off to get ya shoes, how much ya plan on spending on ya thousandth pair today?" Rhonda clowns Tay.

Rhonda's question adding laughter to the air in hope it would cut the tension as she pulled the car out of parking the spot near the restaurant. Tay's shoe collection is the running joke amongst the Sistahs. After partaking in a shuttle cheer at her own expense, Tay focuses her vision on Chyenne.

"How's Polo and Capri?" intentionally, Tay inquires about subjects she know Chyenne would bite into with delight.

Chyenne pretend to be hard but she has a compassionate sentimental side that she showered her children with. Chyenne's son Polo is now twenty three years old. He receives an outlandish amount of Chyenne's love and affection. Cheyenne knows his exact whereabouts at any given moment. Chyenne's daughter, Capri, is nine years old. Capri's little angelic face could bring Mike Tyson to knees with just one smile. Her crippling smile can shatter any discomfort Chyenne is feeling.

"Well Polo is still chasing his dream of the Hip-Hop industry, I keep tellin' him to holla at you to get in to da Modeling thing. He's more sexy then thuggish, but he doesn't hear me. Capri is doing excellent in school. She still ballet dancing her little heart away. Her recital is Saturday morning at 11. After the recital me and Malik is gonna take the kids to a brunch lunch thingy. Then imma drop Capri and Malik off at the house and change for the party. You know Polo, he has his own plans." The loving feelings Chyenne have for her children and man was radiant. Talking of them caresses her mannerisms.

After the "break-up" with Polo's father, Chyenne didn't date for thirteen years. You know Rhonda was giving her hell. Sex jokes, sex insults, dick and balls conversations were thrown all up in Chyenne's face. When Chyenne and Malik found each other, as her friends and as her Sistahs, they all shared the same ecstatic feeling. Sometimes, it seemed the Sistahs were more grateful for Malik than Chyenne was. Chyenne had some hard times, some shit where you had to be Army strong to with stand.

"Imma be in da front row of my little pumpkin recital." Rhonda announces her declaration of support for Capri's ballerina career.

"You better. You know how Capri is, never forget a thing." Warring Rhonda, Chyenne didn't want to deal with the twenty one questions of why Rhonda didn't show up.

Tay smirks to herself. Tay notices Chyenne can spot the unforgiving side in her daughter but couldn't conceive the thought her daughter inherited the trait from mother, Chyenne. In a matter of seconds, Rhonda was driving down in the parking garage behind Bloomingdales. Tay hopped out the back seat like a crack head on the way to nab a hit. I swear to you the car tires hadn't completely come to a stop before Tay's heels was clicking on the concrete.

"Come on, Sistahs. It's shoe time!" Tay shouts back at her Sistahs from the garage elevator door. Rhonda and Chyenne were about a yard away from Tay. They were practically skipping to the elevator.

"Elevator!" Tay shouted at her Sistahs. She is getting annoyed at their slow motion movements.

Chyenne stopped in her tracks. Her legs refuse to obey her brain's commands to walk. Tay's yelling along with the words changed the surrounds drastically, in Chyenne's vision. Chyenne turn her head from left to right frantically, like the sick girl in the Exorcist. Why was she seeing Madison project's hallway walls? Chyenne shakes her head from left to right even faster. She stops shaking her head, using both hands she starts to punch each side of her head. She was hitting herself like you would do to an old T.V, trying to get a better view.

"Are you alright, sweetie?" Rhonda's voice is gentle as she places her right hand on Chyenne's right shoulder. Rhonda's touch bought Chyenne's mind and vision back to reality.

"What da hell is going on over there? You bitches better not be talking 'bout me!" Tay is shaking like a Fall's leaf. She is **jonesing**[16] for her shoe drug.

"We comin', I twisted my ankle." Chyenne shouts to Tay.

Rhonda stares in amazement, she couldn't believe Chyenne just black out and blinked back within seconds, and then pretended like nothing happen. Rhonda's mouth slightly hung open, at the fact Chyenne lied, without any conscious.

"Dis bitch is really crazy, shaking and punching herself. All she had to do was throw-up green. So I could get Anthony Hopkins on the phone. Tay better hurry up and get her shoes. So we can drop dis bitch off. Seeing Crystal got her all fucked up. I can't do the crying bullshit she goes thru today. Since Malik been on deck, we haven't had to deal with the "poor

---

[16] **Jonesing** *is a strong overwhelming craving.*

me" shit. I thought she was cured. I guess not." Rhonda's chitachatter

After trying on seventeen pairs of shoes and hundreds of more laughs, Tay finally made a decision. A pair of Jimmy Choo's six inch high black slip backs with a cute bow on the top, with a peek toe cut, they was covered with sliver spike studs. Rhonda knew she was going borrow those unique creations, called shoes, one day. Chyenne glances at her watch, its 4 o'clock. She reminded her Sistahs it was time for her to punch-in, to start her afternoon shift of motherhood. Rhonda mind traveled to the thoughts of Sammy, Teddy and Brooklyn fight in court. Rhonda has been pressing ignore to her mother's phone calls. Her mother wants to ask her questions. Questions, she didn't have the answers to, yet. She has been calling ever since she met up with the Sistahs around noon. Rhonda must admit Chyenne's departure plan was a great choice; it was time to part our ways. The job is complete, they had lunch with Tay and Tay got her birthday dinner outfit. Rhonda drop Tay off at Jasmine's Hair and Nail Salon. Chyenne was the last one to be dropped off at the ballet institute on Third Avenue. Chyenne is picking up the ballerina, Capri. The Sistah gave each other their good-bye kisses and hugs followed by their signature departure words.

"A piece of cake." Tay expresses her desire for life simplicity.

"A piece of mind." Chyenne request her desire for sanity.

"A piece of ass." Rhonda requests a snack to her sexual desire.

Anticipation had a hold on Rhonda; she needed to know how court turned out. She drove to Ozone Park, Queens in recorded time. Before she could put the car in park her mother, Lorraine, known to her grandchildren as Grams, is standing in the doorway of the house. As soon as one of Rhonda's feet was out the car, she could hear her mother questioning her from about thirty feet away.

"Ronnie, Sammy called ya?" Ronnie is Rhonda's pet name only Lorraine used.

"Not yet Ma, Sammy hasn't called me," the defect was present in her voice level. She was hoping her mother had news for her, but by the question, she knows her mother didn't have any information to deliver.

"Ronnie is ya hungry?" Lorraine questions

The motherly voice always bought comfort to Rhonda. Rhonda shook her head from left to right, gesturing her answer, without parting her lips. Rhonda takes a seat on her mother's sofa. She looks at the T.V. and she laughs on the inside.

"NY1 is on in here" mom is addicted to this channel."
Rhonda's chitachatter

Rhonda had her mother under her surveillances. Rhonda watches her mother stared motionless out the kitchen window. Rhonda is grateful to have a strong black phenomenal woman, as her mother. Lorraine lived up to every word in Maya Anglous's, *"Phenomenal Woman"* poem. Madison PJ's production of authentic mothers was rare. Lorraine raised three children, Rhonda, Sammy and Teddy, in Madison project complex, all by herself, and they never wanted for nothing.

"We all had the proper tools to battle the world. My mother equipped all three of us, with the tools of life and the knowledge of how and when to use the tools to defect the obstacles that would be thrown in our path, without hesitation. I might say we all did well for ourselves. I'm an accountant with a self owned firm; objective is to assistant small black owned business, throughout the tri-state area. Sammy is a custody Attorney, she takes on mostly men defendants. She feels the system is designed against all black men, preying on their down fall. It's unbelievable how many allegeable men, with good jobs, no criminal records are still denied accesses to their own children. Teddy was a revolutionist in the fight for victims of the AIDS epidemic. Seeing Crystal

today brought back all the horror Madison Projects had to offer, to the front of my memory." Rhonda's chitachatter

"Hay Grams, break any hearts today wit cha beauty?" Benny's six-foot body burying his grandmother four feet, eleven inches frame, as he bend over to kiss her on the forehead, with his first love pinned under his right arm, a basketball.

Lorraine shimmied in her chair tickled by Benny flirtation. Lorraine sat at the kitchen table, spitting out of a white coffee cup, with a gold rim, more than likely filled with tea and gin. Indulging in a drink or two was a more frequent action of Lorraine, since Teddy's accident. Lorraine loved her two daughters, Rhonda and Sammy, but her love for her only son, Teddy, definitely shined the brightest.

"What's up auntie?" genuine euphoria singing with his words. Benny flops down beside his aunt, Rhonda, on the sofa facing the T.V., left of the kitchen. He went in for a kiss but was stop by Rhonda's hand.

"You better un-program my car, I almost had to beat Chyenne's ass today 'cause of the radio playing every time I turn the damn car on!"

"I gotcha, Auntie. Don't be acting like dat. Where's mom, still working?" A hint of concern can be detected in Benny's words.

Benny loves to kick it with his eight year old cousin TJ on his free time. Benny likes being TJ's role model. TJ presence makes Benny aware of the words he used and the actions he took in front of TJ's eyes. TJ made Benny feel like a responsible adult. Benny especially likes bringing his friends over and letting his eight year old cousin beat them in any video game of their choice. Benny even capitalized on his little cousin embarrassing wins, over Benny's friends. Everybody was on edge every single time Teddy had to face Victoria in court. Victoria always had a new allegation of neglect for the judge to hear. Victoria is an orbicular liar.

Victoria lies could run laps around you. Teddy and Victoria fought to share their son.

"Yeah, I'm waiting on her to come or call or sommin, my nerves are on edge." The rattling in her throat was hard to hide, Rhonda words shook out of her mouth.

"Wanna take a shot of some Gin, it'll calm ya down a bit." Thirsty to gain a drinking partner, Lorraine held up the liter bottle of alcohol.

"No thanks mom, I'm driving. You shouldn't be drinking so early in the afternoon ya self." Despair apparently visible in Rhonda light scolding, to her mother.

Rhonda wanted to tell her mother she had notice this is her third drink, since she's been there. Rhonda has been there for less than thirty minutes.

"I gotta watch her, if I don't she'll be looking like Eddie King from the classic Five Heartbeats movie or how Michael Wright looks today on the train, disorganized, drunk and deranged. If Sammy was here she wouldn't even be trying this shit." Rhonda's chitachatter

Lorraine decides responding to her daughter distasteful remarks would escalate in to a ruckus and this wasn't the time for messy behavior. The three of them sat in silent. Benny grabs hold of the TV's remote control off the coffee table that stood between the sofa and the TV, and begins to channel surf.

"Imma fix Auntie's car, then imma call up Shorty from da Pees, check out how she works dem soft lips. Yeah boy, but 1st I gotta wait for moms, see if she let me rock da wheels. If not, Auntie might let me rock her wheels wit a little buttering up." Benny's chitachatter

Benny's chitachatter records time. With time accounted for, it's easy to follow the itinerary to the future.

The house phone rings Benny, Lorraine and Rhonda all jumps out of their seats.

Caller ID reads, Wilson, Samantha...

"Red carpet dick could just roll out, go 'head and scream you can't hold out."

What's your fantasy
Ludacris
Back for the first time

"Oh baby let's get naked, just so we can make sweet love, all these sensations, got me going crazy, for you"

Bryson sneaks up on Tay, as she stares in a daze, out the window. He wraps his muscular dark chocolate arms around her waist from behind, softly squeezing her body toward his hard thick dark chocolate rod of ecstasy. Flutters swims in her stomach. His chin rests on her blonde hair, on top of her head. His hug activates warm passion steaming in her veins. The steam's smoke closes her eyes. The steam's heat drops her head back onto the left side of Bryson's dark chocolate mountains of pillowed muscles, resting on his chest. She inhales deep to soak in the loud aroma of lust, pouring from their pores. She left the right side of her neck open, intentionally. The opening on her neck slobbers for his touch. His lips drink her cappuccino colored skin. His butter soft lips slides up and down her neck. He leans forward. His solid thick dark chocolate rod presses against her voluminous bottom cheeks. He gently rubs the solid thick dark chocolate rod on her bottom cheeks. She pokes her bottom cheeks out, just a tiny bit. The bounce of bottom cheeks nudges the solid thick dark chocolate rod to fall into the dark crease between the cheeks. His heavy dark chocolate hands straps onto her hips. He pushes forward, pressing the solid thick dark chocolate rod deeper into the darkness of the cheeks. She pulls back, welcoming his awakened gain of spice. Her bottom cheeks flirtatiously brush across the solid thick dark chocolate rod. He gently glides his right hand up from her hip to her left breast, through the flap of her black silk robe to feed his overwhelming cravings. His sensuous touch is light, but heavy with desire. She didn't feel his hand move from her hip, until his cottony fingertips swab her frozen left nipple. The frozen nipple steams heated passion under his touch. His dreamy touch has her floating. Faint sounds of delight fly from her lips. Her moan of arousal inspires his right hand to collapse to her heart of sexiness. The heart pulsates with thirst. The emotional pleasure motives the rapid heartbeats. His fingertips reach pass her tender juicy lipped gates of sexiness to reach its aim. His skillfully fingertips dances a massaging tango on the pink dimple of sexiness. His fingertips spring a creamy leak from the heart. The dimple is drench to his touch. The heart's warm creamy passion flow naturally. His gracious touches from his soft fingertips inch to fondling the pink cleft of sexiness. His thumb sensual massages the pink cleft. Creamy gratefulness floods the palm of his hand. The heart thirst drools out luscious longing. The heart cries out creamy tears. The heart weeps to clench the firm crashes flowing from the solid thick dark chocolate rod. Sweet moans begging for collisions screams from the stiffness of the rod. The rod swells with pleads to puncture the heart with pleasure. Her hands clutching the black silk robe to give her knees balance. Her knees promised to buckle under his soft touch.

"Inside on top of you, grinding inside and out of you. Baby I know what to do. Baby I know what to do. So come on baby girl let's just take our clothes off, just so we can make sweet love, but I want to know your body tonight is the night, that I change your life."

Between the two fluffy cheeks, he grinds his stiff thick dark chocolate rod in a steady circular motion. His gentle fingertips string at the creamy slippery dimple between Tay's legs. He plants his cottony soft lips on the nape of her neck. He storms up and down her neck with soft kisses. His lips reach deeper than the surface. His scatters heavy drops of kisses on her neck down to her shoulder. He uses his teeth to remove the robe off her shoulder. Her shoulder is under his care. She wiggles her body from under the silk robe. His eyes swallow the naked cappuccino colored skin in a gulp. His kisses graduate to tiny bites of a lustful appetite. The tempo of the kisses is followed by his magical dark chocolate fingertips. His soft rubs on the slobbering dimple, escalates to slowly poke into the heart, with his thick dark chocolate fingers. His thick dark chocolate fingers flutters back and forth inside the flooded heart. His thumb caresses the pink cleft of Tay's sexiness. He inhales her right earlobe into his mouth. Gently tugging her earlobe with his teeth before released it. His warm tongue wets intimate emotions inside of her mind. The sensation tickles her cravings. He whispers in her ear "I want you now". The passion smoking from his words clouds her thoughts. The friction of his warm wet tongue in her ear creates whirlpools on his fingertips between her legs. Overcome by enticing creamy heat from the heart of sexiness, he holds her tightly to his body using both dark chocolate arms. The creamy heart controls his hands. He swings her around to face him with gentle force. She brings his two creamy coated dark chocolate fingers to her mouth. She spurts the cream off his dark chocolate fingers. She looks up at him with her innocent eyes. The urge in his eyes speaks to her. He grabs both sides of her face. He bends his neck down to see her eye to eye. He stares deep into her almond shape honey brown eyes. His eyes looks pass her thoughts into her soul. His vision is breathtaking. She gasps for air. Her plump tities slightly bounce up and down in the air. He brings her face more closely to his. The breath of passionate smoke from his lips clouds down onto her face. He passionately unloads his lips onto her lips. She wraps her arms around his body, as his tongue explores her tongue. His body holds her up. The passion is too heavy on her knees. Every muscle in her body flew to bliss. Their tongue intertwined in desire. He drops his hold on her face, to her waist. He grips on her body. His hands have a hold on her body which can't be touched. She is a servant to his intoxicating handle. His will is her command.

"Just let me control your body, girl are you sure you wanna slow it down? Noooo. And you start screaming when I got downtown. Oh baby tell me why you're so excited. You know I love when you take it off. So, baby go ahead and take it off, tonight. Oh baby let's get naked, just so we can make sweet love, all these sensations, got me going crazy, for you. Inside on top of you, grinding inside and out of you. Baby I know what to do. Baby I know what to do."

At the end of the kiss, she sucks on his bottom lip. His sweet sexy dark chocolate skin groans to be tasted. She pounce her pouted lips on his chin, landing kisses on his sweet dark chocolate skin. She licks her lips teasing her begging taste buds with sweet dark chocolate sugar. She seductively licks and kisses down the avenue to the solid thick dark chocolate rod. Her luscious lips and cushiony tongue strolls down pass his neck and throat. She savors the sweetness of his juicy dark chocolate skin. The tingle of her luscious lip and cushiony tongue on his skin closes his eyes and his head drop back. She brushes her steamy lips on his chest of sexy dark chocolate mountains of muscles. His sexy dark chocolate flesh compulsion made his left hand supports the back of her head. He desires her to feed on his lusty dark chocolate emotions. She nibbles on his dark chocolate nipples. He enjoy the new found sensation, she is igniting. She lowers her body. Her hands slide down the outline of his dark chocolate muscular body. Her tongue inhales the dark chocolate sweetness on his skin. Her tongue trails down to his navel. She lowers herself to her knees, exploring his navel with her tongue. Her tongue tightens the hold he has on the back of her head. Her tongue glides down to his abdomen. Her right hand sweeps from his hip to his inner thigh. Her hand gentle caresses his inner thighs. Her sweet touch fondles his longing. Her hand and tongue meet at his two knots of sugar. Her tongue glazes the knots as her hand holds them up to her tongue. Blissful sounds jumps from his lips. Her hypnotic tongue language speaks to his skin. She draws the knot into her mouth one at time. Her tongue drags up the shaft of the solid thick dark chocolate rod. Her tongue traces the head of the rod. Intense sounds of bliss escape his lips. The sound encourages her taste buds to eat the juicy solid thick dark chocolate rod. Her mouth slowly engulfs the solid thick dark chocolate rod. She eases her hungry taste buds down the whole stiffness of the solid thick dark chocolate of the rod. With the stiff thick dark chocolate shaft in her mouth, her hands hug his sumptuous sugar knots. Her tongue traces the stiff thick dark chocolate shaft of the rod, inside her mouth. Her soft lips plunge down on the juicy stiff thick dark chocolate shaft of the rod. The rod tickles her throat pushing the compulsion to add his right hand of support to aid his left hand to supporting the back of her head. His uncontrolled passion set the rhythm of his stokes in her mouth. Her soft lips yank up and down the stiff thick dark chocolate shaft of the rod. She replaced her soft lips with her right hand. Her hand toys with stiff thick dark chocolate shaft of the rod. She taunts the juicy dark chocolate head of rod with her tongue. Her wet tongue on his flesh is a narcotic to his desire. Extreme groans of harmony stumble off his lips. She inch her soft lips down to the end of the stiff thick dark chocolate rod. With the stiff thick dark chocolate rod lunged in her throat, she caress the sugar knots with her tongue. Silent cries drips clear tears of pleasure in to her throat. The stiff thick dark chocolate rod hurls tears of enjoyment. He brings her to her feet by placing both hands up her armpits. She is stand in front of him, as he wings her off her feet. He positions one muscular arm around her back and the other behind her knee caps. He gentle laid her down on a bed concealed by red, white and pink rose petals. He kneels down on the bed, between her legs. He leans his body forward. His hands planted on the opposite sides of her body. He springs his lips on top of hers with passion. He floods her mouth with his tongue. She savors the taste of his arousal. His mouth locked on her right nipple. His gentle sucks on her nipples. The touch of his lips on her nipple ripples through her body. He circles her nipple with his tongue. He performs the same lusty technique to her left nipple. He kisses down her body until he reaches the creamy heart of sexiness. His tongue runs up and down the pink cleft. His tongue commands her hands to hold on to the silky sheets. The electrifying wet strokes have her body jumpy. She rubs the deep black waves of hair on his head, as his tongue sails through her quivering heart of sexiness. The heart of sexiness creamy tears of ecstasy shed freely. He takes his right hand from the side of her and opens the lipped gate, with his index and middle finger. The pink dimple fully exposed. Her emotions are just as bare as her nude body. His lips dabs the cleft with kisses. Her sounds of delight fight for freedom. Sweet moans echo in the air. His lips suck the cleft as his chin message the pink dimple. Uncontrollable cream gushes from the heated heart. His two dark chocolate fingers are slowly lured into the heart. The heart splashes the fingers with creamy passion. His lips intensify the grip on the cleft as his dark chocolate fingers increase speed, *of gentle thrusting into the heart. The heart clenches his fingers as more cream flows freely.*

"Making sweet love to you baby go ahead and take it off let's get naked 'cus you know I love to turn you on. girl. Let's do your favorite song. Yeah. When the candles lit and then I slow. Baby girl I want for you to roll. Just roll your hips, and just, grind on me, grind on me, grind on me. And baby don't get confused. I'll do everything you wanna to. just as long as you get crazy. and just as soon as you naked. Make love"

He lifts his head up. She looks at his eyes and mouth. His eye smokes with awaited pleasure. On his upper lip, on the right side of his mouth has the tiny thug twist. The sight cries creamy tears from her heart of sexiness. Her hands drop to his shoulders in defeat. She surrenders to being his marionette. He climbs up her body. His soft lips read her thoughts through her pores. His soft lips lands on top of her pillowed lips. He fills her mouth with his tongue. His left forearm is guiding her hips toward the stiff thick dark chocolate rod as his hands grips her right hip. His right hand leads the stiff thick dark chocolate rod into the heart of sexiness. He presses into position with his hold on her plumped bottom cheeks. He parts the plumped cheeks with his firm grip, to fully insert the stiff thick dark chocolate rod into the cream clamped heart. The stab makes her back buck up. He grinds the stiff thick chocolate rod inside the core of the cream clamped heart. He swings the stiff thick chocolate rod with deep strokes to her heart's fantasies. The stiff thick chocolate rod swings deeper strongly, but very slowly. He offers to stimulate her taste buds as the stiff thick dark chocolate rod grinds pierce the heart and taps her stomach. He reaches over to the right side of the bed of red, white and pink rose petals to the nightstand. She opens her mouth to bite into the long stemmed chocolate coated strawberry dangling from his hand. He kneels on the bed. He positions her plumped bottom cheek to rest on his quadriceps. He grinds the whole stiff thick dark chocolate rod deeper filling her stomach. He bounces the stiff thick dark chocolate rod in and out the heart, as the sugar knot bang against her bottom cheeks. He feeds her the other half of the long stem chocolate coated strawberry. The chocolate coated strawberry juices leaks out the corner of her mouth. His tongue licks the fruit juice off her chin. He grinds the solid thick chocolate rod in a stirring motion. He delivers another chocolate coated strawberry to her mouth with blows to the stomach. He gentle lay his body down on top of hers. He flips her on top of him. She eases the creamy heart down on the stiff thick dark chocolate rod. His strong gentle chocolate hands grips her hip. She rolls her hip on the stiff thick dark chocolate rod. He strokes the stiff thick dark chocolate deeper into the hot creamy heart. The stiff thick dark chocolate rod jabs at her voice. Sweet moans of combine pain and pleasure springs from her throat. She glides up and down the stiff thick dark chocolate rod. The stiff thick dark chocolate is coated with creamy goodness. The slippery creamy heat warms up tears of passion in the stiff thick dark chocolate rod. Their feverish thumps gushes. The heart's heated cream erupted down the stiff thick dark chocolate rod, onto the sugar knots. The heart clamps over the stiff thick dark chocolate. The firm grip of the heart allure sugar from the sugar knots to freedom. The sugar knots spit sugar up the stiff thick dark chocolate rod. The sweet sugar is busting from the stiff thick dark chocolate rod. The gooey sugar fills her heart and stomach.

Oh baby let's get naked, just so we can make sweet love, all these sensations, got me going crazy, for you. Inside on top of you, grinding inside and out of you. Baby I know what to do. Baby I know what to do. So come on baby girl let's just take our cloths off. Just so we can make sweet love."

"Helloooooooooooo Ma!" Camille, Tay's daughter is standing in front of Tay's lifeless body yelling.

Tay has a distance look in her eyes. Camille waves her hands in front of Tay's face, desperately trying to gain Tay's attention. Tay is posing in front of her living room window. Tay's mouth is wide open, drool puddles on the left corner of her mouth. Her body weight shifted to the right. Her left leg is slightly sticking out to the left. Both of her hands glued to the top of the broom handle holding her body up. Camille turns off Chris Brown's voice blasting out of the five speakers of the surround sound system. She clears the air. Camille attempts to reduce the surrounding distraction in the living room. Tay's chitachatter has transported her to the past. Tay's vision is watching the body images of her and Mr. Bryson Mitchell consummates their discovery of each other's bodies; a year ago in L.A. Camille shakes her mother's shoulders with both hands. Camille's touch rattles Tay back into reality. Camille sees Tay's spirit spring back into her eyes.

"Ma! I need a pair of shoes to go with my outfit." Camille announces.

"Well, go get the book!" Tay throws the words in the air at her daughter.

"The Book" is a photo album filled with seven hundred twenty six pictures, all of Tay's high heel shoe collection. The photos of shoes are sorted by color. Tay takes pride in her collection. Her photo album is her late night reading. Before she closes her eyes at night she glace through the pretty pictures. Her nighttime reading book rests on the nightstand on the side of her bed, right under her bedroom window. At one point, Camille almost lost her job, due to Tay's collection. Camille was a part-time Sales Floor Manager at Macy's in the woman's shoe department. Tay was abusing her purchase power on the Friend and Family discount program. Camille job's status end result was six months of Friend and Family discount program suspension. Tay puts the finishing cleaning touches on the living room. Her and her children used yesterday night to cleaning the entire three stories, five bedrooms, and three bathrooms cherry brick stone townhouse. This morning she got up early and went over all common used areas of the town house. She wiped down the marble countertops in the kitchen, the digital stove, digital microwave, the digital dishwasher and the stainless steel refrigerator. She polished the golden forks, knifes and spoons. She set out the extravagant china dinnerware for the Chef, Robert. Chef Robert is preparing tonight's dinner. Steak sautéed in garlic favored gravy top with chopped roasted mixed peppers, a Chef Robert's special Sweet and Yukon potato blend with wax beans dripping in a garlic buttery taste. Chef Robert is highly recommended by Brooklyn. Brooklyn is a member of the Sistah-hood. Brooklyn's occupation is a Food Critic. Tay's mother Mary wouldn't get the satisfaction of critiquing Tay's cooking skills tonight. Tay added a small fresh floral arrangement of bright colored exotic flowers to the spotless first floor bathroom this morning. She placed a larger similar floral arrangement on top of the light beige colored Italian tablecloth, covering the dining room table. She sets the golden eating utensils on top of the Italian dark beige clothed dinner napkins. She was going over the living room floor with the broom before the music singing in the air sparked her chitachatter.

*"**Sweet love, sweet love, sweet love.**" Oh hell no! How I let Breezy's sweet singing slap me around, like that. Falling off my feet onto the Red Carpet? I do love ya, Chris Breezy but Saturday night I can't fuck withcha. You leave me no choice. I'm gonna tell da Deejay this song, right here, is off limits. All eyes gonna be on me. It's my birthday party and you know I'm gonna be dressed to kill, for sure. I can't be flying into trances and shit in front everybody. Wow, I can't believe I was all caught up, flying high, on da Red Carpet, like dat. Damn! Girl get ya shit together. C'mon Mr. Bryson Mitchell come tune this koowie down!" Tay's chitachatter*

*The **Red Carpet** [17] is serious business. It's magical. When it gyrates out, it spins you on a ride of your life. The Red Carpets soars through clouds of the mental and dashes thought the physical, mind, body and soul along for the ride. Taking a journey on the Red Carpet is stimulation to the hearing of pure desire screaming from eyes. Closed eyes filled with effortless catering to unspoken fantasy. The fragrance of silent emotions tickles the nose. The exotic flavors dance on taste buds. The Red Carpet is serious business. Not everybody will get a ride on the Red carpet in their lifetime. The selected few whom have been chosen to fly on the Red Carpet speak of its praises but not all will be able to handle it. On the Red Carpet, all part of the inner being is vulnerable and all skin is ultra sensitive. Ride Safe. You can ask*

---

[17] ***Red Carpet** is more emotional than physical sex.*

Luda and he will kindly tell you to your face "The Red Carpet is grown folk business. It aint for everybody,' everybody can't handle it."

"Ma, Chef Robert wants to know where the wine flute glasses are." Camille shouts to Tay as she takes steps upstairs toward the photo album.

"When did Chef Robert get here?" Tay questions she didn't hear him come in.

"'Bout 30 minutes ago, he came in through the kitchen door." Camille answers. Her voice travels over the banister down seven steps to the living room.

"Damn Breezy! How long you had me flying? Definitely off da play list, for Saturday night. Shit, that damn Red Carpet is a mutha fucker. Let me quickly check my phone." Tay's chitachatter

Tay checks her phone call list, phone message list and her social media page, nothing from Bryson. Tay walks with disappointment pass the stairs leading upstairs through the dining room to the kitchen. She greets Chef Robert and retrieves the red velvet box of exquisite wine glass from the cabinet above the sink. Chef Robert gets an eye full of Tay moving around in her cleaning outfit. Tay is wearing her red spandex pumpum shorts, a fitting white tank top, and red patent leather high heels.

"Ma, Aunt Mildred's car just pulled up. Ya better get cha bible. Bible study is going to starts in 5...4...3...2." Calvin jokes, but is the only one laughing.

Calvin is Camille's twin brother. As his left foot steps down off the last step his sarcasm sprays the air. His sole purpose for coming downstairs is to make the announcement, poking fun at Tay. He teases Tay about her biological sister's annoying behavior. Mildred is a Christian fanatic. Mildred's militant recruitment tactics is best described as a Christian extremist. Calvin is in the dining room, walking towards the kitchen.

"Ding Dong," the door bell rings.

"Shit! Well open the damn door. You already know who it is. What time is it?" Tay speaks to Calvin, as she bush pass him.

"7:26, Ma. And watch ya mouth, Auntie Mildred is here!" Calvin turns toward the front door. His words hit Tay's back.

"She knows every damn thing, but can't tell time. I said dinner is at 8. Shit!" Tay irritation itches out her throat.

Everybody living in the town house migrates to the living room, except Camille. They all wait to greet their first arriving guest for Tay's family birthday dinner. Tay darts upstairs. Tay bump passes her other daughter, Amber on her way upstairs.

"Damn! Dat girl can move in dem heels, two stairs at a time. Work it Ma!" Amber shouts the complement to her Tay's back, as Amber continues downstairs.

"God bless you this evening, Nephew. Where's is your mother?" Mildred quizzes Calvin as she greets him with a Christian kiss on his cheek.

Mildred waltz pass the threshold in to the living room area. Mildred's husband, Michael follows behind her. Michael greets Calvin with body language. Michael nods his head, with three fingers holding the brim of his top hat.

"She's upstairs getting dress. Ma is happy you skipped out on Thursday night bible study to be here for her birthday dinner." Calvin answers

Mildred with a joking tone. His words hits Michael's back.

"Now Calvin, there's no such thing as skipping out on the Lord! We moved up the time, in fact we are coming from Bible study. Maybe next time you'll join us?" Mildred shot words at Calvin.

"Maybe, Auntie we should pray 'bout it!"

"Nephew, the power of pray is stronger than you can imagine."

Tay is upstairs on the second floor. She is running around her bedroom skittish. Encounters with her mother and sister Mildred is one thing she choice to avoid. Camille sits on the edge of Tay's king size bed. Camille is absorbing Tay's strange aura. Her mother is calm, confidante, playful and a well organized person. Camille can tell every time her grandmother or aunt presence is near. Tay's aura changes to disorganize insecure nervous wreck. Tay wasn't ready. Tay's outfit was sure to get strong negative reviews from her sister, Mildred. A review Tay wasn't interested in hearing ever. Tay quickly checks her phone call list, phone message list and her social media page, nothing from Bryson, yet. Tay takes a third look at her outfit, not sure if she would wear it down stairs.

Downstairs in the living room:

"Oh my word, these two are adorable, God bless them. I have to get a picture. Look at them Michael. They are too precious."

Mildred scrambles around in her purse. Her hand emerges holding her phone. Mildred is making over the two little children sitting on the couch watching T.V. She repositions the two children to take the picture. The curly blond headed, light brown eyes, little boy smiles up at Mildred. His innocent grin brings out the handsome charm in the little boy's eyes. The handsome three year old boy is Nico. He is wearing black slacks, a long sleeved white button down with a multi-colored silk vest and a cute little black bow tie matching the vest print. On his feet, he is wearing cute little two strap Prada shoes. The darling little three year old girl doll beside him is April. She is wearing a medium pink Ralph Lauren cable knit sweater dress, cute multi-colored little bow printed stockings and the same little Prada shoes as Nico. Her medium pink headband holds back her little soft afro of blond curly hair.

"Ding Dong," the door bell rings. Calvin heads to the front door, a second time, to answer the call of the door bell.

"I hope it's your Aunt Melissa. I've been calling her all day. She never answered. Today the doctor tells if the baby is a boy or girl?" Mildred is talking to Amber.

Mildred is the oldest and Tay the youngest, Melissa is the middle sister. Melissa is six months pregnant with her first promising child. Tay's family is over excited for her. Melissa had three previous failed pregnancies.

"Who in their right mind has a birthday dinner 2 days BEFORE their birthday?" The questioning venom flies in the air from Tay's mother, Mary's mouth.

Mary barges into the living room with Tay's father, Mason, trailing three steps behind her.

"Only Tay Ma," Mildred answers Mary, as she hugs and kisses her.

Mildred greets Mason the same way, with a hug and kiss. Amber, April and Nico follow their Aunt Mildred's footstep, giving hugs and kisses to Mary and Mason. Mildred assists her mother out of her jacket and lays it on top of her coat, resting on the arm of the living room couch. Mildred's father places his jacket on top of Mary's jacket.

"All this fancy furniture and don't own a damn coat rack. **Boochetta**[18] at its finest I tell you." Mary declares her distaste for Tay's choice of furniture, or should I say lack of.

Tay lifestyle does resemble a person living Boochetta to the naked eye. She didn't live in Madison Projects any longer, which is definitely the hood. Tay's passion for expensive things was painted on wall with high-end paintings. Tay's passion for expensive things was hanging from the ceiling of her living room ceiling holds one of a kind a crystal glass chandelier. Tay's passion for expensive things was on the floor, the floors sparkled with custom one hundred bill tiles in some areas, marble title in other area. The two things separating Tay from being Boochetta is she didn't technically live in the hood, granted her brick stone townhouse she owns is only two and three fourths of blocks away from Madison Projects, and her second reasoning was she can afford her lifestyle.

"Ding Dong," the door bell rings.

"You all gonna have to start tippin a brother if I'm gonna be da doorman, ya heard." Calvin mumbles under his breath. Calvin heads to the front door, for a third time, to answer the call of the door bell.

"Now! This has to be Melissa." Mildred voicing her hopes with her eyes glued to living room's entrance.

"Aunt Melissa, finally you're here," Amber speaks with excitement in her voice, as she gives her aunt a warm hug and kiss greeting.

"We made it." Melissa mentions her difficulties with mobility.

---

[18] **Boochetta** is having ghost money. It is living above your economic level. Having the exterior of home lined with top of the line mini mansion material, but can't pay their rent is **Boochetta** Wearing red bottoms on your feet and a fur coat around your body, with a Gucci bag hanging from your wrist but sitting on mass trans, is **Boochetta.**

"Hay big sis and I do mean big." Tay clowns Melissa as she comes down the steps leading into the living room.

Tay's shadow, Camille, follows behind Tay as they enter into the living room. Tay and Camille abides Amber's footstep and give Melissa a warm hug and kiss greeting. Melissa waddles over to her parents sitting on the couch. Mary and Mason rise to their feet to receive greetings from their pregnant daughter, Melissa. Mildred and her husband, Michael, are next in line to greet Melissa. Last but not least, the two adorable kids greet Melissa.

"Whoa, I gotta sit down. Just saying hi to everybody wore me out." Everybody makes room for Melissa to have a sit.

Tay's almond shape eyes make contact with Mary's judgmental stares. Mildred gawks at Tay's outfit. Mildred's eyes have the same judgmental words as Mary's eyes.

"Singing my life with his words. Killing me softly with his words. Killing me softly with his words. Telling my whole life in his words. Killing me softly …with his words." *Lauren preach girl. Why do people think they have the right to past judgments on somebody's life? Mother is the queen of passing her views and opinions off as facts. She can dish out all her judgmental comments tonight. I'll allow her to destroy my Thursday but by birthday, she can't have!" Ok, let's get over this hill and over mother." Tay's chitachatter*

"Well, hello to all of yous too. Don't all jump up at once, take your time." Marc, Mildred's son, sarcasm is ignored.

He entered the living room behind Melissa. Everybody crowds around Melissa's belly leaving him out. Everybody eyes were consumed by the movement in Melissa's belly and blind to Marc's presences.

"What? I'm chopped liver 'round here?" Marc's voice is persistent for recognition.

Marc stands in a pause state waiting for the family to greet him.

"I drove her over here. Can I get some love, for dat at least?" Marc presses on for the room of family to acknowledge him.

"Marc, Man up! Stop begging for attention like a little boy." Mildred scolds her twenty seven year old son.

"Auntie, let's pray on Marc man-ing up." Calvin clowns.

Mildred's eyes shot bullets at Calvin with her stares.

"My favorite cousin." Amber's words are delivered with a hug and kiss greeting to Marc.

"Too little, too late, besides I'm ya only cousin." Marc replays to Amber's greeting.

"Not true, son." Mildred offers to correct Marc statement.

"Not true, for long, is right. Only 3 more months and 21 days and this bun will be out this oven. Oh boy do I dream every night, that day come real soon. This thing is heavy. Sheesh!" Melissa corrects Mildred's statement.

Melissa is repositioning her uncomfortable pregnant self on the couch, searching for the right spot of comfort.

"Ma, you didn't tell them about Melvin?" Mildred questions Mary.

"Who is Melvin?" Tay's curious almond shape eyes questions Mildred's and her mother, Mary's eyes.

"Yeah, who is Melvin?" Marc questions the room.

"Don't go telling stories Mildred; we must verify the boy's words." Mary scolds Mildred.

"Do you all hear me talking to you? Who is Melvin?" Tay's curious almond shape eyes question Mildred and her mother, Mary a second time.

"Melvin is a 20 year old man who contacted Ma and Dad. He's claiming to be Malcolm's son, had a whole heart filled story 'bout tracing his roots and all." Mildred spills information into the air.

Malcolm is Mildred's, Melissa's and Tay's deceased baby brother. Malcolm died twenty one years ago in a motorcycle accident.

"Auntie let's pray 'bout it!" Calvin jokes at Mildred. Mildred's annoyed look on her face is directed to Calvin. She has given him two warning stares. Her next move is to pull out her travel size Holy water and shower him with prayer.

"Mildred, stop telling stories, I have your brother's baby teeth and his hair from his first hair cut. DNA will tell if the boy is telling the truth. Until then, I don't want to even hear the damn boy's name in my presence. You all understand! Now let's eat. I aint got all night to be horsing around this barn." Mary's strongly delivers her words to silence the air.

"My home doesn't look like a barn! And animals don't live here! Mother!" Tay quickly reacts to Mary's statement toward her.

"Fucker! **"Killing me softly with his words. Killing me softly with his words".** *I'm trying my best to maintain but if she keeps throwing stones at*

me I'm gonna have to fight back. She thinks me and kids are animals? She better chill. Let's see how many times she disrespects me tonight? Bryson will never be subjected to mother!" Tay's chitachatter

"Yeah, let's eat so we can give Tay ours gifts." Melissa suggests.

Melissa can smell the tension brewing between Mary and Tay. Melissa knows the mention of gifts will get Tay in a better mood. The mention of food usually works on Mary. After everybody assists Melissa off the couch, they all follow her lead to the kitchen. Melissa's belly can taste the garlicky smell in the air.

"Did you call the caterers? And the car service like I asked you too?" Melissa quizzes Tay on her given party assignments.

Melissa is a party planner slash party promoter. She is responsible for Tay's extravagant birthday ball, Saturday night.

"Yes, Ma'am as ordered." Tay jokes with the round Melissa.

"I need that key." Marc discretely whispers his request in Tay ear.

"It's on my dresser in the green **candy bag**[19]." Tay whispers back to Marc.

Marc ran upstairs. He retrieves the single key, hanging on a green cupcake key ring, out the naive green *candy bag* and returned to group heading to dining room without detection. Tay statically sat everybody where they would be most comfortable. She sat at the bottom end of the table far away from Mary and to her left she sat Marc, her nephew. Marc has a bunch of one liners that always cracks Tay up. Tay needs Marc's

---

[19] **Candy bag** *is a small pouch packed with condoms, koowie wipes, panty liners, travel size deodorant, travel size lotion, travel size toothbrush and tooth paste. Every Sistah has a candy bag.*

sense of humor to make it through tonight's dinner. To Marc's left side sat his father, Michael. Michael's position is to block his wife's sly remarks, coming from his left side, from hitting Marc's ear. On Michael left side sat his wife, Mildred. To Mildred's left sat Mary. Mildred and her mother, Mary, could hold their private conversations with out annoying everybody else. At the head of the table Tay's father, Mason, sat in his proper position head of the family. To Tay's right sat her children, Amber, Camille and Calvin. Camille and her twin brother, Calvin wouldn't be able to literary sit apart. The twins are an inseparable team. Sitting next to Calvin is his aunt Melissa. Melissa can sit anywhere; she is the medium of the family. April and Nico has their own little arrange seating in the kitchen with Chef Robert. Chef Robert is getting a taste of being a single mom, cooking and watching kids at the same time .Chef Robert emerges from the kitchen's double wooden swinging doors. He serves everybody their plate of food.

"How much is Benson running you, Ms. boochetta? Still making ends meet taking naked pictures?" Mary's venom spits at Tay. Mary ends her inquires with tiny malicious laughter.

"His name is Robert. And no, I do not take naked pictures for an income. I am a professional Model, Mother." Tay answers her mother obscene questions.

"*Fucker.* **"Telling my whole life with his words. Killing me softly with his words. Killing me softly with his words."** *My dear mother, I wasn't naked. You never even take a look at one damn picture I took. You had your eyes closed and nose high to the sky when you found out the name of the magazine is NUDE. So how would you know if I was naked or not? Besides, that happens years ago. This is why I be telling Chyenne you gotta let go of the past or you'll end up a miserable bitch just like Mary. Mother is living testimony to the miserable bitch population. That's 2!" Tay's chitachatter*

"Who is very photogenic, I might add." Marc adds his complement to his aunt.

"Shut your pie hole, gay boy." Mary spits her words of venom down the table at Marc.

"Mrs. Mary, I'm going to have to ask that you mind your dinner manners, here tonight. Would you be so kind?" Reverend Michael's gentle stern voice questions Mary.

"Excuse me reverend, It's not your fault you can save everybody, but your gay son." Mary spits more venom down the table.

"THAT'S ENOUGH DAMMIT!" Mason shouts into the air. He attempted to clear all the feelings in the room with his words and tone.

"Tay, it's your birthday dinner. Why don't you say grace?" Mildred suggests hoping to change her mother's venom direction.

"Why doesn't she let somebody with more experience? Reverend Michael, will you do the honors?" Mary questioned.

"Killing me softly with his words. Killing me softly with his words." *So now I don't know how to pray? That's 3. How many more times in one night will she violate me?"* Tay's chitachatter

After the prayer, everyone begins to eat. Silence filled the room. Tay was definitely enjoying the sound.

"Oh my word, Benson is trying to kill me. This meat is so salty, I'm dizzy!" Mary shouts.

Mary body leans over the back of the chair. Her arms spread out wide. Mildred jumps up from the table and dashes into the kitchen. In a flash,

Mildred is back with a glass of water, for Mary. Mary takes the glass of water. Mary is now cured and is now sitting upright.

"His name is Robert!" Tay shouts into the air again because it appears Mary didn't hear her the first few times she told her the chef's name.

"Tell Benson to wash this meat off, so I can enjoy it. Tay probably spent 100 dollars on this puny sad piece of meat. Ya know Ms. Boochetta." Mary commands Mildred. Mary holds the meat up in the air with her two fingers.

"For the last time, his name is Robert, mother!"

*"Fucker. **Killing me softly with his words. Killing me softly with his words.**" Why she can't call this man by his name? Why do we have to be subjected to her live performance of death from "over priced" salted meat? Boochetta? Whatever!" Tay's chitachatter*

Chef Robert brings out the glasses of wine. He severs everybody. Amber is the first to take a sip of wine from her glass.

"Oh hell no. Sorry Reverend, for my language but you are not allowed to drink alcohol in my presence, LITTLE MISSY! So unwrap your soup cooling lips from that glass and sit the glass down! You aint to big to get an old lady shoe up your ASS! I apologize again Reverend for my language." Mary threat shot down the table to Amber along with false apologizes to the reverend for her fowl language.

Amber freeze with the wine glass to her lips. Mary's threat paralyzed her. Reverend Michael ignored Mary's false apology, as a mockery to his professional calling.

"Calm down! She is 20 years old, with a daughter. April is 3 years old, now. Let's not be ridiculous. I'm her mother and I say she can have a glass of wine, Mother!" Tay shouts back at her mother at the other end of the table.

"Fucker. **"Killing me softly with his words. Killing me softly with his words."** *How do you come in someone's home and tell them how to raise their kids? That's 4."* Tay's chitachatter

"Her mother," Mary imitates Tay's voice in a childish manner.

"Tell me this "MOTHER", How you get knocked up by your daughter's class mate? Or maybe you can answer an easier question "MOTHER", how could you walk around with you're your head in the sky, pregnant at the same time as your 17 year old daughter? I'm listening "MOTHER!" Mary questions Tay.

"Santana wasn't Camille's classmate. They just went to the same school. Camille was a freshman, he was a senior. I gain a precious gift from the experience. I love Nico. He is a beautiful kid. So what, I was pregnant with Amber. April is an angel. I'm grateful for them both Nico and April. F.Y.I MOTHER!

"FUCKER! **"Killing me softly with his words. Killing me softly with his words. I felt all flushed with fever embarrassed by the crowd."** *Why she always gotta put my shit on blast? Santana was legal when I tapped that. 18 is legal? Right? So what, I let a youngin lift me off my feet. So what, I got pregnant and had his baby. Me being pregnant with Amber brought us close together, we bonded. I take damn good care of Nico and April. Shit, I take good care of all my kids. So what, my granddaughter and her uncle are the same age. I don't ever hear her talking about Mildred having Marc when she was 16. When I had the twins I was 18. 18 is legal? Right? Mother is always walking around with a fist full of memory to wash my face with. Dessert is looking like it might be cancelled, the way she's going. And that's 5."* Tay's chitachatter

Camille slouches down in her chair. Hearing Santana's name brought back the pointing and staring she received daily at high school. Camille is a book worm. She welcomed the attention. Camille didn't inherit the plump cheeks from Tay, like Amber did. So to be noticed felt good to her. The bonus was having a little brother to care for. Camille loves Nico.

"Damn! Ma aint that kinda hitting too low even for you?" Melissa is doing her duty, trying to iron out the wrinkles of Mary and Tay being under the same roof.

"Oh, you got something to say? Riddle me this, what type of pregnant woman travels New York City streets late at night? Huh? You have nothing to say, right? Just what I thought. Mind your own business. Speak when spoke to." Mary spits venom in Melissa's face from across the table.

"I told Omar I didn't want to stay at your apartment. You would be tracking my goings and comings! I am a party promoter. I go to the parties I set up. I'm sorry working to feed my unborn child is a crime in your eyes." Melissa thoughts spill out her mouth.

"Omar, HMMM. Where's Mr. M.I.A? Poor Marc has been to more doctor appointments than he has! The damn doctor probably thinks Marc's the father." Mary spit more venom in Melissa's face from across the table.

"He's a police officer. Work causes him to miss doctor appointments." Melissa answers to the spit being tossed at her.

"Soooo...What are we getting a boy or girl?" Mildred questions Melissa. Mildred attempts to have Melissa spray good news in the air, to break the fog of tension.

Chef Robert emerges from the kitchen. He clears everyone's plate from the table. He returns to refill everyone's wine glass.

"No thanks, Benson. This wine is too rich for my taste buds." Mary speaks to Chef Robert over her shoulder.

"My name is Chef Robert"

"Why he sounds like the Allstate guy, for the commercials? Say something else, please!" Amber teases Chef Robert.

The room's air clears with sunny laughter springing from everyone's lips, even Mary's lips parted with laughter, filling the room's sunshine. Chef Robert blush and returns to the kitchen.

"Soooo... It's aaaaaaaa BOY!" Melissa announces to Calvin's table top drum roll.

"So, what's his name?" Camille quizzes her aunt.

"Whatever you name him. He better have the family's traditional "M". Sorry Tay, no intent." Mary clouds the air with her venom. Mary and Mildred share a laugh together.

"You are not sorry! That's your intent to make me feel like an outsider! Your intent is to bring me down to hell where you live at!" Tay's words hold back the tears flowing to the rim of her eyes.

"THAT'S ENOUGH! DAMMIT!" Mason shouts in the air. He attempted to clear all feelings in the room with his words and tone.

"Killing me softly with his words. Killing me softly with his words. I prayed it would finish, but it just kept right on. Singing my life with his words. Killing me softly with his words. Killing me softly with his words telling my whole life with his words. *This is why I don't fuck with her. She's a miserable BITCH. Chyenne better straighten* *up or end up like mother. How Daddy put with her shit day in and day out is beyond me. I would have lost it and choke the living shit out of her, a long time ago. Dessert cancelled. Ladies, gentleman and she-devil get the fuck out!" Tay's chitachatter*

Chef Robert emerges from the kitchen with Tay's candle lit birthday cake. Tay roughly removes herself from the table, blow out the candles on the cake as she bush pass Chef Robert's cake filled hands. Tay storms pass Mary toward the living room.

"You are a disgusting predator!" Tay bends her body to speak directly into Mary's ear.

"You're the predator sleeping with kids! "MOTHER!" Mary shot at Tay's back.

"Auntie, let's pray 'bout it!" Calvin jokes at Mildred. Mildred rolls her eyes at Calvin out of irritation. Calvin was interrupting Mildred's pleasure in watching Mary at work on Tay.

"Here's her damn gift. She can call with her thank you later." Mary places a red velvet ring box on the table.

Mary stands up from the table. She is ready to leave. Mason assists his wife with her coat. Marc walks his grandparents, Mary and Mason; two and three fourths of blocks to Madison Projects were they live. Mildred gives goodbye kisses and hugs to Tay's children, before she exits behind Mary, Mason and Marc. Mildred's husband, Michael, tip his hat and trails right behind Mildred's heels. Melissa goes searching the townhouse looking for Tay. Camille, Calvin and Amber continue to partake in the open bottle of wine. Chef Robert entertains April and Nico in the kitchen with homemade vanilla bean ice cream and cake. Melissa finds Tay in her bedroom climbing out of her cute black cat suit. Melissa enters as Tay kicks off her stylish black Jimmy Choo's shoes. Melissa didn't get a chance to tell Tay how good she looked this evening. Mary erupted like a volcano, so quickly. Mary's words are like throwing hot lava on everyone's feelings in her path.

"You okay, sweetie?" Melissa asks Tay as she sits down next to her on Tay's bed.

"I don't understand why she picks at us like that? What makes Mildred such an angel?" Tay's words are weak at holding back the tear at the rim of her eyes.

"She only fuck wit us 'cus she know it gets under our skin. Mildred married a Reverend, whose name begins with an "M". She also married rich, her freedom was won." Melissa explains Mary's behavior.

"It's 10:45. I'm going to head out. Marc should be back, by now. He's walking Ma and Daddy home." Melissa rubs Tay's back as she speaks reasoning in her ear.

Tay walks her waddling sister out to the car. Tay's chitachatter is grateful to the growth in the progress in Tay's relationship with Melissa. Tay is two years younger than Melissa. In high school, Melissa completely disowned Tay because of the attention Tay's mature body received. Melissa bumped Tay in the school hallways like a strange with a problem. Melissa gave Tay dirty looks. Melissa bullied Tay and when Melissa stopped Cookie, Melissa's close friend, stared. Tay had a crush on Roman. Roman was a grade above Tay. Melissa dated Roman after knowing Tay's feelings. Tay decided to seek Roman's revenge. Thanks to Mary's black eye peas, Tay developed a check it out body with fire burn buns. Tay voluminous body was blazing the eyes of every boy in LaGuardia high school. Tay slept with every single boy Melissa thought was cute or was interested in. The boys loved Tay's American idol, Marilyn Monroe figure with her automatic freedom to give her love. Tay's koowie had her name in plenty controversy. The sexing of teachers in their longue to pounding peers during fire alarms were the moments of life Tay she enjoyed the most. Life is a piece a cake when doing what you do best. Tay ignored the hallway whispers of her being a stupid hoe and Mary's super bass of trying to save Tay from herself. Tay declared herself to be a beautiful sinner on a starship seeing right through to one day being the champion of an endorsed dancer. The come up with the twins and Amber father, Christopher was short lived. In case you forgot, Tay's problem is her koowie. Her koowie is her leader. Her koowie ended all her relationship up in flames. Tay used her koowie to re-up the love she wanted from Mary and Melissa but didn't get. Melissa currently begs Tay to forgive her for not being able to attend the birthday party, Saturday night, due to immobility. Marc is already inside the car, warming it up. Tay sees Melissa to a safe departure lead by Marc's hands. Tay thanks Chef Robert for a lovely prepared dinner. She also apologized to him. He didn't get to serve his famous chocolate mousse cake. Mary broke up the party in the dining room early with her vicious words. Tay orders the clean up committee, Camille, Calvin and Amber, to start working. Tay leads April and Nico upstairs to get them ready for bed. She checks her phone and social media page, nothing new from Bryson.

"I don't know what I'll ever do without you from the beginning to the end. You've always been right beside me. So I call you my best friend. Through the good time and the bad ones. Whether I lose or if I win I know one thing that never change and that you as my best friend" Brandy sings the bond between me and my Sistahs. I wonder what the Sistahs are up to tonight. My Thursday night is completely ruined. I don't have the feeling to do nothing. Mother is energy draining. I need a **pink Friday**[20]!" Tay's chitachatter

Tay lies on her bed and shuffles through her gifts from her family. Mildred and Michael gave her a Christian retreat package, typical. Marc gave her a camera, practical. Marc is a photographer. Melissa gave her

---

[20] **Pink Friday** is a day with the Sistahs, not necessarily on a Friday.

just what she wanted, another pair of shoes. Tay opens her gift from her mother. Mary gave Tay her twentieth anniversary ring giving to her by Mason in the original packaging. In the top of the box liner written on the off white satin silk reads: *"Twenty years with you by my side has been great but twenty more would be even better."*

"Whenever I'm down. I call on you my friend. A helping hand you lend in a time of need. So I'm calling you now. Just to make it through. What else can I do? Don't you hear my plea? Friend may come and friends may go. But you should know that I've got your back. It's automatic. So never hesitate to call. Cause I'm your Sistah and always here for ya." *Mother-fucker! Even through her gift she spits venom. What is she saying? I'm at the age where I should have a husband? Mother please live and let live! C'mon please pick up, I need a few words of wisdom, right now."* Tay's chitachatter

The phone rings in Tay's ear. She is calling her Sistah, Sammy. Sammy always knows the right words to say to turn your mood around.

"Hello?" Sammy's voice bounces in Tay's ear, from the phone.

"Hey girl, just finish walking through hell with alcohol panties on." Tay speaks in to the phone.

"How is our lovely Mary doing these days?"

"Mary is more miserable than ever before. Tonight, she called Marc gay boy at the dinner table and me a child molester."

"Mary can be a bit much, most of the time. Just a reminder, everybody has two cent to offer but does it really count? Better yet, what is it really worth?"

"No! Her two cent doesn't count! And it aint worth shit! Thanks Sistah. I need you to clear my vision."

"No problem. Happy birthday to ya. Happy birthday to ya. Happpppy birthday to ya. Goodnite, see ya Saturday. We gonna party like Rock stars! Just two more days to ya birthday."

"And you know that's right, piece of cake." Tay's signature Sistah's quote.

"A piece of solitude." Sammy signature Sistah wish is for peace. She is the voice of reasoning in everyone's problems.

The light turns off on Tay's phone after Sammy's words. Tay glances over her reading book before turning out the light and hops on the red carpet with Bryson conducting the ride.

"Oh baby let's get naked, just so we can make sweet love, all these sensations, got me going crazy, for"

"X in the box, 'cus aint nobody checkin' me." – Nicki Minaj

Girl on Fire
Alicia Keys ft. Nicki Minaj
Girl on Fire

"Jasmine" Brooklyn lies about her name to handsome unsuspected male.

The handsome unsuspected male is sitting on a stool to the left of Brooklyn, at the bar at *"Sweet Watah"*. Sweet Watah lounge is located in the meat packing district of Manhattan. The Sweet Watah lounge has soft red lighten. Plush red couches lines the walls under the soaring granite arches Catalan vaulted tiled ceiling, giving the atmosphere a luxury sexy vampire lair feel. Perfect ora for Brooklyn, she is looking to feed on some flesh tonight. Brooklyn has turn down several men advances; she took a seat next to a clean cut tall gentleman. She hopes his conversation leads in her direction.

*"Yup, I lied. Why not? I definitely can sell it. I got dat Indian suntan. Born in Dominican Republic, lived in the Bronx and now lives in Harlem is too much to follow. And for the icing on the cake my name is Brooklyn. I don't wanna confuse da **Cookie and Cream**[21]. I jus' wanna play. What are you Beast or Bitch ? Are you fuckin' or not? All I need is 7 more minutes before I go in for the kill!"* Brooklyn's chitachatter

Beast or Bitch *is one of the Sistah's games. You target an unsuspecting male, of your liking. You have fifteen minutes to soften him up. The softening him up technique is one you have to own. What works for one, may not work for the other. Then you ask him to perform sexually actives on the spot, anal, intercourse, or oral. That is how you play. The rules are to meet at night and depart before day break. Once the sun rise and day light shine on the reality of the acts just performed the shame brightens their eyes. Number one rule is no*

---

[21] **Cookie and cream** *is blurred lines of an evolution of a white robin with thick black spots of sex therapy. The sweetest love is something else. The dream world of love wars have the lost without you feeling.*

continuous contact. The plan is to never see the person again. Who knows what will be unleashed from the inner being a beast or the bitch? Some man back down from the proposition. They are the one to be considered the Bitches. Other men will find a secluded area on the spot and handle his smooth skin, like a G. These men are considered the Beast. For the female, she can either become a beast and take the smooth skin or be the bitch and just receive the smooth skin. What will be bought out him? What will he bring out of you? The beast or the bitch?

"Yeah, da mole in da middle of my forehead is real." Brooklyn answers the unsuspected male her impatience is ringing in her words.

"See, this is where da game gets tricky. At this rate, I'm ready to Taser his ass and call it a night. He's bullshitting. Am I smelling a little bit of bitch-ass-ness in da air? With his Biggie's rap lines "What's your interest are? Who you be with?" You are cute but blind. You don't gotta have 20/20 vision to see koowie being thrown in ya face? I'm hoping I get to show ya how to work dat bulky smooth skin poking out cha pants. No, no, no, he 'bout to ask for my fucking number. Hold up, clown face. I got 2 more minutes to go, fuck it. I gotta cut him off." Brooklyn's chitachatter

Brooklyn carries a Taser gun. She'll tell you due to her job the taser is for her protection. She is a Food Critic. A business owner might not agree with her rating, published weekly in the New Yorker's Eatery, but to carry a Taser gun is defiantly excessive. She only had the pleasure of actually using the Taser gun once or twice, but her eyes are wide open looking for another opportunity. She believes once a guy asks for your number the game is over. Either, he is not interested and is requesting the number out if politeness or he is seeking something deeper than a one night toss in the *Pink Pussy Cat*. Brooklyn dangles a key on a light blue cupcake keychain, in the unsuspecting cookie cream's face.

"How 'bout we find a spot? So you can hit da spot? I'll show you da *Pink Pussy Cat."* Brooklyn use her bedroom emotional intimate voice and batting her intriguing eyes. This is her seduction closure.

The **Pink Pussy Cat** is Rhonda's production. It's a two bedroom apartment on the upper west side. The apartment is lined with every sexual pleasure known to man. From varieties of sexual creams and oil to dildos. The apartment has scented tea lights posted in various locations to a stripper pole in the living room. From a lip shaped couches to chilled champagne bottles. The living glass coffee table has a candy dishes over flowing with magnum condoms as a center piece to electric chocolate fountain. From a Jacuzzi hot tub in the bathroom surrounded by pink and red butterflies painted on the bathroom walls, to a Chinese spinal Technique Massaging Chair. All of the Sistah's have a key to paradise. The key hangs from a color coded cupcake keychain. Rhonda collects monthly dues, to keep the Pink Pussy Cat purring. It's a home away from home to take care of emotional or sexual frustration.

The unsuspecting male declines her offer but still ask for her number.

"Oh Hell No, you can't get my number. What you will get is the text free number, Bitch Nicca! Thank you Rhonda good looking on the text free hook up. Jokes on you clown face. I aint tryin to chill with you I was trying to get things hot wit you. I was trying to get right for the night. You volunteered your name, I never asked. Damn, I forgot his name that fast. What is his name? Fuck it! His name never matter any way. Getting to know you isn't in the rule book. Who turns down free koowie? A Bitch Nicca! That's who. I would've taken a rain check, but a straight out "no". Bitch Nicca! What is it with this fucking week? First court, I've apologized to Sammy ahead of time, I'm gonna have too Taser Vanessa white ass. I'm gonna melt Lewis's little snowflake. She walks around with that "I'm right 'cus I'm white" attitude. I'm going jolt her ass back into prospective. Harlem is my daughter, not hers. Lewis doesn't do anything about controlling his damn bitch ass wife. Maybe if I slap him with this Brooklyn Dominican koowie, he'll check his snowflake. In your face snowflake bitch I'm still, and will always fuck Lewis's brains out. His smooth skin rise every time we are in the same room. She be forgetting I gave Lewis to her, if I wanted him I could have him. Tomorrow is gonna be more drama. "Mandatory" Friday breakfast with E.P.M.D. and then Tay's birthday party, Saturday night. A boochetta affair, I'm sure of it. Tay 'jus won't give da hood up, no matter what I say." Brooklyn's chitachatter

Rhonda is an expert player at the game, "Beast or Bitch ." In fact, she is the founder. Rhonda advised Brooklyn a phone number must exchange hands, whether the number worked or not. In the time of electronics, everybody even grandmothers have a number; not having one will raise eyebrows. You'll lose the game before you begin. Rhonda discovered a text free phone number, text only, no voice phone calls. Brooklyn loves the idea. She loves Rhonda even more for turning her on to a text free number, a necessary tool while playing the game. Brooklyn's thrill is passing the number around. She isn't interested in a relationship, period. After being married to Carlito, she was completely against connecting with a man on any level, besides sex. In Brooklyn's eyes, men can only provide a service to her. No man was worthy of sharing her world. Brooklyn refuse to have her retrospective to be her reflection today, she wouldn't be able to look herself in the mirror. Brooklyn's childhood was spent working on her parent's farm in Dominican Republic when she received her first taste of growing pains. She grew stronger with each tear. Her journey continues on the farm she shared with Carlito. Brooklyn married Carlito at twelve years old. No, this isn't a "Precious" story. Brooklyn's menstrual cycle begin at the age of eight, by the time she was twelve she had the body breakthrough of a Dominican full grown woman. From toddlers to boys to elderly men, they all stop whatever they were doing to gawk at her body. Men, boys, women and girls all had their eye snatched out of their heads, when her shapely body sways by effortlessly. Even the male K-9 species lost control in Brooklyn's presence. Brooklyn has a unique natural beauty. Her "Hennessy" straight, complexion covers her old fashion soda bottle frame. Her clear, smooth and strong complexion is just like her personality. A natural Indian beauty mole perfectly centered in the middle of her thick jet black eyebrows. Her eyebrows freely grow into a perfect arch. She never cut her hair, just weekly clipping of the tips of her hair. Her shinny jet black hair streams down her back pass her butt to her mid thigh. Men have literally walking into street poles with their eyes glued to Brooklyn. The over flow of attention is blocked by Brooklyn. She didn't see what the big fuss was about. She had the same body shape for years. She selected who would be used and discarded by her.

Men will never have the option to choose her. She had chosen Carlito. In the Dominican Republic it wasn't unusual for twenty two year old men to wed a twelve year girl, with parental permission. Brooklyn brewed resentment toward her mother for not being around to intervening in her youthful chosen destiny. Brooklyn had given Carlito her life along with "E.P.M.D", her four sons, Edwin, Pedro, Miguel, and Dino. When Brooklyn was seventeen, Carlito moved her and the four toddlers from the Dominican Republic to Washington Heights in Manhattan, to Carlito cousin's house. Brooklyn wasn't comfortable living in a three bedroom apartment with three other Dominican families, each family stuffed in a room. She owns a house in Dominican Republic. Six months later, Carlito moved his family to their own three bedroom apartment in the South Bronx. Brooklyn entered American high school. A completely different atmosphere for her, from living on a farm raising four toddlers boys in Dominican Republic, to being a high school student in the Bronx. After Brooklyn conquered the language barrier, it was over. She no longer wanted to be a Dominican house wife; she desired to be an American teenager, like her peers. Carlito's language translated to domestic violence. After two years of being total battered emotionally and physically, Brooklyn's freedom was gained by a can of Beefaroni, shattering her right jaw bone on her nineteenth birthday, launched by Carlito's pitching arm. Along with replacement and plastic surgery, she also received a replacement in her living style. Amazingly, her beauty wasn't tarnished by living Carlito's way. Carlito struck out three years on Riker's Island. Carlito's pitching arm launched Brooklyn and her four son into Harlem. She received public assistance, public housing and counseling. The era of love and life with Carlito was over. In a period of three years, Brooklyn moved forward with her sons to a no more drama Harlem. She begins to sing different ballads with her circle of Sistahs and friends around her. Within three years, Brooklyn became a woman at twenty two. Finally, all the boys were enrolled in school. She had time be familiar with herself. When Carlito returned from the prison dugout, he came looking for Brooklyn. He soon realized Brooklyn wasn't the same player in his battering game. Carlito's gunshot hole in his ass gave him the complete 4-1-1 on how much Brooklyn had changed. Brooklyn ejected Carlito from her life. The faint scar under Brooklyn's right jaw line is all of Carlito she remembers. She covers up the deep wounded scar, only visible to her eyes, with makeup. Brooklyn made up an unbreakable shell around her heart. Her shell foundation is built of refusal to allow herself or anyone in her company to be subjected to any form of disrespect from anyone, earning the nick name Brooklyn Zoo from the Sistahs, the only people she considers family. Brooklyn is not above using her hand, feet and teeth to permanently get her point across, but she is locally known to always pack a weapon. Carlito altered her vision on life. She decided her emotions and love is treasure too rich for anybody. She settled for the quick intense sexual encounters with various men, no strings attached. Men are only pure when engaging in sexual activities, is her belief. She indulged frequently in the purity of many different men. For fifteen years she works as a Food Critic, her total honest tongue is a perfect fit. Being able to have a free dinner every night and play the game, *"Beast or Bitch"* and get pay doing it was a perfect shoe size for her. The lifestyle she adapted to came to a crashing end. Five years ago, Brooklyn stumble on to a man named Lewis playing *"Beast or Bitch"*. Brooklyn and Lewis were hot and heavy. They were meeting each other at the *"Pink Pussy Cat"* at any available moment. Lewis was comfortable with the arrangement of sexual meetings at various times, day and night, any day of the week. After six months of these escapades, Lewis wanted more of and from Brooklyn. Brooklyn ran from the thought of emotion attachment to man. Brooklyn convinced Lewis; Vanessa was the better fit for the "wife" label, but wanted to continue their set arrangement. Brooklyn loved the way Lewis danced for her the long way. The "wife" label, Brooklyn been there and done that and is through with it. Brooklyn was no longer anybodies "wife" material. Brooklyn getting pregnant by Lewis was purely a fluke accident. An accident Brooklyn was eager to ease. Once Brooklyn laid eyes on the red hair and the million tiny red freckles sprayed all over the tiny baby girl's body. The adorable little pale face, Brooklyn instantly fell in love. Her life came alive with Harlem in her hands. Brooklyn wanted this little gift from God to be cherished, guarded and loved. The things she missed out on growing up. Brooklyn was a baby, a mother and then an adolescent. She had grown into a woman after the fact. She wanted to give Harlem the woman she had become. Brooklyn refuses to part with Harlem, sparking the custody battle from hell.

"I'm not gonna let one "no" from a Bitch Nicca, end my Thursday night. It's only 9 o'clock. I need some smooth skin before I can shut it down. Imma hit another spot." Brooklyn's chitachatter

Brooklyn enters *"The City of Sin"*, a female strip club. The City of Sin is located on the Sugar Hill of Manhattan. Men at a strip clubs are easy prey. The exotic dancers get the men sexual juices flowing. Brooklyn smells the sexual juices dripping from their pores and goes in for the kill. She sits in a dark corner sniffing out the easiest unsuspected male.

"Beast or Bitch ?" Brooklyn's chitachatter

Brooklyn is scanning the room. She had her plan all mapped out. She would pretend her car keys were locked in the car. She would then ask an unsuspected male for his help. Meanwhile, she has a second set of car keys in her purse. She hopes the guy fails to get the car open. The checkmate is to solicit a ride "home" from the unsuspected male. No, she doesn't worry about getting into strange men car's because if things don't look right, she don't act right, he'll have an electrifying fright. Inside the car the game is on. She'll utilize the time to spit her hustle, feel the unsuspected male out, planning her next move. Luring him in to the purring *Pink Pussy Cat*, she hopes to stroke him upstairs. Her phone begins to vibrate in her purse. She rummages through her purse and emerges her hand with the phone vibrating in her hand. She recognizes the calling number, Lewis's house phone number. She excuses herself from the music and dancing strippers. She couldn't afford new evidences to be entered into her custody war.

"Hello?" Brooklyn questions the phone.

"Momma, whatcha doooing?" Harlem, Brooklyn's four year old daughter, questions tickles Brooklyn's ear, soothing her nerves.

A sigh of relief flees from Brooklyn's chest. She didn't have to cuss nobody out tonight. Harlem is spending the weekend at her father Lewis house.

"Whatcha doooing still up, my little princess?" Brooklyn question's her daughter.

"Ima stay up all day til daddy come home. Mama Nessa said 20 more min nutes." Harlem's angelic voice speaking words has Brooklyn's blood boiling.

"Mama Nessa." You see how this sneaky white bitch be over stepping the line. I blame Lewis. It's his job to check his bitch ass wife. I 'jus wanna yell into her brain "YOU AINT HER MOTHER". I'm tired of telling her the same damn thing. I'm telling you now, mark my words. I'm gonna have to Taser this disrespectful white bitch." Brooklyn's chitachatter

This is not the first time Brooklyn has heard Harlem refers to Vanessa as Mama Nessa, but each time it's just like the first.

"So, whatcha do today, my little princess," Brooklyn questions her daughter through grinding her teeth.

"Me and Mama Nessa made cookies and cup cakes wit smiley faces on dem. I got new ear rings and lip-gloss with the sprinkerlies." Harlem's innocent voice grit Brooklyn's teeth. Brooklyn didn't want her four year old daughter running around with shinny glitter down lips.

"Once daddy comes, I want you to go to bed its late, my little princess."

"Kay, Momma, I pinky swear, prom mis, night-night when daddy come."

"Who taught you about a "pinky swear"?"

Brooklyn notices everything about Harlem. Harlem's usage of new words sparked interest.

"Mama Nessa showed me, imma teach you Momma when I come home, Kay? Daddy! Momma daddy home! Luv you Momma call you to later, bye-bye."

Before Brooklyn could say a word, Harlem had already hung up. Brooklyn has heartaches. She wanted to be with Harlem. The need to cuddle her sweet Harlem overwhelmed her. Brooklyn wants to hear the sweets ballads of Harlem's love filling her life with meaning. She no longer had the desire to play the game. She didn't want to go home; it will only increase her longing for sweet Harlem. Brooklyn retreats to the *Pink Pussy Cat*, alone. Harlem called it, night over. As she lies in bed, she reviews the importance Harlem has on her life. She vowed to provide Harlem with the sugar and spice little girls are made of. Her farmed childhood is a foreign lifestyle to the city lights in Harlem.

****

Brooklyn opens her eyes to red and pink thick stripped walls. She rolls over on her back. As she stares at the mirrored ceiling, she smiles at her reflection. Her morning natural beauty is charming. She pulls back the wall's matching stripped bed dressings off her body and climbs out off the elevated form mattress, and giggles spring from her dry throat. The dryness in her throat moves her body towards the kitchen. Another giggle scratches her throat. The thought of any one of the Sistah trying to have sex on the mattress is humorous to her. She never uses the mattress when she comes to the *Pink Pussy Cat* to play. To her it was like having sex on a giant marshmallow. Besides, she had a firm belief to never let a man's head hit the pillow, during sexually encounters at the *Pink Pussy Cat*. Once a man's head hits the pillow the pillow talks will being. Pillow talk is how you talk yourself into a relationship. A relationship is something Brooklyn does not want. Brooklyn's groggy body staggers into the bathroom and proceeds to the kitchen. She enters the living room heading toward the kitchen. Out of her peripheral vision, she notice a covered body laid out on the red lip shaped couch. She moves in close to investigate further. It's Chyenne.

"Why da hell is Chyenne sleeping here? She lives in a three bedroom house in Staten Island. What she doing in Manhattan? Don't tell me I'm gonna have to Taser Malik's ass?" Brooklyn's chitachatter

"Buena Dias florcita, Hermosa de mi Corazon[22],"
Brooklyn exercises her native tongue to Chyenne, as she bends down to kiss the forehead of Chyenne's zombie like body.

"Good morning, Sistah." Chyenne crackly voice released the words.

"Everything okay, Hun?"

Brooklyn's question sparked movement in Chyenne. Chyenne excuse herself and goes to the bathroom. She emerges for the bathroom and heads toward the kitchen where Brooklyn is preparing coffee.

"So you had the day off or took the day off?" Brooklyn questions Chyenne.

Chyenne bounce from job to job, but never changed position or salary. Her job title is Quality control. You know when you are on the phone with a company and you hear "this call will be recorded" well the call is recorded for Chyenne to listen to. Her job duty is to critique the

---

[22] **Buena Dias florcita, Hermosa de mi Corazon:** *"Good morning, beautiful flower of my heart."*

performance of the operator assisting customers.

"I took the day off, I haven't been right since I ran into Crystal's trifling ass, but for the record and people at home they believe I'm at work. Today is a "me day!"

"You think she really gonna come thru Tay's party? Her balls don't hang dat low. She knows I'm gonna be there. She aint gonna show I'm telling you!"

"Crystal can show her face around if she wanna! If she does she better walk on pins and needles, around Brooklyn. She think when I broke her noise it was something. I got 50,000 volts for dat ass, I don't use my hands anymore. She'll be shaking like jello in a puddle of her own piss when I'm done with her ass. Brooklyn Zoo style." Brooklyn's chitachatter

"She might come just to fuck with my mental state."

"Chyenne dat girl aint think 'bout you, like you shouldn't be thinking 'bout her bitch ass. If she do show her face we gonna be ladies. But as soon as I see a glimmer of bullshit coming from her, imma light her ass up, promise. BUZZZZ," Brooklyn shakes her body rapidly. She is pretending to be electrified. Brooklyn's and Chyenne's laughter sings in the air.

"What you doing with your silly ass on this happy Friday?" Chyenne questions.

"Breakfast with E.P.M.D. and I'm already late. I truly don't even wanna go. Those eight suspicious slanted eyes staring down on me, watching my every move, some 'ole creepy shit, I tell ya. Their hopes written on their face, 'jus wishing I give them a sign, a clue or anything. I wish just one of them would 'jus man up and grow a pair of balls and just fucking ask me already!"

" I admitted to the popo when I shot his bitch ass back in the day, I had all my gun licensees in order. I showed my x-ray from my shatter right jawbone, with da lifetime order protection. I did a 30 day spin in a nut house wit Chyenne, crazy ass, da girl don't be playing crazy, shit is real. Oh please believe, I would have cocked and squeeze on his bitch ass, if he ever came after me. I guess dat hole in his ass set him straight. He would send money for E.P.M.D thru his sister. We wasn't cool, we just respected each other's space." Brooklyn's chitachatter

"Well I got a set! Did you do it?"

"No Chyenne, you had to ask my Sistah?"

A month ago, Carlito's dead body was found in his car, park inside a parking lot on 129th and Park Avenue. It was very odd a fifty year old man was killed in a drug infested area. At the age fifty years old, Carlito owned a chain of **bodegas**[23] in the Manhattan. Carlito's bodegas are from Washington heights to Spanish Harlem. He kept to himself. Never been robbed, never had a problem in his bodegas. The life style of a street hustler in the industry of corruption wasn't in his character. Brooklyn was the first questioned by Police and then Carlito's family. Police cleared her name. But the odor of guilt lingered in the air, questioning her innocence through his family eyes.

"Shit, I had to ask. You think you know a person and before you know it you got a dagger sticking out your heart, just like Crystal's snake ass did me." Chyenne's Chitachatter

"Una muerte equalls tre, dos mas para ir[24]**"** Brooklyn predicts.

"A piece of mind." Chyenne recites her Sistah farewell.

---

[23] **Bodegas:** *Spanish corner grocery stores.*
[24] **Una muerte equalls tre, dos mas para ir:** *one death equals three two more to go.*

"A piece of pie." Brooklyn expresses her desire to have an American life style. The big house white picket fenced with the all American husband, two point five children and an American dog.

****

Brooklyn heads to Manhattan's Hell's Kitchen to the diner to have brunch with her sons. Brooklyn climbs out of her red Ranger Rover, stomping her heels on the concrete. Her mouth is boxed up. One would think she was entering a boxing match. Playing up her natural Indian outer appears. She is wearing an intriguing solid fuchsia pink Indian tunics. Brooklyn wears her signature gold chandelier earrings and gold bangle on her wrist. Her long beautiful hair, she bundled up into a bun. She was extremely late for breakfast with E.P.M.D, but armed with the "I'm here now" attitude. Breakfast was schedule for 10 a.m., it's now 1 p.m. She usual missed breakfast all together. At least, she showed up today at the request of her youngest son, Dino. At the door of the local diner, she scans the room through her Ray Ban sunglasses. She spots the boys. She deliberately slowly walks over to their table.

"**Buenos Dias, mis hermosos hijos**[25]," Brooklyn greets her sons in her native tongue.

Carlito was a very handsome man. He aged slowly. He was fifty years old, although, he didn't look a day over forty. E.P.M.D are quadruplets of Carlito's timeless skin. They all are young men but have facial features of teenagers. Brooklyn takes the available seat next to her youngest son, Dino's left side. Dino is a twenty two year old college student at NYU. He is majoring in Dentistry. Dino is the only son Brooklyn talks to on an everyday basic. Dino adapted Brooklyn's carefree outlook on life. Dino is far from the serious tensed outlook on life Edwin carried around in his

---

[25] **Buenos Dias, mis hermosos hijos:** *Good morning my handsome sons*

eyes. Edwin's stiff face is strictly business all the time. The emotionless trait inherited from Carlito. Edwin and Pedro had taken over Carlito's chains of bodegas. Edwin, Brooklyn's oldest son, is seating across from Brooklyn. Edwin's eyes stares through her. Brooklyn is the most uncomfortable around Edwin. His stares are Carlito stares. She avoids eye contact with him. Edwin is now twenty five years old and Brooklyn still can't look him in the eyes and he knows it. He stares into her fear to win his way with her. Sitting to the right of Edwin is Pedro. Pedro has the temper of Carlito. Pedro is twenty four years old. His tactic of playing on Brooklyn's fear is break, hit and punch things to let out his hot temper. He has broken many of Brooklyn India artifacts she collects, indulging in the illusion of her appearance. Carlito use to break, hit and punch on Brooklyn to let out his frustrations. Brooklyn's two older sons Edwin and Pedro gave her the most trouble growing up. They were menacing little boys. They disturbed people property, shoplifted and tortured neighbor's pets. Miguel is seating on the right side of Dino. Miguel has his head buried into his iPad. Miguel is the quite one. One could forget he was in the room, he never talked. He has the knowledge of speaking but only exercised the right when it was necessary. Miguel is a twenty three year old computer genius. He works for a computer programming firm.

"Well, thank you for showing up, Mama? I've been calling you! **Telefono Roto**[26]? **Dime tu excusa**[27]..." Edwin questions Brooklyn.

Brooklyn hates having face to face connections with Edwin. Edwin's questioning ignites the explanations to flow from her lips, just as Carlito questioning once did.

"Damn, Eddie, she just got here you already jumping down her throat? Good afternoon Mamacita, how is my gorgeous little sister Harlem?" Dino questions Edwin, his brother reason for verbally attacking Brooklyn as her verbally check up on his mother and little sister.

---

[26] **Telefono Roto:** *phone is broken.*
[27] **Dime tu excusa:** *tell him her excuse.*

Dino spends a plenty time with Harlem. His brothers don't accept her as a sister. Dino was unsure of their reasoning. He narrowed it down to two factors; Harlem wasn't a product of Carlito, therefore, she wasn't their sister or because Harlem is a product of Brooklyn's careless lifestyle.

"I have a business to run; I can't sit on my ass waiting on her all damn day." Pedro speaks around Brooklyn, as if she's not seating at the table.

Miguel looks up from his iPad. Brooklyn sees the tears stream down his cheek. Her mother's instinct kicks in and she wants the details of her son's pain. At that moment, she realizes this wasn't the usual Friday breakfast. Something was going on and she wanted to know what.

"What happen?" Brooklyn questions her son, looking three of them in the eyes for answers.

"Abuela died Ma," Miguel announces the death of his grandmother, Carlito's mother. His words throb with pain as his heart voice the news. His cries of his pain drizzled on Brooklyn's heart.

"Let it out. "**Una persona hermosa tiene un comienzo y un final hermoso hermoso**[28]." She was in the hospital suffering. She's in a better place." Dino words filled with consoling emotion. Dino repeated the quote his grandmother told him when Carlito died a month ago.

"I know it's wrong to speak ill of the dead, but beauty is the essences of the heart, and dat bitch was heartless. Sounds like Dino picked up one of her famous Dominican quotes. "El matrimonio es una montana rusa" was her words of advise the 1st time Carlito drew blood. Yeah, she's right "marriage is a rollercoaster" filled with up, down, wild turns and some more shit. But when you safely get on a roll coaster ride you safely get off.

---

[28] **Una persona hermosa tiene un comienzo y un final hermoso hermoso:** *"A beautiful person has a beautiful beginnings and a beautiful ending"*

I begged that heartless bitch, through bloody lips to send me back home. She tricked me and called Carlito to pick me up. She was a beautiful bitch." Brooklyn's chitachatter

"Just ask her for what we need to know, so I can go back to work, we have a lot of deliveries today." Pedro advises Edwin.

"We need money to send her remains back to Dominican Republic. Are going to pitch in some of Papi's money?" Edwin asks Brooklyn. His eyes glued to her every inch of her face.

"You know what Eddie, you not going to keep washing my face with your Papi's money. I earned every dollar through blood, sweat and tears. No I'm not giving a fucking penny to send dat bitch nowhere. Put her fucking ass on a rife, the same she got over." Brooklyn shouts across the table to Edwin, her son. She braced herself for Edwin's hand to reach out to her, as she looked at Carlito's face on Edwin's body.

"This ungrateful little shit. He has forgotten all the sleepless night I was up with his sick ass. All the cut and scarps I doctored. The cooking and the cleaning I've done for his ass. The washing of his dirty ass clothes by hand 'cus I didn't have laundry mat money. Has he forgotten who provided him with a roof over his head and food in his stomach with hard earned governmental money? All I did on my own, the pennies Carlito throw our way wasn't shit. Carlito buried my childhood. A lost his money can't cover." Brooklyn's chitachatter

"I've been telling you she did it. Why wouldn't she use Papi's money to send his own mother home? **Dime por que**[29]?" Pedro points out Brooklyn's guilty actions.

Pedro is voicing his beliefs. He believes his mother is solely responsible for the death of his father. Pedro pounds the dinner's table with his fist,

---

[29] **Dime por que:** *Tell me why?*

demanding a reason from his brothers for Brooklyn's actions.

"That's my cue to exit. "***Los ninos disfrutar de su comida y dia***[30]" Love ya." Brooklyn's words and body move at the same time.

Brooklyn kissed Dino on his right cheek and pat rubs Miguel's back as she removed herself from the Edwin's stares and Pedro's aggressive behavior. Brooklyn believes a quick round of *Beast or Bitch* will give her back her control of the erratic motional state.

---

[30] ***Los ninos disfrutar de su comida y dia:*** *Enjoy their food and day.*

"They say all wounds heal overtime, but why does it feel like I could die. Bury my heart. Bury my heart. Bury my heart."

Bury my heart
K. Michelle
Untitled

It's the usual arrival time for Chyenne to returns home from work, but today she hadn't gone to work. She takes a deep breath before she removes her key from her blue Ford Focus's ignition. She dreads entering her home. Malik competes against Polo for Chyenne's affection. Polo is Chyenne's twenty three years old son. She takes two minutes to put her game face on before she sticks her key into the lock on the wooden framed double French doors. She lets out a long heavy sigh, indicating she had a long day as her right foot crosses the threshold into the living room. Chyenne enters her house, in Staten Island, at 6 p.m. Malik looks at the cable box on the wall unit, noting Chyenne's arrival time. Malik is Chyenne's husband. After Brooklyn departed from Chyenne, Chyenne decided to have a spa day at the *Pink Pussy Cat*. She relaxed her muscles on the Chinese Spinal Technique Massaging Chair. Then she took full advantage of the Jacuzzi hot tub. The *Pink Pussy Cat*'s furniture was used to straighten up Chyenne's mood. She's been suffering from not sleeping, disagreements with Polo and arguments with Malik to release aggression. She blames Crystal for the change in her unpredictable behavior. Nobody's perfect, her family did have disputes, but since Chyenne seen Crystal, bickering noise has becoming an everyday lullaby ritual. Malik sits on the black leather Jennifer Convertibles sectional watching cartoons with his nine years old daughter, Capri. Capri, tutu included, is snuggled under her father's underarm. Capri is the daughter Chyenne and Malik share. Malik stares at Chyenne, as he clenches his jaw. She walks over to Malik and Capri. She kisses Capri on the forehead, greeting her daughter and a glance toward Malik as greeting.

"How is mommy's ballerina? Are you ready? Tomorrow is the big day!

You guys smell dat? Chyenne questions Capri, as she walks away from the living room area.

Chyenne's body is following the scent. Capri was about to give Chyenne a hug but is leery of her mother's behavior. Capri sinks back into the leather chair.

"Smell what Chyenne?" Malik aggregation is strong in his voice.

"Who had a baby in here?" Chyenne questions Malik and Capri. Chyenne is sniffing the air. The question startles movement in Malik.

"It smells like a newborn. Who had a baby in here? Where's Polo?" Chyenne questions

"Now that's surprising you don't know where Polo is?" Malik mumbles under his breath.

Chyenne is completely consumed by the sent that she didn't hear Malik's comment. Chyenne lets her nose direct her feet through the house. She sniffed Polo's bedroom and then Capri's bedroom. She inhales the air in bathroom. Her nose is not finding the root of the smell. She continues to search the air in house. Malik slides from his comfort zone and enters Chyenne's madness. He walks up to her. He is mesmerized by her peculiar behavior. Chyenne is tip toeing, occasionally dipping low, even crawling around on her knees, sniffing the air.

"There was no baby in here. Where were you today?" Malik questions Chyenne. His eyes fixed on her face to detect any broken lines in her story.

"Hello! Work where else would I be? It really smells like a baby in here."

Malik excuse himself. He takes Capri to her room. He takes out a few toys to keep Capri busy on the Hello Kitty floor mat, in Capri's room. He turned on the T.V. in Capri's room to drown out any disgruntle lullaby that may flow from the living room. He brush pass Chyenne to the kitchen to retrieve a cold beverage and a snack for Capri. Chyenne's eyes didn't bat. She doesn't notice Malik's movements. Her concentration is aim toward discovery of the scent, lingering in the air. Malik returns to the living room to find Chyenne on her knees sniffing under, over and around areas of the living room. His right hand grips her by her right upper arm. He forcefully pulls her up from her knees to her feet. He walks her into the kitchen. He guides her over to the kitchen table. His grip slightly tightens on Chyenne's arm. His foot kicks out the chair for Chyenne to have a seat. He released her arm in front of the chair. He takes a seat at the kitchen table across from her. Chyenne looks across at Malik with puzzled eyes.

"You know today I left work early. Went to the lingerie store, felt out of my element, but I fumbled thru it. Went to the flower stop, got a nice deal on 2 dozen red roses. Went to the liquor store, picked up a nice expensive bottle of red wine to go with the shrimp scampi, I came home to prepare. Yes, I got my chef on, garlic bread included. I took a shit, showered and shaved. Got to your job flowers in my hand, tripping over my smile and you wasn't even there. I felt like an asshole. Your co-workers were laughing and pointing at me. Where the hell you been Chyenne?" Malik is waiting for Chyenne explanation.

"Malik, I took the day to pamper myself. Nothing deep, so don't trip!" Chyenne moves in closer to Malik. She is trying to smooth things over with a kiss. Malik sees the transparent fakeness in her gesture.

"Chyenne, you are not going to be able to use those lips to silent mine, tonight. You are going to talk to me today. I can't go on feeling like this." Malik is referring to Chyenne's "shut him up" technique. She offers overdue sexual pleasure to run his mind from the topic of his feelings on his tongue and mind.

"A day at the spa was supposes to calm my nerves down. Bumping into Crystal three days ago got my head all twisted. My mental is off track."

"CRYSTAL? CRYSTAL IS THE REASON WHY YOU HAVEN'T BEEN ABLE TO SLEEP IN THE SAME BED AS ME FOR THE PAST 5 YEAR. CRYSTAL IS THE REASON WHY WE DON'T HAVE SEX. CRYSTAL, CRYSTAL, CRYSTAL." Malik words are foaming out his mouth. His frustration of neglect no long able to be contained is shooting from his heart but the sound is coming from his mouth.

Chyenne stares at Malik as tears steam down her cheek. Malik feels remorseful watching Chyenne cry. He just wanted to talk to Chyenne and get some answers, not make her cry. Malik falls to his knees in front of Chyenne. He begins to wipe the flow of tears from her eyes, down to her chin.

"Chyenne, I love you girl. I want to make you happy. I want to be your rock when you feel weak. I just need you to accept my love and give a little back. This fixation you have with this woman is crazy, in fact, it's driving me crazy. Chyenne when you let someone into your life, into your heart, you are taking a gamble. You gambled with Crystal and lost. Losing hurts this I know. I have loved and lost a few times in my life time, but time heals all wounds and you live to love again. The past is the past and can't be changed. Let me be you future. Let me shower you with my love. Unbury your heart Chyenne. Let me into your heart. Let me love you until you learn to love yourself." Malik talks up to Chyenne from his knees.

Malik's eyes are glassy. Malik heart is hurting from lack of affection and love. His head feels heavy with mixed emotions. He lays his head in Chyenne's lap. This is the closest he's has be to her body in thirty six days. Chyenne is able to feel Malik's pain. She rubs the back of his head and back.

"To forget about the past is to forgive Crystal. To forgive Crystal is to let go to Ace. My beloved Ace, I will never let go. My teenage love affair diary, I could never say good bye too." Chyenne's chitachatter

Ace is Chyenne's ex-boyfriend and Polo's father. Malik lifts his head up from Chyenne's lap. His face looks identical to Chyenne's face. They both cry to each other but the words of the problems are not being expressed.

"I know you've been hurt. On a daily bases I'm dealing with your buried heart. The heart I didn't break. You've been pushing me away. So I give you your space, but now I want in on that space. I want you to say you done with the past and I want your eyes and face to match your words. Please, truly be done wit this Crystal bullshit, when you speak the words to me. Hearing you cry yourself to sleep at night, your tears hitting the pillow case rips my heart apart. Look me in my eyes!" Malik demands through his fire house of burning pain.

Malik's words are straight from his own wounded heart. He palms both side of Chyenne's face, so she can't avoid eye contact. Chyenne cries at night because she is trying to sleep with a broken heart.

"Do you love me?" Malik heart sings to Chyenne's eyes.

Malik is embarrassed by asking Chyenne "Does she love him?" After ten years he should know the answer, but he doesn't. His heart is half pass dead waiting for an answer.

"I wanna love you, Malik. What's there not to love? Malik is six foot three inches tall. The chestnut syrup coated skin that lies calmly over his slightly muscular frame is mouth watering. Just looking at him was enough to make any female on looker lick her lips, without deliberation. He sports a bald hair cut, like the cream chestnut color on his face wasn't generous enough to satisfy the lustfulness in the on looking eyes. When he spoke, it's in mellow tone, like his words was fondling your mind along

with your body at the same time. It would be nice if a woman could pay attention to the words coming from his sexy lips, but the distraction of his prefect lined teeth, made it impossible. His teeth was so straight, I would bet they were dentures. Any conversation shared with Malik was tranquilly to the receiver of his nesting word flow. He talks like he was singing. And the cherry on top he knows a woman's worth. He has money. He owns an architect firm in the Tenderloin part of Manhattan. He'll give me the shirt off his back if I ask. But he is no Ace. Ace is my forever sweet Tender bone. I know Malik maybe the last boy scout and I'm breaking all the rules by hanging on to a page in my unwritten inkwell diary of caved confessions of love for my boo, Ace. I don't see no one else 'cause I'll never see him again." Chyenne's chitachatter

A **Tender bone** is a special type of man. The type of man Ashanti is sing about when she sings, **"It's like a drug, it relieves my pain. Keeps me live, like blood flowing through my veins."** A tender bones gentleman posture, confidence and excellent bedroom skills. Their anaconda smooth skin hunts for the vital fluid of sweet woman's orchid. Love in the nick of time can have one hooked easily. You can either be stuck on the Tender bone, creating stalker tendencies within one self. Or you can be like Kelly and use it for motivation. Use the energy to create. Don't be fooled by the Tender bone, what he is giving you, he is defiantly spreading around. A Tender bone belongs to no one.

Malik never received an answer from Chyenne. Malik wasn't a boy in the hood, he wasn't one to want to be like Mike and wasn't the best man but he always had a game plan. He worked hard and received excellent grades in school. He was teased by the brothers but wasn't easily broken. He stayed clear of the street war and in the line of karma duty. His earnest green story developed in college point, New York. At college he had the element of freedom. His young charm wholehearted passion was the crime scenes of female broken hearts. All it took was Malik's heart to be broken once. His thoughts were two can play that game. Malik left a trail of wound emotions. Malik climbed forty nine ladders to maturity. Malik blossomed into an authentic black man. Any woman lucky enough to nab his heart was introduced to life as a perfect holiday. His heart was under the siege of love for Chyenne. Chyenne loves Malik but not with her whole heart. She had falling for Ace years ago but never stops listening to her heart. Chyenne and Malik's ten year marriage wasn't simply explain in black and white keys. Chyenne has an authentic black man willing to know her pass and still love her for her. Malik has been showering Chyenne with the unthinkable love but Chyenne never broke down and loved Malik back. Chyenne brand new state of mind after the Crystal era was if she didn't have Ace she didn't have anything. Crystal receives the blame for Ace butterflies swimming in Chyenne's stomach 'til this very day. Malik will love Chyenne as she is and Chyenne knows it. Malik wasn't expecting Chyenne to be a superwoman or G.I Jane, just his wife with loving hands. The lack of love Malik needed to receive had him living in a daily killing yard of the heart. His heart's song sang in a minor fall on deaf ears. Malik currently has an over powering desire to display his love to Chyenne. He believes in his heart if he shows her his love is real, she'll dig up her wounded heart. He knows his love can repair her heart, if given the chance. He is going to make her see, feel and hear his love. He leads her into their bedroom by her hand. They are standing face to face in the middle of their bedroom. He begins to remove her body from her clothing. He unbuttons the four buttons on her brown business suit top. He slowly slides the top off her shoulders. She lifts her arms to the ceiling. He pulled off her white silk tank top over her head. He walks around her body enjoying the view. Her sexy, smoothly, silky chocolate fudge coated skin is exposed. Malik can't resist. He licks her shoulder blade, as he unhooks her bra strap. She wiggles free from the bra straps. The bra lands on top of the pile of her clothes on the carpet floor to the right of her standing body. He unzips her business skirt. The skirt falls to her feet. She steps out of the business skirt at her feet. He sits her body down on the right side of the king size bed. He removes her shoes from her feet. He gently rolls down her pantyhose and then her underwear. He wraps her nude body in her plush white bathrobe.

"I'll be back for you." Malik whispers in Chyenne's ear.

Malik turns on the stereo right before he disappears out of their bedroom. The sweet tunes from Andre Ward's saxophone are soothing to the soul. He quickly checks in on Capri. Capri is practicing her route for recital tomorrow morning.

"You doing good, baby girl. Alvin Alley better watch out!" Malik throws words of encouragement to Capri.

"Oh daddy, let me practice."

"Okay, I'm leaving."

Malik return his attention to Chyenne. She is waiting patiently for his return. He enters their bedroom with two flute glass filled with red wine.

"Sip on this baby, while I run your bath water." Malik speaks softly to Chyenne's eyes.

Malik goes into the bedroom bathroom. Chyenne hears the water filling up the bathtub. Chyenne sat on the bed in a daze, sipping on her red wine. She is soaking up the instrumental music playing in the air. Malik stares at Chyenne from the bathroom door. His eyes trace her sexy silk chocolate fudge coated face. He adores her slightly chinky eyes, Capri was fortunate to inherit. He smiles at her cutie little button nose. From her lips down to her feet she looks like Jessica Rabbit, from the movie "Who framed Roger Rabbit? Malik jokes to himself. Chyenne's sexy body, heavy on the top, thin in the waist and light on the bottom has turned up his manhood. His eyes go back to the beginning of the path of the sexy silk chocolate fudge goodness covering her face. Chyenne notice Malik's stares. The dull lifeless expression painted on Chyenne's sexy silky chocolate fudge coated face remains. Malik wish he could know exactly what was going on in Chyenne's head. Her eyes would never paint him a picture. He walks over to her with a hair band in his hand. He tames her wild curly mix-bred hair on her head into a bun. Capri the ballerina has given him a great deal of practice. He is now better than Chyenne at creating a neat secure bun of hair. He lands a sweet kiss to Chyenne's forehead. He leads her into their bedroom's bathroom by the hand. She uses his right hand for balance as she steps into the bubbles of warm water. She settles her body into the water. He picks up Chyenne's burgundy face cloth. He rinses the face cloth out in the bathroom sink. He lathers up soap on the face cloth. He kneels down on the side of the bathtub. He folds the face cloth in a smaller square. He gentle passes the soapy face cloth across Chyenne's forehead, down her left cheeks, to her chin. He performs the same technique to the right side of her face. He uses the face cloth to clean the corners of her eyes, nose and lips. He cleans the groves in her ear and behind her ear. He return to the bathroom sink and rinsed the face cloth free of soap. He returns to the side of the bathtub to remove the soap from her face. He hangs the face cloth in its place on the storage rack. He takes hold of her bath sponge. He dips the sponge into the bubbly warm water. She closes her eyes absorbing the sweet instrument dancing in her ears. She is relishing the pampering Malik is bathing her in. He mobilizes the sponge. He grazes her neck to her right shoulder with the soapy sponge. He sweeps the soapy sponge down her right arm beyond her elbow to her forearm. He caress her wrist, right hand, and between each finger with the soapy sponge. His expertise with the soapy sponge intimacy explores her left arm, elbow, forearm, wrist and left hand. He individually washes each finger on her left hand with the soapy sponge. He dips the sponge back into the bubby warm water surrounding Chyenne's body. He squeezes the sponge over her chest. The soapy water cascades down her breast and drips off her double chocolate nipple. The white soapy water on her sexy silk chocolate fudge skin has awakens his manhood. The soapy sponge applauds her fit abdomen. The soapy sponge tenderly smooches her vagina. Her lips release a slight moan. Her vagina is unfamiliar with his genuine loving caresses. He lifts her right foot from the bubbly warm water. He washes her toes on her right foot one by one. The soapy sponge continues on the path of wanderlust pass her ankle to her leg up her calf, knee to her right thigh. He places her washed right leg back into the bubbly water. He lifts her left leg out the bubbly water to rehash his sensual washing. Chyenne opens her eyes. Her eyes meet with Malik's eyes.

"What's wrong with me? Why can't I love this man? It's clear he loves me but he is no Ace. The Ace of Spade scooped up my heart. The Ace of diamond is an ornament, I'm happy to wear. The Ace of club has a nightstick, most dream about. Ace of hearts has a deep compassion, which can be felt in every word or touch. Being locked up for a year, Polo's head being busting open, no two year old should ever be subjected to the pain of 45 stitches in their head, my credit being destroy, and the lost of my apartment is everything Crystal did to me. Crystal even sleeping with Ace was something I could have forgiven but to lose Ace forever was something I could never ever forgive Crystal for. In Madison projects there were 3 different stories 'bout what happen to Ace. I've heard he was in Cuba, killed or locked up. Either way, I searched for him when I got home from jail, but came up empty. When I got outta jail, I came home to nothing. No home, no kid, no man and Crystal trifling ass was nowhere to be found. Once Crystal got her inheritance, she ran for the hills. She never was looking back." Chyenne's chitachatter

"Honey, I'm home," Polo shouts from the living room.

Chyenne jumps out of the bathtub, skips over Malik, snatch up her bathrobe and runs to the living room. Soap suds are swimming around Chyenne's ankles. Chyenne leaps into Polo's arms. She plants many kisses on Polo face. With Polo's face resting in the palm of her hands she looks into Ace's face. Malik follows Chyenne into the living room. Malik's heart sinks. Malik wonders what he has to do to gain Chyenne's affection. The same affection she throws so openly on Polo.

"Look at this tutu I picked for Capri for tomorrow." Polo shows off. The little pink and purple custom made tutu.

"Wow, honey that's great! Let show Capri." Chyenne suggest.

"Sorry babe, she fell asleep. She has a long day tomorrow. She has 2 performances early in the morning." Malik announces.

"Let watch a movie together my lovely son," Chyenne suggests.

Malik stares in amazement. Did Chyenne ever give thought to Malik's feelings? Malik's mind refer him back to his unanswered question, did Chyenne love him? Did she ever?

"Sure why not?"

Chyenne suggestion to Polo is a selfish act. Polo will be watching the movie but Chyenne will be watching him. She relives her past life with Ace, through Polo's face. Malik's heart sinks again. Chyenne is gone again. Malik's eyes see Chyenne but to catch sight of her flesh yards away. Malik's heart leaves every time she abandons him for Polo. Malik wonders if she's gone for good or will return to the bed in the morning. Malik predicts a night of tossing and turning he'll be reaching, while imagining that's she's there by side him where she belongs. Malik can't sleep if Chyenne isn't sharing the king size bed with him. He just wants to breathe her air. Chyenne will more than likely fall asleep in the living room staring at Polo's face. Malik wish Chyenne knew how lonely their bed, their sheets, their pillows and his heart gets when she's not sleeping on her side of the bed.

"That bitch bad, looking like a bag of money."

Bag of Money
Rick Ross ft Meek Mills, Wale and T-pain
Self Made Vol.2

It's 5:45 a.m. Saturday morning the sun hasn't fully blossomed for the day.

"I have 17 hours to be drop dead gorgeous. Sorry Tay, but all eyes is gonna be on ya girl, tonight. You should be use to it. I can't help it, am a men magnet. I know it's ya birthday and all, but eyes are gonna be glued to dis million dollar body. My **Blasé**[31] *attitude is how I attract men, not having my ass out. I laid out my little black strapless dress by Yves Saint Laurent, only $2.7k. The dress is from the spring 2008 collection. All black, so I can put a rest to the past. I can begin living free of old baggage. Ya buggin if ya thought I was gonna run out and buy sommin new for a hood affair. Sorry, not gonna to be able to do. I had dis little number in the closet. Shit, them fools up in there tonight gonna be staring I'm the most money they will ever see. Their broke eyes aint never see $2.7k in dollars much less in* **étoffe**[32]*in their lifetime." Crystal's chitachatter*

"SUU-WUU!" Crystal yells out from her thin upper lip's distinguished superior tone to her Vietnamese house maid. Her screeching voice echoes from her master bedroom on the second floor through her two story eight bedrooms, three bathrooms, two living rooms, a dining room and huge kitchen, in Stamford, Connecticut gated twenty four hour secured house. The second floor is where seven out of the eight bedrooms are located. Two of the rooms have private bathrooms. Upon reaching the top landing, entering the second floor is a large living room. The second floor

---

[31] **Blasé** *is French for nonchalant.*
[32] **Étoffe** *is French for fabric.*

living room's floor is wall to wall Tiger's fur. The centerpiece of the room is mounted on the wall. A one hundred inch T.V. connected to Yamaha HD surround sound system. Speakers are embedded in all four walls in the room. Yamaha HD surround sound system is something she picked up while she visited Japan, about two years ago. She has converted six of the bedrooms to "theme" rooms. Each room has a different theme. One room has an exercise theme, lined with all state of the art equipment, the room she rarely visits. Another room has a book theme, similar to a small library. The ton of books filling the shelf was previously owned by her mother. Her mother used books to escape everyday live. Crystal would enter the room open a book and inhale the pages; her nose recognizes her mother's French hand cream on the pages. The last four rooms were occupied by her wardrobe. One room is for tops, one is for bottoms, one room is for dresses and one room is for shoes. The room for dresses has the extra bathroom.

"SuWu, is the only sound I took from da hood. Hiji is the best Arabian sandwich maker in Harlem. I scraped the hood to find Hiji. I finally find him and hired him as my live-in Cook. These two are da only hood things in my life. Dis party should be interesting." Crystal's chitachatter

"Yes Ma'am?" Su-Wu responds to Crystal's hollering. SuWu's accent is very strong on her words. Her name is Sulee Wu, but Crystal cut out the lee part for personal amusement.

"Get Lisa, glam squad, and Armed Security on the phone now. Oh yeah, call dat guy. What's his face? Da damn driver, I'm gonna need his services tonight. Tell Hiji, I feel for a western omelet with green tea." Crystal's demands flies from her thin upper lip's distinguished superior tone before she uncovers her body from a goodnight sleep on her three million dollar Dove feathered custom made bed.

"James? Ma'am." Su-Wu gives Crystal the driver's name.

"Whatever his fuckin' name is, get his ass on the phone. Ya feet aint making smoke! Su-Wu I said NOW! Let's get to working around here today!"

SuWu intentionally moves at her own pace to make Crystal's cold vanilla false Caucasian pigment skin tickle with red frustration.

"Yup, I'm gonna roll up to da part wit security. Da jungle bunny, Brooklyn Zoo gonna be running lose. She gonna have to give me 50 feet or deal with Lance, James or whatever his name is. Dat boy is 300 hundred pounds of pure muscle. He can bend iron, so twistin up Brooklyn should be nuffin for him. Chyenne's punk ass is still bitter. I said it a 100 times, I'm sorry. I know I was supposes to be holding her down while she was locked up but being responsible for another human being was too much for me. I never meant for Polo to get hurt. I wasn't watching him. Next thing I knew he was bleeding and crying. I rushed him to the hospital and called Ace right away. How was I to know Administration of Child Service was would get involved? How was I to know they would take Polo from Ace? I'm gonna try my best to be civil with Chyenne, but if she brings up the past, I'm gonna have Lance, James or whatever his name is deal with her. I'm so pass da Madison Project teenage years of my life. I'm gonna have to show them bitches up. I'm given Tay Scottish Diva Vodka, as her Birthday gift. The bottle is stuffed with crystals and gemstones, real girly like, just like Tay. It cost a mil. My gift is going to be the #1 gift, guarantee." Crystal's chitachatter

Su-Wu returns to find Crystal in the dress theme room. Su-Wu hands Crystal the house phone with Lisa, her accountant, on the other end of the phone receiver.
"Good morning, Miss Moore. It's not even 6 a.m. on a Saturday morning. How can I assist you?" Lisa southern accent with a hint of annoyance questions Crystal.

Today is Lisa's day off. Lisa can't understand what could Crystal possible want from her?

"I'm attending an event and would appreciate if you would accompany me?" Crystal's thin upper lip questions in the distinguished superior tone.

"Will I be paid for the hours spent at your "event"?" Lisa's southern accents questions, hanging with Crystal wasn't for recreational pleasure in Lisa's opinion.

"Lisa, why wouldn't you be paid for your services? I was going to ask if your husband could be my escort, but I'll take you instead."

"My husband is unavailable! It's either me or nothing!"

"Well hurry over, you know I have to dress you from head to toe, make you look like you got a few chips, if ya gonna roll with me."

Lisa hangs up the phone annoyed. Lisa is shocked and appalled Crystal would even suggest using her husband as an escort. Lisa knew firsthand what happens to male escorts of Crystal. Crystal pays for their time and sex.

"Yup, imma dress Lisa's homely ass up. The glam squad gonna do her hair, face and nails. Make da "Sistahs" think she come from money, like I do. They won't know a thing. They don't know a damn thing about having real chip any way, they never did." Crystal's chitachatter

Crystal carries her tyrants down stairs to the kitchen. The click-clacking of heels on her fur slippers echoed thru the dining room in to the huge kitchen. Hiji stands over the electronic stove preparing Crystal's breakfast.

"Hiji, I'll be eating on the pool deck." Crystal's thin upper lip distinguished superior tone, informing the cook where to bring her food.

Crystal waltz pass the guest bedroom, which has an intimate theme. The guest room is where her temporary boy toys stay. She continues to stroll pass the guest bathroom into the glass walled living room. She slides the double glass doors open to her enormous backyard. There is a pool, bar-be-que grill, picnic tables and a bed of roses surrounding a Cupid water fountain. She lays her body out on the beach chair near the pool, the fully equipped bar stands behind her.

"It would be nice to see da Sistahs all together, again. I wonder what their best look like. I hope Chyenne comb her nappy weave. Tay gonna have her ass hanging out, her only asset. Rhonda high yellow ass better have tanned. She looks like she fought of being an albino in the wound but half won. 'Cus da girl aint got a drop no color in her skin. I wanna know who told her dat blond hair goes with her complexion? And the rose of the gutter, Brooklyn, better keep her distance. Oh let's not forget the holy one, Sammy. I wonder what kind of advice will flow from the all mighty Sammy's lips tonight. I can't wait to show these bitches up and erase them from my memory. If Chyenne is still homeless she can have a room in the basement. Sugar and Spice would love a roommate. " Crystal's chitachatter

Crystal laughs out loud at her chitachatter. In the basement of Crystal's house are four living quarters for her live-in employees and her two toy Yorkies, Sugar and Spice. Basically four studio apartments are in the basement. Crystal charges a five percent fee for living in her basement, which she subtracts from their pay. Only Su-Wu and Hiji are currently living in basement with the two toy Yorkies, the noisy neighbors.

"Sometimes, the one you call friend be who envy the most."

BET
Fabolous ft. Jadakiss & Styles P
There is no competition: Death comes in 3's

I'm going to give the facts about Crystal's and Chyenne's relationship. You draw your own conclusions. Crystal's mother moved to Madison Projects. Crystal's mother wanted to teach Crystal the value of a person, as well as the value of an earned dollar. Crystal's mother was raised with a golden spoon in her mouth; anyone or anything was for sale. She planned a different life for Crystal. But to maintain her taste in the finer things in life and raise her daughter with the necessities, she worked two jobs. She was uncomfortable with the idea of her daughter being unattended for hours. She befriended an elderly woman, who lived on the same floor. The elderly woman had a granddaughter living with her, Chyenne. The elderly woman serviced as a babysitter for Crystal. When the elderly passed away the job was passed down to Chyenne. Chyenne's mother lived down south. Chyenne's mother flew up to New York and established the government to pay the rent to the apartment and flew right back down south. Chyenne was envied by many. She was the only sixteen year old with her own apartment. Chyenne's apartment was the original home of *Pink Pussy Cat*. Crystal is four years younger than Chyenne. Crystal followed Chyenne around like a pesty little sister. Sammy warned Chyenne of Crystal. Sammy's wisdom sees past her eye vision. Crystal was too eager to be a part of the Sistahs. The Sistahs keep Crystal at arm's length, not only because she was younger, but because they could see in Crystal eyes the envy she held for Chyenne. Chyenne's teenage years was the beginning of Chyenne doing side hustles with her boyfriend, Ace. Ace caramel color complexion, with cornrow braids and his light green eyes was a lady killer. Ace and Chyenne was an item since preschool, but only made it official when Chyenne gave birth to Polo, Ace's son. They had a on and off relationship, but it was local known they were a couple. Crystal jumped right on board with the scams Ace and Chyenne ran. Their undocumented criminal records ranged from pick pocketing to fake checks. Around this time, Crystal's mother had passed on to a heavenly existence. Crystal practically moved in Chyenne's apartment down the hall. Chyenne took good care of Crystal every day after school. Chyenne and Ace practiced parenthood on Crystal. From feeding her to homework, Chyenne was always there for Crystal. Chyenne even showed up to Crystal's school to protect Crystal from fights. Crystal was known for a mouth writing checks, her ass couldn't cash. Chyenne and Crystal went to Franklin Mills's mall, in Philadelphia, with hot credit cards, obtained by Crystal. The credit cards were already called in to the companies as stolen. Chyenne was detained and charged with Pity Thief, sentenced to three years of imprisonment, but was released after serving a year. Crystal fled from the Philadelphia crime scene. Crystal returned to New York and resumed Chyenne's life. Crystal didn't consider informing anyone about Chyenne's incarceration. Crystal lived in Chyenne's apartment with Ace and Polo. Brooklyn punched Crystal in the face, when Brooklyn saw Crystal playing house in the park with Ace and Polo. Crystal open up twenty credit cards in Chyenne's name while she was in jail. The credit cards in Chyenne's name were equivalent to sixty thousand dollars in debt. Crystal strongly stand behind her words that the forty five stitches straight down Polo's two year old forehead was purely accident, but there is nobody to contradict her claim. Ace was out doing his hustle thing. Crystal and Polo were alone in Chyenne's apartment. By the time Ace arrived at the hospital, his son was already in custody. Crystal didn't seem moved either way. She didn't care where Polo had ended up. She was interested in Ace. Crystal wanted the bond Chyenne and Ace shared. They took apart of Ace heart, when they took his son, along with his hustling attitude. Sooner than later, he lost Chyenne's apartment, due to non-payment. Crystal tried to use sex to get Ace back to his old self, but he had lost himself to his own thoughts, walking aimlessly around the streets of New York. Ace found solitude in drug use. When Chyenne returned home from jail all she had was the Sistahs to help her through the mess Crystal created. Her home, her son and her man was all gone. Chyenne was so depressed. The Sistahs found her living in DUMBO (Down Under the Manhattan Bridge Overpass) with homeless people, sharing a cardboard housing. Chyenne had given up on living life, what an awful feeling. Chyenne felt like her life was not worth living. Chyenne had lost her worth. The Sistahs put the pieces of Chyenne's life back together, but her heart was still broken from Ace's and Crystal's betrayal. Chyenne's tattoo on her waist reads: *Loyalty*. A daily reminder of Crystal and Ace, the three of them got the same tattoo together. Only time told the fact there wasn't loyalty between them. Crystal received her inheritance and ran for the hills. Crystal never looked back for Chyenne. Crystal harbored hatred toward her mother and family for her life in Madison Projects, it was a life she didn't have to live. She felt she should've had the privileges of the money from the day she was born.

"Now I move with aggression, use my mind as a weapon."

Ambition
Wale ft. Meek Mills & Rick Ross
Ambition (Deluxe Version)

"Thank you, Auntie Rhonda. They are beautiful!" Capri gratitude is sealed with her little arms wraps around Rhonda's luminous white chocolate body. She hugs Rhonda extra tight.

"After every performance the Star of the show should receive a bouquet of Roses. You're very welcome, you're a star. You gonna have to teach ya Auntie How to flex and bend like dat, it can come in handy!" is Rhonda's response to Capri angelic face.

"Look Mommy, just like the ones daddy bought you." Capri is showing off her roses to Chyenne.

"You are so beautiful. I got a lil lil sommin for my baby girl!" Polo ignites sparkles in Capri eyes.

"Polo, whatcha got behind ya back?" Capri questions Polo's arm hidden behind his back.

"Close your eyes and turn around." Polo instructs Capri.

Polo ropes Capri's neck with a platinum gold chain with a diamond filled pair of ballerina slippers charm, dangling from the middle of the chain. Chyenne's eyes swells with tears. Her mind travels to her sixteenth birthday when Ace surprised her the same way with a gold chain. She places her hand on the gold heart charm, hanging from the gold chain around her neck. Chyenne is still wearing the birthday gift from Ace.

"Okay now open ya eyes, Princess." Polo instructs Capri.

"Oh Polo, thank you, you are the best brother in the whole wide world. I love you. Thank you!" Capri gratitude is sealed, as she wraps her little arms around Polo's body.

"You are also the best son a mother could ask for!" Chyenne toss Polo a praise.

"Mom, why are you crying?" Polo is questioning the tear drops falling from Chyenne's eyes because he noticed it.

"Just tears of joy, my lovely son!" Is Chyenne response to Polo. Chyenne quickly dry up her tears sexy silky chocolate fudge face. She knows if Malik catch wind of her tears there will be an argument to follow.

"Damn, do you ever give it ya eye's sprinklers break?" Rhonda's chitachatter is referring to Chyenne's tears.

Today is Capri's day. Chyenne didn't want to steal the spotlight from her daughter. Capri, Polo and Chyenne were waiting on Malik to bring the car to the entrance of the New York School of Ballet, to pick them up to go out to eat. Rhonda is keep them company until Malik comes around with the car.

"Pretty ladies and gentleman, need a lift?" Malik shouts from his chestnut syrup coated lips, his voice travels from the driver's seat out the passenger's side window.

Capri and polo climb in the back seats of Malik's bold black Infinite FX35. Capri is shows off her gifts from Polo and Rhonda to Malik. Chyenne continues to finish her conversation with Rhonda.

"Rhonda, you sure you don't have enough time to have brunch with us?" Chyenne questions

"No sweetie, I gotta lot to do before tonight. I still haven't picked a gift for Tay. You know how Tay gets over birthday gifts. She gotta get as many as she can, and I'm gonna drop my car off to Benny."

Benny is Rhonda's nephew, Sammy's son. Chyenne and Rhonda share a laugh at Tay's childlike behavior over birthday presents.

"What did you get her?" Rhonda questions Chyenne.

Rhonda picks Chyenne brain for a gift idea. She refuses to buy Tay another pair of heels. Everybody will show up with a pair of heels. A pair of heels is a quick way to Tay's heart.

"I bought her the new Nicki perfume, and a Coach tote. Did she hear anything from Mr. Bryson Mitchell, yet?" Chyenne questions Rhonda about Tay's contact with Mr. Bryson Mitchell.

"Nope she hasn't heard anything yet. It's only been 3 days! She losing her mind like it's been weeks or even months. I bet he show up at the party. She'll be alright." Rhonda speaks her optimistic view.

"I don't think he'll show. I just don't trust his ass."

"Chyenne, who do you trust?"

"I only trust the Sistahs and Malik."

"Girl, ya crazy!"

"Okay ladies, it's time to go we are starving. You can catch up at the party tonight." Malik rushes Chyenne's small talk with Rhonda.

"A piece of mind." Chyenne recites her signature good bye.
"A piece of ass." Rhonda replies with her own signature good bye.

Rhonda gives out her hugs and kisses to Chyenne and her family before she heads toward her parked car.

****

"Benny I want the whole story. Don't leave a thing out," Sammy uses her scolding voice.

Rhonda walks into Lorraine's house. Rhonda takes a seat by the window next to her brother, Teddy. Rhonda has no idea what's going on, so she just listens in to be filled in on the details.

"Mom, I'm sorry. You can ground or punish me but nothing you do can make feel any worst than I already do. The girl told me she was on birth control pills. I know dat don't make it alright not to use a condom. I didn't use one anyway. She claimed to be pregnant. So I took her to abortion clinic. When the doctors were done with her and she came out from the back, I could tell she was in a hell of a lot of pain. My heart couldn't send her home like dat. So I wrote a fake letter, stating she was going on a weeklong trip with the school. I made up a fake trip to several colleges orientations. Mom, I've told my crime in whole. I'm so sorry. I definitely learned a hard lesson." Benny explains the strange phone call Sammy received from the yelling parent of the girl.

Rhonda tries to ease her way out the door. Benny's brilliant plan wasn't executed alone. Rhonda knows Sammy is smart enough to figure that out. Rhonda didn't want to be fingered for her involvement.

"Hold it right there, Rhonda! Benny is a very smart kid but I know you were involved. This pile of mess gotcha name written all over it! I deal with you next." Sammy shouts to Rhonda.

Sammy caught Rhonda trying to exit the house without detailing her involvements in Benny's situation. Sammy is the middle sibling, between the oldest Rhonda and the youngest Teddy. Sammy has a tendency to mother everyone in her family, even Lorraine, her mother.

"Sammy, all I did was gave him the key to the *Pink Pussy Cat* to stash the girl. I swear!"

"Rhonda, that was far too much! When it comes down to my son and decisions that will affect his life forever you have to tell me! I would never do that to you! If Paris came to me with a big problem similar to this, you would be the first to know because she is your child. I wouldn't be able to hold out on you! You are 100 percent wrong and I'm calling you out on it. You're so wrong!"

Sammy is truly annoyed by her sister's behavior. Instead of being a role model to her son, Rhonda was being his friend. Holding Benny's secrets is not an Auntie's duty; Rhonda never listened to Sammy's aunt etiquette speech.

"Mom, can I still go to see my father play?" Benny asks Sammy. His head already hanging low because he thinks she is going to deny his request.

"I'm not going to stop you. The trip was planned for weeks. Plus, lil TJ has his little heart set on seeing a basketball game from courtside. Plus, you gonna check up on Paris while you are in Atlanta. You better drive extra careful and watch my nephew. Whatever happens to him happens to you 10 times worst."

T.J is Teddy's eight year old son.

"C'mon guys its 3:30 already. We gonna miss our dinner reservations!" Rhonda announces.

"Silly girl, the reservations are for 6. We still have plenty of time," Teddy informs Rhonda.

"But I still haven't gotten a gift for Tay."

"Who waits until the last minute to buy a gift? You knew all year this day was coming. Why aren't you prepared?" Sammy questions Rhonda.

"She's not prepared because it's Rhonda we talking to. Better late than never, is her motto." Teddy pokes fun at Rhonda.

"Well it's late already. I can't afford never. Tay will bite my ass off if I show up without a gift."

"And you know that's right. Tay plays no games with her birthday gifts." Teddy agrees with Rhonda.

"My dear sweet mother we'll be back shortly, can you please be ready." Sammy leaves instructions for Lorraine.

"Mom, we are heading out. We gonna get on the road." Benny informs his mother, Sammy.

Benny's six foot frame hovers over Sammy body, as he kisses her on the cheek good-bye. He also kisses his grandmother, Lorraine and his aunt, Rhonda. Teddy walks TJ and Benny out to Rhonda's car. Teddy double checks TJ's book bag. Teddy wants to make sure his son is well prepared with entertainment for the long drive.

"Uncle, I'm gonna take care of ya boy. You know I gotcha!" Benny's words are to assure trust from Teddy.

Everyone is surprise Teddy was allowing TJ to take the trip with Benny. Teddy is an extreme over protective father. But after a week over TJ being out of school and under Teddy twenty four hour care, Teddy was interested in a short break.

"I know you better. Ya mother is serious business. I know she's short but she'll whop da ass." Teddy reminds Benny of Sammy's threat.

Rhonda runs out to her car.

"Shit, I almost forgot my damn outfit is in the backseat. Benny, don't forget to give your cousin a big 'ole kiss from her mother." Rhonda reminds Benny.

Rhonda snatches up bags from the backseat of her car. Rhonda buys things and throws bags in the backseat of her car. There are a total of six bags, collected over a week of Rhonda's spontaneous shopping. Rhonda gives Benny and TJ a hug and kiss good bye. Rhonda looks around the car to make sure she didn't leave anything behind. Teddy has already started heading inside Lorraine's house.

"Good lookin'! You didn't snitch me out!" Rhonda is thanking Benny for not telling the whole story including her involvement with "girl" situation.

"Oh auntie, I would never serve you up. I always gotcha!" Benny assures Rhonda, they little secret is safe.

"Rhonda, let's go! You have 1 hour to get Tay's gift, then we coming back here to get Ma for dinner. It is 4:15 now. You snooze, you lose!"

"SHOTGUN!" Rhonda shouts into the air. Her words are to inform Teddy he will be seating in the back of Sammy's shiny silver S-type Jaguar car.

"Go, Go, Go, Go, Go, Go, Go Shorty. It's your birthday. We gon' party like it's your birthday. We gon' sip Bacardi like it's your birthday. And we don't give as fuck 'cus it's your birthday."

Rhonda, Sammy and Teddy sing along with 50 cent, as his voice and beats scream from the car speakers. They are getting mentally ready for Tay's birthday party in a few hours. Sammy pulled her S-type Jaguar in to a parking spot at Queen's center mall's parking garage. The trio walks in the shopping area of the mall.

"So I found out why Victoria didn't show up to court, last Wednesday. She was being processed in Central Bookings for shoplifting." Sammy is updating Teddy and Rhonda.

"Shoplifting? Why would she be shoplifting when I give her child support money every week? I know she don't spend even half of the money on my son. So what da hell is she doing with my hard earned dollars? It's bad enough my tax dollars are being used for to feed other families!" Teddy speaks his annoyance.

"Forget about the child support money she's getting from you, where da hell is her HUSBAND at?" Rhonda comments.

Victoria is the mother of TJ, Teddy's son. A little over two months ago, Victoria wed a local bum from Madison Projects, the hood. Victoria challenged Teddy's court ordered visitation rights. She demanded TJ to walk her down the aisle on a Saturday morning. Teddy didn't feel it was unreasonable to deny her request; the weekend is his time with TJ. Teddy plans every minute of the forty eight hours spent with his son. Teddy weekend visits are from Friday afternoon, 3 p.m., to Sunday afternoon, 3 p.m. So Victoria decided to reinforce her "mother" authority over TJ's, her son. She marched up to TJ's school and picked TJ up an hour early, on a Friday afternoon. Teddy arrived to the school at ten minutes to 3 o'clock, like any other Friday. Teddy close his office on Fridays, he leaves no room for errors. His employees love the fact they work ten hours a day to have Friday off. Teddy milk chocolate skin beats with a lighthearted civil state of mind. The sunlight shines from his cheerful smile. All week long, Teddy's state is aggravated by concerns of TJ. Victoria has restricted phone calls between Teddy and TJ to one hour a day, before eight p.m. All phone calls are monitored. Teddy knows Victoria listens in on the phone; sometimes he can hear her breathing. Two months ago, Teddy nearly lost his mind when he saw his son's classmates march out at dismissal at 3 p.m., and his son wasn't on the line. Teddy went civil on the principal, threaten to sue, and some more things. The principal band Victoria from school property after Sammy got involved. Teddy gets to see TJ every day after school. Teddy appreciates the thirty minutes after school. Teddy use the few minutes to his advantage. He makes sure his son has survived another night at Victoria's apartment, in Madison Projects. He makes ascertain TJ was feed dinner and breakfast. He surveys how clean TJ's school uniform is. He sustains the lines of communication between him and his son by light questioning. Teddy's ears tickle with joy to hear stories of life told from an eight year son's eyes. The same thing that gives pleasure torments him during the week.

"Husband was arrested and Vicki's her crack headed sister too." Sammy reveals.

"We should win in court now, for sure. If the judge still rules in her favor, then I will have proof the system is corrupt, like I've always being telling you all. She should've never gotten custody in the 1st place." Teddy preaches from his seat.

"Oh bro, don't you worried I'm gonna catch her. Imma whip dat ass, real good. As soon as dis little court thing is over, I put my life on it." Rhonda makes promise to beat Victoria down.

About year ago, Victoria sneaked attacked Rhonda. Rhonda was watching TJ at Lorraine's house. It was Rhonda and TJ in the house alone playing video games. TJ was giving Rhonda an old fashion beat down on the video game. Rhonda couldn't believe her eye of how an eight year old was beating her down on Ms. Pac-Man; she was a professional back in the day. Victoria arrived at the doorstep with two uniform officers, demanding her son. Teddy was in a car accident, in Egypt. He was in a coma for three weeks after a car accident. Sammy and Lorraine flew a sixteen hour flight to Egypt. Teddy's rancid baby's mother, Victoria, was seizing the moment. Victoria went to court and filed a petition for full custody of their seven year old son, TJ. Victoria hadn't laid eyes on TJ since she spit him out. Sammy's argument in court the day she returned from Egypt was Victoria didn't know TJ. The last she seen TJ, he was two weeks old, but the judge didn't even hear Sammy's dispute and awarded Victoria custody in milliseconds. If you batted your eyes once then you would have missed the whole procedure. Sammy has been in court ever since she's been working her lawyer skills. Sammy's heart and soul is dedicated to get her nephew back. She won weekend visits, along with any school vacation, Thanksgiving, Christmas, spring break and summer recess, for her brother and nephew. Victoria won Teddy after school visits with her childish behavior at the school, but to Sammy it still wasn't enough time.

"Victoria is a selfish bitch. She is an evil individual. Never once has she considered her own son's feelings. She up rooted him from the only family he knows. To be honest, the bitch is a stranger to my boy. He knows of her because in the 7 years she was gone, I told him who his mother was. He hadn't seen his mother since he was 2 weeks old. She ran off to chase her "video vixen" dreams. While she was off dreaming, I was home with my son. Thank God, for my mother and 2 sisters. What man knows how to care of a 2 week old baby off the top of their head? None. Men are not built "motherly." I had to learn as I went along and I'm still learning. Parenting isn't an easy thing period, but for a man it's 10 times harder. TJ is a well respectable young boy. The courts got us living back in slavery times. The masters will divide the black's families by removing the fathers from the unit. By doing this, the moral of the black man is broken down. The courts got me feeling the same way, broken. Victoria doesn't deserve TJ. He is such an intelligent and funny little boy. Victoria has pulled a master move

on TJ like the courts have done to my spirits." Teddy's chitachatter

Teddy's chitachatter shines light on unjust situations of a black man in America.

"Smell, you like it?" Sammy presents Rhonda with a perfume option for Tay's gift.

"It smells great, but Chyenne got dat for Tay already." Rhonda denies Sammy's suggestion.

"Excuse me sir, do you work here?" A pale faced woman questions Teddy.

"You see this? No ma'am I do not work here! What gave you that impression? Could it be the name tag button on my shirt? No, 'cus I don't have one. Or is it the chocolate color on my face? Now **Getdee**[33]!" Teddy verbally checks the woman and walks away.

"Racism is alive and kicking the chocolate faces down. A chocolate face have to fight against the salty sugar to maintain the smooth distinguish flavor." Teddy's chitachatter

"Cool it, Minster Martin Malcolm." Sammy teases Teddy.

"Shit, wit all those M's you can get into Tay's family and Mary will like ya." Rhonda clowns Teddy too.

"I don't know why we walking around bullshitting, I'm hungry. Get a pair of heels for Tay and let's go. Y'all got people thinking I work here by walking in circles." Teddy voices his completion of shopping.

"I can't bring her heels. Everybody and their mother is gonna bring Tay

---

[33] **Getdee** *is Teddy word. It means "Get The Fuck Outta Here"*

heels!" Rhonda denies Teddy's suggestion.

"Look over there, that's nice, she'll like dat." Sammy is pointing out a pair of high heel oil burning lamps.

"Good eye Sammy. Teddy we are leaving now, okay. Try not to get ya Black Panther on at the register." Rhonda jokes at Teddy.

Teddy is a modern day Dr. Rev. Martin Luther King. In elementary school, Teddy boycotted the lunch room for only serving milk, no juice or water. In high school, he protected against school policy. The policy states males short is not proper uniform. Teddy felt this was unjust. Females were given the option to either wear a pants or skirts; where as male students had no choice but to wear pants all year long. He won the war; male students were able to wear shorts in the spring and summer time. From the time he was fourteen years old, he volunteered at Churches, soup kitchens and anywhere else he thought he could have been some help. Lucky for the department of Education, Teddy graduated from high school at sixteen years old. In three years, he graduated from Columbia University with a Bachelor of Liberal Studies. Lorraine was overly proud of her son. Teddy was a nineteen year old, proud black man with a full education. Teddy's graduation day was bitter sweet. He was very proud of his accomplishment but his mentor, Lawrence Steiner, died of AIDS. Teddy learned plenty from his mother and sisters but becoming a man was all taught by Mr. Lawrence Steiner. For the past nine years of Teddy's life, he's been preaching AIDS awareness. His whole life is dedicated to his devotion to his son and his mission to open the world's eyes. The world's eyes are closed to the number one killer of black people worldwide, AIDS. The nation has their eyes close to the epidemic killing a race of people. Teddy refers to the spreading of the epidemic as modern day holocaust.

****

Sammy set up this dinner date at Paulie's Steak House, in Forest Hills, Queens. Paulie, the owner, made an aged steak so savory the mouth waters for more, but the stomach is out of room. Paulie's recommendations were given by Brooklyn. Brooklyn wrote a beautiful detail review on Paulie's restaurant. Brooklyn's tongue is true to her words. With the kids gone on the roads trip to Atlanta, Rhonda, Sammy and Teddy are going to Tay's party tonight. Lorraine was going to be alone tonight. Sammy's plan was to feed Lorraine well and get a few good strong drinks into her. The combination of good food and strong liquor will have Lorraine go home and fall right to sleep, not noticing the emptiness in her house. Lorraine is a giver. She needs her family around to receive the love she's giving. Without the exchange of affection, Lorraine turns to sweet sedative of intoxication. Family surrounds Lorraine to avoid her taste of alcohol bliss.

"Mom, How's ya steak?" Teddy question Lorraine.

"Tender, just the way I like it," Lorraine answers
"Me too Ma! I love Tender meat! Ya heard!" Rhonda chimes in.

*"Shit, thank goodness I had a good **house call**[34] today or I would be a cranky bitch. I went out last night. I played Beast or Bitch but there were only bitches in the club. Thank goodness for house call. I know dem delivery guys be fighting when they see my address. They did real good yesterday. Dat beast throws me down on the bed like DMX did Keisha, in Belly. Oh yeah, thank goodness for house call." Rhonda's chitachatter*

Sammy laughs out loud. Teddy gets a small chuckle off of Rhonda's words. Sammy and Teddy know Rhonda wasn't talking about the tenderness of the steak on her plate.

---

[34] ***House call*** *is another Sistah game. One has to order things that will be delivered to your home by the package delivery companies. Barging with the delivery guy to obtain a signature for a must given sexual favor.*

"Ma, I have a surprise for you." Teddy announce to Lorraine.

"Well, whatcha got boy?" Lorraine inquires.

"We all chipped in for a seven day cruise trip with Miss Betsey." Teddy reveals.

"Oh, you kids are a mother's dream. You kids always make me proud. Rhonda passed the CPA exam on the first attempt. Sammy has passing the bar with a history making score. And Teddy, my miracle, you being here with me is a blessing its self. I love you kids, thank you." Lorraine speaks though her tears falling from her eyes.

Rhonda is the fire cracker of the family. She has always been a good student. She received her high school diploma along with a bun in her oven. Being pregnant didn't stop Rhonda from going to night class, at Baruch College, after working to earn her Bachelor degree in Accounting. At one point, Rhonda had a day job; an internship and night college class, all while being a mother to Paris, her daughter. She graduated with a job offer. After five years, she opened her own Accounting firm. Sammy serves as Rhonda's road signs to stare her on the straight path, in the right direction. Rhonda is easy distracted by the opposite sex. Sammy had Rhonda on a strict study diet to pass the CPA exam. Sammy is just like Teddy. They both are unstoppable focus and driven toward their goals. Rhonda is the oldest sibling. Sammy is one year younger than Rhonda, but years wiser. Sammy graduated a year and a half early from high school. She enrolled in the New York University of Law. She gave birth to Benny at twenty. Being a full time single mother didn't stop her from working hard to open her own small Law firm. All three of them work hard to beat the odds of Madison Projects. Lorraine gets all praises for her three children's life success. Lorraine and Daniel were married early. After marriage, Lorraine continued to pursuit her dreams to become a school teacher. After fulfilling her dream, she satisfies Daniel's desire to begin a family. Daniel utilized his natural knowledge of cars to get a job at a mechanic shop. They lived humble in a two bedroom tenement apartment. Their home was low on furniture, but high on love, support, and unity. The morals they instilled in their three children has out lived their father, Daniel but kept life in their mother, Lorraine. Teddy is Lorraine's last miracle gift from Daniel. Seven months after Daniel's funeral, Lorraine was escorted to the emergency room by her two daughters, Rhonda and Sammy, with complaints of stomach pain. The doctor delivered her diagnosis to Rhonda, who was thirteen years old at the time, and Sammy, who just turned twelve years old. The doctor identified Lorraine was in labor. Lorraine, Rhonda and Sammy in disbelief, Lorraine was fifty years old at the time and experiencing menopause. Thirteen hours later, Teddy was born into the world to the three woman of his life. The three women all showered Teddy with the love, support, and harmony the same Daniel gave to the three women. Now that Teddy is twenty seven years old, he returns his heart to the three woman of his life.

"Okay Ma, you are ready to go!" Teddy notices the affect of the four glasses of wine on Lorraine. She wobbles as Teddy puts her coat on.

"Imma sleep like a new born baby tonight." Lorraine plans, just what Sammy hoped for.

Rhonda, Sammy and Teddy get Lorraine home, changed her into her night grown and tucked her into bed, all by 10 p.m. They locked the door at Lorraine's house and headed to Sammy's house to get ready for Tay's party. Tay's party had just begun.

"Some jiggy and some straight grindin'. All up in the crib just to have a good time and, Ay, Where the party at?" - Brandon

Where the party at?
Jagged Edge Ft. Nelly
Where the party at? - EP

The line to get into 40/40 this Saturday night is down the block and around the corner, almost hitting another corner. The line is filled with all types of characters. Women on the line are willing to endure the brisk breeze of the night air. Sporadically, seasoning the line in the breeze night air are women wearing bright miniskirts and pumpum shorts. Men suited and booted in their Sunday's best. Security is the barrier between the patient party goers on line and the soul music bouncing out onto the street. The soul music is slightly whispering into all ears on line. Soul music feeds your mood. Soul music can have a person crying one minute and then laughing the next minute. Lyrics and rhymes so moving, your mind forgets today's and yesterday's trouble. Your body sways to memories dancing in your ear. Your lips savor the sweet sedative of words of time. Security is run by Omar, Melissa's husband, the police officer. Melissa is Tay's sister. Omar is the only suitable security. He is a Madison Projects, the hood, original. He has been working in the area for so long; he has become a part of the area. There are some suspicious characters coming in the club tonight. Suspicious characters who are opposed to being searched. Omar has searched them all before. He knew who needs to be thoroughly frisked and who could get in with just a pat down. He demands to visual inspect proper identification and party tickets. If there is no ticket, there is a fifty dollar entrance fee. Omar's team of officers gave their neon pink UV stamp of approval. Once inside, two magazine cover men models, dressed in black Speedo and Dr Martin's boots, greets the entering guest. The muscular naked man are wearing multi- colored masquerade masks and covered in gold glitter shimmer, resembling chocolate gods dipped in gold sparkles. The chocolate gods offer a selection of masquerade masks, for men and woman. The men's masquerade masks are Venetian styled, with a unique curvy line design on the mask. The women's masquerade masks are decorations in Spanish lace with the signature feathers on the right corner. The masquerade masks are available in different colors with different meanings. The black masquerade masks affirm marriage status. The gold masquerade masks states single and ready to mingle. The red masquerade mask communicates interest in a one night stand. The sliver masquerade masks put into words a "just chilling" state mind. Tay stood with the chocolate gods for the first three hours of the party. Her availability to the entering guest was to receive her gifts and give photograph opportunities. In the hallway, to the main event is a thirty by thirty inch cake. The cake is a blow up of Tay's head, neck and shoulders. People's talents are amazing. The cake's frosting is in perfect color matching Tay's cappuccino complexion. The cake has been greatly detailed, from Tay's long blond hair to her sexy pouty lips; the resemblance is accurate. Eye shadow and long lashes is an unbelievable copy of Tay, a cake of pure art. The cute chocker name chain on the neck of the cake reads "HAPPY BIRTHDAY." Everyone enters the party and stops to photograph the spectacular cake of Tay in the hallway, until the music beckons the body inside. The two story oval shaped room is twenty seven thousand square feet. The ceiling in covered with magenta and gold colored balloons. The strings attached to the balloon rain down on the guest. The entrance of the mezzanine is directly across from the platform. DJ K-Slay and D.J Maino are on the platform, showcasing their talents on the ones and twos. The DJ's music sections range from the cha cha slide to stepping in the name of love. The sweet sounds will have you standing on couches and hitting the dance floor because it feels like it's your birthday too. To the right and to the left of the entrance are fully lined bars. The mezzanine is over flowing with people. From the doctor that spanked Tay's ass when she was born to the cashier who checked out Tay's groceries yesterday afternoon was all invited, it looks like they all showed up. The mezzanine is half intoxicated, a quarter Latin, fifteen percent boochetta, and a dime worth of stragglers. Up the stairs is the veranda, a ring around the club. The veranda is split up into five sections. Each section has a half a moon shaped banquets with a table in the center. On the center of table is a bucket of ice. The ice surrounds a complementary bottle of liquor. The veranda looks down onto the mezzanine. The veranda is the V.I.P. area.

"Oh wait a minute (oh wait a minute) Oh wait a minute (oh wait a minute hey hey hey) Girl wait a minute. Oh wait a minute (oh wait a minute) Oh wait a minute (oh wait a minute hey hey hey)Yo you know the words say it (wait a minute)Blaw tadow watch out now, uh-huh! It's the little one and I'm not Bow Wow." Yup! You all heard right, I'm on my Lil' Kim shit tonite. If Mr. Bryson Mitchell snoozes he loses. I'll bounce up outta here wit a Ray J look-a-like if I can find one." *Tay's chitachatter*

Tay has had a few drinks at the door, but she wasn't drunk yet. She is now dancing in V.I.P. Tay is partying in her section with the twins, Camille and Calvin, and Marc, her nephew. Tay's section is in the middle of V.I.P., above the DJ's platform. To the left of Tay's section is where Chyenne and Malik are seating. Chyenne and Malik are sitting close together talking and kissing each other, like they just meet. The liquors that danced down Chyenne throat have her in a different state of mind tonight. Chyenne and Malik are loved up like two teenagers in puppy love. To the right of Tay's section sits Sammy and Teddy. Sammy and Teddy are entertaining themselves by mimicking old school dances from their youth. Rhonda is outside in front of the club waiting for Brooklyn to arrive. On the right side of Sammy's and Teddy's is Roc's section. Roc is a local celebrity. His career of selling street pharmaceuticals earned him his fame. His partner in crime is Phil. Phil is off in a dark corner, two stepping with Camille. Roc has two goons on standby, laying low in the shadows of his section. The last section in V.I.P half a moon shaped red couches are decorated with the Ballers. Rah-Rah and Freaky are rappers of a legendary record label. Jessie and Hi-Z are profession basketball players. The rappers and basketball players has found their path out of the hood, but always come back to show love. They have brought up five local groupies with red masquerade masks to capture their lustful eyes.

"Yo. You still blow?" Roc questions Tay.

"You got trees roll it up You a G throw it up." *I'm smoking tonite. I don't know why but I feel 22 again." Tay's chitachatter*

"You need to stop frontin' and let Roc hold ya down. You got a nicca running laps around you for years. Can da Roc get a taste?" Roc questions Tay.

Roc passes her lit marijuana covered by a cigar leaf. Tay inhales from the custom cigarette. Tay passes the custom cigarette to Marc. Marc hands the custom cigarette to Calvin after inhaling his desired amount of smoke. Camille declines. Calvin then passes the custom cigarette to its starting point, the hand of Roc. The circular passing of the custom cigarette continues, until it burns out. Roc wasn't ugly but he wasn't cute. He wasn't tall but he wasn't short. He wasn't fat but he wasn't skinny. He wasn't broke but he wasn't wealthy. He is just Roc. Roc is a meatball brown complexion with a round couch potato frame. His name weighs heavy on ears, just as much he weighs in pounds in Madison Projects. Tay has known him for years and for years he has been trying to get with Tay. Tay always shot him down, but Tay wasn't above accepting his gifts of persuasion. Tonight, Roc has con conversation from Tay with a white mink coat with chinchilla fur staring around the collar that flows down the front of the coat.

"Nicca slipped me his number on the low. I tore it up." *Roc aint gotta chance in hell, but thanks for da fur anyway." Tay's chitachatter*

"Oh wait a minute they playin that shit slow it up. Oh wait a minute (oh wait a minute) Oh wait a minute (oh wait a minute hey hey hey) Girl wait a minute. Oh wait a minute (oh wait a minute)

Oh wait a minute (oh wait a minute hey hey hey)Yo you know the words say it (wait a minute)" Tay sings out loud. The DJ hears Tay's chitachatter request.

"Girl you see I got on my red mask, you coming home with me tonite?" Roc presses Tay, while his eyes drink on Tay's voluminous tasty cappuccino lady lumps and curves.

"I'm not dat high or drunk yet. Slow ya row!" Tay responds to Roc's advances.

At the entrance to the mezzanine:

"Brooklyn, we up in here!" Rhonda spontaneous shouts into the mezzanine. Her luminous skin, ultra light blond baby curls are just as bright as her mood and her powder pink off the shoulder thigh high dress. She waited outside for Brooklyn just so she could speak the words. Rhonda is from Harlem, without Brooklyn by her side the words flowing from her lips just wouldn't feel right.

"I see niccas in here that might be having my baby!" Brooklyn's jokes in Biggie's voice, but her intriguing "Hennessy" straight complexion covers her old fashion glass soda bottle frame is screaming the truth. Brooklyn is looking for unsuspecting victims to play her game with.

"I hear ya girl. There are some scrumptious *Tender bone*s to the left and to the right. What's up you playin da game tonite or you chillin?" Rhonda questions

"I'm down. Ya already got a target?" Brooklyn questions Rhonda's premeditated plan.

"Nah, not yet but im looking." Rhonda has spoken to soon. Her eyes land on her target for tonight's game.

"Oh shit Brooklyn, look it's the Johnson boys. I'm gonna have to man up and holla at them *Tender bone*s tonite." Rhonda points out her findings to Brooklyn's eyes.

The Johnson boys are a two brothers and a cousin. De'Andre and Le'Roy are the brothers and their cousin is Anthony. The brothers are a year apart but can play the part of twins. Their caramel coated skin and light green eyes are lady magnets. In high school and college they played football. Their muscular frames didn't tarnish in time. The Johnson brothers are years older than Rhonda. She felt like they were out of her league, but she's grown now. Rhonda's attitude is she's a bottle of wine, the quality of tastes in better with age. Rhonda has always had her eye on De'Andre but tonight she hopes her koowie will be the one checking him out. Brooklyn's eyes are undressing Le'Roy in the public eye. Brooklyn's and Rhonda's eyes skip over Anthony. Anthony has the Johnson's trait of the body fame and bedroom green eyes but in their mind his heart will always belong to Tay. Anthony followed Tay around in high school like a lost dog. Not once did Tay even notice him.

"You've been screaming dat since we were teenagers. You are a go getta, so go get it." Brooklyn encourages Rhonda to go after her desires.

"Not now after a few drinks, I promise." Rhonda back down from the challenge.

"Why you scared? I got a gun." Brooklyn and Rhonda laughs at Brooklyn's words of truth.

"I'm gonna holla at De'Andre tonite! A piece of ass." Rhonda voices her promise.

"A piece of pie." Brooklyn voices her support to see Rhonda through her promise.

"Hey ladies, where's da birthday girl?" a female voice asks Brooklyn's and Rhonda's back.

They turn around to see who is questioning them. The eyes reveal its Cookie. Cookie is a light skinned woman with a large mole on her right cheek. Her facial features resemble a chocolate chip cookie, granting her the nickname Cookie. Cookie is Tay's arched rival. Cookie and Tay compete against each other for everything. Who dressed the best? Who has the best hair? Who has the better boyfriend? Who has the best career?

"Hey Cookie, how you been? How are your kids?" Rhonda turns on the phoniness with her questions. Rhonda's chi chi is at a two hundred tonight.

"All is well with me." Cookie answers.

"Follow us. We are on our way to her right now." Rhonda instructs Cookie.
The three ladies march up the spiral staircase to the veranda.

"Happy Birthday, sweetie. Damn, Princess Barbie you working dat tutu." Cookie tosses fake compliments. She speaks; hugs and air kisses Tay on the cheek all at the same time.

Tay is wearing a magenta colored bustier. The bustier is accented with gold colored Venetian styled, unique curvy lines. The sheer Ruffles around the bottom edge of the bustier makes Tay shine like a princess. Tay's rotunda behind peeks out from under the tutu's sheer fluffy ruffles. Her gold thigh high fishnet tights have a cute little magenta colored bow on the top's center. On Tay's feet she has on her birthday gift shoes from her sister Melissa.

"Thanks for coming." Tay replies to Cookie's fake heartfelt greeting.

"Your cake is gorgeous. I see my birthday party last month has raised the bar. Well, here's your gift. Imma head back down and party with the common folk." Cookie states the competition between herself and Tay is still in effect.

"Girl wait a minute. Oh wait a minute (oh wait a minute)Oh wait a minute (oh wait a minute hey hey hey)Yo you know the words say it (wait a minute) Poppin on the scene. Careful how ya'll talk cuz we pop them things." *Cookie better go ahead wit her bullshit. She fucks around tonite and imma let the Brooklyn Zoo lose on dat ass. I know she don't want dat." Tay's chitachatter*

"Here are some condoms Cookie to go with your red mask. Common folk have common germs. Be safe girl." Sammy's five feet of cinnamon spice dismisses Cookie.

"Now Getdee!" Teddy's nutmeg civil spice words gave Cookie the extra kick out the veranda.

"Cookie! You ever notice everybody has a nickname in the hood? Like they hiding who they are. Pretending to be something they not, just to fit in. Nicknames are the stamp of pride to fit into the poverty and regression stigma. Only in the hood, you're rewarded for failures. Rewards in abundances are received from the government, applauding failure to the nicknames for the chocolate skin we are and economic stand still. If you received govern mental assistance for doctor care, food, housing, and in your pocket, you are in the same boat as the chocolate face working the 9 to 5. The 9 to 5 chocolate faces doctor care, food and housing is at top dollar leave the pocket equivalent to govern mental chocolate face's pocket. Ironically, the government enables laziness in our community, then turns around and complains about the lackadaisical attitude in the community.

"Why trying?" become the attitude. I don't think like that. I think it's 3 times as hard and 3 times as much work, to be anything, but "Why trying?" thinking I can relate to. Society continually asks why we are so angry. Try being trapped in an economic elevator for life on the same floor, you'd be pissed off too." Teddy's chitachatter

Sammy had the gift of knowing how to politely check a person with words. The V.I.P chuckles at Cookie's descending back down the stairs.

"It smells like bud. You all were blowin wit out me?" Brooklyn questions the V.I.P

"Chill BK, no need for violence. You know da Roc gotcha back. Tell Phil I said to roll up." Roc offers calamity to Brooklyn.

Brooklyn interrupts Phil from two stepping with Camille to relay the message from Roc. Brooklyn and Rhonda follows Phil to Roc's V.I.P section to smoke marijuana.

Omar startles Tay. He used the rare spiral staircase behind her V.I.P's section. She didn't hear or see him coming up behind her.

"I need you downstairs, now!" Omar demands movement of Tay's body.

"What's the problem?" Sammy inquires. She notices the worried look written on Tay's face, caused by Omar whisper in her ear.

The music drowns out Sammy's question to Omar and Tay. Sammy's curiosity follows them down the back spiral staircase. The three of them walks out of the mezzanine.

"Some woman rolled up on the door in a limo. She's being an obnoxious outside. She is beyond being reasonable. She is refusing to wait on line or pay the entrance fee. She's demanding you to come to the door. She claims to be a personal friend. If you don't know her I'm locking her up for disturbing the peace." Omar explains the disturbance at the door to Tay.

"All her personal friends are already here. Who could it be?" Sammy's chitachatter escapes her lips.

"I wonder too, who this might be." Tay's anxiety has her feet moving fast.

"Baby girl, you good? You need da goons?" Roc offers Tay his protection. He has followed Tay downstairs.

"Nicca please! You better sit your ass down before I run your name for warrants." Omar denies Roc's offer.

"Yo O, I know you bees po po and all, but you can't be talking to me all crazy and shit, especially, not in front of my wifey." Roc jokes.

"Wifey? Nicca please! Not in this lifetime or the next three." Tay follows Omar's lead down the spiral staircase out to the front of the club to investigate the situation. Sammy is right behind Tay's high heel.

Upstairs in the veranda:

"That is a man." Chyenne sexy silky chocolate fudge words points out to Malik's eyes.

"I know dat is a man. I'm a man, I can definitely spot one a mile away, but I know he has fooled plenty tonight." Malik states his knowledge.

"You are so right. That dress is hugging his body so tight, aint a trace of a dick or balls."

"Aint no way in heaven his father is a Minster. Chyenne are you telling the honest truth to God?" Malik questions Chyenne.

"Yes, babe I'm telling the truth."

Malik is in disbelief. Marc is dressed in full drag wear. He has on a fire red wig on, eye make-up, in a fitting fire red sequin dress. He had on a pair of fire red six inch hells. His shaved legs covered in black fishnet stockings. He has curves and lady lumps so perfectly positioned men and woman are double taking. Tay and Sammy returns with Crystal. Crystal's entourage is Lisa, her accountant, and Lance, her bodyguard for the evening. Chyenne so intoxicated she didn't notice the added guest to the V.I.P section.

"Me and Brooklyn is going down to get our dance on, y'all coming?" Rhonda asks Chyenne and Malik.

"I'm down." Malik stands his six foot two inches of chestnut syrup up. He extends his hand to assist Chyenne to her feet. She denies his offer.

"I'm gonna stay right here and wait for you sexy chestnut syrup ass too come back. Brooklyn you better watch him!" Chyenne's words slurs from the sweet liquor on her tongue.

"Wanna shake dat thang downstairs?" Rhonda baits Marc.

"I thought you never ask, Hun." Marc relies.

"We're going down to shake our money makers. We'll be back, deuces." Rhonda announces into the circle of Crystal, Lisa, Sammy and Tay.

Rhonda would ask Camille but she was dry humping Phil against the wall. Camille is without a doubt has exceeded her alcohol limit. She is usually by Tay's side, barely speaking a word.

Downstairs in the mezzanine, on the dance floor:

Uncle Luke's Do Do Brown has Rhonda and Marc dancing their hearts out. A tall young *Tender bone* has crept up behind Rhonda. Rhonda dips her ass low and lifts it up slowly. She lifts up the young *Tender bone*'s penis and testicles with her ass. Marc is shouting praises at Rhonda's performance. Brooklyn, Malik and Teddy are at the left side bar purchasing drinks.

"This is a drink to all custody cases. Fuck baby mothers, baby fathers and the judges. Fuck them all." Teddy shouts his toast over the music to Brooklyn and Malik.

"I'll drink to custody cases!" Malik shouts. He downs his shot in a swallow.

Brooklyn and Teddy puzzled eyes meet, to their knowledge Malik didn't have custody cases issues.

"**Eh Mira**[35]! I know jou see me!" Joanny shouts to Brooklyn, from the far end of the bar, approximately twenty feet from Brooklyn.

Joanny is Carlito's younger sister.

"Speak English! Its "YOU" not "JOU." 'Jus 'Cus I see you don't mean I gotta speak?" Brooklyn relies.

"Here these simple bitch go. I came here to dance, get drunk and find someone to fuck. I didn't come here to whip nobody's ass. Besides, I left my Taser in the car, thanks to Omar's ass. Aint nobody trying to spend

---

[35] **Eh Mira** *means hey you, in Spanish*

two nights in Central Bookings for dumb shit. I know I'm not down for a weekend stay behind bars. It Saturday night, I won't get out until Monday morning." Brooklyn's chitachatter

"Outta respect you suppose to speak, **Puta**[36]!" Joanny's words and body moves in on Brooklyn's personal space.

"Your brother and dead mother is a bitch! BITCH!" Brooklyn words and body meets Joanny half way.

"'Cum on Brooklyn, she aint really worth it!" Teddy and Malik are the voice of reasoning in Brooklyn's ear. Teddy places his body in harm's way. He is standing between Brooklyn and Joanny.

"No, she aint worth it, but my mother is worth every penny of Carlito's money!" Joanny shouts over Teddy's back to Brooklyn.

Brooklyn grabs a glass filled with alcohol off the bar's counter. She tosses the alcohol out the cup onto Joanny's face. Malik try to grab Brooklyn's hand from behind, but it was too late.

"Teddy move! I wanna get at this bitch." Brooklyn shouts almost as loud as the music jumping out of fifty foot speakers.

Joanny reaches over Teddy and try to take a swing at Brooklyn, but miss. She results to spitting over Teddy's shoulder at Brooklyn.

"Oh hell no! Brooklyn Zoo unleash! Whip her ass." Teddy has given Brooklyn permission to attack Joanny.

Teddy moves to the left. Teddy removes himself from the line of fire. Joanny's spitting has spoken fighting words. Joanny and Brooklyn are

---

[36] **Puta** *means Bitch, in Spanish*

face to face with each other.

"You grimy Puta, you better send my mother home!"

"Like I said, Fuck you! Fuck your brother! Fuck your mother! Jump Bitch!"

Joanny jumps. Brooklyn head butts her to the floor. Brooklyn knocked Joanny out. Brooklyn didn't smudge her make-up or got a wrinkle on her all white Indian tunic dress with colorful rhinestones around the collar, sleeve and around the bottom of her dress. Her ballerina bun on the top of her head didn't even budge.

"OOOOOOHHHHH, Shit!" Were the words of the witnessing crowd surrounding the whole commotion between Joanny and Brooklyn. Strangers aids Joanny sluggish body on to the stool at the bar. "Now, I need another shot! Sorry 'bout ya drink. Whatcha was drinking? Imma replace it."

Brooklyn buys the guy standing at the bar his drink back. She is replacing the drink she showered Joanny's face with. After partaking in another round of shots, the trio, Brooklyn, Malik and Teddy, joined Rhonda and Marc on the dance floor.

Upstairs in the veranda:

Crystal and Lisa take a seat in Sammy's V.I.P section. Tay sits in the middle of Calvin and Roc. Sammy takes a seat next to Chyenne. Sammy refills Chyenne and her shot glass with alcohol. They are off to the left watching Crystal from a distance.

"1, 2, 3. **Disparos a la hermana amar**[37]. " Sammy counts down and

---

[37] **Disparos a la hermana amar:** *Shots to sister (Sistah) love.*

quotes Brooklyn on the Sistahhood toast saying. She and Chyenne throw the shot glass of alcohol down their throats on the count of three.

"Can you believe Ms. Money Bags was downstairs hollering about paying 50 dollars?" Sammy questions Chyenne in a light whisper.

"The bitch is a con artist. She got da money but she wanted to try to get in for free. Did she even bring a gift?" Chyenne ask Sammy.

It was as if Crystal was listing in on Chyenne and Rhonda's conversation because right after Chyenne's question, Crystal presents Tay with a birthday gift.

"Tay, this is Scottish Diva Vodka, a little something I picked up during my stay in Scotland, years ago." Crystal presents Tay's birthday gift with an introduction from her thin upper lip's distinguished superior tone.

The seven hundred fifty milliliter bottle of vodka is stuffed with pink, purple and white crystals and gemstones.

"Thanks, Crystal! It's beautiful. So pretty I don't even wanna open it. Aww, thanks again." Tay gives Crystal a hug. Tay naïve thinking thinks Crystal actions are genuine.

"Yo Chris, do somin with cha mans. He up on a nicca neck, I can't breathe. I'll turn his ass into Swiss cheese." Roc is warning Crystal about Lance, her bodyguard.

The bodyguard is stand too close to Roc for Roc's liking. Tay lets out an intoxicated giggle.

"OH, you like dat? I know ya into Thugs and baby I'm a Thug!" Roc whispers into Tay's ear.

"Lance, please stand by the staircase. Is that better Roc? Are you comfortable?" Crystal patronizes Roc.

"Chris, hold ya tongue. While you up in here playing Big Willie, giving away bottles dat cost a mil and all, let's not forget you pulled a fast one on ole' Roc. A debt you never repaid. But now a G anit shit to you. It's funny how things change." Roc reminds Crystal of a failed deal between them.

Many years ago, Roc came across two credit cards with spending limits of one thousand dollars each. Draining credit cards wasn't Roc's criminal expertise. He entrusts Crystal with the task of unloading the credit cards. The profits would be split down the middle, fifty percent for Crystal and fifty percent for Roc. Roc revived an update from a valuable source that Crystal unloads the credit cards and cut him out the equation.

"This bottle cost a mil?" Tay questions the cost of Crystal's gift.

"You see this bitch always showing out." Chyenne voice her disgust of Crystal.

"Chyenne, I gotta agree witcha! A mil for liquor is a bit much. WOW." Sammy co-signs Chyenne disgust.

"Crystal, you changed your hair color it fits your face. It's the Barbie's friend Tess's hair color. A sweet chocolate with dark blond low lights is a nice color blend. Cute shit." Tay compliments Crystal.

"Barbie? Shit she more or less look like a Bratz doll. With her plastic body and bobble head size. Money can't fix dat head shape!" Chyenne comments make her and Sammy giggle. Sammy refills their shot glasses again.

"1, 2, 3. Disparos a la hermana amar." Sammy counts down. She and Chyenne throw the shot glass of alcohol down their throats on the count of three.

"Thanks it's a Brazilian blend...."

"Yeah yeah, we know went to Brazil and cut the hair off the Brazilian woman's head." Calvin clowns Crystal. The V.I.P all roar in laughter. Calvin has heard Crystal's endless gloating since she arrived. Calvin knows just what Crystal needs to humble her mean ass. He sits and begins to plot against her.

"Where's your prince?" Crystal's thin upper lip distinguished superior tone, questioning the whereabouts of Tay's man.

Crystal tilts her diamond shape head, as if she was giving Tay her full attention. Her hooded mud brown eyes wait for Tay's naïve response.

"Chris, how you gonna try to play me? I'm sittin right here!" Roc questions Crystal's line of conversation.

"Roc STOP IT! His name is Mr. Bryson Mitchell and he's working." Tay replies to Crystal.

"He's working alright, somebody's pussy. You see if I was your man, I would be wit my Boo on her b-day." Roc words moves close to Tay's ear as he leads in.

"Oh wait a minute (oh wait a minute) Oh wait a minute** (oh wait a minute hey hey hey)Girl wait a minute. Oh wait a minute (oh wait a minute)Oh wait a minute (oh *wait a minute hey hey hey)Yo you know the words say it (wait a minute)* where the fuck is Mr. Bryson Mitchell? I got all caught up today I forgot his ass wasn't around. I haven't heard from his ass since Wednesday. It's been three whole days since I've

heard from Mr. Bryson Mitchell. Fuck him! His lost **"Sex you're getting some. It's on tonight. Oh wait a minute (oh wait a minute)"** *'jus won't be Roc. I promise dat! Shit, only one problem, I need to borrow a key from one of the Sistahs. Marc has mine and claims to still need it. Who I'm gonna ask, on the low?" Tay's chitachatter*

"Let's hit the dance floor." Lisa suggests. She wants to remove Crystal from the tension in the air.

"Go head girl, shake whatcha mommy gave ya. You killing dat dress." Tay compliments Lisa.

"Than…" Lisa's southern milk chocolate lips begins to accept the compliment but is cut off by Crystal.
"I bought it this morning at Barney's. Can you believe it was only $300? What a steal." Crystal announces to the V.I.P

"Damn, why she do shit like dat? That's fucked up, putting that woman business out in front of total strangers. That is a foul bitch!" Chyenne distaste for Crystal's words is clear.

"I can hear your comment from the peanut gallery over there." Crystal's thin upper lip distinguished superior tone, speaking over her cold vanilla false Caucasian pigment shoulder in Chyenne's and Sammy's direction.

"Who in the hell you think you're talking too?" Sammy five feet of cinnamon spice questions Crystal's thin upper lip distinguished superior tone.

"I'll smack the shit outta you, bitch. I owe you an ass whippin!"
Chyenne's tall sexy silky chocolate fudge intoxicated heavy one top light on the bottom frame stands. Chyenne to try to take a swing at Crystal but her knees failed her and she fall back down on to the banquet couch. Chyenne is temperately blinded by her coily soft curly hair.

"Come on, Lisa let hit the dance floor. V.I.P is getting to **insalubres**[38] for me." Crystal's thin upper lip distinguished superior tone, speaking to Lisa as they gather their things and is ushered down the back spiral staircase by Lance.

"Last call for alcohol! Last call for alcohol! Last call for alcohol! Last 45 minutes everybody get ya ass on the dance floor. If ya feet hurt take off your shoes. Let's go." DJ K-Slay announces though the microphone.

"Ay, where the party at? Girls is on the way, where the Bacardi at? Models and models, talkin all a that. Know I can't forget about my thugs (Where the party at?) And all my girls. (Where the party at?) Off in the club (Where the party at?) If the party's where you're at let me hear you say. Uh oooooooooooooh. (uh oh oh oh) Uh ooooooooooooooh (uh oh oh oh) Uh oooooooooooooh (uh oh oh oh) Uh oooooooooooooh. If the party's where you're at just let me know"

Calvin, Camille and Tay obeys DJ K-Slay's orders of reporting to the dance floor downstairs in the mezzanine. Sammy refills their shot glasses for the third time.

"1, 2, 3, Disparos a la hermana amar." Sammy counts down. She and Chyenne throw the shot glass of alcohol down their throats on three.

After thirty minutes of hardcore ass shaking and two stepping the party is finally coming to a close.

"Oh hell no! Sammy let's go. I'm gonna whip her ass tonite. Would you look at her?" Chyenne is looking down from the veranda onto the mezzanine. She spots Crystal smiling and dancing in Malik's face. She is pointing out her findings to Sammy.

---

[38] **Insalubres** *is french for unsanitary.*

"Calm down! Malik isn't that type of man, and even if he was, he has more respect not to do it in your circumference."

Sammy's words of wisdom were in vain. Chyenne excuse herself to the ladies room. Chyenne destination wasn't the ladies room. She was heading to the dance floor. She plans to confront Crystal. She uses the walls for balance and support to get down the back spiral staircase. It was a miracle she made it down the stairs without falling. As Chyenne tries to focus her eyes and legs, she is using the glow from her cell phone to navigate through the dim lighting of the club.
"Guess who?" the voice belongs to hands covering Chyenne's eyes. The voice gently whispers into Chyenne's ear. The breath stiffens Chyenne's body.

"I know dat deep manly voice. I know this sweet strong manly smell. I definitely know the feeling of these soft hands on my skin. Could it really be my beloved Ace? Has God open the sky and smiled on me?" Chyenne's chitachatter

Chyenne wants to guess but doesn't want to be wrong. She is trying to talk but her words won't find her voice in her throat. She wants to snatch the hands off her face but her arm has failed her commands. She wants to turn around and look into the eyes of the voice but her whole body is ignoring all her request for mobility. The voice behind the soft hands on Chyenne's face takes control. The hands grant Chyenne sight. The voice turns her about face. She is face to face with the voice.

"Ace, my love is it really you?" Chyenne's chitachatter

"It's been a long time don't see. How you been girl? Is my son here with you?" Ace questions Chyenne.

Ace scans the mass of people, appearing to be searching for a sight of his son, Polo. Chyenne's eyes are locked on Ace little curly light brown hair, his honey coated muscular fame and his sunshine shinning of his bright white teeth. Ace is wearing an all white Ralph Lauren linen suit. Ralph Lauren is the only fabric that covers Ace's skin. His love for the label made him vow to name his first born Polo. Chyenne appreciates the lighting from her cell phone, enabling her to look into Ace's soft alluring gray eyes.

"You're **smacked**[39]. Here's my number. We gotta lot of catchin up to do girl." Ace grabs Chyenne's cell phone out her hand. He enters and save his number in her phone.

"I gotta say, you look good. I truly miss you. Please call me." As the words dance in Chyenne's ear. His hands tango with her fingers.

"Hey Babe, you changed your mind. Come rhumba wit me." Malik directs Chyenne to the dance floor with his arm around her waist.

Chyenne is looking over her shoulder but Ace is gone. She feels like she is hallucinating.

"I know I had a few drinks, fuck it I'm drunk but not fucking crazy. I know I just saw Ace. Malik got me out here fucking two stepping, I wanna find Ace. Oh, my beloved Ace, oh how I miss u, my love." Chyenne's chitachatter

Chyenne is moving her body with Malik's body but her eyes are dancing over the crowd. She is savaging for a glimpse of Ace. Her arm wrapped around Malik's neck. She plants sweet kisses on the available skin on his neck to keep him distracted from her search. Her chin rests on his shoulders. She is grateful for her high heels tonight. Malik is taller than

---

[39] **Smacked** *is being heavy intoxicated.*

her without her heels. She needed the extra hight to continue her search.

"Thank you, for coming out to party with me on my Birthday, Luv Luv you all. Thank you!" Tay voice travels through the club from the speakers connected to DJ K Slay's microphone, replacing the soul music.

"Not everybody knows this but me and Tay go back like cornrows and our friendship is even tight as a braid. I am happy she invited me to DJ her birthday party. Happy Birthday Baby Girl." These are the words to the tear filled speech from DJ K-Slay to Tay.

"Look Tay, Anthony Johnson from the Johnson boys all grown up." Brooklyn states as she presents the handsome gentleman.

Brooklyn and Rhonda were laying down the foot work on the Johnson brother, when out of nowhere Rhonda disappeared. Brooklyn was happy to reintroduce Tay to Anthony just so she wouldn't be the centerpiece of three men. Brooklyn plays a lot of games but three at once isn't a game she plays. Anthony always and forever had a crush on Tay. Besides Anthony being two years younger than Tay, Anthony had a slight nerd look going on.

"Damn, time did you well!" Tay stares at Anthony's mature body through her naïve koowie sight.

"I see now is not the time, but here's my number. Please use it. I would love to take you out to breakfast, lunch or dinner. It's always a pleasure to be in your presence." Anthony romances Tay with his words and kisses the back of her hand. His kiss is pillowed with his soft caramel heart shaped lips. He walks off, but her eyes and throbbing heart stays with him.

Everybody is together and ready to go but nobody can find Rhonda. Tay ditched Roc and is eager to disappear. The twins are holding her up. Tay has drank pass her walking limit. Marc has loaded up all Tay's gifts into the limo. Tay made twenty thousand dollars off of entrance fees and purchased drinks. Her birthday cards filled with cash totaled five thousand. She was given a hundred pairs of high heel and twenty designer handbags. Tay believes the fifty foot oil-base painted portrait of her face is from Bryson.

"Chyenne, what's wrong?" Tay questions slurs off her tongue.

"Nothing, I'm just drunk." Chyenne answers Tay with the same slur speech but Chyenne's eyes are on a sober search.

"Ace, where are you? Come back to me my love." Chyenne's chitachatter

"Oh wait a minute (oh wait a minute) Oh wait a minute (oh wait a minute hey hey hey). So much you go through. Only problems know you." *I wonder what Crystal did now too ruin Chyenne's night. 'Cus when I left Chyenne on the veranda in Sammy's company. Chyenne was good and drunk but still good." Tay's chitachatter*

"Everybody ready?" Rhonda questions the crowds of Sistahs looking for her.

"Where were you?" Sammy questions Rhonda.

"I was in the ladies room."

"I can't tell my little sister some young Tender bone bent me over a bathroom sink, like the shooter bent Jeanne Tripplehorn over the chair, in Basic Instinct. Shit, I couldn't get enough of that young fire and desire stabbing my insides up." Rhonda's chitachatter

"UH HUH whatever, can I get ya key. The night is still young for me?" Tay asks Rhonda for her key to the *Pink Pussy Cat*. Rhonda needs has been satisfy. She hands over the key to Tay with no problem.

Everybody splits up taking the provided car service to their destination.

"A piece of cake." Tay's signature Sistah wish

"A piece of mind." Chyenne's signature Sistah wish

"A piece of ass." Rhonda's signature Sistah wish

"A piece of pie." Brooklyn's signature Sistah wish

"A piece of solitude." Sammy's signature Sistah wish

"You can't tell me, you aint feelin' the same shit. Girl it's our chemistry like icing on the cake."

After party
Koffee Brown
Mars/Venus

De'Andre and Le'Roy, the Johnson brothers, sit across from Brooklyn and Rhonda. De'Andre is two years older than Rhonda; he is forty two years old. De'Andre is one year older than his little brother, Le'Roy. It's 7am Sunday morning. It's the morning after Tay's party. They are having breakfast together at a local diner in Morningside Heights, called *Uncletiti's*. The theme of the diner is the fifties era. The waitress are wearing a light pink fifties signature "poodle-skirt", embellished with a huge, fuzzy chenille French poodle, riding over a cloud of stiff, bouffant petticoats. Staying true to the theme of the diner, the waitress feet is covered in the original fifties black and white saddle shoes. *Uncletiti's* is a restaurant owned by Marc and Mildred. Marc and Mildred share many feminine ways but cooking in the only trait of Marc, Mildred takes pride in. *Uncletiti's* serves southern soulful breakfast, lunch and dinner.

"So how you guys lives turned out?" Rhonda's luminous skin and ultra light blond baby curls questions the Johnson boys.

"I'm a race car engineer at New Jersey Motorsport Park." De'Andre reveals.

Le'Roy rapidly chews the pancakes in his mouth before speaking.

"I work at a television station." Le'Roy finally answers.

"So you're an actor?" Brooklyn questions Le'Roy.

"No, he's an electrician. That's his smooth operator line for da ladies. Most women just run with it and don't ask if he's an actor or the janitor."

De'Andre reveals.

"With his sweet caramel coated skin covering his 6 foot frame, sexy light green eyes and perfect white teeth you can sell it." Brooklyn appreciates Le'Roy's game.

"The same way you own the Indian look. You are the most beautiful woman I ever seen in my life and sexy as hell." Le'Roy words make Brooklyn's "Hennessy" straight complexion change to a rosy color on her cheeks.

"You too good to be true, are you married, with a hundred kids stashed around the states?" Brooklyn quizzes Le'Roy.

"No I do not have any kids, and I've never been married, yet." Brooklyn has lost herself in the comfort of Le'Roy's answer.

"What about you Mr. Johnson? Do you have a wife and kids? A wife at home pacing floors waiting on you? Do you have your kids looking out the window waiting for daddy to come home?" Rhonda questions De'Andrea with a fabricated scenarios.

"Your sense of humor is charming. Yes I was married, but have been divorced for three years. I have one beautiful little princess name Andrea. She is one years old." De'Andre tells Rhonda.

"So the ex-wife and the baby mother is the same person? I ask 'cus of the two year gap." Rhonda pry's deeper into De'Andre's life.

"You see how my break up work is; I'm leave on good term so I'm able to talk the long way. So the answer is yes they are the same person." De'Andre replies.

"Good answer." Rhonda voices her approval.

"Where did Anthony run off to?" Brooklyn questions the Johnson brothers about the third member of the Johnson boys, their cousin.

"Anthony is an artist painter and cartoonist. He is revealing his art today at Metropolitan Museum of Art at 9:30." Le'Roy speaks into Brooklyn's eyes. She is unfamiliar with the warmth in her stomach caused by a man, but she liked it.

"It's 8:23 now. Lovely ladies, you're more than welcome to meet us there, if not you have our math, gives us a call. We had a lovely evening. Thank you for gracing us with your presence." De'Andre's words set up his exit.

De'Andre speaks as he drops a hundred dollar bill down on the table and puts on his blazer. He walked around the table. He grabbed Rhonda's right hand and brought her to her feet. He planted a passionate kiss on Rhonda's luminous lips. Le'Roy only kissed the back of Brooklyn's left hand.

"Maybe I should've done the interview before De'Andre fucked my brains out at the Johnson and Johnson hotel. He had me shout early this Sunday morning like I was in Church. He was 10 times more experienced than that young thang in the bathroom at the club. Shit, I had 2 in one night. Brooklyn loses the game. The one she got, I help get. I want my twenty in cash not change. I might see De'Andre again or maybe not. He was a gentleman. After he dug my stomach out, he had the decency to fill my stomach, like a true gentleman." Rhonda's chitachatter

****

"Ace, please come back to me."

The sound of her own voice awakes Chyenne. Lucky Chyenne's sleep talk didn't disturb Malik's sleep. She crawls out of bed. She tip toe out her bedroom. She creeps into the living room. She is scrambling for her cell phone. She has to prove to herself Ace was in her presence, last night. She dumps the contents of her purse onto the black leather couch. Her phone meshed in with various things.

"Shit!" her phone is dead.

Chyenne scans the living room for an outlet, as she tries to create a plan to retrieve her phone charge from her bedroom, without waking Malik. Just as the wheels started turning in her head, she is startled.

"Babe, whatcha doing? Come back to bed." Malik beacons Chyenne. She reluctantly complies.

Malik's chestnut skin has been starved from the sexy silky chocolate fudge of Chyenne. He is overjoyed by the love making he shared with Chyenne, last night and this morning. It has been at least a month since Malik had a taste of the sexy silky chocolate fudge belonging to Chyenne. He is still thirsty for sweet goodness of the sexy silk chocolate fudge.

"You're always gonna be a little secret of mine."

My Little secret
Xscape
Traces of My Lipstick

Tay opens her eyes to the red heart shaped alarm clock reading 11 a.m. She is lying on her left side. There is a man's right arm laying over her right hip and his right leg over her legs. She feels his manhood spring to life on her nude voluminous butt cheeks. She grinds her cheeks against the thick manhood resting on her nude voluminous butt cheeks. She rolls over onto her back. She wants to be introduced to the face of her stiff interest. She looks into the mirrored ceiling. She's astonished by the reflections burning her eyes.

"It's whuteva, whuteva, whuteva, it's whuteva, whuteva, whuteva, whuteva, it's whuteva. Fuck em' all day, fuck em' all night, treat niggas like hoes." *damn damn damn, Tay, why? How could you let your koowie do this? Fuck em' it's done. I gotta get this nicca outta here. I'm taking this shit to the grave. I could blame it on the goose but I'm a grown ass woman. The blame is all on Mr. Bryson Mitchell. I fucked up because he fucked up and didn't show up. And it's...* **"It's whuteva, whuteva, whuteva, it's whuteva, whuteva, whuteva, whuteva, it's whuteva. Remy ma I'm rollin wit ya attitude 'bout this 1 here, it's whuteva!"** *Tay's chitachatter*

Tay slowly pulls back the red and pink thick stripped bed dressings off her body. A feeling of sickness is giving Tay the chills. Her nude body is covered in goose bumps. She inch her nude body off the elevated foam mattress. A stomach ache of nausea threatens her mobility. She reaches quietly into the room closet for a pajama silk robe.

"And you already know the rules don't apply to us. See I got money but its always robbin' season" *For this humiliation I gotta be paid. Shit,*

Tay you really let your koowie fuck you over this time. I'm taking this to the grave." Tay's chitachatter

Tay goes through the pants pockets of the man sleeping in the bed in front of her eyes. Her eyes glued to his frame as she commit her crime. She stuffed her robe's pockets with her monetary winnings. She tip toe out the room. She runs to the bathroom. The pink and red butterflies painted on the bathroom's wall are flying in Tay's eyes. She prays to the porcelain gods, as she regurgitates the contents of her stomach and flashbacks of last night to her mind. Viewing Roc's hands, penis and tongue in and on her body caused her stomach to release more contents. She rinse off her face and her memory.

"It's whuteva, whuteva, whuteva, it's whuteva, whuteva, whuteva, whuteva, it's whuteva. Right hand got a blunt, left hand got a cup" *I know how the slime ball gotcha girl, stupid Tay feel for the oldest trick in the book. Get a silly hoe drunk and high and have ya way wit her. Damn Tay, let it go!* **"It's whuteva, whuteva, whuteva, it's whuteva, whuteva, whuteva, whuteva, it's whuteva."** *Tay's chitachatter*

She proceeds with the evacuation operation of her actions with the meatball brown couch potato frame of Roc. She head to the room and notice the naïve green ribbon on the second room door. The ribbon on the door is the Sistahs code for someone is using the room. The color of the ribbon matches the color coded cupcake key chains. Tay color is naïve green.

"Okay, kay, kay now. Who's up in there with Marc? Better yet, I can have Marc put Roc and the memory out of my sight." Tay's chitachatter

Tay knocks and then opened the door. Marc and his guest are still sleeping. Tay tip toe closer to the bed. She pulls back the red and pink thick stripped bed dressings off the two naked bodies in the bed.

"Teddy? *It's whuteva, whuteva, whuteva, it's whuteva, whuteva, whuteva, whuteva, it's whuteva. We gon' do what we do, it's whuteva 2 fuck. Put your right hand up, Put your left hand up. Put your right hand up, Put your left hand up. Put your right hand up, Put your left hand up. Put your right hand up. It's whuteva, whuteva, whuteva, it's whuteva, whuteva, whuteva, whuteva, it's whuteva"* Tay's chitachatter.

"I almost gave up, but a power that I can't explain fell from heaven like a shower."

I smile
Kirk Franklin
Hello Fear

This Sunday morning was no different than every morning. The duties of a preacher's wife have a never ending "To-do list". Mildred rises with the sun at six thirty-ish in the morning. She slips her feet into her house shoes. She quietly climbs out of the bed. She grabs her house robe off its designated hook on the back of her bedroom door. She creeps down the stairs of her small humble brownstone in Strivers Row, Harlem. She enters the kitchen. She turns on the kitchen's sink faucet. Cold water fills the small pot. The ticking coming from the stove is the only sound in the house. Mildred loves the of the morning time, peace and quiet. As the pot of water comes to boil on the stove, she collects the Sunday's newspaper of the front step. She reorganizes the newspaper's sections into her husband's order of reading. She enjoys a cup of coffee before she begins to make breakfast. On today's breakfast menu is pancakes, home fries, scrambled cheese eggs, beef sausages and toast. Sunday morning menus are larger than everyday breakfast menus. The reverend's longest day is Sundays. Sunday school begins at 9 a.m. Sunday services begin at 11 o'clock and evening Sunday service begins at 3 p.m. Mildred makes a big and healthy breakfast. The next time the reverend will eat it will be 5 o'clock this evening. Mildred cooks for the reverend and the congregation during evening service. While the reverend enjoys his breakfast, Mildred will be ironing the Reverend's collar shirt for church. She will lay out his cloths from his socks to his suite blazer. She shines his shoes before beginning to get herself ready. After picking up Mildred's parents, Mary and Mason, and sister, Melissa, they head to church. Mary, Mason, and Melissa sit in the front pew directly facing the prophet. Mildred sits with pride and honor in the prophet besides her husband, Reverend Michael Jacobs. In the middle of Easter Sunday service the church doors bust open. Easter Sunday is the busiest Sunday of the year for churches.

Reverend Michael Jacobs's congregation has overflowing out the pews. Congregation members being force to stand along the walls of the church. The loud entrance startles the congregation.

"NO SINNERS IN THE PROPHET! NO SINNERS IN THE PROPHET!" the intruders shout.

The group of intruders has pick-it signs reading the words they are yelling. One of the pick-it signs has a picture of Marc, the reverend's son, dressed as a woman.

"NO SINNERS IN THE PROPHET! NO SINNERS IN THE PROPHET!" the intruders shout in the house of the Lord.

"ENOUGH! PLEASE LEAVE NOW! DON'T DISRESPECT THE HOUSE OF THE LORD!" Reverend Jacobs yells into his microphone from the prophet.

Volunteers from the congregation ushers the disturbing intruders out of the church doors, onto the street. The volunteers close the door and stand guard. The whispers of congregation's concern screams in the Reverend's ears.

"I am a man of God. I took an oath to my heavenly father to serve him and spread his word. My son did not. On judgment day I will stand alone before my heavenly father and my son will do the same. My heavenly father is the only one who shall judge the lives of others. My son passed through me but is not of me. My son is not of my oath. My son is a man like any other man, free to his own choice of a life path. My heavenly father is of forgiveness and love. My heavenly father has forgiven all of us for our sinners, and I shall do the same for my son. My heavenly father has loved me through my sins and for my son I shall do the same. My son is the only one who can make things right between himself and the Lord, but I shall make things right between me and my son. You ask why? I'll tell you why because I'm a parent. Parents love and nurture their off springs, just as my heavenly father has done for me and I shall do the same for my son, no matter the circumstances." Reverend Jacobs talks to the congregation through the microphone from the prophet. Reverend Jacobs's voice and message has echo in the house of the Lord, tickling the ears and hearts of the congregation.

"I smile, even though I'm hurt see I smile, I know God is working so I smile, Even though I've been here for a while I smile, smile... it's so hard to look up when you look down. Sure would hate to see it when you give up now you look so much better when you smile."

"I ain't gotta do a lot of flexin', Shorty you already know what it is. All that I wanna hear is you say Daddy's home, home for me. And I know you've been waiting for this lovin' all day. So you ain't got to give my loving away."

Hey Daddy
Usher
Raymond v Raymond

"Shit turned crazy fast and nobody was around. Where did you go?" Sammy's cinnamon spice lips questions Rhonda. Sammy's voice travels by cell phone to Rhonda's ear.

"Myself and Brooklyn hooked up with the Johnson brothers. Why what happened?" Rhonda reveals her dirty deed commit after the party.

"Well, how was it? You been dying for years to get with De'Andre."

"It was a 7 ½. I know two "house call" guys who are better. Besides, he is recently divorced and has a 1 year old. I'm not ready for nothing too serious. What happen after I left?"

"Girl, shit went haywire. Phil was trying to slide with Camille and Calvin went crazy. Phil punched Calvin in the eye and they started fighting. Camille drunken ass tried to break up the fight and fell on her ass. I'm helping Camille up and hollering at Omar to help me out. Omar breaks up the fight. Phil sucker punches Omar. Omar pepper sprayed his ass and locked him up. I don't know where Tay's ass was? But I ended up leaving with Camille. Calvin was still out there yelling, kicking and all type of crazy shit, when we left him. I left Omar to deal with Calvin drunk violent ass."

"Wow, where was Roc to control his pet, Phil?"

"I have no idea. I was in the middle of the bullshit by myself."

"And Teddy got home safe?"

"Of course, he was the first to leave. He's on his way here to pick up T.J, after he picks Mom up from church. Benny should be here soon."

"Can you believe Brooklyn head butted Joanny?"

"Yes I can. They kept bothering that girl about Carlito's money. I have news for them, it's her money now."

"How about Bryson never showed up. I hate to say Chyenne was right, he aint no good."

"Damn, Rhonda give the brother a chance. We don't know why he didn't make it to Tay's birthday party. After we find out then we can call him all type of dogs and bitch niccas."

"You think the fifty foot oil-base painted portrait of Tay's face is from Bryson?"

"I don't know who gave it to her but it magnificent. It takes natural talent to create in that magnitude."

"Sammy I'm gonna sleep this alcohol off, I still feel drunk and it 3 o'clock in the afternoon."

"I'm gonna wait on Benny and Teddy and then I'm gonna go check up on mommy."

"Call me if you need me, I'm home."

"Will do. A piece of solitude." Sammy's cinnamon spice lips recite her signature Sistah wish.

"A piece of ass." Rhonda's luminous lips recite her signature Sistah wish.

Rhonda and Sammy end their conference call.

As Sammy place her house phone on the base, Sammy's door bell rings. She opens the door. Her mouth fell open. She can't believe her eyes. Benny, T.J and Benny's father is standing in front of the door.

"You lost your key again Benny?" Sammy cinnamon spice lips questions to her son is in a scolding tone.

"Daddy's home" Benny's father shouts through his grin plastered on his face.

"Hi mom, how was the party?" Benny asks his mother. He bends down and kisses Sammy on her cheek.

"Auntie, I'm hungry." T.J reveals as he hugs Sammy.

"Are you going to invite me in?" Benny's father asks Sammy.

"Oh yeah, I forgot a vampire can't come into your home unless you invite them in." Sammy responds to Benny's father sarcasm.

"I see you didn't lose you sense of humor." Benny's father sarcasm is meant to agitate Sammy.

"Benny, you and T.J put your things in your room and I'll order some Pizza." Sammy shouts to Benny.

"Yes Pizza." TJ approves Sammy's choice of food.

"Gotcha Mom." Benny responds to his mother.

Sammy can now focus her attention on Benny's father. She is anxious to know his reasoning for his pop-up visit.

"What blows you this way?" Sammy questions Benny's father.

"I just had to tell you the news in person. Next fall I'll be back in the city to live. You know I was a free agent and no team wanted to sign a contract for the amount I'm worth. No more traveling. I was thinking we can work on us. You know, give me another chance." Benny's father appears to be as sincere as his words.

"I'm not willing to put my heart in your hands again so you can crush it, and your knees are weak from playing ball, I don't know if you can handle me now."

Benny's father is a famous professional basketball player. Sammy met him in college. They instantly fell in love. But Benny's father's idea of love was giving his heart to Sammy but sharing his smooth skin with many different females. During his six year relationship with Sammy, He has fathered another child with a gold digger. He then had the nerve to marry and divorce the gold digger in the public eye. The divorce nearly left him broke. He had to push his injured knees an extra five years pass retirement, just to live financially comfortable. The gold digger tried to stalk Sammy. Rhonda's foot to her face put an end to gold digger's efforts. Sammy has given Benny's father several chances, he has blown each one. She also didn't care for her relationship embarrassments to be displayed in the Paparazzi's eyes again.

"I gotta love dat sense of humor. Well it didn't hurt to ask. Are you alright?"

"Why do you ask? I look bad?"

"No you don't look bad. You have always looked sexy in pajamas and rollers."

"Flattery will get you nowhere. What's going on?"

"Ok, I really ask 'cus I sent Benny some money. I was just checking."

"So that's where he got the money for the girl's abortion. I'm gonna kill him."

"Noo, You can't say anything. It's a father son thing."

"Well, you aint gotta go home but cha gotta get the hell outta here."

"Are you kicking me out?"

"No just telling you to get out."

"I was hoping I could crash here for the night. My interview at the high school is tomorrow morning."

"Mr. Baller doesn't have funds for a hotel?"

"Why you gotta be so cold? It aint about having funds, It's about spending time with my son."

"Whatever."

Sammy has granted Benny's father permission to spend ONE night in her house.

****

Brooklyn took Le'Roy up on his invitation and went to Metropolitan Museum. She rushed home showered and changed in record time. She washed the dry gel out her hair. Her hair has the wet curly Dominican look. She is wearing a pair of denim skinny jeans, an electric intriguing blue v-neck t-shirt and electric blue wedge heel pumps. She tossed on a denim blazer to complete her outfit. She didn't feel the need to dress up for Le'Roy. He has already seen her naked. Brooklyn spent her Saturday shopping, dining and sleeping before going to Tay's party. She's been awake for twenty hours but no one would be able to tell. She is full of energy.

"Excuse me, can you tell me where Anthony Johnson's exhibit is?" Brooklyn's "Hennessy" straight color coated lips inquire information from the museum's security guard.

"Yes sweetie, it's on the second floor on the right." The museum's security guard speaks, but his eyes sips on Brooklyn's old fashion glass soda bottle frame.

"Thanks." Brooklyn's "Hennessy" straight color coded lips appreciate the directions.

Brooklyn has lived in New York for years and never visited a museum, Empire State building or the Statue of Liberty. The museum intrigued her. Brooklyn's "Hennessy" straight old fashion glass soda bottle frame has intrigued the eyes of everyone that received a view of her. She took her time getting to Anthony's exhibit. She loves the creativity her eyes are capturing. As her feet bring her closer to Anthony's exhibit, Le'Roy picks up her scent.

"Oh shit, she really came." Le'Roy's anxiety bounces in his words as he speaks to his brother De'Andre. Le'Roy's sexy light green eyes are wide open. His sweet caramel coated skin covering his six foot frame glows at the sight of Brooklyn. His smile of perfect white teeth shines brighter than an diamond.

"You have been stung." De'Andre teases Le'Roy.

"Stung? What cha talking 'bout bro?"

"You've been stung nicca, by the Queen bee. Pussy whipped, nose wide open. Pick a name that you like but it's all the same thing."

"Shut up, she's coming."

"Stung!"

"You just mad the friend aint show up."

Brooklyn walks up on De'Andre and Le'Roy.

"Good afternoon Beautiful, I'm so happy you decided to come." Le'Roy words are accompanied with a kiss to the back of Brooklyn's hand, covered in an intoxicating complexion.

"It's my pleasure, Hello De'Andre." Brooklyn responses to Le'Roy open display of affection.

"Where's ya girl?" De'Andre inquires about Rhonda's whereabouts.

"She is worn out from the party. Us girls aren't as young as we look or feel."

Le'Roy takes Brooklyn's attention away from De'Andre. Brooklyn and Le'Roy wonder around the museum, hand and hand. Enjoy each exhibit and each other's company. They have wondered out the museum and into Central Park.

"So Miss Brooklyn, you had the pleasure of interrogating me. Is it my turn for the 21 questions?' Le'Roy asks.

"Depends on what cha wanna know." Brooklyn words bounce out her mouth in a playful manner.

"I wanna know everything 'bout you." Le'Roy speaks with the intoxicating absorption of Brooklyn's "Hennessey" beauty in his eyes and words.

"Ask away, I don't know how to be anything but honest. I hope you can handle the answers."

"Are you ready?"

"I may be more ready than you. Ask away."

"Married?"

"Widower."

"Are you going tell me you killed your husband too?'

"People believe that."

"I don't. An elegant flower such as yourself, isn't capable of killing a bug, much less a man."

"A "man" you say. Oh, do I smell little sexism in the air? Honey, let me enlighten you, we live in the 21st century. The 50's is gone. Woman is capable of anything a man can do, except, pee standing up."

"You're wrong. Dem chicks on the point can pee standing up, easy."

Brooklyn falls out in laughter. "You lie." Brooklyn squeezed out though her giggles.

"I'm telling you, I've seen it. Are you ready for the next question?"

"You are so silly. Yes I'm ready for the next question."

"Kids?"

"Five kids"

"All from your marriage?"

"No, I give my husband 4 sons. My daughter wasn't planned but I have no regrets. Harlem is my world."

"Wow, I don't believe you. Wit a body like dat, aint no way in hell 5 kids came outta you. How old are they?" Le'Roy holds up his right hand to put emphases on the five.

"The boys, E.P.M.D are 25, 24, 23, 22 and my Harlem is 4 years old."

"E.P.M.D?"

"Yes, EPMD is the abbreviations for Edwin, Pedro, Miguel and Dino."

"That's funny," Le'Roy speaks through his laughter.

"It's different."

"Not it unique, just like you."

"Next question Sir?"

"Do all kids live with you?"

"No, the boys moved with their father, before he died."

"You sound bothered by it."

"I was, but not anymore."

"What's ya relationship status with Harlem's father?"

"We never had a relationship. Harlem just happened."

"So you are available?"

"Yes, I am."

"Where do you live at?"

"Harlem, of course, what you was expecting me to say Brooklyn, huh?"

"I was hoping you said Brooklyn because that's where I live, I want you close."

"Ask the next question, Mr. Ronny Romance."

"You always lived in Harlem?"

"No, born in DR. I moved to the Bronx first and found my way to Harlem."

"What do you do for a living?"

"I'm a Food Critic. The benefit is to dine at great places and never having to pay."

"Sommin like free school lunch every day?"

"Yes, silly but much better cuisine."

"How long have you been working as a Food Critic?"

"10 Years."

"Wow, so I take it as you like what you do?"

"Love it. I'm not confined to an office space with catty woman. I'm traveling the city and eating great food while getting paid. It's perfect."

"Have you always wanted to be a Food Critic?"

"I guess. I've always wanted to be free and being a Food Critic is a freedom type of job."

"So I take it as you don't cook."

"You take it wrong. I'm a Dominican woman, we are born to cook. I've been cooking since I could reach the stove."

"Maybe I'll be lucky enough to eat your cooking."

"Maybe you will."

"Will you be willing to see me again?"

"Sure, why not?"

"So you are willing to date me?"

"Yes Le'Roy, I will date you?"

"When are you available?"

"Weekends"

"Can I kiss you?"

"I like a man who goes for what he wants. Asking is kinda corny."

Le'Roy swiftly tossed Brooklyn up against the gate. He uses his body to pin her against the gate. He grips the gate with his index, middle and ring fingers with both hands. His tongue explores Brooklyn's mouth. His tongue flickers at her heart. Le'Roy lets Brooklyn free from his hold but Brooklyn's body was still in Le'Roy's hands, and he didn't even know it.

"How was dat for you?"

"Lovely."

"Brooklyn, thank you for coming, can I take you to dinner Friday night?"

"Yes you may."

"So that means I can get you number."

"Yes you may."

"Whatcha wanna do now, my lady?"

"Wow, time sure flies when you're having fun. It's 5 o'clock. I gotta head home to Harlem; her father is dropping her off at 6."

Brooklyn and Le'Roy say their good-byes with a long passionate kiss.

Brooklyn is driving home. She's been away from Le'Roy for a good fifteen minutes but his presence was still on her lips, mind and skin.

"I've been humped on by plenty of boys but Le'Roy is a man who made love to me. The Sistahs always talk about the Red Carpet dick. This was my first ride. I like the butterflies swimming in my stomach. I like Le'Roy's sexy naked ass run thru my mind. I never felt love but if this is it, then I'm in love with Le'Roy Johnson. What is this world coming too?" Brooklyn's chitachatter

****

"You were so drunk; do you even remember what happen last night? Do you?" Amber questions Camille.

Amber is Camille younger sister but plays the role as the older, wiser, more experienced sister. Amber is in Camille's room, sitting on the left side of Camille's queen size bed.

"No, but I know you going to tell me?"

"Calvin fought Phil over you."

"Are you talking about Phil, the goon? What da hell was I doing wit Phil? I really shouldn't drink in the public!"

"Yeah right you shouldn't drink, you were trying to leave with Phil and Calvin stopped you. Phil got tight and wanted to fight. In the end, Omar locked Phil's ass up."

"Wow, I was drunk before I got to da damn party. Me and Mommy had like 3 drinks before we even left the house. I love Calvin. I'm sooo glad he was there. I can't live without my twin."

"More like 4 drinks, sweetie. I know I made the drinks and they were strong. I told you to slow down but you were following Mommy like you a true G. You better love Calvin, you don't wanna lose ya virginity to a goon like Phil. Phil's life expectancy is 5 more years. The street life of hustling and shooting people only land you in 2 places, dead or in jail. I wish Cayne's mother could understand there's no life in the street!"

Cayne and Amber are the parents of the adorable three year old little girl, April. Camille seats up in her bed. Amber trembling voice is calling for Camille's attention and affection. Camille is sitting upright. She has wrapped her arms around her little sister. She wanted to jump on her sister's words about her virginity but Amber was emotionally hurting. Camille is uncomfortable with the fact that her younger sister has a baby girl and she still hadn't even had sex yet. Camille's head has always been buried in books. Whereas, Amber's head in buried into Cayne.

"What happened now Cayne's mother kicked him out again?"

"Yep, he showed up here at like 2 in the morning. The same stupid fight, just a different day. She wants Cayne to be his dead father. Cayne is not a hustler. His father died hustling! What mother encourages their son to be a part of that dead end lifestyle? She's crazy. She got a different man every 4 months, but it's the same guy just with a different face. She let them hustle out her apartment and then ask me when her grand baby is coming over. Never! She's run a trap house. Cayne speaks up and gets kicked out." Amber speaks with tears flowing down her cheek.

"Camillie, I'm telling you that house is gonna get raided any day now and if Cayne is in there, he's going to jail. There are drugs and guns all up and thru that apartment. I'm just so scared for him. The worst part is Cayne is in college, working part-time and a good father. Why would she rob him of being the great man he is? I just don't get it!"

"Where's Mommy? Let's talk to her. Maybe Cayne can stay here."

"She didn't come home last night."

"Stop crying. Mommy is gonna fix it! Where's Calvin and the kids?"

"Calvin didn't come home last night, neither. The kids are downstairs. Oh, I almost forgot. C'mon, I gotta **Anklebiter**[40]. Capri was up in here running her mouth last night. C'mon, you gotta hear it, I need a witness." Amber dries her tears. The thought of someone's life made Amber stop think about her own situation.

Anklebiters *are tricky. They can be a hundred percent true or a hundred percent false, but most of the time, within the Anklebiter there is about five percent truth. The hard part is to find the truth laying in the scattered story.*

Amber drags Camille out of bed as she dries the last of her tears. They both came downstairs together. April and Nico are playing with toy building blocks with Cayne on the living room floor in Tay's cherry brick townhouse. Capri is practicing her ballerina moves. Amber was a paid babysitter for last night's party. Chyenne and Malik paid Amber to watch their nine year old daughter, Capri while they attended Tay's party, and Tay gave her a few dollars for watching Nico.

"Ma ma Dad dad home," April speaks through her baby gibberish language.

"Yes, I know baby." Amber agrees with April's baby gibberish.

"Who's Sunny?" Amber questions Capri.

"Sunny is my baby sister." Capri has responded with confidence in her answer to Amber's question.

---

[40] **Anklebiter** *is when a child say something they should not have said.*

"You don't have a baby sister." Camille corrects Capri.

"Yes, I do. My daddy took me to see her in the hospital when she was born. I just saw her again when she came to my house." Capri has responded to the question with wholehearted confidence in her words.

"Really," Camille questions with puzzled eyes.

"Yup, I have a sister. Her name is Sunshine and she is 3 months old and she looks just like me, Beautiful!" Capri concludes the conversation and continued practicing her ballerina moves.

"Anklebiter!" Camille and Amber speak in unisons.

Camille and Amber look at each other with puzzled faces.

"Ding Dong!" The door bell rings. Amber walks to the door to answer the call of the door bell. She opens the door to a surprise to her eyes. "Daddy's home." Santana announces. He is standing outside the door in full army attire.

Santana and Tay created the charming adorable little 3 year old little boy, Nico. He is returning from the army. Santana enlisted in the army a year after Nico was born. Tay haven't heard or seen Santana since then. In the past two years Santana has coincidental visited Nico four times while Tay wasn't home. Today his luck is unchanged.

"Dad dad," Nico shouts in baby gibberish.

Nico shouts, as he runs to his father. Every day for the past two years, Tay reminds Nico of the fact that Santana is his father. Tay planted several pictures of Santana around her townhouse and quiz Nico when a picture is passed. Tay practices this ritual with Nico on a daily basic. Santana wearing his Army uniform helped sparked Nico's memory.

Santana drops his duffle bag and bends down. He holds his arms open waiting for Nico's little legs to deliver. Santana picks Nico up and plants thousands of kisses on Nico's little face. Santana walks into the living room with Nico in his arms. Nico notice April and Cayne playing with his building blocks. Nico wiggles free from Santana's arms to return to April, Cayne and his building blocks.

"Here comes some more drama." Camille announces in annoyances.

"Well, hello to you too Camille." Santana's army strong lips spits sarcasm.

"What's up fam?" Santana greets Cayne. Santana words are followed by a hand clapping between himself and Cayne.

"Amber, where's ya mom?" Santana's army strong lips questions. "Yesterday was her birthday party. She's hasn't came home yet." Amber spits the words at Santana's emotions.

Amber isn't a fan of Santana. Santana wants to live with Tay and Nico and play house like a grown man, but wants to date woman in his age group and run the street like a little boy. Amber recognizes the fact Tay needs an attentive, interesting, and strong relationship. In Amber's opinion, Santana doesn't fit the mole.

Everyone is in the living room focus their attentions to the key jiggling in the lock on the front door. Someone is coming in. The door opens.

"Honey bunnies, Mommy's home." Tay announces to the living room.

"Ma ma here." April and Nico speak in baby gibberish language. April and Nico both runs in a competitive race to greet Tay.

After Tay kisses and hugs April and Nico, she surveys the living room.

"Today's afternoon snacks are cupcakes." Chef Robert announces after he enters the living room.

"Cake cake," April and Nico sing in baby gibberish.

"Come on little ones, let's wash up for cake cake." Chef Robert ushers April and Nico toward the downstairs bathroom. Capri followed behind Chef Robert and the toddlers.

"I gotta get ready for work." Cayne reveals his reasoning for exiting the living room and going upstairs. Amber follows behind Cayne upstairs.

"Pretty young thang I love the way you make me feel. It's off the wall dangerous. I wanna moonwalk all over your body. I love when you rock my world. Damn, Santana is looking tasty; I want a piece a cake. Thank God I took a shower and changed. Thanks to Rhonda's brilliant idea to keep an extra outfit at the Pink Pussy Cat. I would have looked foolish strolling up in here looking and smelling like yesterday. One problem is I started spotting blood after taking the morning after pill. I took it to be safe. I didn't find a condom in the room after Marc put Roc out. Please believe me, I looked. And tomorrow morning I'm going to the doctor's office I wanna be check from head to toe, aint no telling what Roc might have. I wish I could ease last night, but it's just another part of me in the closet. My secret is between me, the ceiling mirror and Marc. My secret is safe with Marc and Marc's secret is under lock and key." Tay's chitachatter

"Hello sexy lady," Santana's lusty eyes speaks to Tay as he licks his lips.

Santana's eyes are enjoying the view off her plumped voluminous bottom cheeks in the shiny black spandex. Chef Robert march though the living room with Capri and the two toddlers to the kitchen, to enjoy the afternoon snack of cupcakes. Camille joins the parade to the cupcakes.

"Hello Mr., Are you here to visit or you gonna stay awhile? I see you have luggage." Tay questions Santana.

"I just got into town. The Army will deploy me back to Afghanistan, in 'bout a month. I'm gonna stay at my parents new house in Jersey. I stop here 1st, I had to see Nico. I was hoping you let me take him to my parent's house 'til I'm deployed. Before you answer I gotta say sommin to you about the video message I received this morning, or it's gonna eat me up from the inside." Santana's army strong lips speaks with irritation. "Video message, Of ?" Tay inquires.

"Of you fucking Roc. You are an embarrassment as a baby mother. Joey sent it to me. You tend to forget your age."

Joey is Santana's closest male friend. They have been friends for their entire life.

"Fuck you, Santana. Do you give the same speech to your porn star girlfriend, Dirty Diana? You can download her movies for 99 cent off the internet. Everything aint always black and white, huh? Ya come up in here after two years talking shit. I know how old I am. I do what I do and think nothing of it. See your son and then see the exit, little boy! I'm taking a shower and I'll consider if I want my son to meet his grandparents, for the 1st time."

Tay marches with disgust in her cappuccino skin for her koowie's actions. Her heart hurts knowing Roc is spreading her shame.

"Damn, Santana wanna be starting something. Being a smooth criminal is Roc's human nature. I don't wanna remember the time. Just thinking about Roc, I can smell his fat rolls on his body. Maybe another shower will wash away the shame. Jelly belly is not my lover. Who would believe the oh la la Tay, wit the body of a Liberian girl, had sex with the fat sloppy

smelly Roc? Do you? I don't. I'll deny it to the day I die. Nowadays, anything can be digitally altered. Right?" Tay's chitachatter

****

"I'm outta here. The pussy was great, the head was even better and that ass I might come back for." Calvin expresses his gratitude for the evening.

"You sure you can't stay? We can go shopping or something." Crystal's thin upper lip distinguished superior tone offers payment for his time.

"You see how you can fuck up a good time? Stop trying to buy a nicca! Imma holla at cha. I gotcha number right? So chill!"

Calvin exits the mini mansion in Stamford, Connecticut. Crystal stands in the doorway watching Calvin drive away. Calvin put Crystal's body in low sexual positions to belittle her superior crown.

"I don't care what he say I can, no I'm gonna buy dat dick. Everything and everyone is for sale." Crystal's chitachatter

****

For the past eight hours, Chyenne's been trying to get alone time with her cell phone. She must prove her heart right. Chyenne puts her phone on the charger but any time she goes near the cell phone, Malik comes near Chyenne.

"Sweetheart, I got a plan. Capri wants to see the new 3-D movie, how about we go?" Malik suggests to Chyenne as he assist her with the breakfast's dishes.

"Sure, why not?"

"Shit, I just need 5 minutes alone with my fucking phone. I used the excuse of making breakfast to get out the bed. But Malik insisted on helping. I put Ace face on Malik's body and fucked the shit outta him to put Malik to sleep, but that plan back fired and I fell asleep. All I wanna do is check my fucking phone. I'm gonna take a shower and lock the door. I'm gonna check my fucking phone before I lose it." Chyenne's chitachatter

"I'm going to get Capri from Tay's house, while you get ready. I'll be back for you sexy." Malik reports his plan movements.

Chyenne runs for her cell phone as soon as Malik's right foot exit's the front door. She turns the cell phone on. Her heart is beating a hundred miles per minute. Finally, the cell phone is on and all applications are loaded. She goes into the contact section. The first contact reads Ace. She is calling the number.

"Hello?" Ace answers.

Chyenne freeze up from the sound of Ace's voice and hangs up the phone. She talks a deep breath. She is thinking what will be her opening line?

"I wanna song "I just calinh to say I love you" but I'm doing that. Okay I can say, I am calling to just say hi, no! Good afternoon. No, that's not it. Shit, I feel like a fucking kid. I am calling... I am calling 'cus..." Chyenne's chitachatter

Chyenne's cell phone is vibrating in her hand. Ace is calling her cell phone back.

"Hello?" Chyenne answers her cell phone.

"Hello, did somebody just called dis number?" Ace questions

"Yes, it's Chyenne."

"Hey baby girl. I've been waiting on ya call all day. When you free I wanna talk to you face to face. I love looking into you beautiful eyes. I miss you girl."

"Tomorrow is Monday. What time?"

"How about I get the whole day? 9 a.m. Where you live at? I come pick you up."

"Ace, you can't just come pick me up. I live with my man. I'll meet you somewhere."

"Are you talking about Ol'e dude from da party?"

"Yes, we have a kid together."

"I'll meet you at 42nd. That's good?"

"Fine, I'll see you then"

"Thank you God. It was real. I saw my love, Ace. I have to sit down with him and see if our love is as strong as it once was before I kick Malik's ass to the curb. I can't believe I will be with Ace all day. I can't fuck him. I just can't. I gotta make him work for it, to see if he really wants it." Chyenne's chitachatter

"If you had twenty four hours to live, just think. Where would you go? What would you do? Who would you screw? And who would you wanna notify? Or would ya' ass deny that ya' ass about to die?"

24 hours to live
Mase ft. Black Rob, DMX, The Lox, Puff Daddy
Harlem World

It's a Thursday afternoon and Sammy is waiting on her one o'clock appointment at a nice quiet restaurant tucked away in Korea Town, Manhattan. Sammy has chosen the restaurant called *Thai*. The restaurant comes highly recommended by Brooklyn. Sammy loves the atmosphere at this restaurant. Sammy is seated outside on the rooftop. On the rooftop there are various plants and flowers everywhere. Sammy requested the rooftop garden she loves the scenery. There are two secluded areas set up on the rooftop garden dining area of the restaurant. The areas are divided by the tall grass, exceptional tropical plants and tropical flowers in rare colors. The beautiful Thai woman is dressed in her native land fabric. The beautiful Thai woman has a golden cluster of flower hair dressing from Thailand. The beautiful Thai woman and ground stones guides the feet to your designed dining area. One area is covered by the Tiki hut and the other one is open to the clear blue sky. In the dining area there is one jungle green colored couch and two moss green single chairs perfectly positioned around the wooden oval shaped coffee tape in the center. Off to the left of the couches and the coffee table is a high table with four chairs. On the coffee table there is a glass pitcher of ice cold water with four empty glasses and a glass bowl of sliced dragon fruit. Dragon fruit is a Thailand treat in Manhattan. Sammy sits on the couch and enjoys the heat of the summer like day. Eating at this restaurant is rejuvenating to the soul. The plants and the chirping songs of the Thailand's songbirds singing into Sammy's ear have relaxed her mind. She has taken off her Channel suite blazer to get the full feel of the sunny rays. She puts on her Channel sunglasses to be able to read the evidence. The evidences she has just placed on the coffee table in front of her. Sammy plans to drop off a different set of some court briefs at the court house, after her appointment, so the location is ideal. Close enough to the court house; she can avoid searching for another parking spot. The restaurant's ora put the mind far from the city's roar. The ora of the restaurant give enough distance to almost completely forget you are in the city. Yesterday morning at work Sammy received the weekly court dockets for the judges she will appear before in the coming month. To her surprise there was a familiar name on one of the judge's court docket. So after work, yesterday evening she investigated the familiar name's custody case. Sammy heard Traci Adams's side of the story now it is the man's turn to tell his side of the story. She'll add and subtract and sum up what is the truth. Sammy is set up at the restaurant table like she would in court at the defendant's table. She is armed with solid evidence. She has laid out photo copies of the original filed custody petition, the woman's side of the story on a mini voice recorder, and her woman's intuition on to the coffee table. The familiar face matching the familiar name on the court docket has arrived. He is wearing a gray business suite vest with the slacks to match, a lavender long sleeve button down, a lavender and gray blended tie and lavender suede hush puppy cut shoes.

"Good afternoon, Sammy. This place is extraordinary. How did you discover such a pleasant marvelous place in the heart of the most brutal city of the world?" the voice of Sammy's one o'clock appointment questions her.

"I found this place thru Brooklyn. She wrote a wonderful piece about it, about two months ago. Is it lovely?" is Sammy response to the deep voiced genuine gentleman.

"This fruit is great. Have you tried it?" Sammy's one o'clock appointment, deep voiced genuine gentleman questions, while tasting the Thailand fruit.

"Yes, it is great."

"I'm really anxious to find out what is this meeting all about." Sammy's one o'clock appointment has a ring of suspicion in his deep voice. Skepticism is in every word flowing from the lips.

"I'm not going to play games with you. I'm going to tell the facts as I know it." Sammy has shifted to using her lawyer tone of voice.

"I'm all ears." The deep voiced genuine gentleman has crossed his legs in a manly manner. His body language speaks in volumes of being in defense mood. The twisted look on the deep voiced genuine gentleman's face spoke louder words of curiosity.

"This custody petition reads Malik Williams is beginning petition to forfeit his parental right of Sunshine Adams, leaving Traci Adams sole parental parent. Do I need to read any further?" Sammy's words are filled with her cinnamon spice flare.

Traci Adams is a Real Estate Agent. She worked on a short term project with Malik at his Architect firm. Together they work on the project of remodeling a home on the market. The temporary project required Traci and Malik to work closely together at the Architect office space in Midtown Manhattan.

"Listen, Sammy. I slept with her only one time, 13 months ago. I'm man enough to admit I was wrong for sleeping with another woman, while being in a committed relationship with Chyenne. But Chyenne played a major part in my decision. Sammy, I have worn my heart on my sleeve, giving Chyenne every part of me and she has yet to fully let me into her heart. I'm hurting inside and have been for a long time. Between me and you, the whole time I was with Traci I was pretending she was Chyenne." Malik's chestnut syrup lips speak with glassy eyes.

Malik's words spoke to Sammy's heart. Sammy could feel the hurt, regret and shame in Malik's voice. Sammy is familiar with the feeling of loving somebody and that somebody not loving you back. Malik has leaned forward in the single chair. He uses his thumb and index finger to pinch the bridge of his nose between his eyes. Malik fights back an emotional breakdown.

"At least your story matches Traci's because I was ready to play the tape on your ass." Sammy jokes in attempt to lighten the tense lines invading Malik's face.

"Traci called me 3 months ago in the middle of the night, begging for me to drive her to the hospital. She was in labor and the ambulance won't come to her neighborhood. I thought I was just doing a favor for a friend. The hospital was when she dropped the bomb that I was the father. The nurse over heard us auguring and had a DNA test performed right there on the spot. Traci has decided that Sunshine shouldn't have anything to do with me. I am conflicted. I wanna make Traci happy and sign the damn papers but I don't want to have a daughter in world thinking her father abandon her. You know the saying, girls idolize their fathers and then they marry a mirror image of their fathers. I've seen the little girl two times and I feel some kinda connection. I wish I could talk to Chyenne about my mixed feelings. I really need her right now. I'm sorry to lay all this on you Sammy but I don't have nobody to express my feelings to without receiving their opinion in return."

"So you sneaked out in the middle of the night? Where was Chyenne?"

"I was up alone, as usual. Chyenne was sleeping in Polo's room. Sleeping in Polo's room isn't unusual for her. She gets up in the middle night and I find her there. I understand she lost Polo once in his life and don't wanna lose him again but when is enough? Polo is a grown man. My heart is broken. Sammy, can you tell me why she can't love?"

"I can't answer that question. You really should be telling all this to

Chyenne, but if you don't I will in 24 hours. It's nothing against you, Malik. I believe you but what I believe doesn't mean shit. I hate to be the snitch but there's no secret between the Sistahs. "

Sammy was about to get up from her chair to head to the restroom. She is surprise by the sight of her 3 o'clock appointment heading her way. They are forty five minutes early. Melissa, Mildred and Tay have just entered the area where Malik and Sammy are sitting. Malik immediately stands to allow the ladies to have a seat like the gentleman he is. Melissa immediately took a seat on the couch next to Sammy. Tay also sat down on the couch. Mildred sat in Malik's vacant seat, the single chair.

"Hey, my Sistah. What cha doing here, Malik?" Tay greets Sammy and questions Malik at the same time in one breath.

"I was just leaving. Good day ladies and little one." Malik voices his goodbyes to the ladies as well as Melissa's unborn child. His words still linger in the air as his feet follow the ground stones to the exit.

Sammy hugs and kisses Tay and Tay's sisters, Melissa and Mildred.

"What was that all about?" Tay is questioning Sammy appointment with Malik.

"I'll tell ya all about it later. How many more months do you have now 'til you give birth?" Sammy dismisses Tay's question to question Melissa's huge bugle of Motherhood.

"In one more week I'll be 7 months, so that leaves me 2 more months of hell. I don't know if it's the heat but this belly have me sweating 24/7. Sammy I love you but cha gotta move over. I'm feeling squished and hot." Melissa's pregnant words express her uncomfortable sitting arrangement.

"Understandable, love you too." Sammy repositions her body on the couch to giving Melissa more space on the couch.

"Mildred, how are you holding up? My mother told me about last Sunday." Sammy inquires into the embarrassment state of Mildred's being.

"God is good all the time. So I'm good all the time. My son has the right to live his life how he pleases, none of us is perfect. My husband is going to keep preaching at that church until they put him out. We shall not be moved." Mildred speaks in her Christian accent.

"Okay. Let's get down to business. Let's plan this baby's shower." Tay interrupts Mildred's sermon.

"Wait, before we get to planning of the baby shower, I got two true or false questions for you Missy over here. The hood's rumor buzzing everywhere is you slept with Roc on a video for a G, true or false?" Melissa's pregnant words relay the hood's interpretation of Tay's shame.

"Now I have to say that's just nasty. Tay do you have any control of your body?" Mildred's Christian judgmental accent questions and irritates Tay's eyes.
Tay replies to Mildred's comment with a roll of her eyes, Mildred's judgmental words are borrowed from Mary's lips.

"Wow, you see how people make **_Puerto Rican soup_**[41]outta a small incident." Tay's aggravation in the tone of her words was clear on her cappuccino skin.

Puerto Rican soup gossip is when a story passes through many ears and mouths but each time it's passed along to another, a little more is added. Just like Puerto Rican soup, it starts with boiling water. By the time the soup is done it has corn, rice, beans, and meat all added

---

[41] **_Puerto Rican soup_** *is created gossip by several people.*

by a different person's mouth. A simple pot of boiling water converted into a full meal of false information.

"What I do with my koowie aint nobody's fucking business, but my own. Mildred has some fucking nerve passing judgment on somebody. Aint passing judgmental opinions suppose to be against your Christian way? Her son out here sexing men but I guess dat also aint nobody's business either, right?" Tay's chitachatter

"Well, all our ears are open. Tell us what really happen?" Melissa inquires with more conviction.

"True. I did sleep with Roc. I robbed him for a G. I didn't know 'bout da damn video 'til Santana told me. I hate Roc but I blame Mr. Bryson Mitchell's ass 'cus if he would have showed up I would have been in his arms, instead of lying up with Roc's fat ass. I told all of you, but if anybody else asks I'm gonna deny it." Tay puts her humiliation in exposed words.

"My second true or false, are you gonna let Santana take Nico to finally meet Santana's parents?" Melissa's pregnant words probe deeper into Tay's life.

"Why are you interrogating me?" Tay's annoyances of Melissa's pregnant questions are visible in her words.
"What can I say? It's the talk at Ma's house. I just wanna know. I didn't mean any harm." Melissa justifies her pregnant prying line of questions into Tay's life.

"You better be nice before you end up with a sty on ya eye." Sammy's cinnamon spice warns Tay.

"Don't tell her anything. At her rate, she's gonna end up wit sommin." Mildred adds her Christian prediction to Sammy comment.

"Let's not forget what we here for. I got a 5 o'clock appointment with a real estate agent. I'm trying to find a place for Amber and Cayne." Tay is stating her limited time through her cappuccino lips.

Melissa's pregnant decision finalize when, where, how and colors of her baby shower. Mildred is appointed food duty; after all, she did already run three different kitchens on a daily basis. Mildred is a spectacular cook, a trait Marc naturally inherited. Tay duties are the decorations and music. Tay and DJ K-Slay go back to when he was selling shirts out off a shopping cart on the avenue, outside Madison Projects. So music is always covered by Tay for all events. Tay finds fulfillment in interior decoration. Her party décor is always exquisite. Sammy is the most responsible. Melissa left Sammy in charge of the invitations. Sammy congratulates Melissa's release of her passionate controlling stand point. Sammy admires the trait she has yet to discover. The four of them exit the restaurant. They are all gloomy to be leaving a slice of heaven in the city behind. Marc, Mildred's son, is waiting on Melissa and Mildred. Marc shots Tay a left eye wink and an air kiss from the palm of his right hand. Tay returns the sweet greeting from Marc. Sammy hops in her shinny ice white Mercedes Benz, that was parked four cars down from the restaurant deciding against dropping the court documents off at the court house. Tay hails a yellow cab. She is leaving her fire red two door Lexus in the parking garage, two blocks down from the restaurant. In Tay's opinion, it was easier to keep her car from the real estate agent's sight, considering pricing. A real estate agent sees money and the price of apartment goes up. Tay couldn't dress down. She has on a silk chocolate Gucci one shoulder dress and a pair of Jimmy Choo on her feet. The Jimmy Choo shoes are ankle laced heels with two adorable bows on the side. The shoes are one of Tay's birthday winnings. Tay purchased the matching bag to the shoes yesterday at Bloomingdales. Tay arrived to Washington Heights in record time. She is thirty minutes early. Tay is meeting Traci Adams Real Estate Agent, a recommendation by Rhonda. Traci found the *Pink Pussy Cat* for the Sistah's pleasure. Traci, Crystal and Lisa are standing in front of the building when Tay arrives.

"Good afternoon. You're early. Traci Adams." Traci's comic spiritual voice introduces herself to Tay.

They have spoken over the phone several times but it was the first time they are meeting face to face. Traci offers her hand as she states her name. Traci is a five foot two inches tall. A sweet savory milk chocolate coated complexion. Her natural hazel eyes have a unique glow. Traci is wearing a bright orange Donna Karen woman business suit. The side slit on the skirt gave the outfit a cute sensual twist. She is killing a short hair cut with a long side bang. Her multi colored heels has grab Tay's attention.

"Good afternoon. Taynasha, Tay for short. Nice heels." Tay cappuccino heart shaped lips introduces herself to Traci.

"Macy's, Donna Karen." Traci comic spiritual voice notifies Tay.

"Let me find out Crystal, you moving from your mansion to slum with us, po'folks?" Tay's eyes examine Crystal's diamond shape head and cold vanilla false Caucasian pigment with hooded mud brown eyes. Tay can feel the tone of Crystal's superior presence.

"Not in this lifetime. Connecticut is a long drive away from the city. Most of my affairs are in the city. I need a place I can lay my head when I don't feel like driving home. What's ya excuse? Finally willing to leave da hood?" Crystal unveils her purpose through her thin upper lip distinguished superior tone.

"I could never leave the hood. Two reasons my parents and my love for the drama. I'm apartment hunting for my daughter and her family. Where are my manners? Hello Lisa. How are you doing?" Tay directs her questions to Lisa as a form of a greeting.

"Tay you're a grandmother? Now that some drama in its self. I've heard 'bout cha your love for drama part of performing arts. Staring in any movies lately?" Crystal's thin upper lip distinguished superior tone, spits sarcasm at Tay referring to the porn video starring Roc, co-starring Tay.

"I'm living life after death. Is there anyone who hasn't seen that fucking video? I wanna kick in the door waving the 44 on Roc's fat ass. I gotta come up wit sommin to get his ass back. He doesn't even know he has got himself into dat Biggie beef. I'm going to call Brooklyn as soon as I get home. I know she has sweet revenge plans in her pocket. Can you believe this fat bitch nicca? Look at Crystal fake ass and I do mean fake from head to toe. Her 2 million dollar body was a waste of money. She spent a mill on the face and a mill on the body. Now she is 100% fake on the outside like her 100% fake insides." Tay's chitachatter

"It's nice to see you again. Girl, I had a wonderful time at your party. I'm just working. This is the 7th apartment we've seen today. You look good, nice dress." Lisa's southern milk chocolate lips returns a response to Tay, in attempt to ease Crystal distasteful words.

"And we'll see 7 more until I'm satisfied. And dat dress is from 'bout 8 seasons ago." Crystal's cold vanilla false Caucasian pigment glows with annoyance to Lisa's southern glimmer of a complaint. Crystal couldn't believe Lisa had a hint of dissatisfaction in Crystal's apartment hunting.

"We will have to reschedule. I'll email you the available listings and you'll pick the ones we will see. Does that work for you?" Traci's steps in to defuse a situation sparking.

"Yes. Tay we gotta stop meeting like this. We keep bumping into each other." Crystal's thin upper lip distinguished superior tone, as she comments to Tay and answered Traci in one breath.

"Will you be in the city tomorrow? The Sistahs are having lunch at the *French Trimestre* restaurant. You are more than welcome to join us, Lisa you too." Tay's cappuccino heart shaped lips extends an invitation to Crystal's cold vanilla false Caucasian pigment.

French Trimestre is the restaurant were Crystal meets Lisa for weekly updates, in regards to her finances. The restaurant is also Tay's favorite place to dine. Tay, especially, likes the location since it's next to Angie's woman's clothing boutique. Tay is setting up another opportunity to even the odds with Crystal for her pop shot at her outfit.

"An offer I will consider." Crystal's thin upper lip distinguished superior tone, pretending to accept the invitation.

Crystal's better than tone bounces out her mouth with every word. Traci confirms Crystal's email address, soon after Crystal and Lisa disappear into the back of a Lexus RX 350 driven by a Crystal's driver.
"You guys are friends?" Traci pries into Crystal's and Tay's semi-relationship.

"No, long time acquaintances," Tay's bitterness over Crystal's knowledge of the video of shame itches her throat and cough up with her words.

Traci gives Tay a tour of the two bedroom apartment on the second floor. The building has a doorman, elevator and Laundromat in the basement. Upon entering the apartment, Tay takes note of the hard wood floors. Tay also observes the bright white walls. The walls can easily be changed in color with a coat of paint.

"This is the living room." Traci points out.

"I like it. It's spacious. April can run around in here."

"April is your granddaughter, right?"

"Yes. She needs plenty of room to play. She's an active little girl. Do you have any kids?"

"God has just given me my 1st bundle of joy, my baby girl Sunshine. She is 3 months old today." Traci displays her cell phone to Tay's eye sight. Sunshine adorable face is Traci's screen saver.

"Wow, she is beautiful."

"Thank you. I have truly fallen in love with her."

"You look damn good to have just given birth. I gotta introduce you to my sister; she's 7 months and she doesn't believe she'll ever get her old body back. Once she sees you, she'll have hope."
"I'll definitely meet your sister. I will love to give her secrets to getting your curves in the right spot. The trick is to snack on fruits and nuts every time you feed the baby and sleep when the baby sleeps."

"I'll set it up. I call you with the details. Let's finish checking out this apartment."

"This is a newly remodeled kitchen. It has a brand new stainless steel dishwasher, microwave, refrigerator, and stove."

"This is nice. Amber is gonna get good use of the dishwasher and microwave. She isn't much of a cleaner or cooker."

Tay and Traci walks down the short hallway in the apartment. Tay admires the flower shaped light fixtures in the short hallway.

"Okay. This is the master bedroom and second bedroom."

"I like these spacious closets."

"The bathroom is also newly remolded."

"I love this wall mirror. Amber will love it too. Did you show this apartment to Crystal?"

"No, Crystal is interested in a one bedroom. I showed her a unit on the 4th floor."

Tay approves the apartment for Amber, Cayne and April. Tay hails another yellow cab, after she set up another appointment so Amber can view the apartment. She hops in her fire red two door Lexus and head home. Tay arrives home. She enters into a heated discussion between the twins.

"Ma, tell Calvin I didn't give Phil head." Camille is looking to her mother for assistance. Calvin is scolding Camille on her reckless behavior.

"I know you aint looking for Ma for help. She's in trouble too. I heard 'bout ya video. I wanna put hands, feet and teeth on Roc, but I gotta deal with you first. Why did you do it Ma?" Calvin scolds Tay.

"Ma, how was your day? Would be nice to hear when I step foot in my house." This is Tay's response to the confrontation at the door.

"I've thanked you from saving me from Phil, why are you still talking about it? What you want me to do?"

"I'm talking 'bout it 'cus everybody in the hood is talking 'bout it. The word in da hood is while Ma was fuckin' wit Roc for a G, you suckin' Phil's dick for free."

"Calvin, you can't let *Puerto Rican soup* gossip excite you. Stop believing lies. Phil was arrested after you fought him. So when did he supposedly get head for ya sister? Where is everybody?"

"Amber took April and Nico to the park." Camille answers.

Chef Robert enters the confrontation in the living room. He hands Tay a certified letter that was delivered while she was out. Tay rips open the letter. Tay's button nose can smell Mr. Bryson Mitchell's scent steaming of the pages and out the envelope. The letter reads:

Tay, #69

I don't know how to begin to apologize for missing your birthday party but I'll try. From the 1st time I laid eyes on your cappuccino skin, I knew there was something special about you. When I look into your honey brown eyes, I see your soul. You was straight up with me the whole time and I been living a lie. After I tell you the truth about me I don't except to hear from you again. But your beauty has made a change in me. I'm coming clean to all 68 women I slept with. You are the hardest and the last one, #69. I've been living with H.I.V virus for 5 years. When I 1st found out I had the virus, I was mad at the world. I vow to pass on the virus to every woman that cross my path, just as a woman passed it on to me. But once I met you, I no longer had the bitterness in my heart. After the third time we sleep together, I started using condoms because you didn't deserve the bitterness of the virus. I have excused myself from your life. My heart won't let me rest until I tell you to get tested. Sorry a million times.

-Bryson

****

Crystal walks into her mansion in Stamford, Connecticut. She is surprise to see Ace lounging on her Italian leather couch, in her living room under the wall fish tank.

"You been outta jail for a week now and you haven't come home 'til now?" Crystal's thin upper lip distinguished superior tone, questioning Ace.

"This is not my home. This is the address I use for parole. I've been here, you was just too busy to notice."

"Speaking of parole, your parole officer came by here this morning. He said you have 24 hours to report to him or he's gonna lock your ass back up. I was waiting. If you didn't show up here today I was gonna call him and tell him you haven't been staying here."

"Look at you. Talking like you got a nicca by the balls. Chris, you can't play me no more. I aint high today, my vision aint blurry, I can see clearly. Try something else."

"If I call him you go back to jail."

"If you call him I'll divorce ya ass and take your house, your money and your two little dogs, leave your ass wit nuffin. I think you'll commit suicide wit out ya money, that would be even better for me."

"I do have you by the balls. I always had ya balls in my hands. The jokes on you, the marriage certificate is fake, like a Maddoff investment. Ya can't divorce someone ya never married. You'll never get ya hands on my money." Crystal's chitachatter

"You hate me so much, tell me why you married me?"

"I married you 'cus I don't trust ya ass. We did a lot of dirt together. If you ever would've gotten caught, I know you would sell me out. Marrying you was for my protection."

"So, me traveling going to federal prison once a month to fuck your brains out was for nothing?"

"I wouldn't say it was for nothing. I don't know if I would have made it thru 10 years without some pussy. Don't flatter yourself. That pussy aint the greatest but it made due."

"Now I know he's lying! I've fucked plenty niccas and never ever did I get a complaint. This here is million dollar pussy, literally! If I fucked ya once I can always fuck you again. Ace, you'll be beggin for this pussy sooner than later, I promise you." Crystal's chitachatter

"So pussy, that's all I am too you?"

"No, that's all you were to me. Now we just people who share a past."

"So what? You're not fuckin me no more? Tell me you don't want this pussy."

"No I don't want your pussy."

"LIAR! I know you want this pussy." Crystal's chitachatter

"You better call that youngen that was in here blowin ya back out last Sunday morning. I got somebody to handle my needs and it aint you."

"Thanks for the tip. I just might call Calvin over. Let him fuck me while you jerk you dick. You'll be beggin in no time. Guarantee!" Crystal's chitachatter

"I've been holding you down for 20 years and this is my thanks?"

"Ya right were holding me down, down under 'til the point where I couldn't breathe. 10 of those years I was locked down and the other 10 I was running the street with you. We were supposes to be partners, a 50/50 slit, but because I was high the whole damn time you would do a 70/30 slit. Is that the thanks I get? You're a cheater, heartbreaker, and a liar who could never be trusted."

After Crystal fled from Madison Projects she landed in her grandfather's vacant mansion in Richmond, Virginia, taking Ace along for the ride. Ace and Crystal had discovered uncharted territory of unsuspecting victims in Virginia. They had a ten year run of scandals and scams, until Ace was arrested. Ace was arrested for cashing hundreds of Social Security checks into a dummy account created by Crystal. Ace was sentence to ten years in Federal prison. With Ace in jail, Crystal moved to Stamford Connecticut. She hired Lisa and begins to sell off her family's name.

"Just let the past. Just be the past. And focus on things. That are gonna make us laugh. Take me as I am , not who I was. I'll promise I'll be, the one that you can trust."

Don't Judge Me
Chris Brown
Fortune

"BANG, BANG, BANG, BANG!" Teddy's condo apartment door is shaking from the pounding coming from the outside of the door.

Marc is startled from his sleep by the banging on the front door of the condo apartment. He awakes Teddy.

"Teddy, Teddy, Teddy!" Marc shouts up to Teddy.

Teddy's sleeping body lies behind Marc's body. Marc squiggles his petite five foot two inch nude, medium coco powder brown body back into Teddy's awaken manhood on a sleeping body, in pursuit of a conscious Teddy. Teddy surrenders his sleep to Marc's voice. Teddy blinks his eyes into focus.

"Teddy, I'm scared go check it out. Who could be banging down your door 6 a.m on a Friday morning? I wanna know, how did they get pass the doorman?" Marc's voice trembles with fear.

"I'm going. Aint nuffin to be scared of, I'm going to check it out." Teddy speaks as he attempts to move his comatose body out of the bed.

Teddy lives in a two bedroom condo apartment downtown in NoMad, Manhattan. Teddy lollygags out the bed, his five foot eight inch slightly muscular nutmeg colored nude body practically crawlers out the bed. Marc's lustful eye enjoys the movement of the seasoning of the nutmeg spice. Teddy dawdle his nude body toward the leather recliner chair across from the bed, in the right corner of the bedroom. He dilly-dallies around the pile of discarded clothing on the leather recliner chair. He discovers a white tee-shirt. His sluggish arms throw a shirt over his head and he covers his lifeless legs with a pair of Persian silk electric blue pajama pants. He slowly slipped his foot into his UGG house shoes, which were conveniently at the foot of the bed. He drags his half asleep body out of his bedroom, down the small hallway, pass the bathroom, and through the living room toward the front door. TJ's room is to the left of the front door, down a small hallway. TJ's room is the master bedroom with a private bathroom included. Giving T.J the master bedroom is one of many small scarifies Teddy has willingly made.

"BANG, BANG,BANG, BANG!" The door sounds again.

"I'm coming, calm down!" Teddy shouts to the person on the other side of the door, right before unlocking the door.

Teddy opens his condo apartment door. His eyes are astonished by sight outside his threshold.

"Teddy you gotta help me, please." Tay words are poring with tears and snot.

Teddy's body is deadlocked. His eyes locked on Tay's five feet body, standing on six inches of high heels. Tay's cappuccino complexion is flushed with red concern. Her honey brown almond shape eyes, peeking out from under her Chinese cut bangs, pours tears. The rain of tears drops off her half an inch long curled eyelashes runs down her rosy colored cheeks. Her waist length honey blond weave tied up in a ponytail. Teddy hasty pulls Tay's trembling body into his condo apartment. Marc hears Tay's sobbing and emerges from Teddy's bedroom and rush to Tay's aide. Marc sashayed across the living room in a matching pajama robe to Teddy's pajama pants and pink bunny rabbit slippers. Marc's head is covered in a black curly bob wig. Teddy assistant Tay's sobbing body to the Jennifer Convertibles suede couch under the widow in the living room. Teddy waves Tay's blind eyes clouded with tears around the glass coffee table. Marc takes a tissue from the box on the glass coffee table and pat at the tears and snot streaming down Tay's face. Teddy rubs Tay's back to consoling her. Tay's shoulders heaves up and down as she gasp for air as Marc combat the flow of body fluid flowing freely from Tay's eyes and nose.

"Auntie, what's wrong?" Marc questions Tay.

"We can't help you unless you talk to us." Teddy's words are to encourage Tay to reveal her pain identifying the problem is part of any healing process.

"Hun, you gotta talk to us." Marc's sweet whisper caress Tay's ears as his gentle touch smooth out the tension wrinkles in her back.

Tay hands Marc the letter from Mr. Bryson Mitchell. Marc and Teddy read the letter together.

"O.M.G!" Marc's horrified voice rings out in the living room.

"Wow." Teddy voices the distress of the letter.

"Oh, baby don't worry you came to the right place. Teddy has a home kit. We gonna test you right here." Marc attempts to play down the importance of the letter.

Teddy has plenty of clients who are too shamed to be tested for H.I.V in a faculty. It's new to the market but accurate, a home H.I.V. testing kit. Teddy keeps a few at home for situations just like this. Teddy walks over to the antique bar cart in the left corner of the kitchen window, into the living room. Tay is pacing the floor awaiting the test results.

"Your pacing got me all nerves I got to get a drink to settle my nerves."

Teddy speaks of his actions as he adds ice to his half a cup of dark brandy.
"You know it's too early, but under these circumstances I'll give you a pass." Marc's words speak over the stove, out the kitchen window. The kitchen has a window looking into the living room.

"Make me a drink too, shit. I need it." Tay states her request to Teddy.

Tay takes a seat on the black stool, under the kitchen window looking into the living room. Teddy also takes a seat on the stool. Teddy sits in front of the kitchen window looking into the living, between Tay on left side and the antique bar cart on the right. Marc begins to make breakfast. Marc cooks to calm his nerves. His nerves are on edge awaiting Tay's test results. Tay has temporarily stopped crying. She enjoys her screwdriver drink Teddy made for her. Teddy makes another screwdriver drink for himself as his second drink, before 7 a.m. Marc serves his famous home fries with chopped mixed peppers, sausages and sunny side up eggs. Marc comes out the kitchen and sits next to Tay. The three enjoys Marc's home cooked breakfast. The southern savory food has silenced all three of their tongues. Teddy washes his hands and then reads Tay's test results. The test results are positive. Tay begins to cry again.

"I know a guy named Fredrick Thomas, which can help you. He is a personal friend. He has a center that can set you on a prescription drug regiment, along with counseling. It's not the end of the world, Baby girl. There are plenty of men and women who live healthy lives with H.I.V. don't worry you are going to be just fine. It's not a death sentence." Teddy offers words of advice to stop Tay's flow of tears.

"I just wanna die." Tay's pain travels through her sobs and tears.

"Hun, don't give up on life. You have your kids to live for. Your life is not over. I'll go with you to see the guy. Let me get my face and clothes on.

I'm feeling manly." Marc rush off to Teddy's bedroom.

"I gotta get ready too. I got an hour to be outta here. Court is at 9. I gotta face Victoria today." Teddy announces purpose for indulging in two alcoholic drinks in the early morning, along with his plans as he disappears into the bathroom.

Marc and Tay headed to Fredrick Thomas's office while Teddy heads to court.

****

The family court room on the fifth floor is boxed in by three wooden walls and a wall of two enormous windows. The Judge sits on the bench in the front of the room, in the traditional black robe. His reading glasses sit on his nose as he rereads the court docket in his right hand. Above the judge's head hanging on the wall, is a large plaque reading the logo of the dollar bill "In God We Trust." On the left and right side of the judge are two American flags. Adjacent to the judge's bench is the witness stand, desks where the court clerk and court stenographer sits. The lectern is in front of the court clerk desk. The lectern is where the lawyers position their selves to address the judge. There are two tables behind the lectern. One table is for the defendant and the other table is for the plaintiff. At the defendant's table sits Victoria Stevens and Victoria's lawyer, Dick Richards. Victoria's mocha complexion is barely covered by a video vixen red short sleeved mini dress. Her coco buttered greased legs are bare, she's not wearing stockings. Her layered black colored weave lies perfectly on her head, her extra large gold hoop earring peep from behind the layered hair. Through her side bangs, her beaded dark brown eyes speaks evil. The sun's ray gleaming of her clear heeled pumps was blinding the Judge. The Judge kindly asked her to remove her shoes in his court room. Her court appointed lawyer, Dick Richards, is about fifty years old. He is the same age as his tired pinstriped suit. His cheap toupee is crooked. The side part on the toupee is in the front instead of on the side. To the right of the defendant's table is the plaintiff's table, where Theodore "Teddy" Wilson and his attorney Samantha "Sammy" Wilson sit. Sammy's cinnamon complexion is covered by a medium grey Yves Saint Laurent full business suit. Her hair put into a bun. The bun rested in the back of her head. She is wearing her sophisticated custom Cartier glasses. Her fresh water pearl earrings and choker necklace also speaks nobility like her words. Sammy calm brown eyes meant business just like her outfit. Teddy is dressed as he is always dressed, in colors complimenting his flourishing nutmeg complexion. Teddy has a fifties ring to his style. Killer two toned Claston brand shoes on his feet; Claston was a popular men shoe brand name in the fifties. A chocolate colored pair of fitting slacks with crease so sharp they could cut leather. Two toned suspenders, matching his footwear are over a detailed ironed light coffee brown button up shirt. Teddy's color of choice is chocolate and light coffee brown today. Teddy has his chocolate colored top hat sitting in his lap, out of respect to the court house rules. The bailiff is the court officer stands guard at the bar. The bar is a wooden rail barrier, separating court officials from the public. The gallery of pew style benches is the seating area for the public curious spectators. The Gallery is divided by an aisle into two areas, one on the left side and one on the right side. Rhonda is sitting on the second row pew on the right side, behind Sammy and Teddy. Rhonda's ultra light blond colored short hair is slick down with a side part today. She has cute little Betty Boop curls gelled to her forehead and sides of her face. Her white gold feather earring dangled from her ears. Her luminous white chocolate skin is covered by a hot pink two button blazer. Her cleavage is sitting above the two buttons on the blazer. On her legs she has on a pair of skin tight blue denim jeans with hot pink Dior pumps on her feet. Her hot pink rhinestone covered clutch purse rest on her laps. She eye hustles the bailiff, the court officer; muscular sculpted body as her ears listens to the court proceedings. Rhonda appreciates the handsome facial features of the cookie and cream bailiff officer. His high cheek bone and shy blue eyes appeals to Rhonda's eyes sight and desire. Kira sits next to Rhonda. Kira is Teddy's female companion. Kira's soft warm vanilla brown sugar complexion is wrapped in a checker board black and white blazer, with a dainty red belt above the waist line. On her legs is a pair of solid black slacks. Her feet has on fire red Louis Vuitton red bottoms, with a fire red odd shaped Louis Vuitton tote. Her ear length of sun kissed brown soft curly hair is held back by a thin red head ban.

"Your Honor, I believe I have presented enough evidence that supports the facts the best place for any child is with the mother." Dick Richards speaks to the Judge from the lectern.

Dick Richards returns to his seat behind the defendant's table. He sits on the right side of Victoria.

"Victoria has had custody of Theodore Jr. for one year and within that year; she has proven to be an unfit mother. Her address has changed 4 times. She has kidnapped her son from school. She has been arrested with her son while stealing electronics from Best Buy. She is currently out of jail on bail. Every time she is arrested, her son, an 8 year old active little boy, is left in the care of Victoria's elderly grandmother, a 70 years old woman. A 70 year old woman who is suffering from the early stages of Alzheimer's is not proper daycare for any child. At this point in time, Theodore Jr. best place is with his father. His father is a model citizen. He has maintained employment and permanent residency." Sammy addresses the judge.

"Your Honor, Mr. Theodore Wilson's lifestyle is not kid friendly, due to this fact he is not the best option. He is known to have sexual activities with man and woman." Dick Richards notifies the Judge from behind the defendant's table.

"Why it always gotta come down to whom ya are fucking when dealing with baby mothers? That isn't the case at hand. What should matter is what is best for my son? Some of my colored Sistahs always lose focus. They let social media decide what's important. Careers, fashion and sex is

leading priorities. Families are taking a backseat to jobs, shoes and smooth skin. Children raising themselves with the internet and television as there guide. Our children are our future. Back seat children with no morals and no proper guidance leaves our tomorrows where? If today's children are our future, do we have a future? Who will lead the next generation? My son will be a leader of the future. I'm going to make sure of it, as my Sistahs have done for me." *Teddy's chitachatter*

"Oh, so this is what this is all about? Huh, Vikki? Who am I sleeping with?" Teddy words questions Victoria from across the room.

"You damn right, you promise to end your secret affair with Marc, once TJ was born but you lied. You're still probably sleeping with him and its 10 years later."

"This bitch is shameless. She know damn well her and Teddy been over. How can you respect a woman who leaves her 2 week old child to be a groupie in a video, and never returned? She pops up like nothing happened. When I get my hands on her she's gonna be looking like Taye Diggs from the movie, "the Best Man". Since she can't see her wrongs imma close her eye. If Mr. cookie and cream smile at me 1 more time, Imma jump on his sexy ass right in the court room." Rhonda's chitachatter

Victoria's words have rubbed Kira the wrong way. Kira reposition herself on the pew style benches, beside Rhonda. Sammy was more surprised at Victoria's comment than Kira. Sammy knew about Teddy seeing Marc but she had no idea they had been seeing each other for so long. Teddy exposed his lover affair with Marc to Rhonda first and then three years ago, he revealed his relationship with Marc to Sammy.

"You know all about who I was when we got together. I never lied to you. I love the scent of a woman and the feel of a man. It's my civil right to share my bedroom with whoever I like!"

"So my son has to be raised in a homo home?"

"ORDER IN MY COURT, NOW! EVERBODY OUT! CLEAR THE COURT ROOM. WHILE I DELIBEATE OVER THE EVIDENTS PRESENTED TODAY." The Judge shouts as he slams his gavel.

The bailiff, the court officer, directs Victoria, Dick Richards, Sammy and Teddy pass the bar into the gallery, down the aisle to the large double door exit. Rhonda follows behind the bailiff to the double doors. The bailiff holds the double doors open for Kira and Rhonda to exit. Kira exits right before Rhonda's seductive thanks to the bailiff. Outside the exit of the court room, in the court house hallway one is faced with the right side of the hallway, four large double doors on the opposite wall. On the left side of the hallway are four more sets of double doors. On the right side of the hallway wall two elevator doors set in the middle between the set of four double doors. Each set of large double doors is an entry way into person's family life being probe under a microscope and calling it a fair trial.

"You ort to be ashamed of yourself, do you know what a mother is? It takes more than just giving birth to be somebody's mother. You show ya raggedy ass up after 6 years, proclaiming to be somebody's mother! Then you got da audacity to be dragging Teddy's sex life into this. You're fucking bums in the hood, we didn't bring that up. How ya husband is a 2 time convicted felon? You're fighting dirty and we can sure nuff fight dirty too. I gotcha boo. Bank on dat." Rhonda's furious words fly over Sammy's head. Sammy is using her body to pin Rhonda's frame to the right side wall of the hallway.

"Mr. Richards, you hear her threaten me?" Victoria questions Dick Richards, her attorney.

"Please, don't say nothing else to this woman until the case is over. Rhonda please!" Sammy pleads with Rhonda's out spoken tongue.

"Sweetie, you're no different! You are sharing him with a man. Do you want a relationship like that? Teddy, I think you used me for a kid. Just like a woman would use a man and that's fucked up!" Victoria's words are thrown in the air to excite violence in Kira or Teddy.

"You sound like a woman scorned! What you want Teddy back?" Sammy questions Victoria's venom.

"What da fuck I'm gonna do with a fuckin faggot?" Victoria's heart fires more hurt in the air.

"Like you're in the position to judge anybody's fucking lifestyle?" Rhonda questions Victoria's words.

Teddy's word articulation is silenced by the sight of Victoria's ignorant words and careless expression on her face. Kira is silenced by the animosity in Victoria's voice. She couldn't understand how a person's love could transform into blatant hatred. The bailiff, the court officer, pokes his head out the double doors. He beckons Victoria, Dick Richards, Sammy and Teddy to reenter into the court room, Kira and Rhonda in tote. The Judge is ready to pass his verdict. Victoria and Dick Richards returns to their assigned seating at the defendant's table. Sammy and Teddy take their places at the plaintiff's table. On the opposite side of the bar sits Rhonda in the gallery of pew style benches with Kira at her side. Rhonda's eyes are glued to the bailiff's body but her hands sweat for Victoria.

"I've heard both sides and I'm ready to pass judgment. I believe it's in the best interest in Theodore Wilson Jr. that he should permanently reside with his father. Victoria Stevens will have visitation right. Victoria Stevens will not be allowed to leave city limits with Theodore Wilson Jr. without the approval of Theodore Wilson. Case dismissed!" The Judge slammed his gavel as the final word.

The bailiff, the court officer, oversee Victoria, Dick Richards, Sammy and Teddy pass the bar into the gallery down the aisle to the large double door exit once again. Rhonda chase behind the bailiff to the double doors. The bailiff holds the double doors open for Kira and Rhonda to exit again with a grin plastered on his face. Rhonda seductively slips him her number, the real one, not the text free number.

"This isn't over. Me and my lawyer is going down to the 3rd floor to file an appeal, right now!" Victoria shouts at Kira, Rhonda, Sammy and Teddy.

"You don't let me catch you on dis here street! You hear me?" Rhonda barks at Victoria.

"We gotta celebrate! One of yous better call me. Its 12, I gotta go 'cus TJ has a half a day of school today. Call me!" Teddy disclose to Rhonda and Sammy.

Teddy rushes down the court house's stairwell to the street level, pass the revolving doors onto the street, with Kira right on Teddy's heels.

Rhonda and Sammy waits in front of the elevator doors for the next ride down. They are not interested in riding the elevator with Victoria and her lawyer. They walk in silence out the court house to the parking lot. The quiet air whisper's in Rhonda's mind, the air in her mind bounces from the sexing the bailiff to whipping Victoria out. Sammy's mind is reviewing the evidence she missed with Marc and Teddy's relationship. Sammy slides into the driver's side of her shinny ice white four doors Mercedes Benz. Rhonda sits in the passenger's side. Sammy drives towards François Trimestre, the restaurant in SoHo, to meet Brooklyn and Tay for lunch. Chyenne has been unreachable lately but several messages have been left on her phone from the Sistahs. Each Sistah hopes Chyenne shows up today for the Sistah's session at the restaurant. Rhonda turns down the volume on the radio in Sammy's Mercedes Benz.

"What's up lil' sis? You never told me your answer to Mr. Ball player's invitation to a date. Are ya going or not?" Rhonda ransacks Sammy's intimate ingredient to life.

"I don't know yet. Half of me really knows him and wanna give him another chance and then the other half of me remembers the hurt and humiliation I went thru while the world was watching. I don't know if he even deserves another chance, after he has blown thru the millions of chances already given. I can't let him wasted my time. Maybe, I'll see if he is willing to work for another given chance." Sammy expresses her genuine democracy of feelings from her heart.

"A free meal aint never hurt anybody. You guys started as friends and when he was going thru his divorce, who was consoling his broken heart at nite? You were. So if anything, he could treat cha to a meal and maybe some dessert." Rhonda puts words to instigate Sammy into the date.

"I have all day to decide. If I go, it's tomorrow night at 7 p.m. I'm going to meet him at JFK airport. When we were in college, we would eat hot dogs and pretend we was on the planes. I hope that's not his idea of a date. I'm not in college anymore." Sammy verbally reminisces of time spent with the professional basketball player.

"Oh, fuck that. Forget it than. You can eat hot dogs at home. I hate the airport. There aint nothing but lines and attitudes offered at the airport." Rhonda jokes.

"What you been up to, besides running these streets fucking anything moving? You've been running around the city slamming niccas on their back like dominos." Sammy clowns.

"That's right making up for lost times and loving it. Tonight at 10, I'm meeting Brooklyn at Sugar Watah. It's date game at the club. You should come out with me. Want to?"

"I'll think about it. We gotta do something for Teddy. Maybe we should have a nice little family party at Ma's house in celebration? "

"Yeah, a nice family party at Ma's house should be nice for Teddy and TJ"

Sammy pulls up to the restaurant and to her surprise she slides into a parking spot near the entrance to François Trimestre. Rhonda and Sammy enter the restaurant. They are awaiting the **Accueillir** [42], Ethan, to seat them at their reserved table. As Rhonda and Sammy await their table, Tay arrives. The sound of Tay's powder pink Dolce and Gabbana glitter six inch heels hitting the marble floors of the restaurant, broadcasts her arrival. Her cutie powder pink baby doll dress compliments her head full of honey blond Shirley temple curls. Her Chinese bangs and inch long eye lashes gives her innocent feature to her ensemble. Her cappuccino complexion is the seal, coordinating her outfit.

"I gotta shake you off. Cause the loving ain't the same, and you keep on playing games like you know I'm here to stay" *Mariah singing dat Soul music. What da fuck is wrong with Bryson? I couldn't pay the nicca to call or text, now I can't get him to stop. What did he think would happen after he dropped a death bomb sentence on me? Mr. Fredrick Thomas put my soul at ease. He ran test all morning. I'm a healthy person living with H.I.V. He prescribed some medications so I stay that way.* **"I gotta shake you off. Find somebody who, appreciates all the love I give."** *I don't know where I'm going to find him, but my man is out here somewhere. Yes, I'm going to still look for love! A loveless life is a sure death to the soul but to living and loving is dying in pleasure. As for Roc, I'm just glad I didn't catch sommin else from him.* **"You wasn't worth**

---

[42] **Accueillir** *is French for restaurant host.*

my time, so I'm leaving you behind." *For each dollar of the G I took from Roc I got embarrassment in exchange. He gonna have to pay double for the shame I'm wearing.* **"Gotta do what's best for me"** *and that why* **"I gotta shake you off."** *I'm not ready to tell the Sistahs." Tay's chitachatter*

"Good Afternoon, my Sistahs." Tay voice is bubbling with cheer as she distributes hugs and kisses to Rhonda and Sammy.

"Good Afternoon lovely ladies, your jackets, please." Accueillir Ethan requests to hang up Rhonda's, Sammy's and Tay's jackets in a half Eastern Europe accent.

The three Sistahs hand Accueillir Ethan their jackets. Shortly, Accueillir Ethan returns to escort the three women to their reserved table on the right side of the dining room. The women get comfortable in their seats.

"Will the fourth guest arrive? Or will you like me to remove the additional chair? Accueillir Ethan questions the Sistah's about their fourth missing guest to dine.

"No, leave the chair. She's running behind schedule but she is still coming." Rhonda informs.

Sammy sits at end of the table and Rhonda at the other end. Tay takes the seat on the right side of the oval table. The chair on the left side of the oval table is vacant.

"Where is Brooklyn? We gotta do somin about Roc!" Tay comments with revenge in her tone.

"Don't you worry baby girl. If you put Brooklyn on da case, he will be dealt with. Believe dat!" Rhonda states.

"You know Brooklyn." Sammy agrees.

"So what's the news in you all lives? It always feel like it's been ages since we seen each other." Tay's cappuccino heart shaped lips questions.

"We won today in court. Teddy now has full custody of TJ and the best part is, aint shit Victoria can do to change that." Sammy announces.

"That's great news, let celebrate! We need a victory drink." Tay suggests.

Tay beckons the waiter over to the table. She orders a bottle of pink champagne.
"We will formally have a family celebration. I wanna plan a little sommin at Ma's house, maybe Sunday." Sammy mentions.

"So what's new witcha?" Rhonda questions Tay.

"I'm going to kill Roc. I got into it with Calvin over that fucking video. I really hate Roc for recording my shame. I still don't know who gave me the painting, and I decided to let Santana take Nico for a weekend. Three months is too long for my son to be around total strangers. I know Santana's parents just wanna meet their grandson, but he is 3 years old and all he knows is us. I just hope it goes okay."

The painting Tay is referring to is the fifty foot oil-base painted portrait of her face. At one point, she anticipated it to be a gift from Mr. Bryson Mitchell but his letter murdered her expectation. Upon invading into Tay's world from Afghanistan, Santana promoted a month long stay at his parent's new house, in Camden, New Jersey, with Nico. Tay declined his promotion and told Santana to settle for a weekend visitation plan, visits lasting a month. The Army will deploy Santana back to Afghanistan in thirty days. Tay is willing to accommodate Santana with quality time with Nico for twelve of the thirty days.

"There aint nuffin to be worried about. It's the boy's grandparents, all they gonna do is spoil him. What else grandparents do?" Sammy secures Tay's decision.

"Tay got a secret admirer. Did the painting come with a note?" Rhonda teases.

"No note, no message, nothing, but the painting is beautiful. I hung it up in the living room."

"A secret admirer is a stalker wit stationary, but in this case a paint brush." Sammy jokes.

"You're so vain, a 50 foot painting of yourself hanging in your living room. Really Tay, how far are you will to bend to kiss ya own ass?" Rhonda clowns.

"Don't judge me!"

"So Missy, are going on the date with the ball player or not?" Tay's quizzing eyes on Sammy.

"Rhonda put you up to asking me that, huh?" Sammy rolls her eyes in her head after shooting knives at Rhonda with her eyes.

"Are ya still undecided?" Rhonda pries for an answer.

François Trimestre's left side dining area is privileged with the presence of the custom cold vanilla false Caucasian pigment, sitting across from Lisa's southern milk chocolate sitting physique. Crystal's cold vanilla false Caucasian leather elbows holds up her diamond shape head, resting on the back of her hand. Her hooded mud brown eyes stare at the words being discharge from Lisa's southern milk chocolate lips. Crystal's Dolce and Gabbana multi colored cosmic floral printed dress and matching pump heals has Lisa light headed. Lisa looks mostly at the documents of information in front of her to dodge the pastel colors of Crystal's outfit blinding her vision. Crystal's wheat brown hair resembles a bird's nest, in Lisa's opinion. Crystal continuously runs her French manicured hand to combs throughout her hair due to the facts of her discussion with her accountant, Lisa. Lisa's milk chocolate physique sits at the oval shaped table. Lisa's suit blazer to her dark gray business suit is on the back of her chair. The heat from Crystal's brown eyes has over heated Lisa, causing her to remove her suit blazer. The softly candle lit restaurant is where Crystal meets with Lisa for financial updates. Crystal appreciate the dim lighten hiding her frustration.

"Dat muther fucker did what?" From Crystal's thin upper lip distinguished superior tone and her bottom lip painted with pale pink lipstick shouts the question Lisa.

"He has withdrawn 100,000 dollars from your bank account. Two days ago at 11 a.m. on 145th street and 7th avenue." Lisa reveals through a sly twist in her southern milk chocolate lips, expressing amusement at Crystal's lost of funds and prestige demeanor.

"And whatcha plan on doing to make sure this doesn't happen again?" Crystal's French manicured hand scampers through her wheat brown hair as she inquires.

"I've change all accounts and blocked him from them all."

"I can't believe dis muther fucker had da balls to touch my fuckin chips. I'm gonna kill him. Ace, you have gone too fuckin far." Crystal's chitachatter

Crystal notices out the corner of her eye Rhonda, Sammy and Tay at the same time they notice Crystal and Lisa.

On the right side of the dining area:

"I'm gonna over there and invite them to our table." Rhonda confesses her thoughts.

"Do you always have to be so chi chi? You know we don't like the bitch but you wanna invite her over here. Nobody is interested in what she bought or how much it cost? You know da bitch saw us, but too uppity to speak. Last time I ran into the bitch she told me my dress was outta season. I can't wit her today." Tay's voices her disinterest through the twist in her cappuccino heart shaped.

"Chi chi is what I do! Don't judge me!"

Rhonda pulls her French chair back. She stands and proceeds to walk over to Crystal's and Lisa's table. Sammy and Tay continue to have their conversation, while watching Rhonda's back.
"Outta season? Please tell me what season did her shower curtain dress she got on today come from? Please! You can't today? I can't no day." Sammy clowns Crystal from the right side of the restaurant across from restaurant several feet away.

"You has chi chi up her whole body. Is anything part of you real?" Tay questions Crystal from across the right side of the restaurant.

"Baldie what da hell do you want?" Crystal's chitachatter address Rhonda approaching the table.

"Hey girl, how you been? Haven't seen you since the party, it's been like two to three weeks ago. What cha be up too?"

"Some o'le thing. Just being Au courant wit my chips." Crystal's snobbish voice spilling from her thin upper lip distinguished superior tone, turning Rhonda's attention to Lisa.

"Lisa, how have you been? You are working the hell out them cheetah fames. Who is the designer? They are really nice."

"Oh, they are by Prada. Len crafters, buy one get the second pair half off, just 80 dollars off the bargain table cute and cheap right?" Crystal's thin upper lip distinguished superior bottom lip painted with pale pink lipstick boomerang a reply to Rhonda's question to Lisa.

Lisa didn't have time to acknowledge the compliment from Rhonda. Lisa was robbed of the opportunity to respond to Rhonda's question, before she parted her southern milk chocolate lips Crystal had her voice in the air. Rhonda directs her attention back to Crystal. Crystal's over talking Lisa was a cry for recognition.

"Nice dress. Whoa now, matching shoes too cute."

"It has too many colors. The dress looks like a damn flower pot. She looks like Anne-Marie Johnson from the movie "I'm Git you Sucka" in a summer dress stolen from "Mrs. Doubtfire." Every body part surgical sculptured. She's a pure jackass!" Rhonda's chitachatter

"This dress and shoes is off last season's runway in Paris. I'm close and personal with the designer. I took it right of the model at the show. Aint this dress beautiful?" Crystal's thin upper lip distinguished superior tone spills her boisterous glows.

"Okay, I came over to invite you lovely ladies to dine with us." Rhonda's chi chi shinning from her luminous white chocolate skin is losing its luster.

"I smell a set up. Whatcha really want Baldie? Dining with "us" is **insalubres**[43]*." Crystal's chitachatter.*

---

[43] **Insalubres** *is french for unsanitary.*

Crystal's custom hooded mud brown eyes and her cold vanilla false Caucasian pigment wrinkles with revulsion from Rhonda's invitation. Crystal's unwillingness is spoken through her facial expression on her diamond shaped head and body language.

"Maybe next time our meeting has just concluded. I'm waiting on the check."
"Whatcha can't pay for ya meal so ya want me to dine witcha so I can pick up the tab. Not in this life time, Baldie!" Crystal's chitachatter

Crystal commence to gathering her belongs. Crystal reaches down in her pale pink Ferragamo over size handbag that sat in the chair that separated her from Lisa. She pulls out her Gucci sunglass case. Lisa apprehensively looks at Rhonda. Lisa is excited at the opportunity to dine with the Sistahs. Crystal showed up forty five minutes late to the meeting with Lisa and Crystal had already eaten. For forty five minutes Lisa debated with Accueillir Ethan to seat her at Crystal's reserved table. Accueillir Ethan refused due to Crystal's phoned in instructions. When Crystal called the restaurant questioning Lisa's whereabouts, Crystal was notified of Lisa's waiting presence. Lisa found it to be ironic Crystal could call the restaurant with seating instructions but couldn't answer the fifteen missed calls from Lisa.

"I don't mind. I just had a glass of wine. I can go for a bite to eat." Lisa agrees to join Rhonda.

"A glass of wine you shall pay for, 15 dollars, please. Did you really think I was gonna watch you waltz you happy ass over to another table without paying for your glass of wine 1st?" Crystal's thin upper lip distinguished superior tone snarls.

*"**Je n'ai jamais**[44]. I never thought Lisa to be a fuckin turncoat. Lisa you're*

gonna regret your decision. This might cost you your job. You wanna eat wit hood rats, instead of rolling wit the head cheese. I'm gonna get your ass but 1st I gotta deal wit Ace's sticky fingers." Crystal's chitachatter

Crystal's attitude is transparent in her snobbish composure. She snatched up her purse and signaled for her weekly waiter. Lisa kindly left a twenty dollar bill on the table when she knew her glass of wine only cost eight dollars. Lisa gathered her dark gray Macy's business suit blazer and her document filled brown saddleback leather briefcase and begin to walk to the right side of the restaurant with Rhonda.

"Call me if you need me." Lisa offers over her shoulder to Crystal.

"No bitch you'll call me when you need a job." Crystal's chitachatter

Lisa and Rhonda join Sammy and Tay. Lisa sits in the vacant seat on the left side of the table. Lisa back is facing Crystal's cold vanilla false Caucasian pigment irritated storm out of the restaurant. Sammy and Tay have puzzled looks in their eyes. Lisa senses the discomfort.

"If I'm making anybody uncomfortable I'll leave. I just work for Crystal, I gotta feed my family. In no shape or form are we friends of any kind." Lisa southern milk chocolate lips reveals.

"Wow, Crystal seem more crabby than usual. Is she okay?" Rhonda voices her chi chi concern.

"She is having some financial troubles, that's all. If you know anything about Crystal, you know her money is her world." Lisa responds.

"I like her." Rhonda voices her approval of Lisa's characteristics.

---

[44] *Je n'ai jamais is french for 'i have never'*

Accueillir Ethan escorts Brooklyn and another French chair to the table. Brooklyn's five foot two inch old fashion glass soda bottle frame is covered with "Hennessy" straight complexion. Brooklyn is standing on six inch intriguing turquoise blue Christian Louboutin Bollywoody pumps. Brooklyn is working her Indian theme with her exclusive pumps. Her shinny jet black hair streams down to her tight passing her turquoise blue shirt and pass the skin tight white jeans on her butt to her mid thigh. Brooklyn's signature bangles jingle on her wrist and Indian feathered earrings dangle from her ears.

"You made it. We are just about to order. Killer pumps!" Tay franticly jumps up out her chair to give Brooklyn a warm greeting, Rhonda and Sammy follows Tay's footsteps. Each one of the Sistah gets hyperactive when they meet up. They truly enjoy each other's company. The waiter is standing at Lisa's right jotting down the ladies orders.

"I just need a drink." Brooklyn requests

Brooklyn left work to meet the Sistahs. She was at a new restaurant and tasted every dish they offered for her review. Brooklyn only has a taste for alcohol.

"What's wrong, sweetie?" Tay's heart shaped lips questions.

"Today was Harlem's 1st day of school. Lewis asked could he be a part of it. You know, meet Harlem's teacher, scoping out the classroom and classmates. I agreed he is her father. He should be a part of it. He shows up wit Vanessa. That snowflake bitch is always over stepping the fucking line. The snowflake bitch introduced herself to the teacher and shit. She was just all in my mix and Lewis never opened his fucking mouth. After I leave here, I'm going to meet with him. This shit is outta hand. Lewis has to check her. She should have never even been there. I'm tired of telling her I'm Harlem's mother and she is not. Sammy, I don't wanna blow the case but I see me tasering her white ass, soon." Brooklyn's voice scratches with irritation as she retells her morning events.

"Just talk to him and see how things go." Tay's naive heart shaped lips offers advice.

"I've been talking to his ass for 4 years. Today I gonna threaten his ass. Either control ya wife or identify her body in the morgue." Brooklyn practices her threats to Lewis.

"What school is she attending?" Lisa chimes in hopes to relieve some of the tension in the air.

"Westbrook." Brooklyn answers.

"My son attends that school too. It's the best in the city, if you ask me." Lisa southern accent voice her praises out her milk chocolate lips.

"Really, how old is your son? My nephew attends that school also." Rhonda inquires.

"He's eight. How old is your nephew?" Lisa responds to Rhonda with a question.

"The same age as your son. His name is Theodore Jr."

"I know your nephew. My son Quincy is his classmate and TJ's biggest fan."

"Wow. Small world they went to a Yankee game together with your husband...Don't tell me. I can remember his name." Rhonda's tongue struggles to release the name from her lips.

"I know what he looks like I drop TJ off to him to go the game. How could I forget the name of that root beer brown color hulk of muscles, with sexy sunrise brown bedroom eyes? Damn what is his name?" Rhonda's

chitachatter

"Arron Scott." Lisa kills the suspense.

"I said don't tell me, it was on the tip of my tongue." Rhonda reveals her nasty thoughts with her words.

"Sorry for coming here ranting. How is everybody? Lisa it's good to see you again." The sip of wine is calming Brooklyn's raging tongue.

Rhonda, Sammy and Tay give Brooklyn minutes of conversation before the food arrival. The waiter returns with the ladies desired dishes of French food.

"Oh, baby don't you worry one little curl out ya pretty little head. Roc will pay in full for his camera skills. Trust and believe!" Brooklyn vows revenge.

"Have you heard from Chyenne? I've been getting her voice mail for a week now." Sammy questions the table.

"We gonna double dating tonight." Brooklyn reveals.

"Double date? Who are you taking?" Rhonda probes Brooklyn's words.

"Le'Roy"

"Hhmmm, you like him. It's been 4 years since you seen the same guy twice. Love is in the spring air?" Tay teases Brooklyn.

"No, dat Red Carpet Dick got me soaring thru clouds." Brooklyn confesses.

The ladies all laugh at Brooklyn honest response.

"Are you still going to Sugar Watah? Tonight is date game nite." Rhonda questions Brooklyn

"Yeah, I'll be there after the double date."

"So I see Malik hasn't told her yet." Sammy voices her disappointment in Malik's decision.

"Told Chyenne what?" Tay's cappuccino heart shaped lips questions.

"I meet with Malik because his name was included in a custody case. I didn't go looking for the information, it came looking for me. I talk to the mother of Sunshine, Traci and her story matches Malik. They had a one night stand over a year ago that resulted into a baby. They both claim they didn't have contact with one other, until the day Traci gave birth. Traci wants Malik to sign away his right and forget about Sunshine. I give Malik 24 hours to tell Chyenne, before I told her. I've been calling to see what has happen, but I can't get to her." Sammy discloses.

"Wow, Amber was telling me that Capri was telling her she has a little sister name Sunshine. We didn't believe her. I tell you the truth always come out the mouths of babes. Then I meet a nice Real Estate agent name Traci, while looking for Amber's apartment. Traci has a 3 month daughter named Sunshine. This is definitely a small world." Tay presents her evidences.

"Ma always said what dirt doesn't come out in the wash will come out in the rinse." Sammy comments.

"You don't know if he told her or not. Maybe Chyenne did the right thing and forgave him. Malik is a good man and hellava good look. Chyenne better put on her big girl draws and handle her BI. I would hate to see her state if she lose Malik." Rhonda states.

"Well, I'm off to face my own drama." Brooklyn announces. Brooklyn gives the Sistahs a warm hug and kiss good-bye.

"A piece of pie." Brooklyn's signature Sistah wish.

"A piece of cake." Tay's signature Sistah wish.

"A piece of ass." Rhonda's signature Sistah wish.

A piece of solitude." Sammy's signature Sistah wish.

"Lisa, don't be a stranger." Brooklyn shouts as she disappears out the restaurant.

"Yeah, Lisa you should come out tonight, Sammy you too." Rhonda suggests.

"Maybe, I might come out and shake my ass." Sammy states.

"You gonna take me to the tanning solon? I'm whiter than a piece of chalk. I need some color and Benny has my car." Rhonda questions Sammy.

"Rhonda, when you gonna stop lending dat damn boy your car." Sammy warns.
"Maybe, I'll come out too. It's been awhile since I been out personally and not professionally." Lisa comments.

Rhonda and Lisa exchange cell phone numbers before Lisa left the restaurant.

****

Brooklyn climbs into her brand new Maybach 62 S, 2011 model, parked nine cars down from the restaurant entrance. Brooklyn pulls up into parking spot in front of the Central Park's Zoo. She spots Dino, Brooklyn's youngest son, assisting Harlem, Brooklyn's four year old daughter, with an oversize scoop of vanilla ice cream on a sugar cone.

"Ma, you are styling." Dino comments about Brooklyn new set of wheels.

"You like that, huh?" Brooklyn questions Dino as she plants a motherly kiss on his light hazelnut coated cheek.

"Yes I do, Ma it's clean."

"Ma ma, you here?" Harlem's baby gibberish voices question.

"Say, Thank you Carlito." Brooklyn thanks the financer of her expensive new vehicle.

"Thank you Carl lito." Harlem's baby gibberish voice mimics.

Brooklyn swats down to Harlem and plant a thousand kisses all over Harlem's darling face. Dino stands before Brooklyn in a pair of baggy True Religion denim jeans and a solid black tee shirt. On the front of the tee shirt is a picture of the Johnny Kilroy Jordans. He has the matching image on his feet. In his right hand he holds Harlem's little pale hand covered in red freckles. Harlem beige brown skin is covered in adorable red freckles from head to toe. Her red freckles are covered in a cute little pastel purple pea coat jacket. The jacket covers Harlem's little jean skirt and pastel purple cardigan. Her cute little multi colored tights peek out from the pea coat and pastel purple knee high UGGs. Harlem's little poetic gray colored eyes shine bright at the sight of Brooklyn.

"I know you gonna let me front in dat!" Dino confirms borrowing Brooklyn's new car.

"So you don't want my red Range Rover?" Brooklyn quizzes.

"Yeah, but If I get a date or sommin or just wanna front, can I rock?"

"Of course, my son"

"How was ya 1st day of school, my little princess?"

"Fun Ma ma, Dino got a pic ture I make for you."

On que Dino pulls out Harlem's painted picture from Harlem's cartoon character backpack.

"One for Dad ddy and Ma ma Ness and one for you Ma ma."

Hearing Harlem voice say Mama Ness boils Brooklyn's blood.

"We going to daddy right now."

"Ma, I'm staying in the city tonight. Okay?" Dino clears his evening plans with Brooklyn.

"Dino, you don't have to ask to stay at my apartment. You still have a room there. What happened? Is your brother giving you hard time?"

"Naw, I'm going to hang out with Benny, Polo and Calvin tonight. Benny was supposes to be here already to pick me up."

Brooklyn heart warms. She loves the fact her son and the sons of the Sistahs build a relationship. She just hopes their bond is just as strong as the Sistahs. Benny is Sammy's son. Polo is the product of Chyenne and Ace. Calvin is the twin of Camille. The twins are Tay's offspring. Within seconds, Benny pulls up alongside the driver's side of Brooklyn's

Maybach. Benny is driving Rhonda's midnight blue X5 BMW. Dino hugs and kisses Brooklyn and Harlem, before jumping in the passenger's side of midnight blue X5 BMW. Brooklyn secures Harlem in the back seat before she pulls out her parking spot. Brooklyn drives and talks to Harlem through the rearview mirror. Brooklyn benefits from any moment to observe the conspicuous diverse Harlem.

"You like school?" Brooklyn inquires.

"Luv it Ma ma." Harlem's baby gibberish is music to Brooklyn's ears.

"What's your teacher name?"

"Ms. Pea ches."

"No its not." Brooklyn tease.

"Yes Ma ma! For real Ma ma her name is Pea ches."

"You like Miss Peaches?"

"Yes her is nice."
"Ready to see Daddy?"

Brooklyn didn't get a response. She looks in the rearview mirror at Harlem's motionless angelic sleeping face. Brooklyn pulls up to the *Uncletiti's* restaurant in Morningside Heights, where she meets Lewis to exchange the responsibility of Harlem. Brooklyn carries the sluggish Harlem into the diner. Lewis's dark brown wistful eyes spots Brooklyn's struggle and run to relieve Brooklyn's arms of the charming load of Harlem. Lewis's teddy bear brown skin is clothed in Armani Exchange metallic navy blue slacks. An Armani Exchange pinstriped long sleeved button up shirt, with diamond cufflinks on his wrist covers his upper body. His diamond cufflinks match his diamond encrusted Fossil watch.

Metallic navy blue and grey Prada sport shoes on his feet. His hair has a crispy dark caeser haircut. His hairline is too sharp to be touched.

"She fell asleep in the car. I was only driving for about 15 minutes." Brooklyn explains.

"I got her." Lewis speaks as he reaches to take Harlem into his arms.

With Harlem in Lewis's arms, he starts to head for the exit.

"No, I gotta talk to you."

"No problem. Let me take Harlem to Nessa. She's waiting in the car."

"Oh, now the snowflake wanna wait in the car. That's where she should've been this morning. She's playing games. She knows I couldn't beat her ass in Harlem's classroom so she had her pale face all up in there. She knows if she brought her snowflake ass up in this diner I would've mopped the floor with her ass." Brooklyn's chitachatter

Brooklyn took a seat at the table Lewis was sitting at, while Lewis drop Harlem off to the waiting Vanessa in his Ford Pacifica car. Lewis returns to the table eager to hear Brooklyn out.
"So what's up?" Lewis's teddy bear brown lips questions.

"Your wife is not what's up."

"Please, not today Brooklyn. I already know what you wanna say. You've said it a thousand times.

"So why haven't you done nothing about it?"

"You promised Vanessa something and you didn't deliver. She is holding on to that. I can't do anything about Vanessa's feelings."

"Listen Lewis, when I first found out I was pregnant with Harlem, I couldn't contemplate the thought of child bearing any other way but Carlito's way. I was willing to give the baby up but after I laid my eyes on Harlem, I knew I would never part with her. I'm sorry Vanessa can't have kids but you guys can always adopt."

"Brooklyn, you're missing the point. You as a woman should be able to identify the pain of a man cheating on his wife. She's hurting from that fact alone. Then to add insult to injury, Vanessa finds out you were pregnant. You gave me the most beloved gift of my life. Vanessa will never be able to give me such a gift. Then you blatantly lied to her and told her you will give her the baby. Vanessa is hurting inside. The happiness in her life is in Harlem."

"I never told her I would give her Harlem. I said I would Consider!"

"Do you really think Vanessa would have stood by and watch me practically spend 9 and half months with you off a Consider? The appointments, the money and the occasional overnight stays, you really milked the situation."

"You're the father. You wanted to be a part of Harlem's life, The appointments, the money and the occasional overnight stays, that was all a part of being a father."

"I just want to look into that icebox you call a heart and feel the coldness of your wrong in this."

"Don't fucking judge me. Harlem is my daughter. I'm not wrong for wanting to be her ONLY mother! Check your Snowflake, before you find her in the East River."

"Brooklyn, you always go the extra 30 miles. Calm ya self. Vanessa will never harm Harlem. So what she showers Harlem with love. What's the problem?"

"Lewis, this is the last time I'm going to spell out "the problem" for ya. The chain of communication is I talk to you, you talk to her. She doesn't talk to me. She is you wife. She only talks to you. I am Harlem's mother and your Harlem's father. We discuss Harlem's future. We go to doctor appointments. We go to her 1st day of school. Public events are for family and friends. Public events is where Vanessa is welcome to come too. If she step outta line again she will be dealt with. And because I had to continuously talk to you like you don't speak English, or like your some little boy, you also will be dealt with."

"Brooklyn, before anything I'm a man. I didn't disrespect you in any form. Please don't threaten me. Don't say things you'll regret."

"Oh sweet baby, I don't threaten. I deliver." Brooklyn leans in on her left elbow.

Lewis stands up. Brooklyn places her turquoise blue purse on her lap. She slips her right hand into her purse on her lap. Lewis walks over to the left side of Brooklyn's sitting body. He bends down to talk in Brooklyn's ear.

"I aint Carlito. My family will come straight at you with everything they got."

Brooklyn swiftly pulls her right hand out her purse. In her hand is the taser. She deposits 50,000 volts into Lewis's left ribcage. Lewis falls down to his left knee. A urine spot appears on the front of Lewis's Armani Exchange metallic navy blue slacks. Brooklyn stands up on the right side of her chair. She walks around the chair to stand in front of the kneeing Lewis. Brooklyn bends down.

"Grown men don't piss on their self. Ya wife is next. If your family wants some, tell them I got bullets from them. Don't fuck wit me!" Brooklyn speaks to the back of Lewis's bowing head.

"Sorry Sammy! I had too!" Brooklyn's chitachatter

Brooklyn storms out the diner and into her brand new Maybach 62 S, 2011 model. She climbs into the driver's seat. She turns on the radio. She scans for the perfect song to relax her mood. She didn't want to arrive to her date with Le'Roy with her violent twitch jumping.

"So can I get a refill? Can I get a refill? Can I get a refill? I've never had game, no never. I feel like the girl at the bar who's been there too long. Can't stand up! I should be gone but I just can't get enough. Fumbling, giggling, silly as ever I get like this after one too many. But right now I ain't even been drinkin'. He approached me and asked for a minute, which turned into five, then turned into ten." The singing is coming from the surround system in Brooklyn's new vehicle.

"Then turn into two weeks. I'm all caught up just like Elle Varner's voice is singing. I'm flying high on that Red Carpet Dick and I only been on it once. I'm not the relationship kinda girl. I think it's cute when Le'Roy gets upset when I don't call him in a day. I like the late nite talks. I don't know what it is about him. I open up to him, telling him my past. I don't know what will become of this ride but I'm riding it. Hopefully, tonight I'll get a refill. The last time I saw Le'Roy was that day at the museum. Last weekend I had to cancel 'cus Lewis flew to Japan for a job offer. So I spent the weekend with Harlem. Time with Harlem is a delightful treat. But tonight Harlem sleeps in good hands and I wanna ask Mr. Le'Roy Johnson ..." Brooklyn's chitachatter.

"So can I get a refill? Can I get a refill? Can I get a refill? Yeah, of your time. Cause you're intoxicating my mind. Feel like a

conversational lush. Cause I don't know how much is too much."
springing from Brooklyn's car surround system is the singing clouding
the air is.

Brooklyn finds parking two blocks across from the restaurant named
Thai, in Korea Town, Manhattan. Brooklyn steps out of the car on a
positive foot. She walks to the restaurant. During the walk across the
two city blocks passing through two avenues, Brooklyn is mustering up
her thirteen day of sobriety from the pleasurable touch of a man. She
hasn't played the game, *Beast or Bitch* . She would say she's been
devoting her time to Harlem, but who would believe her? Brooklyn is
apparently craving the sweet caramel coated skin covering his six foot fit
frame of Le'Roy. She has a tendency of being rough. She doesn't want to
frighten Le'Roy. Le'Roy hasn't met the aggressive side of Brooklyn yet.
The Thai woman with fascinating beauty, dressed in her native land
fabric, magnifies the feeling of Thailand in the restaurant. The beautiful
Thai woman has a dazzling golden cluster flower hair dressing clip water
falling from her head down to her earlobe. Brooklyn is a frequent flyer of
the transportation through the authentic Thailand rooftop garden
restaurant. The gorgeous Thai woman guilds Brooklyn's body, while the
brightly laminated ground stones guides her feet to the designated
secluded area, covered by the a tiki hut. The laminated ground stones
guides makes it easy for the beauty of the exceptional tropical plants, tall
grass and tropical flowers in rare colors to shine while the sky is dark.
Thailand's songbirds chirp sweet songs into the air. Brooklyn's enters the
florescent designated secluded area. The designated secluded area is
parted into a lounge area and a dining area. To Brooklyn's surprise, the
lounge area on the jungle green seat for three colored couch, sits Ace and
Chyenne. Brooklyn hadn't seen Ace in over twenty years. There are two
moss green single chairs in the florescent dining area. Le'Roy is sitting in
one of the moss green single chairs. Le'Roy's sexy light green eyes grab
Brooklyn's attention. Brooklyn walks pass the wooden oval shaped coffee
table, perfectly positioned in the center of the couch and single chairs,
with a glass bowl of sliced dragon fruit from Thailand, a large glass

cylinder with a lit candle inside, and three half drinking glasses of white wine until she reached her destination, in Le'Roy's arms. After Brooklyn's and Le'Roy's overdue passionate embrace, they retires to the dining area. Off to the left of the lounge area is the dining area. In the dining area is a medium sized circle tall table, with a large glass cylinder that has a lit candle inside, sitting at the center of table. Circling the table is four tall chairs. Brooklyn and Le'Roy occupy two of the tall chairs. Brooklyn takes the liberty in ordering the entrées for herself and Le'Roy. Brooklyn is gazing into Le'Roy's sexy light green eyes. Le'Roy's eyes are glowing in the candle light.

"Gorgeous, how was your day?" Le'Roy's tasty caramel coated lips questions.

"Long and hard, No point intended." Brooklyn answers.

"I like this look on you."
"What look are you talking about?"

"You're a true Indian in heat."

"You got jokes."

The Thai woman with fascinating beauty, dressed in her native land fabric appears with two white plates of Thai cuisine. Brooklyn and Le'Roy excitement of finally seeing each other after thirteen days have them talking and eating at the same time.

"Not really joking, you wear the hell outta the Indian look and you do it so well, How did the talk go with Lewis?"

"The talk went straight to his knees."

"What?"

"Never mind Lewis. What's the question of the day?" Brooklyn is eager to play the little game created by Le'Roy.

"You ready? Who's glove, MJ or OJ?"

"MJ, 'cus it's glittery."

"Really? I pick OJ. It's the only time in history a black man will get off for killing a white woman."

"You got that one. How's your food?"

"It's pretty good but nothing in this world taste as good as you."

Le'Roy's words has made Brooklyn take a large gulp of her glass of white wine and a gulp of redness shallows her "Hennessy" straight complexion on her cheeks.

In the lounge area:

Ace's satin light honey brown curly hair on his head is the beginning of Chyenne's trail of mesmerized lustful eye. Chyenne stares at his six foot one inch powerfully firm built body frame, sitting beside her on the three seated jungle green colored couch. Chyenne leans her back against the oak tree light brown skin on Ace's chest. She inhales the alluring scent of his cologne. Ace's chest is covered by a grown men's black Ralph Lauren's v- neck collar cardigan. The grown men's cardigan is fitting enough to display the frame of his shoulders. The properly worn cardigan sculpts the bulge of muscles on his chest and arms. The improperly worn cardigan is too tight; the men's nipples literally are poking out from under the cardigan. Ace's acid washed Ralph Lauren's jeans fall neatly on top of his metallic purple Nike's Foamposite sneakers. Chyenne reposition her body to look into Ace's enticing soft gray eyes. The light evening breeze blows Chyenne's wild curly mix-bred hair into her dark brown slightly chinky eyes. Ace's irresistible touch assists Chyenne to regain sight. Chyenne's tightly fitting thigh high light peach provocative dress, allowed her sexy silky chocolate fudge skin to tease the sight. The low neck line of the dress has her desirable sexy silky chocolate fudge coated mountains of breast exposed. The light peach dress attractively hugs Chyenne's thin waist. Chyenne's gorgeous light peach and brown leather colored pumps sat in the single chair. Chyenne's complaint of her feet hurting ringed in Ace's ear. The ringing has Ace engaged in messaging Chyenne's feet.

"Oh thanks to the heavens the moon and the stars. My treasure has returned to my arms. My love my Ace." Chyenne's chitachatter

"I can't believe I'm sitting here with you. It felt like it would never happen. I have dreamed of this day for years." Chyenne speaks through the tantalizing grin on her face.

Chyenne's comment is implied to the fact this is their first meeting since two weeks ago. Ace and Chyenne agreed to meet up at 42nd street. Ace had Chyenne waiting in the rain. She stood there for a whole two hours but Ace never showed up. Then they made a second date but Chyenne was experiencing difficulties shaking Malik off her tail. Now this meeting is the third. Chyenne claims if Ace wouldn't have shown up she would have given up but who would believe her?

"I am happy to see you too, Chyenne. You're just beautiful as my mind remembers." Ace's alluring oak tree light brown lips comment.

"Ace, I miss you but I don't want you to think you can just smile your pearly whites and everything is back to how it use to be. Where have you been?" Chyenne's yanked her words and her foot from Ace's charismatic gasp.

"I spent 10 years running street scams in Richmond Virginia, high as a kite while I was doing it. Those years I was getting high 'cus I failed you as a man and failed Polo as a father. The drugs silenced my conscious and the people I was around kept an endless supply of drugs around. I never had an uninfluenced thought in those 10 years. Then I did 10 years in a federal prison. The crazy thing is, the whole time I was doing my bid I was motivated by getting out and somehow making it up to you and Polo. Would you give me the opportunity to do so?" Ace explains.

"Ace, I really don't know."

"I'm scared to let go and just let Ace back into my life. After he had me standing in the rain and not answering my phone calls I wonder if he was serious about taking a second chance at love. It felt just like old times. Not knowing where Ace is. Ace telling me he's was one place and finding out he was another. I'm too old for the cat and mouse game. But damn Ace look sooo fucking good. If I listen to what my koowie is saying, I'll be in the Pink Pussy Cat with the bottom of my feet reaching for the sky. Shit, I want Ace more than ever right now and he don't even know it." Chyenne's chitachatter

"I'm not saying drop 'ole dude you living wit and let's get an apartment together. I'm just saying let me into your world. I wanna try to re-build a relationship with you and with Polo."

"What cha talking, sommin like a family day? Ace, Polo is a young man. He lives his own life. You have to approach him like the man he is. Aint no way around it."

"I want you to kinda warm him up to the idea for me before I approach him."

"I'll mention it to him but I aint making no promises."

"And how about you? How can I soften you up?" Ace questions

Ace leans in and plants his oak tree light brown soft lips on top of Chyenne's sexy silky chocolate fudge lips. He glides his tongue into her mouth intensely. Her sexy silky chocolate fudge finger fondles his satin light honey brown curly hair. His strong oak tree light brown touch starts griping the left side of her jaw. His strong oak tree light brown touch wonders down to her sexy silky chocolate fudge breast. His oak tree light brown thump strings at Chyenne's hard nipple, protruding through her light peach dress. His strong oak tree light brown touch travels under her dress. His strong oak tree light brown touch fingers her heart of sexiness. Her heart of sexiness gushed milk of delight. He releases his oak tree light brown colored lip hold he has on Chyenne's soul. Ace pulls his milk coated fingers out of Chyenne's sexiness and places his milky coated fingertip onto his tongue.

"Your sexy silky chocolate fudge is just as sweet as my mind remembers. I want you."

Brooklyn and Le'Roy waltz over to the lounging area to join Chyenne and Ace. Brooklyn and Le'Roy has plans to go to Brooklyn's apartment for a quick roll in the bed before Brooklyn goes to *Sugar Watah* bar to meet up with the Sistahs.

"Eating at this restaurant is rejuvenating to the soul." Brooklyn comment startles Chyenne and Ace, as their bodies jump apart.

"I agree I feel like I just woke up from a nap." Le'Roy agrees.

"I'm more like ready for a nap." Chyenne states

"I gotta get outta here. I'm meeting Rhonda and she hates when I'm late. Chyenne are you driving? Brooklyn questions Chyenne way of getting home.

"Don't worry, I get her home." Ace assures.

"Oh hell no, Malik would just love that." Chyenne's chitachatter

"I'm good. I know my way home." Chyenne politely turns down Ace's and Brooklyn's offer for a ride home.

"C'mon Chyenne, I wanna give you a ride in my new car. I'll drop you off down the block so 'ole dude don't see me. Cool?" Ace asks

"Maybe that can work." Chyenne agrees with Ace's suggestion.

Brooklyn, Le'Roy, Chyenne and Ace emerge from the Thai restaurant exit. Brooklyn and Chyenne exchange hugs, kisses and small talk before departing each other's company.

"A piece of pie." Brooklyn's signature Sistah wish

"A piece of mind." Chyenne's signature Sistah wish

Chyenne entangle her arm with Ace arms, as Ace chaperone Chyenne to his new vehicle.

"Chyenne?" a deep male's voice shouts at Chyenne's back.

Chyenne is familiar with the person the deep voice belongs too. She releases her grip on Ace and turns to greet the familiar deep male's voice. Chyenne hugs the body of person the deep voice belongs too. Ace looks at Chyenne with confused eyes, just as the woman accompanying the deep voiced man looks at to the greeting embrace.

"Whatcha up too?" The deep male's voice questions as his eye speaks a once over of Ace's body.

"I was just having dinner with old friends." Chyenne's sexy silky chocolate fudge lips responds to Dwight but her fidgeting spoke louder.

"I see. Have a good night. Call my brother, he's worried." Dwight, Malik's brother, suggests.

****

Brooklyn hops into the driver's side of her Maybach car. Le'Roy takes a seat in the passenger's side of the car.

"This is a clean ride. Shit, all this room in here, we don't gotta go all the way to the crib." Le'Roy suggests.

"This man is after my own heart and desire. I wanted to suggest the same thing but didn't wanna say it. I don't know what it is about this man; sometimes my mouth won't even speak my mind." Brooklyn's chitachatter

After a quickie steamy work out in the backseat of Brooklyn's Maybach, Brooklyn drops Le'Roy off at a pretzel brown colored brick townhouse in Crown Heights, Brooklyn. Brooklyn flew down the highways to the *Sugar Watah* lounge. Brooklyn checks her hair and make-up in the rearview mirror before rushing out her car into the lounge. She plans to use her *candy bag* to freshen up in the lounge's ladies room. At the door Brooklyn spots the Sistahs at the bar, accompanied by an unfamiliar female face. Sammy's five foot tall frame of one hundred and twenty pounds of cinnamon spice, is sitting on the left side of Rhonda's one hundred and sixty seven pounds of bronzed luminous white chocolate skin of availability. Sammy has let her ebony colored hair down, into an evenly cut boob, stooping at her neckline from the secure security of the bun she wore to court earlier. She traded her custom sophisticated glasses for prescribe clear contacts. Her sophisticated shaped lips have a burgundy wine tint and her high cheek bone has a kiss of burgundy blush. Her sliver eyeliner on her eyelids matches the sliver chin belt loosely hanging around her waist and the silver heels on her feet, given her four inches in height. A silky sleeveless Donna Karen black dress, with a v-shaped cut in the front and the back has her cinnamon spice provocatively seasoning eyes. She traded her pearls for large thin white gold hoops and a thin white gold necklace that has a heart dangling between her breasts. Rhonda's luminous blonde hair has a mini afro of baby curls, glowing in the dimly lightening of the lounge. Her spontaneous eyes scan the lounge for a potential player of *Beast or Bitch*. Rhonda traded her pink blazer and jeans in for a seductive hot pink one shoulder tightly fitting Gucci dress. Her two inch wedge leather black heels made her frame stand five foot seven inches tall. Her feather earrings down sized to diamond heart shaped studs. The diamond heart shaped studs matching necklace dangles from her neck. She bites down on her seductive red stained lips, as her spontaneous eyes search for an unsuspecting flower to pluck and drain the flower of all its sweet nectar. Her spontaneous horny eyes catch sight of De'Andre, a member of the Johnson boys, seating in a plush red single chair to the far left side of the lounge. Her eyes sticks to the sweet caramel coated skin, covering his six foot muscular frame. She anticipates De'Andre to be her back up plan if her hands come up empty from her stroll through the garden of men flowers in the lounge. De'Andre almond roasted colored eyes catch Rhonda's desire filled stare. His agreement to be her back up plan is sealed with a wink of his right green eye and glimpse of his teeth. Brooklyn creeps up behind the ladies. Rhonda senses are on high alert; she felt Brooklyn's presence before Brooklyn's turquoise blue Christian Louboutin Bollywoody pumps covering her feet could reach the bar. Brooklyn greets Rhonda and Sammy with a hug and kiss.

"Brooklyn met Traci, Traci meet Brooklyn." Rhonda formally introduces the two women.

Traci's sweet cosmic savory milk chocolate complexion drips down over her five foot seven inch frame, standing on six inch white sliver studded

Dior heels. Her squeezing strapless metallic white dress has three circular windows to her sweet cosmic savory milk chocolate coating. The three circular windows to flesh flows down the each side of the dress from her rib cage where the dress begins to her mid thigh where the dress ends. Brooklyn shakes Traci's hand, after formally being introduced.

"Nice to finally meet the #1 Real Estate Agent of the city." Brooklyn compliments Traci.

"Thanks, flattery will get you everywhere." Traci's unique natural hazel eyes glows at the compliment.

"Where's Tay?" Brooklyn inquires.

"Tay didn't come out. She said she is tried. She was up since 6 am with no nap. She's 40 now. At 40 you gotta take a nap before you do everything." Sammy pokes fun at Tay.

"So what's the verdict Sammy, you going on da date wit da ball player?" Brooklyn asks.

"Don't start Brooklyn. I'm still thinking about it." Sammy responds to all the inquiring minds but her words were thrown in Brooklyn's direction.

Brooklyn excuse herself to the ladies room. She needs to wrap her skin clean from her backseat car adventure. Rhonda follows Brooklyn's trail leaving Sammy in Traci's company at the bar. Once they're in the bathroom, Rhonda fires a round of automatic questions.

"So, did Chyenne show up to the double date?" Rhonda asks through the bathroom stall's door.

"Girl, missy showed up with Ace, the rose of the hood." Brooklyn replies.

"Getdee, Ace? Where in the hell did she find him?"

"Girl, I don't know but they was all luvie dovie."

"I don't wanna start boiling water for the *Puerto Rican soup* but I think Malik told Chyenne about the baby and she ran to Ace's open arms. Why that girl always walking around with her head in the clouds? Malik is a good man. I believe his story." Rhonda's words put a pot of hot water on the stove any way because her statement is from thought and not facts.

"I believe his story 'cus Sammy believes his story. Sammy's eyes have the gift of seeing pass a person's words to their core." Brooklyn's words support Rhonda's choice for Chyenne's love life.

"You right, my little sis is one tough cookie. She'll crumble your lie in your face. Trust and believe, I know 1st hand."

Brooklyn and Rhonda return to bar to see a familiar face has joined their gathering.

"Hey girl. I'm happy you have decided to come out and play with the Sistahs." Rhonda voices her delight.

"No, thank you for the invite," Lisa expresses her gratitude.

Lisa's five feet three inches of her pure southern milk chocolate skin is wrapped in a southern red fitting blazer, accompanied by a black and white striped fitting mini skirt. Her brown almond colored hair with waves of sand colored streaks highlights reveals her spark dark brown southern eyes of concealed loneliness.

"I moved up here from Richmond, Virgina to work for Crystal. I don't know a soul in this city. I just work and go home. I'm happy to have a little fun."

"You cross borders to work for a bitch like Crystal?" Brooklyn's "Hennessy" straight lips question.

"It was an offer, I would have been a fool to refuse. On top of a nice salary, I get free condo apartment and a car."

"You right an offer like that doesn't drop in your lap every day." Rhonda agrees.

"A strong sounded decision." Sammy's comment states her appreciation of a Lisa's thoughtful actions.

"I know working for Crystal could make the offer seem unworthy of the headaches that accompany Crystal." Traci adds.

"Sometimes, like for instants, before I arrived here I stopped by her house on the hill because I left some paper work in her car. Just because she was auguring with her husband, she insulted my outfit. The outfit she personal picked out."

"Husband? A man was stupid enough to agree to be stuck with that bitch for the rest of his life? I know he is regretting that decision." Brooklyn voices her surprise in Crystal's relationship status.

"Please, tell me the name of the fool that married Crystal Moore. I'm begging you" Rhonda's words bounce out her mouth with a hint of laughter.

"Ace Washington is Crystal's husband."

Lisa's open words have Brooklyn's and Rhonda's eyes lock in disbelief.

"Are you talking about body to body Ace Washington?" Rhonda questions Lisa to confirm her hearing.

"It's all or nothing. Ever since the day we met. Give you my all or nothing. Want all of you or nothing. I really love you, really really love you. Now that I know I love you. I'll never love another girl. I dropped the ball I'm so ashamed. I fumbled your heart."

Fumble
Trey Songz
Chapter V

Traci's superficial lustful engagement with De'Andre on hourly rented sheets has put a peep in her step early this Spring Saturday morning. Last night, De'Andre quenched a fourteen months of pinned up thirsty desire. De'Andre mood color changing eyes burst with colors like fireworks. De'Andre went from light green eyes to savory light blue passing soft gray in between. De'Andre's fireworks of colors from his round eyes had awaken the horny appetite hidden in Traci's sweet cosmic savory milk chocolate skin. De'Andre's fireworks were loud enough to drown out the sound of Traci's loud desire for Malik. De'Andre's sweet caramel coated manhood gave sensual potent stabs to her creamy sexiness. De'Andre's sweet caramel thrusts of lust were fulfilling to her instant satisfaction but Traci desires an oath of commitment not the meaningless sex De'Andre offers. Its true love making is better than sex. She enjoyed De'Andre kisses down low but Malik's chestnut flavored lips makes her toes curl whether he was talking to her or kissing on her. De'Andre was skillful with laying down his caramel rod but Malik arched her back when he grinds his loving chestnut rod into her sexiness easy and slow. The thought of Malik spends chills down her spine. Her last sensual encounter is one she holds dear to her heart. Fourteen months ago, Malik stoked and caressed her entire being. Malik is an authentic black man. Malik's chestnut syrup coated skin is a craving on Traci's tongue. There was only one special occasion when Traci's body lying in the strong muscular chestnut syrup coated arms belonging to Malik. The special occasion will always be remembered as the sun gleams bright in the eyes of Sunshine. Sunshine is Traci's three month old daughter. Traci and Malik naked bodies were coached by R. Kelly's twelve plays of a slow dance of passion and desire. Their steps in the name of love composed Sunshine. The infamous night they spent exploring each other body's landscapes is on reload in Traci's memory. Traci has just entered her one story house off of Castle Hill Avenue in the Bronx at 6 a.m. She hopes to gain three hours of sleep before her 9 a.m. hair and nail appointment at Jasmine's salon in Manhattan. She is meeting her best friend slash cousin Kira and her newly found comic spiritual friend, Lisa. Traci is a strong believer of the moon, stars and sun.

"I'm happy to see you're okay. Ya could've called. I love the rays of Sunshine just as much everybody else. But she is not my responsibility. I agreed to watch your daughter while you work. Overnight escapades aren't acceptable." Betsey's elderly voice shouts with wisdom in her tone.

Betsey is Traci's aunt but plays the part of an adopted mother in Traci's movie-life. Kira is co-starring in Traci's movie-life. Kira is Betsey's daughter. Kira owns the role of a best friend, cousin and sister to Traci movie-life. Traci's biological mother has chosen the cruelty studies at the University of Hard knock life. Traci's mother is alumni of the cold back dark street from Marcy to Hollywood had to offer. Traci's mother accepted ninety nine problems of the street verses parenthood. Traci can't knock the hustle but wanted to know her mother so she could answer the questions about herself like "Where I'm from?" Traci hears stories from Betsey's elderly lips of who her mother "uses to be". Traci wants to meet that woman from Betsey's stories. Traci's mother and her toothless companion Otis run this town with their ride or die love as a Bonnie and Clyde team. Their narcotic empire state of mind had their minds on a green light take over and their feet on the go. Their minds are eight miles and running from the sweet song cry of reality. As a child, Traci spent her days spending out prays and used her nights wishing on a star for her mother's return but there is no church in the wild. In Traci's teenage years she could hear the whispers of the streets. The streets are talking and watching. Some of the words dropped on Traci's ear were half true and the other half was just ignorant shit. Traci dusted the dirt off your shoulder, change clothes and held her head up high. Traci thoughts wished that this can't be life but it was as real as it gets in Traci's heart. She flipped her thinking to guilty until proven innocent judgmental prospective and she was welcome to the jungle. She realized things would never change and she found glory in the heart of the city of progression. The city is hers. Who was going stop her growth? She did it her way. Just when Traci thought she made it, guess whose back? Traci's mother surprised Traci at her job. When the woman with the wears and tears of the street aged on her skin shouted "Excuse me miss", Traci had no idea who the woman was but with a deeper look from her round hazel eyes through the dirt and grime she recognized her biological mother. Traci was reliving an encore performance of embarrassment when her mother showed up at her school when she was twelve years old. Traci's round hazel eyes laid on a woman whom once was a part of the group of pretty girls but now only a customer popping tags to narcotic paradise. Traci's mother's young forever thinking grants her the best of worlds, fantasy and reality. Traci has a million and one questions for her mother but started with "Where have you been?" and "Why are you an imaginary player in my life?" Traci has a question for herself for every three questions she asked her mother, "Why do I love her?" But her mother fumbled around without given one answer. "Thank you" and "You must love me" was the only words Traci received. Get this money thought screamed from behind Traci's mother's round eyes as she held out her narcotic paradise hungry hand. Traci's heart sings you're welcomes for the guns and roses her mother bare every time her round hazel eyes laid on her mother's circumstances battered inverted face. Why does Traci's mother's hand only open with her heart? Why wasn't Traci's mother's love for free? Traci believes her cosmic destiny would lead her to be somebody's girl. To be the girl of somebody's world in her life time was in the stars. Somebody who knows what a girl likes. Someone that is willing to shower their knowledge on Traci's heart. Traci round hazel eyes searches the world for someone to shine the love of the twenty six letters of the comic alignments of the stars into her life. She is willing to notice the first nine letters of cosmic destiny love; she needs a man to carry their love from J to Z.

"I was networking at a party. I lost track of time. I don't wanna argue with ya. I got three hours before I have to start my day." Traci responds

"Ya working on a Saturday?"

"Yes Ma'ma. People on the "A" list don't live on a schedule like normal people."

Traci's cliental ranged from celebrities to television stations and in middle rest the average Joes. Traci wasn't completely telling a fib. She does have a noon appointment with Ms. Crystal. Traci is going to show Crystal the tenth available apartment in the city today.

"Well get some rest. Sounds like you gotta full day ahead of you. No worries. I will bask in the glow of my beloved Sunshine."

Traci takes heed to Betsey's words and crash onto her bed in her clothes. Before her mind travels to the sub consciousness, a touch of remorse tickles her heart. Traci is second guessing her decision of leaving De'Andre's snoozing nude body alone in the hotel room. Traci fleeted the hotel room to avoid the awkward word linger of meaningless sex. They both received the expected pleasure; there wasn't anything left to say. There was no words to be exchanged the body juices said it all. The absent of Traci's presences would announce any answers to De'Andre's questions.

****

Jasmine's salon is located on the upper Westside of Manhattan. Kira and Lisa meets at the nails and toenails care area after getting their hair washed, dried and styled. The two ladies are basin in the pleasures of pampering as their nails and toenails are being tended to at the same time, while sipping on flute glasses filled with white wine.

"What cha plans for today girl?" Kira soft warm vanilla brown sugar lips questions, as Kira flings her sun kissed brown hair out her right eye so she could force in on Lisa's response.

"Me and ya cousin is going apartment shopping with Ms. Crystal. What cha doing today?" Lisa's southern milk chocolate lips responds.

"Myself and Marc are taking Teddy and T.J out to celebrate winning the custody case. Teddy is so happy that the damn nightmare is over."

"I don't mean to pry but how do you do it? I'm a jealous lover; I couldn't imagine sharing my Aaron with another woman, much less a man."

Lisa's question is hinting at the fact of Kira's relationship with Teddy is a three way tie. Teddy openly admits to being in a relationship with both Kira and Marc.

"I make the sauce and Marc makes the gravy. It's the twenty-first century; at least I know who I'm sharing Teddy with. It's plenty of women sharing their man and don't have a clue who the **chia**[45] is. Besides, Marc is the girlfriend ya always wanted. I enjoy chillin' with him; he has great qualities as a trustworthy friend, even if one day Teddy decides to choose him over me, I would still be Marc's friend. Plus Marc can cook his ass off. One day I'll treat cha to a meal at *Uncletiti's*, his restaurant."

"Well, this country girl doesn't know a thing about whatcha saying but it made sense. As long as ya happy hold on to it and enjoy it 'cus happiness is hard to come by."

---

[45] **Chia** *is a mistress.*

"Ya right about that. Happiness in love is hard to find, if ya get a taste of it in ya lifetime ya lucky. Funny thing is I love Marc and Teddy in different ways and it makes me happy."

"No offense but to be in a three way relationship makes me grateful for my marriage."

"No offense taken. 'Cus I'm a New Yorker. In New York everybody has their own way of doing their thing. How long ya been married?"

"Today makes 20 wonderful Years. I knew the 1st day I laid eyes on Aaron at the possum hunting festival that one day he was going to be my husband." Lisa's southern accent ringed with every word and sincerity in her words bloomed with the south on her milk chocolate cheeks.

"You shouldn't be working today. You should be in ya husband arms."

"Tonight we are going out to a restaurant recommend by the "Sistahs".
"What restaurant?"

"Last night Brooklyn and Tay was chatting it up about a restaurant called, "*Thai*" down in SoHo. But the party's next weekend back home. That is how we southerners celebrate, with our family and friends."

"Wow, you were hangin out wit da Sistahs? I know you had a ball, dem ladies is a lot of fun. Brooklyn recommendations is a blessing, she knows great eateries. Where did ya'll go last night?"

"The *Sugar Watah* lounge and I had a ball. Rhonda taught me how to Diddy. Diddy has dance moves even a country bumpkin could mimic. I haven't had a ladies night since I been up here. I was happy your cousin came out with me. I love the Sistahs and all but without your cousin's presences I would've felt like an outsider. You know all my family and friends live in Richmond, Virginia. I can't wait to see them."

"The *Sugar Watah* is a cool lounge. Sweet strong drinks at a discount price. I can tell you some stories that begin and end at that lounge. So how long you have been living in the city?"

"I've been here for 10 years. I just spend my days working and spending my nights with my family. It felt good breaking free and indulging in the sway of the music."

"Wow, 10 years and not enjoyed the pleasures New York has to offer? I gonna have to get ya out more. Its 10 minutes to 9 ya think she gonna make it? "

"Traci hasn't been late for an appointment yet."

"She's my cousin and I can tell you she always late."
Just as the words flew from Kira's sweet warm vanilla brown sugar lips Traci stumble through the two glass doors into the aroma therapy room at Jasmine's salon.

"How much did ya'll bet on me?" Traci's cosmic lips questions but her naturally unique hazel eyes interrogates with stares.

"I had faith in you girl. I know you was gonna make it." Lisa's southern milk chocolate lips attempt to soothe Traci wrinkle brows.

Traci partakes in a complementary glass of white wine, as Kira and Lisa update her on their small talk. Kira, Lisa and Traci exchange of words last through their manicure, pedicure well into the scent of lavender in the candle lighted room. The surrounds is harmonious to the soul. The three women sit in the massage chairs with their skin covered in white toweled robes bathing in the ambiance. After an hour past, Kira express her gratitude for a delightful morning of lady talk and pampering before parting ways with Lisa and Traci. On the second hour after Traci's arrival, the two ladies have completed their beauty transformation and were ready to take the hour long drive to Stamford, Connecticut to Crystal's mansion. The two ladies changed into their personal clothing and climb into Traci's car. Traci raced up the highway in her midnight black 2011 two door drop top BMW M6 with Lisa in the passenger seat. Traci car choice was before Sunshine entered into her life. This spring Saturday morning the sun is shining bright but after just getting their hair done the top of the car is denied the function to drop down.

"We don't wanna neva end . We don't wanna neva end. It's like our life has just began. You walkin' out, you comin' back again. 'Cause we became the best of friends. I could tell you was into me, from my instant chemistry. I took a sip of your tea and I ain't been right ever since." The lyrics flowing from Future's heart is filling the air in Traci's car. While the whole song is floating in the air, certain words sing directly from Traci's inner thoughts. Traci's mind travels up the highway of different lanes flooded bumper to bumper of confused feelings parted by white lines of white lies to separate the facts. On the highway of "What if?" your heart is the driver and your brains is the passenger not wearing a seat belt, just not thinking straight. When your heart drives your world into the brick wall at the end of this highway, your brains is chopped and screwed by pain. This type of pain can't be cured. Only time could heal the heart. Traci has her foot on the gas as she speeds up the highway of "What if?" The first time Traci's natural unique hazel eyes tasted Malik's six feet two inches solid muscular frame dipped in scrumptious chestnut syrup, she felt the instant chemistry in her stomach. In her thirty two years of living she had never felt anything like it. She was addicted to being in his atmosphere soaking up the flutters in her stomach. During the six month of twelve to sixteen hour days working together they became the best of friends. How else would Traci know Malik's favorite color, drink and movie? She even knows his zodiac sign. The zodiac chemistry was clear to Traci. She has endless testimony built off zodiac connections, constructing a strong foundation to her believes. The project wasn't unusual work for Traci. She has performed plenty of these

transactions in her ten year career. Chief executive Real Estate Agents often alter property to make the house more marketable. Hiring Malik's Architect firm specifically was Traci's only error. The memories that stained Traci's thoughts are things that can be perceive either way. Woman whom are not accustom to being in the presence of genuine intelligent sophisticated black man wrapped in traditional morals could get confused. Traci's spiritual being has never witness the abstract art of Malik. Malik possessed charisma and style in his strut, along with his voice can calm a screaming hungry newborn. Several women have mistaken Malik's casual conversation and natural common courtesy for genuine interest. Some are brave enough to take a short leap of faith and read deep into Malik being an authentic black man and get their feeling hurt in the long run. The first month of Malik and Traci working together Malik received a phone call. His cell phone ranged at the end of an important stressful meeting. The meeting was regarding the project not flowing smooth as projected. The phone call was from his eight year old daughter, Capri. Malik's wife, Chyenne was supposed to pick Malik up from work and together they would watch their daughter's ballet performance. Malik's car was under the hands of Dwight. Dwight is Malik's younger brother, the mechanic. Capri was calling Malik to voice her concern about his presence. Malik placed many calls to Chyenne but she never answered. Chyenne falling behind in schedule caused Traci to shift and spring to Malik's assistants. Traci assisted Malik with a ride to the performance. Although the car ride to the Ballet Theater was less than ten minutes, it was more than enough time for Traci and Malik to exchange small talk. Malik's conversation was words revolving around Chyenne and Capri but Traci heard something unspoken. Traci heart ranged as Malik's family dedication drip from his pores and panic sweat formed on his brows. Traci noted the quality trait in Malik. She also noticed his ease as words rambled from her chestnut syrup lips. On Halloween, Malik dared Traci to a trick or treat challenge. Traci had been trick or treating over a dozen times but the time with Malik was the most fun she ever had. She felt like she was a little kid. Malik has a way of bringing out all parts of a person's character. She bath in his laughter, lather her skin in his smile and soaked up his shinning eyes of pure happiness. That Halloween is the mark of Traci's knowledge of the un-acknowledged instant zodiac chemistry shared with Malik. Traci willingly drives into the light sparkling from Malik's smile. Malik never uttered a word to support the glow blinding Traci's vision. This bright light affects all Traci's senses once she started viewing the sunrays. Halloween also marked the second month of the project. Traci keeps a dollar worth of dimes but combined they didn't equal a quarter of Malik's unique masculine ora.

"Oh never say never. From the day we got together I thought it will be forever but oh baby you showed your true colors. I can't believe you played me. I let you meet my mother." Kelly's angelic voice harmonizes Traci's fluttering emotions. Thanksgiving landed in the third month of working on the project. For Thanksgiving Chyenne packed up Capri and Polo, her son, and went down south to spend the holiday with her mother, leaving Malik home alone. Ironically, Chyenne went to her mother's home to prevent loneliness. Malik was unavailable for the trip; the following day was a big day for the project. He couldn't abandon the project right in the middle. Traci convinces Malik into being introduced to her family and friends over Thanksgiving dinner. Malik accepted the invitation out of sheer acquaintanceship. At Traci's grandmother's house in New Jersey Malik spend eighty five percent of his time in the basement with Traci's uncles, cousins and male family affiliates watching a football game. At dinner Malik said the grace and it was a supernatural experience. He prayed from his heart in front of a room filled with complete strangers. He announced the bravery of self comfort ability. Traci was all ears to Malik telling her another trait worthy of notice. While Traci's natural unique hazel eye was open, she held a pure platonic relationship with Malik but as soon as her eyes closed her relationship with Malik was a dirty sexual affair. Christmas rolled around in the fourth month of the project. During their many late evening inspections of construction completed on the project property, Traci has respectively mention her weekend entertainment of exercise on her cousin Kira's Wii. She bragged about her virtual dancing skills. She often displayed a sample of her gyrating lady lumps disguised as the game dance moves. Malik teased her game skills. Thanks to Capri, Malik is savvy at the dance game too. The infatuation game Traci displayed was over looked, Malik wasn't playing. Christmas morning Malik surprisingly showed up on Traci's doorstep of her house off of Castle Hill Avenue in the Bronx with a Wii console complete with the dance game. Malik's out of the way gesture dug a forever hole in Traci's heart. He challenged her to a game. Traci flexes and bends in pumpum shorts and a cut off t-shirt. Her nipples played peek-a-boo with the bottom rim of her shirt. She pretends to be installing the game system. But Traci's was installing a full practically nude image in Malik's brown eyes. His brown eyes gracefully sneaked installments of the sweet warm vanilla brown sugar scented exposed skin. Traci's ego was bruised when Malik stuck to his word and exited after one game. She definitely planned to play a different game involving a lot more sweat and heavy breathing. The blow Traci took only made her want to try harder to gain a taste of the sweet chestnut syrup on Malik's body. Malik's company's New Year's Eve party was amazing not only in décor, entrees, but the unlimited drinks is what remained in memory. Traci had every man's eyes on her dress or lack of material, except Malik. Traci's sweet warm vanilla brown sugar lady lumps sculpted in proper position made the leopard printed dress value increase. Malik stood his ground with Chyenne by his side. At the end of the party Malik walked the room welcoming his colleges into the New Year. Traci used a juvenile trick to taste the chestnut syrup dripping off of Malik's luscious lips. Malik was giving Traci a hug and a normal friendly kiss on the cheek welcoming her into the New Year as he just previously done to his receptionist standing beside Traci. A quick jerk of Traci's head and Malik's lips landed on Traci's awaiting lips. The tiny nibble of Malik's sweet chestnut syrup lips didn't seized her nights disabling her sleep. She craved a mouthful of Malik's sweet chestnut syrup candied body. The day after Valentine's Day was Traci's day of wrecking. The project was complete. A television station had signed a year lease for the project property. Traci's time with Malik has come to an end. She planned one last attempt to ignite the fire she felt in her stomach in Malik's heart. She laid out a home cooked meal picnic style in the living room of the project property as her farewell. They ate the well cooked meal over laughter and personal short stories on the blanket of her hidden emotions. Laying out her heart was the final line. Her nerve knowing what is at stake had her sipping more white wine than normal. Her intoxicated tongue slurred her hidden agenda. Her emotions for Malik were thrown on him in the form of sexual aggressive advances. His neglected skin welcomed the unfamiliar womanly touch. Traci opened a bottled up sexual desire deep within Malik. It had been at least a month since Malik had the pleasure of releasing loving sexual gestures on Chyenne. So when Traci awoken the desire resting under his solid muscular frame, Malik's wall against temptation melted away likes ice cream under a ninety degrees on a summer day. Malik's muscular chestnut syrup body against Traci's sweet chocolate skin stimulated different pleasures. Malik caressing Traci's body into three rounds fighting off her moans of newfound pleasure. Malik's long solid chestnut syrup coated rod stab respectively to different rhythms at the core of Traci creamy lusty sexiness. Their down low kisses, ached backs and curled toes are images Traci rock to sleep at night. At night she hears Malik breathing in her ear. His breath spends chills down her spine. After the nine hours of being under Malik's sweet chestnut candid touch, Traci was head over heels in love. Malik's chestnut fingertips dripped pass Traci's sweet savory warm vanilla brown sugar skin and covered her soul. His fingers fondled the emotion sensation resting in Traci's psyche. When the deed was done their eyes meet. Traci could clearly read the apologetic, regret and shame in his eyes through the tears of pain. Traci naïve thinking believed that after sexually consummating of the bond with Malik things would be altered. She believed her sexiness had talked them into a forever lasting bond. Malik's rejection was the true colors of men that has cross paths with Traci's heart in past. Her mind can't wrap around the fact Malik had gently let Traci's heart down. Her heart felt played with by Malik's soft chestnut fingertip. As her mind reminisces of her actions, she finds countless mistakes in her movement. She would forever remember the pleasure her weekend of wicked games with Malik's sweet chestnut skin.

"You know I still love you. You make so mad, it like I can't get over you. I can't get over you and the things you do. I swear I don't want nobody but you."

Traci relates to Kelly's emotional confession. She was experiencing a man infecting her system with no remedy of comfort. She was so angry at Malik for his choice of Chyenne. In Traci's opinion, Chyenne didn't fit the shoes she is wearing. Malik needs an attentive, dedicated wholesome woman and Traci wanted to try on the shoes, she believes the shoes would be a perfect fit on her feet. Traci felt like Malik was created just for her and her for him. When she saw he didn't feel the same. The shower of his tears poured rejection on Traci's heart. She couldn't have her dream lover so she killed the lines of communication. Traci refused to maintain the business relationship with Malik. To move on with her life she had to remove Malik from her sight and her system. However, two months after making love to the ideal man of her dream, she found out Malik had given her the gift of life. She tussled with the thought of informing Malik of his Sunshine in Traci's dark loveless world. During the eight months of holding Sunshine inside Traci submerged into her career. Sunshine couldn't wait to be revealed to the world she came a month early. Traci took four months to learn the characteristics of Sunshine before returning to work. It has been a whole month of Traci back at work, working the property market to her pocket.

"Thanks again for coming out last night." Lisa's voice snapped Traci back into the car.

Traci is grateful Lisa's voice grabs her from the reenactment of the events leading up to Malik's unique flash of charisma imprisoning her heart. Sweet Sunshine's rays are her only proof Malik even happened to her.

Malik is a muscular mountain of delicious chestnut syrup she just couldn't get over.

"No problem. Hanging with Rhonda is always a blast. That girl fun-nay. My night ended in delight. So I should be thanking you." Traci's cosmic voice slides sarcasm into the air.

"I like the "Sistahs" they are must better company than Crystal. I tell you that much. You and Rhonda were playing that *"Beast or Bitch"* game. When I left I saw the killer look in your eyes. Delighted with the end of your evening, really? Do tell."

"I ended up in a hotel room with De'Andre."

De'Andre mood color changing eyes catered to Traci's thirsting lust. If De'Andre eyes didn't captivated her she might have found her intoxicating fingers dialing Malik's number. Traci's mind could hear the slurred voice of Traci blatantly begging for a shot of Malik's love.

"The light eyed fella that brought all of us a round of drinks?"

"Yup him, well I had to thank him for our drinks."
Traci's sly remark made the two ladies enjoy a quick chuckle.

"So what is he?" Lisa's southern milk chocolate lips questions De'Andre's earned title from his performances.

"He's a Bitch. He didn't bring the beast out of me and that's what I was looking for."

Traci's verbal assault on De'Andre's sexual performance causes the violent chuckles to fall from the ladies lips and fill the car's air. Traci pulls her car up to Crystal's security gated mansion. The two ladies await Crystal's phoned approval to gain entrance through the gate.

"Why she never tell the guard when she is expecting company?" Traci's comic warm vanilla brown sugar lips questions.

"You know she likes to flaunt her authority."

"I hope she's ready. I have plans. I don't wanna sit around waiting on her. I want to go see the apartment in Harlem and drop her ass off."

"Get in and get out is always the plan when it comes to being around Crystal."

"I don't know how you manage 10 years with a boss like her. It's been 3 weeks and I'm tip toeing around cussing her ass out. Being that rude don't make no sense no matter how many dollars you have."

SuWu opens the double French glass doors allowing Lisa and Traci to enter the front doors to Crystal's mansion. SuWu is Crystal's four foot ten inches Vietnamese house maid. SuWu chaperons Lisa and Traci across the whimsical floral design embedded in the white Italian marble inlay floors to the living room. SuWu nods signaling her exit before leaving Lisa and Traci in the first floor living room. The two ladies have a seat on the ice white Italian leather couch. The couch face a glass wall equipped with sliding doors. The ladies eyes soak up the view. Their eyes ignore the enormous backyard lined with fresh cut grass. A bed of roses circling the Cupid water fountain in the shadows of the oversized pool manufactured with a diving board is completely bypasses the ladies lustful stares. To the right of the picnic tables in front of the bar-be-que grill stands the physique of a Greek god dipped in honey. The chorine raindrops drizzled down his soft light brown baby curls, cascading down his bare built broad shoulders and slides down his chest. The chorine raindrops roll down his chiseled muscular abdomen and puddle at the rim of his solid navy blue Ralph Lauren swimming trunks. Traci's vision showers her sight with every move of the chorine raindrops trickling down the physique of honey dipped Greek god. The chorine raindrops rained down between Traci's legs.

"Who is that?" Traci's naturally unique hazel eyes questions.

"Oh that's just Ace. He's Crystal's husband aint he great to look at? You can stare til your eyes get sore."

"I see better with my body."

"Calm yourself. I know it's been a while but a lady should always move with grace."

"You're right. I got that little taste last night and now I'm open. Look at him, he aint helping my situation looking like that. Do you see those muscles?"

"Yes I do. He picked up the six packs and muscle mountains over ten years in Federal prison."

"Wow, a sexy bad boy. He is a guarantee panty droppa. Don't tell me no more. I'm sorry; I take that back please tell me how Miss Plastic gets a man like dat? Spill it."

"I don't know how she got him but she had him for a long time."

"Don't mind me; I'm just happy to be out dating and living again. I love my own skin again; I'm not sharing it with another person, literally."

"No offense but dating in New York City in this day in time is somin I couldn't do. Everyday I'm grateful for my humble marriage."

"No offense taken. You've been blessed to find your designed man. Everybody aint so lucky to find their perfect fit designed man. So I have fun fumbling thru the blue prints in the meantime. My ultimate goal is to find the man designed for me."

Traci heart has surrendered to Malik and swears to love nobody else. The ladies met each other three weeks ago but a connection was made. Traci absorbed Lisa into her life. Traci best friend is her cousin Kira. Family friend relationships are sticky. No matter what happens, you still stuck with them.

"I might as well change my clothes now. It's almost 1 o'clock. I'm meeting Aaron at 3. He has a special surprise before dinner."

"Good thinking to bring your clothes with you."

"I've been thru many of Crystal's delays. She's gonna be late for her own funeral."

Their laugher springs into the air to avoid facing the annoyances of Crystal's tardiness. Lisa step off into the dark curves of the mansion to change her attire. Traci glares out the glass wall at the scenery. The sweet sight of the Greek sculpted Ace was fervent entrainment but untouchable statues perish quickly. Just as Traci patience boils to the rim and threatens to overflow, the sound of expensive heels dancing on the white Italian marble inlay floors is warning of Crystal's arrival. The sounds of superiority echo in the strut of her alighting. Her custom carve top and square bottom is wrapped in barbarian red Gucci silk loose fitting one shoulder dress. Her feet are covered in red Channel open toe sandals to match the nail polish on her exposed toes that starves to be noticed.

"All set? Where's Lisa?" Crystal's thin upper lip distinguished superior tone questions.

"She's changing." Traci's annoyed warm vanilla brown sugar lips responds.

"I hope somin worthy of my eyes."

Lisa's southern milk chocolate fame emerges from the dark curves of the mansion.

"Love the shoes. Doir right?" Traci questions Lisa's shoe wear.

"Good fashion eye. They were featured on 2008 fashion week. The outdate shoe looks expensive again on Lisa's feet but the cheap dress makes you wonder if da shoes are real." Crystal's thin upper lip distinguished superior tone snarls.

Crystal's small chuckles slides out her pale pink painted bottom lip. The roll of her hooded mud brown eyes is hidden behind her black Gucci shades. Between the designer oversize garden hat on her diamond shaped head masking her new ginger colored hair and the oversize designer shades the cold vanilla Caucasian pigment of her superior attitude peeps out.

"These raggedy chicks don't known nuffin about fashion. No matter how ya dress it up brokenness shines thru. Lisa can fuck up a wet dream, those shoes are a girl's dream. Do you know how hard it is to make a designer part with their work? And she's wearing a $5.99 discount store rack dress over 2 **gees**[46]. *And the other one's Donna Karen dress is passing but those are bargain table shoes for sure." Crystal's chitachatter*

"Funny you say that. I bought the authentic Vera Wang dress thinking of you. It feels and cost like your taste." Lisa's southern sarcasm tone replies to Crystal's comment

---

[46] **Gees** *is a thousand dollars*

"Where did you get a Vera Wang dress from? I know you bought it off an African on a street corner."

The southern ruby red draped evening dress with a fabric flower on Lisa's right shoulder compliments her southern lady bumps and lumps.

"I bought it at a boutique in SoHo."

"Really so after eating with the Sistahs you were shopping with them? **Insalubres**[47] " Crystal's thin upper lip distinguished superior tone rattles her diamond shape head as the question is asked. Lisa has insulted Crystal by her company. The insult stains Crystal's cold vanilla false Caucasian pigment.

"Crystal, I'm not your child. I don't have to explain my movements to you."

Crystal's pale pink painted bottom lip plops down from her thin upper lip.

"What da fuckin is going on around here today? One spring day and people forget themselves. Lisa is feelin herself today like her job don't mean nuffin. Talking out her neck will only get her ass retired." Crystal's chitachatter

"Is that right? We'll talk later." Crystal's thin upper lip distinguished superior tone.

"There's nothing more to say." Lisa's southern tone ends the discussion.

---

[47] **Insalubres** *is french for unsanitary.*

Crystal's heels sulky dance over the whimsical floral design embedded in the white Italian marble inlay floors toward the exit. Lisa is first to follow in Crystal's shadow staining the white Italian marble inlay floors. Traci pulls the double French glass doors close behind her. Crystal made a grand exit swinging both doors open when only one was needed. This is Crystal's daily conduct, her trademark is overdoing it. Before Traci could turn her back on the closed double French glass doors, Ace exposed honey dipped physique of chiseled muscular mountains jumps out from behind the double French glass doors, triggering Traci's body to jump in lust. A minute ago when she first laid eyes on Ace, she missed the sip of his manly qualities. Her stares doesn't drink up Ace's bedroom soft gray eye and huge bulge imprint in his solid sexy navy blue Ralph Lauren swimming trunks.

"Chris, I'm gonna need dat card back." Ace's honey dipped lips shouts over Traci to Crystal's ears.

"I can think of a hunnit thousand reasons why you can't have dat card back. You wanna take Chyenne out? Who authorized you to do so? Do what cha want wit you own chips not mine! **Je n'ai jamais**[48] !"

Crystal is still bitterly furious over Ace robbing her for a hundred thousand dollars. She is even more irritated at his proclaimed innocence. Then to add insult to injury of misguided trust, Ace used the credit card she gave him to take Chyenne out to dinner.

"We weren't talkin 'bout dat. I need dat card now. I'm having a pool party tonight."

"Where is dis pool party?" Crystal's hooded mud brown eyes questions from behind the Gucci shades.

---

[48] **Je n'ai jamais** *translation from french to English is 'i have never'*

"Here, today's technology is amazing. Back in my day I had to spend a day calling everybody to invite them to party but today I can post it on da book and everybody texting my phone to confirm. I wish I had this technology back in the day I could've made a ton more money. "

"Oh hell no! You aint gonna have dem fuckin hood rodent crawlin around my shit." Crystal's thin upper lip distinguished superior tone shouts with conviction in her words.

"Did I use punk pussy perfume today? Lisa is showin her ass off for Traci. Now, this mutha fucker is ridin his long dick too far. 1st off he straight up snatch a hunnit thousand dollars worth my chips. Then had the balls to take Chyenne out to dine on my dime. Chyenne, dat spineless rodent have never eaten 4 hunnit dollars worth of food in her life. This morning I check da card again and dis disrespectful nicca brought a 6 hunnit dollar ring from Tiffanies. Now he talkin 'bout having da rodents from the Madison Projects tramplin on my Italian marble inlay floors. I'm gonna have to check him. Right after I dismiss the help." Crystal's chitachatter

"This money has given you amnesia. I'll remind you of who you are. You rise from those same rodent infested Madison Projects. You hide behind your piles of chips but I see you for the grimy mangy rodent you are. Your pale charity privileged hands are insensible to the shady cracks of struggles and manholes of depression paving the concrete street of Madison Projects? You were once among the rodents savaging for a morsel of a chip. You have climb so high on your own clouds of royal seniority that your ass is showing but my dear, you're insides are just as low as the dirt on the concrete street of Madison Projects. How does it feel living alone in this humongous world?" Ace pierced though to the core of Crystal's existence.

"How dare you talk to me like dat in front of the help?" Crystal's hooded mud brown eyes felt the hit of Ace's words, the pain threaten to drip. Ace's words battered her cold vanilla false Caucasian pigment. Her thin upper lip distinguished superior tone questions with hatred in her breath.

"Who the fuck are you calling the help?" Traci's warm vanilla brown sugar lips questions with offense in her tone.

"Ladies, I'm gonna have to take a rain check. Right now my business is here. I'll call you two's later." Crystal's thin upper lip distinguished superior tone cracks under Ace's exposure.

Crystal about face her five foot three inches frame of superior cold vanilla Caucasian pigment coating her custom carves up top and her square bottom and return to the hollow mansion throne. In silence, the two ladies climb back into Traci's midnight black 2011 two door drop top BMW M6. Lisa returns to her assigned seat. Traci's voice breaks the air with praises for Lisa standing up against Crystal.

****

Malik trouble heart bleeds with confusion and in need of mending he seeks a band-aid of Dwight's words to temperately patch up his aching heart. Malik drives a bold black Infinite FX35 car to Dwight's Auto Shop on Jerome Avenue in the Bronx from the gym in Astoria, Queens near his house. He has been placing the wooden living room floor of his one story house as his achy heart hardens.

"I keep going in circles, circles. Round and round. And while you're doing me so wrong. I just keep holding you down. I feel so stupid, foolish. Loving you all this way. But what I can I say. But I wanna go. But I keep coming back. I feel so used by you just like a toy. It's a shame that you don't care enough .To even give me half the love I give to you. I live for you oh baby. I'm ashamed to say that I'm to blame for how you act. Cuz I keep coming. I keep coming back." Jazmin's songbird voice narrates Malik's inner thoughts. Malik's hand grips the staring wheel as he clench his teeth mix emotions is battling

within his soul. He has held Chyenne down through two nervous breakdowns, three miscarriages and over twenty jobs while his love for her stayed as pure as the first day they meet. Her infidelity minced his heart and it hurts. He knows he slashed her heart by sleeping with Traci but it was a horrible mistake. He wishes he had the opportunity to tell Chyenne his side of the story, but he believed Sammy beat him to the stab at Chyenne's heart. He predicted the truthful words from his chestnut syrup coated thin lips would have eased the wound. Face to face Chyenne would be able to witness the sincerity speaking from his true thin brown almond eyes. He condemns himself for Chyenne nonchalant care for their love. He catered to her disrespect. He understood her strong consumption of losing Polo after what she's been through twenty years ago but how much could she eat before one would be full. Malik blames himself for pushing Chyenne back to the nights of watching over Polo by pressing the issue of trying for another baby. He also holds himself accountable for never uttering a word of protest as Chyenne pushed him further and further away, subtracting bites of her love with every step backwards. His authentic love remains pure like the first day he surrendered his heart to her existence. Malik pulls his car into a parking spot. Malik's chiseled muscular six foot two inches physique of chestnut syrup drips out the driver's side of his car. A pair of sincere gray Sean John sweat pants covers his legs. A plain narcotic white tee shirt covers his muscular shoulders, chest and stomach but the frame is not hidden. Malik's chestnut syrup coated face glows with brotherly love once Dwight is caught in his vision. His sneaker covered feet practical skip over to meet his brother half the distance between them. Malik claps his right hand with Dwight's right hand and wraps his left arm around Dwight's back. Dwight's back is covered by an oil stained aggressive green mechanic jumpsuit.

"What up big bro? Still no call?" Dwight questions.

"It's killing my insides, how could she be that angry without even hearing my side to spend a night out with homie?" Malik questions

"You think she fucked him?"

"I love her but I aint no dummy. A man goes all out and take a girl to Thai restaurant at night is trying to smash. She probably wanted to get back at me and fucked him outta spite. I aint mad I put myself in this position. I just wish she'll call and let me know she's breathing."

"Yo, you a good guy for real. I would duce a chick after she blatantly violate, get caught and spend the night out into mid day of the next day. Oh hell no, and you worried about her breathing. You are too good for her. She doesn't appreciate the type of brother you are. She takes your gentle nature as a weakness. Chyenne needs a thug type brother to slap her ass in line to set her straight and I don't put my hands on woman but dat one right there needs some act right. I would've choked the shit outta her and thought nuttin of it"

"I just want a talk to her, see her and smell her scent. I miss her."

"My own brother stung."
"Whatever. I'm on my way to meet Traci. I'm going to tell her my decision. I wish I could've talked it over wit Chyenne 1st."

"Why ya unemployed wife is never around?"

"Never mind that. How I look?"

"Why do you care how you look? You only gonna "talk" to Traci, right?"

"I haven't seen her in a minute. Just wanna look good. You have a problem wit that?"

"Bro, you can talk to me? Where's ya head at with this Traci woman?"

"Traci has a cute face and a nice thin waist but her beauty is in her mind. We could talk about anything. I like the special way I feel when she holds me in conversation. I would lose track of time in conversation with my homie and my friend but everything she said to me was her raw emotions. There aint a price you can put on a woman who knows just what to say when you need to hear it the most. Yes, I was addicted to how we kicked it. The friendship we had is hard to find. I was skeptical when we first started hanging out, wondering about her intent but she was genuine. I've had friendships with different kind of woman with hidden agendas. Aint any of them other woman at all like Traci, she's somin special. I have never had anybody show me all the things that she done showed me. The six months of her in my life, life seemed so much better. She showed them other ladies how to treat brothers. Never knew it could get so wicked. I was hoping to keep the friendship after I fumbled the ball and cross the line but the pain of rejection in her eyes broke me down. I knew we wouldn't be able to face each other again without the cloud of our sexual encounter hovering over us. "

"Bro, I sorry to tell you but your heart belongs to Traci. You're in love with that woman."

"What's wrong with you? I love Chyenne."

"I hear your mouth but your heart is saying something completely different."

"I am so sorry for what I did to Traci's heart. She trusted me as a friend and I crossed the line. I hope I didn't scar her heart. I love the friendship, not her."

"Whatever. Bro, listen to your heart. Who could pass up on a sister that like. Plus, she understands the game of football!"

"Chyenne has watched the game wit us before."

"But she didn't like or understand the game. Traci knows everything that was going on."

"You never backed Chyenne."

"And never will, you deserve more than she is willing to offer. How about you come out tonight with the player's club and free your mind? We are taking a party bus to a pool party in Connecticut. Tonight, we all get to meet the chick taking up all Le'Roy's time."

The ingredients to the player's club are Douglas, Dwight, Tugee and the Johnson brothers. They noticed one another just cooling in the playground. Their friendship was sewn together over a pigskin ball and ice cubes. The five boys are all defensive players in Madison Projects; you had to be protective and watchful of your own. The five different personalities brewed together is Madison Projects recipe for another bad creation. All of them played the game with boundaries, bravery and dignity but in different zones. Douglas also known as Beans is a player of the club. Beans earned his name by the magic he has in his arm to find the right player at the right time. Beans is the best quarter back. His position on the field matched his position in his work field. As a stock broker, Beans advised people where their monetary beans should be placed to earn them a buck. Beans playing zone is the sidelines. He is an observer but could flip and be just as defense as his teammates. Dwight holds the ground of the nickel back. Just off the fact he wasn't half as broad as his older brother Malik. Dwight is a gambler tacking the out bound areas. Dwight took a chance on his hobby and he love for cars. Who know his joy would blitz into a three link chain business. Dwight has found his way to the end zone, the zone of endless comfort ability with one self. Tugee is the mastermind of the red zone. Tugee's corner back gunner mentality plans and directs the suited up players. Suited up players shooting the gap between blitz, rush or tackles and Tugee. Le'Roy is the team's special player. Le'Roy's expert position is the return specialties and he never left the comfort of the neutral zone. De'Andre owns the dime back spot. His mood color eyes always made the ladies kneel shouting Hail Mary's. The five boys played football in the street of Madison Projects. Then when they were old enough to leave the block they would play in Central Park. They played for high school teams together to Virginia Tech college football. Their team bond will last to the goal line and beyond. They played through hail, rain and sleet. Helmets on ready for whatever was put on the field against them. They would run the hundred yards for one other. There were three red flag penalties almost costing them the championship friendship. The first was a juvenile tripping of a missing football, not a major foul. Illegal hands to face over Iesha also became an optional play but the tackle ended before it could start. Iesha tick play of sacking more than one player on the same team almost cut the grass of a lifetime growing bond. The last penalty play was a personal illegal motion. Tugee was holding metal safety defense on the playground. He need safety defense from a jealous girl. The other players gave him an ear full on a three minute warning. Metal safety defense at the playground is always wrong. The five adolescent teammates were popular with the ladies but their male peers had quick kicks at their clothes. The teammates were into the pigskin not shirt, pants and shoes. They still played the field with the ladies and the pigskin. It's wasn't what they wore it was how they played their position. They promised to be single and play with pigskin until they die. But since they had the caption of "Player's club" they have been fumbling on remaining player on the field at the same time. They lived different lives but every Friday the player's club share drinks and laughs about their pass and on Saturday's they toss their pigskin work week aggression on the football field in Central Park.

"He missed another game?" Malik's chestnut coated lips questions Le'Roy's attendance to the mandatory player's club meetings.

"Yup, I can't wait to meet this woman that has Le'Roy caught up. So are you coming out tonight or what?"

"I just might roll out wit the Player's club. But right now I gotta face Traci."

Malik claps his right hand with Dwight's right hand and wraps his left arm around Dwight's back along with plans to meet up later. Malik climbs back into his car. He drives toward *Uncletiti's* to talk with Traci over a southern meal. The anxious nervous sweat oozing from his pores is the only sound in the car. Two chains are pulling his heart and mind in two different emotional directions. "Traci aint just another girl." Malik's mouth argues with his thought. Traci was a down to earth type of woman. "That angel of mine." His mouth speaks in Chyenne's favor. Malik heart knows and loves the Miss Thang swing in Chyenne. His mind and heart are disturbing the peace of mind he use to have. His life was once sturdy and solid. His mind questions how did his life turned rocky asap? He is so gone from his adolescent titi boy days at college park campus being the king of the players circle. In college, he supplied the demand of dozen roses and short talk the long way while never telling a lie. Take offs and landings on plenty young woman as they swamped his way like bees in a trap. They all knew what Malik was and what he was all about. They lined up to be used and they didn't take it personal. Mercy to his heart won and awarded him a relationship of the true religion of devotion to a one woman army. Finding Chyenne was the making of a new life. Malik found a new life of sharing a love's good music melody with Chyenne. Malik believes Chyenne to be his designated soul mate. Malik's pulls into the park lot across the street from *Uncletiti's*. He wonders what will be the making of him after the storm. Who will be still standing? Malik pours six foot two inches of chestnut syrup through the doors of *Uncletiti's*. He jingles loose change between his sweaty palms. He hides the nervousness clammy hands in the pocket of his sincere gray Sean John sweat pants. His hands are out of sight but the anxiousness on his chestnut syrup skin screams to be seen. The wetness drooling on Traci's legs and thighs under her Donna Karen cosmic spiritual lavender mini dress is proof she spotted Malik. Malik aimlessly searches the restaurant with his big brown eyes for the sight of Traci. Traci waves her arm in the air to attract Malik's attention. Traci is successful. Malik's sunray from his perfect lined teeth shins on Traci as he approaches the table. Traci jumps to her feet to greet the earnest big brown eyes. Traci couldn't hold her emotions back her body lunges into Malik's chestnut syrup coated muscular toned arms. Malik civilly wraps his chestnut syrup coated muscular toned arms around Traci's frame. While being in secondary heaven, Traci inhales the scent of an authentic black man. Malik's flavored aroma stimulates all Traci's tastes for his desire. The brief bush with heaven touches the wetness between Traci's legs and thighs. Malik's takes his assigned seat across the table from Traci. Seeing Malik in the flesh made Traci's memory a liar. Malik is ten times sexier in person then in mind. Traci sits across from Malik with a silly grin plastered on her face.

"Good Afternoon how was your day?" Malik questions

Malik wanted to shower Traci with compliment but didn't want to cloud the intent of his requests of her presences. Malik's chestnut syrup lips are moving. Traci hears the words flowing in the air but she is deaf from the sunray shinning in her face. The manly tone of his voice is provoking pulsation in her heart of her sexiness. Traci is desperately trying to control her senses but they have been taken into Malik's chestnut syrup. She fidgets in her seat. Between her legs and her tights she is sticky with desire.

"Every day is great with Sunshine in my life. How about your day? Are you a man of habit? Today is Saturday. Let me guess a.m. gym, taking Capri to ballet class and car wash?"

Traci's words of familiarity tugs the two chains of mixed emotion. His is paralyzed. He fumbles with Traci's exquisite ability to hold his movements in her mind where as Chyenne has complete forgotten how to answer a phone. Malik just smiles at Traci he still had control of his lips.

"So am I right?" Traci's cosmic warm vanilla brown sugar lips looks for validation in her knowledge.

Malik searches for his voice. His mind down talks the apprehension beating in his heart. The Sunshine of anxiety shines heavy on his heart. Fatherhood wasn't something he would be new too. He practically raised Capri. Chyenne's body was oblivious in the present but her mind cruised in the Deloren DMC-12. Her mind accelerates eighty eight miles per hour. The vanishing blue glow blazing her whole body mesmerized Malik's eyes. The offensives behavior left fire trails of heated outrage. Malik would have to literally bring her back to the future of her thoughts. Chyenne's mind and presences fades. Chyenne consistently reminisce about previous milestones, periodically visiting the present, her future is always unpredictable. Chyenne is burning in Malik's mind. Malik remove his phone from the clip attached to the waist band on his sweat pants. He places the phone on the table in front of him. He hopes Chyenne calls. He folds his arms on the table and leans in toward Traci. He's ready to free himself from the agony of the brown studies in Traci lustful unique hazel eyes. The inability to determine his credibility in his own ten year relationship is eating at Malik.

"Good afternoon Malik, what can I get you? Camille questions.

Camille is a part-time waitress at *Uncletiti's* restaurant. Camille is a homebody. Her part-time work is second to school. School and work is her way out the house. Plus, by her working at the restaurant she gets first eye to the boiling water to *Puerto Rican soup* that brews. The doors of the restaurant are open late nights to early mornings. The restaurant walls has invisible butterflies unfastened the secret friends and lovers. The dim lighting in the southern food restaurant enhanced the hush-hush airy flow. While Traci tells Camille her menu selections, Malik researched his throat for words to response to Traci. He tests his voice box on Camille as he orders a coffee and a slice of pure heaven posing as sweet potatoes pie.

"Traci, I asked you to meet me 'cus I wanna be a part of the glory Sunshine has to offer. I'm willing to do whatever Sunshine needs. I'll pay what bills you need to pay. So what do you think?"

"1st off I don't need money or nothing. I only contact you because Sunshine's presence is so bright the person that help created that should know about it. I'm fine with you being a part of Sunshine's life. But what about Chyenne, is she going to be all right with this?"

"What about Chyenne? Sunshine is my daughter, a part of me. To love me is to love all of me."

"So this was like a prep talk for court next week?"

"No, I was fumbling with signing away my parental right as you requested but I decided that it wasn't in my nature to turn my back on my responsibilities. We are adults; we both know what could come from our actions. So as adults, we as a team will deal with the Sunshine."

"Our actions" you make it sound so heartless. I know you felt the cosmic ora of our skin touching while making love, say it aint so?"

"Traci, this is how I feel, sex aint never felt better, it was like a army tank hit the house while I expose your insides and I enjoyed every minute of it but it was just sex. I have nothing but love for you, it's just platonic."

"I can't make you love me now or never. I just don't like being your emergency sex music. Tell Chyenne to take care of you so I don't have too. Maybe you deserve to be unhappily married."

A woman buried alive six feet deep in filth and gunk bangs on the left side of Traci's face on the opposite side of the glass window. Wash away the dirt, grime and detox the desire from the body's soul and create a human. End the woman's drastic obsession of immortal vacation on narcotic paradise island with detox. Traci's unique hazel eyes looks out the polished glass restaurant window and recognizes her tarnished biological mother. Traci takes her last bite of buttermilk pancake and washed down the bite of pancake with a swallow of orange juice. Traci offers money for her meal but the gentle Malik has declined her offer. Traci hugs Malik just to get close to the chestnut syrup again. Malik's eyes escort Traci's body out the restaurant's door to the curb. His view is interrupted by Camille presenting the bill. Camille words to Marc have set a pot of water on the stove. There is a small pot of *Puerto Rican soup* simmering in the kitchen of the restaurant. Camille returns to the kitchen.

"Did you send the picture to ya mother?" Marc questions Camille.

"Yes, I did. There's never a dull moment in these walls." Camille responds.

Camille has taken a picture of Malik and Traci sitting at the restaurant's table. She sent the image through the wire to her mother. Chyenne had popped up at Tay's door step right before Camille left to go to work. Camille sense something salty was going on with Chyenne but didn't have time to get a taste. She wished she was home to witness when it all falls down for Chyenne. There isn't anything cheesier than finding out your man is out in the public dinning with another via text message.

"While you two are over there stirring up *Puerto Rican soup* the rest of us are working. I suggest you two do the same as everybody else and get to work." Mildred's Christian tone orders Camille and Marc back to work.

"I kinda feel bad snitching him out after he gave a 20 dollar tip." Camille voices her guilt.

"You did what you were supposes to and that aint snitching. Snitching is when you hang somebody to get yourself of the hook. You are just looking out. All in a day's work for a foot cadet using her senses to become woman soldier in a world of man." Marc schools Camille.

****

Tay gasps when she opens the text message on her phone. The image displaying on the screen took her breath away. Through the wire Camille is exposing Malik's afternoon dining at *Uncletiti's*. Tay's legs disobeyed her command to move. She stands in the middle of the kitchen floor in her three story cherry brick townhouse. Tay's honey brown almond shape eyes are bright from shock. Her full voluminous cappuccino lips wide open and her five feet cappuccino frame standing on six inches powder pink glitter red bottoms. Chef Robert snaps his fingers in front of Tay's lifeless face. The sound of her name spoken in Chef Robert's deep masculine voice awakes Tay from her trance. Tay's soft voice fights to explain her shocker. Instead of fighting against her vocal cords, she just places the phone in Chef Robert's eye sight.

"Oh wow. That's a hard hit. What cha gonna do with the information?" Chef Robert questions.

"I'm gonna march in there and show the picture. I'm not gonna say nuffin. Let her draw her own picture of the situation. Maybe it's really nothing. That could be the case right?" Tay's naïve cappuccino lips responds.

Tay pushes pass the two kitchen swing doors and walks into the dining room. Her honey brown almond shape eyes photograph a rare image, the five Sistahs sitting together in the same place at the same time. The Sistahs sitting at the dining room table in position. Sammy is sitting at the head of the table. She is the levelheaded Sistah. Sitting to right of Sammy is Rhonda. Rhonda is the right hand to Sammy. She is the

Sistah that use her right hand to pick and play with various coaxed smooth skins. Brooklyn is sitting to the left of Sammy. When things went left for the Sistahs and someone needed to be dealt with, Brooklyn's name is the first to be called. To complete the body of Sistahs the legs are needed, Chyenne and Tay are the legs. Chyenne is always running from her problems and Tay's koowie always run her into problems. Tay's mouth is unable to hold water. She passes her phone to Chyenne to view the image on the screen. The Sistahs treated the phone like they were sitting in a kindergarten circle of show and tell. Chyenne pass the phone to Brooklyn the phone went around the table until it landed back in Tay's hands.

"You can't keep running from the situation. You owe that man at least a conversation." Sammy's mind offers sounds advice to Chyenne.

"When's the last time you been home?" Rhonda questions.

"Thursday," Chyenne responds.

"Since Thursday, You say? So for 2 days Malik's been looking for you? Where ya been Chyenne?" Rhonda's luminous white chocolate lips questions but the irritation of Chyenne's insane distortion of the truth is in her tone.

Rhonda questions Chyenne but she already knows the answer. Benny borrowed Rhonda's *Pink Pussy Cat* key Wednesday. When he arrived with his little girlfriend he was scared half to death when Chyenne popped out of the bathroom. Chyenne has a habit of tell **halftrues**[49] when the whole truth is already known. Chyenne's mouth said she's been away from home for two day but really it has been three days.

---

[49] **Halftrues** *are when someone tells 50% of the truth in a story.*

"I was spending time with Ace, just to see where his head is at." Chyenne's sexy silky chocolate fudge lips responds but her body language tells a completely different retell of the story.

"I would like to know where his head was at too." Rhonda's eyes roll with her statement.

Rhonda insinuates that Chyenne was spending time with Ace the long way. Ace's words have the power to remote control Chyenne's every move. Rhonda's comment causes laughter to erupt in the air of the dining room. The ladies sip on the custom cocktails concocted by Chef Robert.

"Rhonda stop being so comical. I'm in love all over again you know like that teenage love."

"Don't believe his lies. Don't forget he's married to Crystal. Leave that nicca in ya past!" Brooklyn's "Hennessy" coated lips advices Chyenne straight up.

"I can't deny what my heart wants. Don't get me wrong, I love Malik but I'm not in love with him. My heart has and will forever belong to Ace."

"Don't let your heart fuck your brain. I love you so I'm gonna give it to you straight no chaser. Right now you are unemployed. Malik provides you with a home, your lifestyle, and the food you eat. Ace is a wild card, he was a wild card back when we were young and I'm sure much hasn't change. I'm gonna, no we all gonna be by your side no matter your choice but think about this. Don't give up stability for the unknown. The let down can be damaging to you mental progression." Sammy's has a sound mind and her mind just spoke.

"He gave me a promise ring. He promises to make up for the twenty years apart. Just being in his presences smoothes my heart, my mind and my skin."

"You only feel like that because he is a *tender bone,* that's his job. He suppose to ride your world and leave you bewilder but the most important fact about *tender bone* is..."

"HE DON'T BELONG TO NO ONE!" the Sistahs shout in unisons and toast to their cocktail glass in agrees.

Chyenne didn't raise her glass. She was hoping to gain the Sistahs blessing. This is the first major discussion she made by herself, it just wasn't a rational one.

"I know bad boys are no good but yet so much fun. The last three day lying up with Ace while he showered me with his love felt like I was 18 again. Sneaking time with Ace before his father caught him; I was to dark for his precious Ace. Good boys are no fun. Malik lives life by the rules. I have a criminal record. Obliviously is my way of life. I don't do rules. Lord knows, I've been praying for Ace to return to my arms for twenty years. The Lord is giving me a second chance at real love. Now that he is in my arms aint no way in hell I'm gonna give him up. My heart won't allow me to moving on without Ace, Mr. Wrong. We got something so special it's tangible. I know Ace is wrong for me but it feels so right. Malik is the right man for me but living with him has always felt wrong. Look at the Sistahs screaming like they are strangers to the feeling, like they never had none. Every woman has fallen for a Mr. Wrong. I could dig in the crates and remise on some of their wrong choices. I cant live right and I feel wrong but I rather live wrong and feel right. I'm running off with the right one, Mr. Wrong." Chyenne's chitachatter

"So ya plan on leaving Malik?" Tay's naïve cappuccino lips questions.

"Not completely, I wanna test drive Ace and if everything is good then roll out. I'm going tell Malik I need space."

"And in what space will you be living in?" Rhonda's disapproval of Chyenne's life decision screams in her question.

"Amber is moving out in next weekend. I'm gonna stay wit Tay." Chyenne's insane plan was new news to Tay's ears.

"You got it all work out? But what if while you giving Malik space Traci moves into that space? Then what?" Rhonda's questions are meant to poke at Chyenne's nerves.

"Rhonda, please stop badgering me!"

"Chyenne, we are just trying to make you think this thing thru." Sammy's sound mind speaks again.

"I've thought about it for 20 years. I won't be right until I see if Ace is the one."

"Malik is the one!" Rhonda's strong tone is to slap Chyenne into reality.

"Rhonda, it's my life. I gotta see for myself."

"It's okay. Don't get upset." Tay attempts to consol Chyenne's glassy eyes. "Who knows it might just work out." Tay's naïve cappuccino frame means the words spilling from her heart shape lips.

"Oh please, no waterworks Chyenne, this is the only woman in the world who cries more than a newborn. Mark my words when the smoke clears sweetie gonna be by herself. I'm in a good mood today, I had a good night. Club Sugar Watah didn't let me down. A tall glass of cookie and cream whispered in my ear "Hey love, can I have a word with you?" his mellow

voice had me wet from the "hey". I usual don't allow man to pick me up but he had that vibe. I'll never forget that body bumping honey love. It's about time I found love dedicated to me. He was all work and no play. He didn't hold back and neither did I. I wanna publicly announce I'll slow dance the long way with John Doe anytime." Rhonda's chitachatter

"On a different note I teasered Lewis last night. I'm sorry Sammy but he had it coming. "Mama Nessa" is next please believe me." Brooklyn confesses.

"Brooklyn! Whatever the circumstances was, teasering Lewis was wrong. You should apologize when you pick up Harlem tomorrow."

"Why should I apologize, I'm not sorry at all. I'm sorry I didn't do more."

"Brooklyn apologize and move on."

Brooklyn accepts Sammy's demand with a roll of her eyes.

"All of you are deep in my love affairs. What 'bout Brooklyn new relationship glow?" Chyenne questions

"Oh, I notice it; I was just waiting on someone else to point it out." Tay states

"The glow depends on what kind of new relationship guy you are wit. If ya new relationship guy is a beast then you lose a little bit of weight from excising the long way. But if ya new relationship guy is a bitch he trying to win ya over by taking you out to different restaurants so you gain weight." Sammy sheds light.

"So that's why Brooklyn is lil' heavy and Chyenne is a lil' light?" Rhonda questions over her small chuckles.

"Brooklyn is a beast. She will only attract a bitch." Sammy added comment adds chuckles to the air from everyone's lips.

The other Sistahs smirks at Rhonda's question but try to hide their faces from Chyenne; a small joke can trigger her eye sprinkles.

"This rare occasion all the Sistahs in one place at the same time. I'm gonna save myself the phone calls all next week. Next Saturday is Melissa's baby shower and Sunday is Amber's moving party. Both of them are Prima Donnas, I'm gonna need each of you to hold my hand through the headaches to come." Tay announces.

"A piece of mind." Chyenne promised.

"A piece of pie." Brooklyn promised.

"A piece of ass." Rhonda promised.

"A piece of solitude." Sammy promised.

"I don't know what I'll ever do without you from the beginning to the end. You've always been right beside me. So I call you my best friend. Thought the good time and the bad ones. Whether I lose or if I win I know one thing that never change and that you as my best friends." *The 4 of us been friends since preschool. Brooklyn is the 5th element, entering the Sistahhood in the teenage years. Thinking about all of the things that we did back then is unbelievable. Its some things you just can't make up. Rhonda getting suspended in junior high for getting finger fucked in the stairwell at school. Brooklyn giving the sisters Hope and Faith 110 stitches between the both of them in high school. I remember me sneaking boys in me in bathrooms, home and at pebble beach. Whispering in my sister's (Melissa) boyfriends ear "Hurry up, meet me at the room." In kindergarten I gave Chyenne half off my Oreo and she handed it right over to Ace. Chyenne was hustling and scheming for Ace*

all her life with Crystal at her tail. The two was digging for gold in Madison Projects. Crystal was being dug out for her gold. Chyenne had Ace as her gold to show off. Sammy would always turn heads when she falls through any door because she always makes moves how a boss do. Sammy has been mothering us for years. We've been though Edwin jeans holding our young butt to shape it in a woman's curves and 54.11 live saver colors on our feet with the hopes of snagging a street industry player or a ball player. I can't keep anything from them because they wouldn't keep anything from me." Tay's chitachatter

Tay pulls out her letter from Mr. Bryson Mitchell. She hands the letter to Sammy first. The letter was passed around like communion on Easter Sunday. The air is still. All eyes are on Tay. Each set of eyes have their own questions but the words are stuck in their throats.

"When I have a sparkle of being a woman fed up it's gonna hurt like hell for somebody else. Bryson and Roc wouldn't be able to exhale. I done clapped at the best of them caused the death of the rest of them. Roc knows I'm gunning for his ass but Bryson will definitely be a sneak attack." Brooklyn's chitachatter

"Have you been tested?" Rhonda questions in a sincere tone.

The Sistah sit at the table with the same pain in their eyes and stomach as if the letter was addressed to each of them.

"Yes, it was positive and I'm positive about the whole thing. I've been going to a therapist. It not as bad as it could be. I just want him to pay for all the women he infected."

"Oh, please believe he will pay, I just don't know how yet but I got him." Brooklyn promises.

"We need a Pink Friday to get our spirits up." Rhonda suggests.

"You all can come out with me. I'm meeting Le'Roy in Connecticut at a pool party. We can show off our sexiness in bathing suits. Who wanna come?" Brooklyn questions

"I can't come out because I'm going out wit the ball player tonight. But you know what meeting the friends mean? " Sammy announces.

"Finally! You going out wit the ball player." Rhonda comments.

"I even know what it means when a guy introduce you to his friends. It means he is serious about you and his friends are a test run before meeting the parents. Watch out, somebody is about to tame Brooklyn Zoo." Tay's naïve thinking bounces in her words.

"I can't be tamed. Who's rolling witcha girl?"

"I'm not up to hanging out tonight. I'm just gonna lounge around. I think I'm going to go home and face Malik tonight." Chyenne's words declines as her sexy silky chocolate fudge body moves with regrets of returning to her home.

"So it's just me, Rhonda and Tay rolling out to the pool party. This is the last call for alcohol?" Brooklyn announces her last drink amongst her Sistahs before her departure.

"*Disparos a la hermana amar*" Brooklyn repeats the Sistah's signature toast quote: "Shots to Sistah love."

"Welcome to my house party party. Welcome to my house party party. It's bottoms up but is going down."

House Party
Meek Mill
Dreams and nightmares

Brooklyn hops into her brand new Maybach 62 S, 2011 model that is park in front of Tay's brownstone, Rhonda jumps into the passenger seat. Brooklyn decided to canvas the mouse trap called Madison Projects before taking Rhonda home to change and stopping by her condo to change herself. Since Tay lives two and three fourths of blocks away from Madison Projects, Brooklyn looks on both sides of each street. She spots Roc's cranberry colored BMW X6. Brooklyn streaked the tires into a parking spot across the street from Roc's car. Brooklyn pops the trunk open and hops out the driver's side.

"Here's my phone, if you hear sirens call Omar." Brooklyn instructs Rhonda.

Rhonda can't believe her eyes. Brooklyn has a chest gun holster with a nickel plated nineteen eleven colt forty five automatic pistol on each side of her body cocked and loaded. A pump shotgun griped in her hands. The sight took Rhonda's breath away.

"BOOM!" Brooklyn let off a shot from the pump shot gun into the window shield of Roc's cranberry colored BMW X6. The kickback from the shot moved Brooklyn's body a few inches.

"BOOM!" Brooklyn let off a second shot from the pump shot gun into the rear window of Roc's cranberry colored BMW X6.

Roc's meatball brown colored couch potato frame came rolling out the building with his pants open and only socks on his feet. Roc's goons turned the corner at the same time. Brooklyn drops the pump shot gun at her feet and with her right hand she pulled a nickel plated nineteen eleven colt forty five automatic pistol from the left side of the chest holster and pointed at Roc. Brooklyn's left hand pulled the nickel plated nineteen eleven colt forty five automatic pistol from the right side of the chest holster and points it at Roc's five goons.

"Yo BK, what's good wit cha? Why you out here trippin?" Roc's meatball brown colored lips questions Brooklyn as his hand signs for his goons to stand down.

"It's just us! Me and the guns, you knew we were coming for ya fat ass when you sent out da video."

"Yo, dats my word I sent it to one nicca and he blew it up."

"And now I'm blow you up."

Roc begins to tear up.

"What ya want from me BK. I'm sorry I drugged her, popped da molli in her drink it was over after dat but I'm sorry. How you violated my X like dat BK!"

"Beg for mercy!"

"Yo BK, I told you I'm sorry shit just got blown up."

"You lucky I don't lay you down. But you credibility on these street is done."

"You going too far BK."

"Too far?"

"BAM" Brooklyn pops a shot into Roc's white sock on his left foot. Roc cries and screams like an infant. Brooklyn retreats to her Maybach 62 S, 2011 and speeds off.

"Yo, ya fucking crazy!" Rhonda eyes are widen for the clip from Dirty Harry playing before her eyes.

"Stunt 101 baby! I'm G'd up. I gotta remind niccas why they salute me!"

"Shit, what a fucking reminder!"

"*Disparos a la hermana amar*" Brooklyn repeats the Sistah's toast quote: "Shots to Sistah love"

Brooklyn wasn't sipping on alcohol, she was enjoying the sweet taste of revenge.

****

Ace and Crystal standing face to face in the backyard lined with fresh cut grass. SuWu has lined the picnic table with the traditional red and white checker board tablecloth. The traditional tablecloth is topped with bar-b-que condiments, variety of potato chips, finger foods and disposable cups and utensils. To the right of the tables Hiji is firing up the bar-be-que grill. During the conversation, Crystal's eyes bounce from the bed of roses circling the Cupid water fountain to the shadows of the oversized pool, manufactured with a diving board to Ace's physique. Crystal bites down on her bottom lip. Her hooded mud brown eye is enjoying the view of Ace's Greek God body dipped in honey; it is bringing on lustful stares.

"Yo Chris, what cha really want from a nicca?" Ace's alluring soft grey eyes questions Crystal.
"What dat suppose to mean?" Crystal's thin upper lip distinguished superior tone responds with a question.

"Ya up on a nicca back. Like ya some serial killer. That's dat shiznit I don't like."

"You didn't even ask me."

"Ask? What's my name? I don't ask I take shit. You know dat. I'm a D.O.G. Dig out Girls. Dig dem out between the legs and dig out their pockets. Either way this dog cames out on top."

"Fuckin bitches by the group, I use to be down. I still gots money by the pound but that lifestyle was how I use to live. I don't want ya dog rodents or anything else that might have lice or disease in my home."

"Those ice rings in ears is freezing ya brain. Ms. Uppity you forgot ya fucked da whole Madison Projects in my face and behind my back. Either you fucked them outta their money or fucked them outta their mind with ya sexual antics. Them same niccas is coming to my pool party. So you should be good. Who knows you might get lucky. Somebody might come up in here willing to bend ya over for old time's sake."

"You can't have ya fuckin party in my house!"

"Please spare me da bullshit. I'm gonna have dis party up in here and I don't wanna hear ya mouth. All my dogs from da hood is gonna be runnin' thru here. We gonna party in dis bitch like its da 90's. Bending hoes up doggy style in the middle of the party or at the after party. Digging out her insides and nobody can hear her cries of pain and or pleasure over the music. Ya know what they say, aint fun if da homies can't have none pass her off with da blunt. Sippin on gin and juice the way, the way we do. That reminds me. I can't forget to check wit da DJ when he gets here to makes sure he got all dat 90's music, I wanna time travel tonight. I gotta hear da "Lodi Dodi" the Slick Lion style. Da 90's was a great decade. That's when me and the homies was for really living like corrupt dogs, using Chyenne's crib as a dog pound for my homies. We converted Madison Project into a dog eat dog world, a place where hoes were down on their knees and true G's rein as kings in there designated sets. I know you remember how the original G's hustler such as myself roll. So make a choice now, ya gonna stay upstairs or ya gonna enjoy dat party. Don't get embarrassed trying to step outta line. Stay in ya lane if ya going to partake in da party. I'm telling you now."

"Ace, I don't think my home is a place for or ya "dog pound homies". You see how I live. This here is a palace. Them dogs of yours aint never seen nuffin similar to this here, they are use to the sewers."

"Everything is set for the pool party. People should start arriving. Decide now upstairs or downstairs?"

Ace has a sound mind. Whatever he is thinking is what he is going to say. Ace walks away from Crystal. He said everything he wanted to say to Crystal. He walked away because he just couldn't look at Crystal's snob face. Saying the words Madison Projects started getting Ace excited like a little kid in a toy store. It has been twenty years since he been back to New York. He missed the essences of New York. He missed the multi diversity of the people bumping, pushing and rushing into him to get around on the streets. He missed panhandlers on street corners, store fronts and on trains grubbing for loose change but not hungry enough for a donated sandwich. He knows the panhandlers were smiling behind his back after swindling him for a dollar. He missed eating a hot dog and dry pretzel from dirty sandy colored foreign vendor hands. He missed the sour aroma of piss in the train. He missed beating a Park Avenue wife in the race for a taxi cab. He enjoyed watching the over fed, pulled, lifted, shine pale face struggles to show emotion. The taunted face of a fifty dollar Deluca's artichokes diet woman was hard on the eyes. Their thousands of dollars spent on hidden age, has nobody fooled their age is transparent. He missed the fragrance of a yellow cab's back seat. The fragrance of fresh cut onions and raw sardines stinking up his day, streaming from the driver's naturally curry pores. The sight of decrypted cabs bombing down the avenues at terroristic speed is missed. The rank odor of squeegee men dirtying up his clean windshield of his car for a buck is missed. The Chelsea piers sport of waxed chests and pumped biceps is a sight he didn't missed but remembered. The pier is where every day is Halloween. Everyone dress as something they're not. He remembers the Chelsea boys and girls invading his public access channels with nude games of gay and playful pleasures. He missed the Wall Street suits self styled masterminds legally robbing the working class blind of their hard earned money. He missed the sight of the thick breaded man in religious black hats with two long Shirley temple curls dangling on the side of their ears. The curls sweep the dandruff off the dirty gabardine fabric coat. The thick breaded man strolls up and down Forty-Seventh Street bleeding the motherland of blood diamonds and selling it to highest bidder displaying the diamonds on the red carpet. The rich are wearing the winnings from their starved brothers and sisters across the seas. He missed the over price pyramid fruit, tulips and roses wrapped in plastic. Fruit and flowers sold to you by a person living in the country for ten years and still "No speakee" English. He missed wheeling, dealing and scheming with bright beach mobster thugs, sitting in the Café's sipping tea in glass cups with sugar cubes on wood sticks between their teeth. He missed the brawls with the Soprano want-a-bees, flying around with their pomaded hair, nylon warm-up suits and Saint Anthon gold medallion dangling from their necks with Jason Giambi's Louisville slugger in their right hand bowling from their stomach, their territory "Bensonhurst". He missed playing basketball with his uptown brothers. We brothers are playing in a court fighting for freedom. The thirteenth amendment to the constitution freed slaves one hundred and forty-eight years ago but shackles of stagnation holds brothers back today. He missed the two worst times in the city, the green day when genetic red heads roam the city street displaying outlandish intoxicated behavior. The second is the parade up Fifth Avenue. Traffic jams all over the city, twenty people to a car sucking the city dry of taxed benefits. Under the city is the blue carpet that is supposed to protect us all but is feared the most. It is the eighth upside down wonder to the world. The partners in blue stretched from long beach to the brick city. The largest gang force in America. The courtesy of the blues is lessons in gangbang one-on-one. From OG's in blue to gangbanging rookies, the professionalism of ghetto symphonies of gunshots ring into our black skin. The blue is armed with anal violating plungers and deadly shots. Their color protects them from the rules and regulations, while other colors are subjected to punishment accordion to rules. Other colors have two guidelines to live by. The other colors are restricted by the respect codes of the street and codes of the blue. The color residents of the city drowned the true blue lies with Hennessey and light up Buddha praises to the special true secret about the blue that could never be told. In the first twenty hours of freedom, Ace ran to his mother, Madison Projects. He loves his mother. Madison project gave birth to him. Ace had females from the road house in Astoria, tenements in Alphabet city and projects in the Bronx, cheering on the Bronx bombers to high heel ditty chicks in penthouses on Park Avenue, Lofts in SoHo, and Brownstones in park slope. Ace ran up and down the rat infected city of New York from one pair of fresh panties to the next. He chased females on the split levels in Staten Island but nothing was sweeter than being home in Madison Projects. Ace's childhood is a bitter sweet memory. Ace was born and raised in Madison Projects. Ace is the only child. Ace had the latest Ralph Lauren polo shirts, the latest sneaker, and anything else his mind could come up with from video game systems to custom leather jackets. Ace's father ran out and bought Ace's minds desires. Ace's father was an Entenmann's delivery truck driver. His hours were late nights and early mornings. And on weekends he would occasionally sign up for overtime. Weekend overtime is from Friday night until Sunday afternoon, driving cross state lines. Ace would be left alone, as a young boy being alone was depressing but as a teenage the weekend became paradise. Ace's mother had passed away when he was very young, so young Ace barely remembered her. Ace befriended his next door neighbor, Spade. Spade is two years older than Ace. Spade taught Ace the freestyle of conversation to manipulate a girl out her mind and underwear at the same time. Chyenne was in Ace shadow following him around like a love sick puppy since she laid her kindergarten eyes on him. Not only did Ace love having a number one fan in Chyenne but he loved having a guarantee. She would always ride for him. Ace had mind control over Chyenne. When Ace turned twelve, Easy Montana moved to Madison Projects from California. Easy Montana moved into the ninth floor apartment in the middle of Ace's apartment and Spade's apartment. Easy introduced Ace and Spade to doggy land. Ace had gold fever after he was exposed to an older female's treasure. Ace had fooled around with Chyenne's body but to get the homerun from an experienced female was a different ball game. Ace was running down on all females who crossed his path. But Easy was the one who schooled Ace on the art of finessing the suppression of desire with the help of Mary Jane clouds. "Never put on your emotion just wear your clothes." Ace switched up his hunger for female's sexy treasure. Ace would wear a stone face, all emotions suppressed. Females were willing to do anything to make Ace smile or get a word out his mouth. The cold game face is his gimmick. Females who were willing to part with their money were able to buy Ace's attention. Females without money were willing to pay for Ace's attention span with their bodies. By the age of thirteen Ace owned the title "Dog Father". Ace was a natural dog. He played the field of girls at school. Then when Ace came home from school or city ordered vacation he frolicked with the local advance females. At night, Ace raffled his life on the street. He didn't have to hustle in Madison Projects' street industry but he loved the attention. When Ace turned fifteen he had scramble up enough money from Chyenne, Jenni, Nita, Monica and Wanda to bust out in the industry when a solider fell to the unethical judicial system. Ace thought he was getting attention from the females but the Madison Projects industry workers weren't too receptive to Ace entrance into the industry. Industry worker's eyes was talking and watching Ace. This type of attention was unwelcomed by Ace. Ace reputation of dogging gave the reflection of a pretty boy and the industry didn't have pretty boy workers. Industry workers said Ace never struggled; he wasn't hungry enough to have a spot in the industry. Ace started from the bottom and now he has arrived. Ace had to work twice as hard then the average industry workers to give his name merit. After three months of dogging and paper chasing in the industry, Ace needed a vacation. Juggling five females and two workers was exhausting. Getting his hands dirty in the industry marked the vapors of the business. Respect was earned from peers in the industry. His name was ringing bells in the streets for his G thang he had over his group of girlfriends and the industry. The names Easy, Ace and Spade had a loud buzz not only in their local industry but to other industries of the same product. Making money at their speed made the three targets for five finger discounts and bargain sales for their life. He couldn't take the heat of the block. Ace went to his father for advice. His father was no help. "The game is to be sold, no to be told." This is his father entire speech. Ace had to play the game of life without losing his woof, get the industry to show him love and build an army pound of dog gangsters. The foreign industry workers would bark at Easy and Spade in Ace's absences but when Ace drove by in his BMW with the gold BBS's you could hear a pin drop on the concrete. Ace passed by meeting and greeting industry bosses. They smiled in Ace's face but plotted his future behind his back. The smog of envy was thick in the air. He fell into the shadow of the industry spotlight. He was eating off the plates of his five girls. Chyenne just gain ownership of her own apartment when Ace was seventeen, he is one year older than Chyenne. Ace had brain washed Chyenne into allowing four of Ace's female homies to live in her apartment. Ace had sexual relationships with all five female soldiers in his pound but he remembered their quality instead of their names. To Ace her name is "Buck 'Em Cali" but to the world her name is Monica. Monica is a firing red headed cutie with a big bootie. Her secret weapon was a Mack ten, she liked to make it go boom. She loved Ace but was in love with the scent of females. Crystal was in love with the beautiful thug side of Monica's lollipop tongue hustle. Monica's moments in love were in the art of gun noise. Ace army needed a gunman and Monica was perfect. Ace fondest memory of Monica is when Crystal and Monica had a lover's quarrel. It was no secret Crystal got around the block on a tricycle but sometimes it was overwhelming for Monica. During the fight, Monica bit down on Crystal's nipple like a pit bull and refused to let go. Monica sat up all night in the emergency room while Crystal got two stitches on her right nipple. Nita is her given birth name but to Ace she was referred to as "1800". His reasoning is because she was smooth but hit hard like tequila. Nita was originally from a plush brownstone in Park Slope but made Chyenne's apartment her home. Nita was laid back on the white horse but didn't waste time dropping heat like it's hot on victims blind by her perfect hourglass figure. "Bang Out" is Wanda's selected name from Ace. Wanda was a champion boxer. She held down the title of being an undefeated Bronx bomber. She bathes in the spotlight of another won on her belt. Ace relives the time when Wanda knocked out Heavy on the avenue on a Big Willie style summertime day. Heavy was supposed to be superman but Wanda was his kryptonite. Ace needed a fighter on deck to keep order and law in the pound of females. Jenni was Ace's medicine. She cratered to his every whimper. Jenni was most hated in the pound, especially by Chyenne. Ace asked Chyenne to trust him she was the one and only. The homies in pound was all business. Chyenne needed to be a part of the building up paper so Ace had her in charge of white collar offense of popping fake checks or cashing in fake dollars. Crystal was Ace eyes in the industry. She was a toy in the hood that everybody broke fluids with at one point or another. She was the life of every industry party. Sexually eruption of information was her set up. She let out all the information she gather to Ace. Her frequent fluid conversation with numerous industry workers often was a profitable gain to Ace. No one imagined the control Ace had over his pound, hardly any barking. He paid the cost with long stokes to be the boss. Ace was spending his day bopping to the bee gee's enjoying too much of heaven with his pound of girls. Easy and Spade was begging Ace for a return to the industry as a worker but Ace was ego tripping from being pampered by five women on a daily basics. Easy and Spade partner up with another industry boss after one final question of Ace next move. "See ya when you get there." Was their advice to Ace. Ace wanted to hustle and ball like his friends but he wanted to do it bigger than flipping nickels, dimes, and quarters. Ace wanted his earning in the industry to be unlimited while being the top dog over his female pound. Ace continued to build his foundation of sexual partners across the boroughs. He hit the industry like a smooth operator. Treat the pound of females like prostitutes; sell their skills to the game. They would sell their unique art of biting to the boss dogs in the industry. Ace knew when, where and how the boss dogs would hit. Ace took over all different corners of the industry with his knowledge. Ace had a last meal with the top dogs, no guns allowed. He broke down the rhythms and moves of his larger pound after the meal. Ace and his pound came off with food right off the top dog's plates. The industry reincarnated the dog, Ace into a mindful lion. Chyenne being arrested, Polo being prisoner of the system and the pound was a lost distant memory to Ace. Ace lashed on to the only thing that resembled the way life used to be, Crystal. Crystal kept Ace's nose candy dripping like water and his mind translucent with her freak sexual harassment. Ace buried his self inside Crystal. The next ten years is a blur to Ace. He has spot memories of schemes, sex and drugs in Virginia. He remembers doing too much and nothing getting done. After ten years in prison Ace stepped his game up, cleaned his system of poison and industry gangster love dreams. He waited for better days to return home to the king.

"DJ Here," SuWu announces to Ace. Ace is outside the glass doors in the back yard.

Ace claps his right hand with Maino's right hand and wraps his left arm around Maino's back. Maino is Ace's childhood friend. Maino has always been into music, it started when he got a sweet tooth for the Sugarhill's rapper's delight. His sweet love of music had him living Big Willie style like a fresh prince. He flossed like it's summertime all the time showing of his paid in full paper look. He was beyond locate party but for Ace the top dog he fold and play his hand, old fashion way records and needle points.

"Welcome home bro!"

"Thanks bro, good to be home."

"Looks like you've done well for yourself." Maino's eyes speak of the sight it captures.

The sixty foot by sixty foot fish tank wall across from the glass wall leading to the backyard.

"I'm humble."

"Where can I set up at? Oh and by the way, I invited some top head models, I hope you don't mind."

"C'mon, ladies are my game. The more ladies the more fun for me."

The five top head women models promenade their promiscuous perfectly fruit shaped bodies pass Ace's eyes. The oversexed fruit that is ripe for liberating picking. The five top head models danced around in their unrestricted pumpum shorts and provoking bikini tops. Sensualist chocolate complexion ranged from white chocolate to hot fudge. The top head models heart shaped faces and lips stimulated sexual desire. These top head models weren't trained by Ms. Bank but by Ms. Steffans. The top models beauty dances in front of Ace's lusty eyes. His eyes sway to hoedown party in his mind.

"These two are sisters Pina Cum Lotta and Paloma." Maino introduce two of the top head models.

Pina Cum Lotta and Paloma are to Latin intoxication known to cold rock a party. They earned their names staring in Back and Rack City productions. Their young wild free spirited hair has been captured on film. Pina Cum Lotta full lips has the effect of making a male's smooth skin to cream a lot. Paloma birth name is Margarita. Margarita with white grape juice sprayed on her face is favors the drink Paloma. Ace eyes sips up their intoxicating vibe.

"Alize and Mai Tai" Maino introduce two more of the top head models.

Alize and Mai Tai are drinkers of vanilla ice cream dreams. These two are on a heavy calcium diet but are paper thin. Their special technique is to transform grown man into dancers performing moves from the cha cha slide to straight up ballerina moves, thanks to their heart shaped lips skills. They keep on keeping on no matter the flow of vanilla ice cream dreams dripping down their throat.

"This is my personal favorite Sunny D Lite. The others are all yours." Maino places his claim.

Seeing Maino with his personal entourage of sexiness made Ace miss the pound. A rush of guest just started rushing in to take Ace's mind off the thirst of pound. Ace is jumping around greeting and hugging everybody entering the backyard. Crystal came downstairs. She wants to keep eyes on Ace's rodents. She's going to ensure her home isn't turned into a funhouse losing control like its kid and play time. Crystal eyes scan the room to detect body and outfit flaws.

The Project's rubbish is in my backyard. All these bitches hating I got the #1 prize, Ace. Da sisters Hope and Faith have on name brand sun dress from Macy's. Da price tags stickin out the back of the dress. Broke hoes. Ya know they gonna return da shit ASAP. Broke bitches trying to make broke look good. Look at Cookie's thirsty ass all up in Dwight's face with her girdle type one piece bathing suit holdin' down all that cottage cheese. Please check out Miss Cleopatra she done brought the fucking bun back. Her name fit her perfect, her rep of taking advantage of young boys. I wanna know how many 20 yrs old paid $20 for 20 minutes to buy her them red bottoms and that red Maseratti. Monica, A bitch I use to knew. She brought her little sister Sonia. I just might have some fun after all.

Wanda looks like she rode here on a bus pass. Da player's club in da house! Beans and the three Johnson boys are cuties but they aint got shit on Tugee, the illegal alien. His mother is some kinda Koran and his father is a strapping black man, together they created a masterpiece. Tugee inherited his mother chinky eyes and yellowish complexion but his father's muscular frame along with the signature waterhole genitals. I wanna whisper in his ear "I'm wet. I wanna fuck you" I'll give him a 2 minute's warning before I rock his world. Traci I'm threw witcha. How da hell is my employee at the party hanging off De'Andre's arm. Jus plain 'ole trashy. Ace ignorant friends Spade and the joker, Easy Montana lookin' dumber than they really are and for them that's hard 'cus them two are broader line retarded. Nita, that's the homie. Jenni showing her face at my house? She's lucky I aint bustin' rocks at her face. Oh hell to the no, which one of you asshole up in here totally disrespected my house and invited the Sistahs up in here? Da body, da bad and the bald eagle." Crystal's chitachatter

Crystal eyes have just pick up the image of Brooklyn, Rhonda and Tay just taking a dip in the pool. Tay is up to her neck line in chorine water. Tay doggy paddles to the edge of the pool in her naïve hot pink two piece bikini bathing suit with no secrets. Camille has French braided Tay's honey blonde weave but kept her Chinese bangs out. Brooklyn awaits Tay arrival at the edge of the pool. Brooklyn sits on the edge of the pool sipping on a slushy alcohol cocktail. Rhonda has found a cocktail in King. King is Ace's father. Rhonda's challenge to Tay's swimming skills was a way to find her way to the other side of the pool and the other side of King. King built a great deal of hated for Chyenne. In King's opinion, Chyenne was too gloomy, too heavy, and too needy. Ace was always striving to please her but nothing was ever enough. When Ace announced his choice in the light bright Crystal, King showered them with gifts, money; he even financed their move to Virginia. The rest of the Sistahs shared the opinion of King but because they are Chyenne friends, he characterized the Sistahs. "Birds of a feather flock together" Is King's words.

*"Look at this **Slick Dick** [50]ass nicca right here. He is for the grown and sexy. I damn sure am grown and sexy. I am glad he is here to keep me off Traci snake ass. How she fucked De'Andre? It's not like I wanted him, it's just the principal. Now I don't like her before she was cool. OOOH shit, this nicca is like a 60 year old bottle of wine. He aged with poise, quality, and wisdom. Besides the dusty grays, his skin is as silky as my sheets. True indeed, uhm. Black don't crack. I always had a thing for Mr. King. His 6 foot and 5 inches of pure autumn wheat syrup dipping down his bare diesel chest is sooo sexy. I hope they aint got no color guard in this pool 'cus he is talking but I'm looking and I'm leaking. Shit, I'm trying to calm myself. Mr. King is a man not those men boys I've slapped down on their back and took advantage of their sausage links in the meat packing district. Sammy on a damn date and I need her here. Mr. King is major league and I've been play stick ball. Shit, I can't blow this 'cus I want this." Rhonda's chitachatter*

"You have turned out very well. I'm proud you. How's the rest of the "Sistahs"? King questions Rhonda. King is laid out on a beach chair near the edge of the pool.

"Well, I'm here with Brooklyn and Tay. The rest are working." Rhonda's luminous white chocolate skin responds but her sexual eyes are speaking different words to King's body.

"Yup I lied. So what I'm not gonna tell my future husband Chyenne aint change, still chasing after your gigolo son and Sammy somewhere getting her brain fucked out on a yacht. No I will not. I'm trying to hook him. What the Sistah do is always between the Sistahs. If you don't know and wanna how holla at the streets 'cus the Sistah's lips are air tight. The streets will defiantly fill ya up on that good 'ole Puerto Rico Soup." Rhonda's chitachatter

---

[50] **Slick Dick** is a older man with the mannerisms of young man.

"So where's your husband?"
"Don't have one. Did you ever remarry?"

"No, I didn't. But I'm looking; I got about a good 10 years left in me. I can make some lucky woman live comfortable for the next ten years."

"Well where and how long have you been looking?

"I gotta know 'cus I've always been easy to find." Rhonda's chitachatter

"'Cus I can't imagine a lady not snitching you up by now." Rhonda's sexual stares continue.

"I been looking everywhere and nowhere for 5 years. I will strike gold soon enough."

"Slick dick nicca ya have struck gold good big time right now and you don't even know it. Ya already mines and ya don't even know it." Rhonda's chitachatter

"Well how about a refill on ya cocktail?" Rhonda's luminous white chocolate skin drools with words.

"Yes, thank you sweetie."

Rhonda slowly lifts her spontaneous rainbow string tie bikini top bathing suit and impulsive hot pink boy shorts, barely covering her uncontrollable bottom cheeks out the water, on the right side of King's pool chair. The chorine rain drops of her plumped butt cheek drizzles on King's face. She bends down over King's body picking up his cocktail glass on his left side. King's grin is a sure sign he enjoys the rainbow after the rain. King's eyes glued to the jingle and wiggle of Rhonda's steps to the picnic table. Rhonda had her mouth watering for a burger when out the side of her eye she could see Malik racing toward the picnic table area.

"I don't know you and I don't care too. I'm asking you a man to man too stay away from my wife." Malik's eyes spoke louder than the words flowing from his lips as the aggressive heat on his slightly muscular chestnut syrup coated physique fumes.

"Listen, before she was your wife she was my bitch. I love her up and down and inside out. I can't lie to you and say imma stay away from Chyenne 'cus I jus can't." Ace reveals.

"Are you trying to tell me you fuckin my wife?" Malik's words flows from his lips as the words clench his fist.

"If she rings you around and say I ain't hit, you'll be the clown to believe her. That girl can't get enough of me."

Before anybody could react to Ace's words Malik's solid right fist did. Malik's right fist connects to Ace's jaw line on the left side of his face with a force of anger. Malik follows up with a left hook of brutal envy to the right side of Ace's face. Ace rush Malik's body into the picnic table. The picnic table easily snapped in half, like a tooth pick. Malik lands on his back. Malik bear hugs Ace's body. Malik flips Ace onto his back. Dwight grabs Malik from behind off of Ace's body. King aids Ace to his feet and holds Ace's body back. Ace is fighting to get free. Ace's bloody mouth shouts fighting words across to Malik. Rhonda notices the strength in King's biceps. Ace is furious he didn't get a pinch off in the short fight. Traci runs to Malik's side with a towel of ice for his hand.

"That does it, all you heathens get the fuck outta my mansion, now! *Je n'ai jamais*[51]." Crystal's thin upper lip distinguished superior tone shouts.

"Heathens? Bitch don't let ya chitachatter get ya jaw shattered."
Brooklyn speaks to Crystal.

Le'Roy wraps his right arm around Brooklyn back and grips her left hip.
He nudges her towards him.

"Crystal is so lucky Le'Roy is here. I would have whipped her superior ass up in here for ole time sake. Le'Roy hasn't been introduced to Brooklyn Zoo yet. He's not ready neither is Crystal." Brooklyn's chitachatter

"Babe, let's just get outta here. She aint worth your trouble." Le'Roy words of wisdom influence Brooklyn to forget Crystal's diamond shape head, hooded mud brown eyes, cold vanilla false Caucasian pigment, and the words from her thin upper lip distinguished superior tone.

"Every time our eyes meet. Be talkin talkin talkin talkin to me (talkin to me). Talkin talkin talkin talkin to me. Just ain't no need for words to speak (oh). Cause every time. Be talkin talkin talkin to me. Be talkin talkin talkin to me (Talkin to me). Your always actin so composed and cool. Never got to many words for me" *Amerie aint never lied. She is telling the tale of a different languages when eyes speak. I'm seeing what she's singing. I always had that sexual eye chemistry wit Tugee but he rather makes touchdowns on the wrong field. In high school he always use to turn his head and make sure I see. But after my koowie tango wit Beans (Douglas) there was no need for words to speak, I saw the hurt in his eyes. I was so ashamed how I let my koowie sleep wit one of Tugee's closest friends. Da Sistahs couldn't see how a love unspoken can be so deep. I didn't wanna show my face in school. But the fire and desire is back in his pretty brown eyes and they are talking to me." Tay's chitachatter*

---

[51] ***Je n'ai jamais*** [51]*translation from french to English is 'i have never'."*

Le'Roy wraps a beach size towel over Brooklyn's "Hennessy" straight old fashion soda bottle shape frame. Brooklyn's intriguing soft tangerine bikini bathing suit was accessorized with an Indian belly hip chain. Indian belly hip chain had tiny soft tangerines bells dangling from the chain like fruit in a tree. Brooklyn and Le'Roy scans the humungous backyard of bodies scattering. They are searching for their friends.

"Yo, we out, everybody is on the bus. Are ya coming?" Dwight questions Le'Roy.

"Yeah, but I gotta make sure my girl finds her friends first. Jus give me a minute I'm coming." Le'Roy words were aimed to Dwight but his eye continued to search.

"Ya girl?" Dwight's surprise responds shout over Le'Roy's search.

"A'ight, see ya on da bus." Dwight talks and walks at the same time.

Dwight disappears into the lollygagging stampede of crowds moving toward the side exit. Crystal refused to have trails over her white Italian marble inlay floors. Departing guest use the service exit in the backyard alone side Crystal's mansion.

"Ya girl?" Brooklyn is questioning Le'Roy about her new title.

"You heard right. You are my girl, soon to be my wife. Brooklyn, I'm in love wit you and I'm not letting you go." Le'Roy confesses.

"We gotta go now! Where's Tay?" Rhonda questions Brooklyn with panic in her eyes.

Brooklyn immediately notices the panic in Rhonda's eyes and voice. Brooklyn agrees to call Le'Roy as soon as she gets home. They kiss to seal the agreement. Brooklyn joins Rhonda in the hunt for Tay. Rhonda fills Brooklyn's ear with hysteria. Benny called Rhonda's cell phone. In Benny's shaky voice Rhonda understood there is big trouble at the *Pink Pussy Cat*. Brooklyn and Rhonda finds Tay curled up in a corner with Tugee.

"Hate to interrupt but we gotta roll." Rhonda informs Tay.

"I'm rolling wit Tugee and his friends on the party bus." Tay announces.

"The boys are in trouble. We gotta go, now!" Brooklyn reiterates.

"I got faith you two can handle it. I'm rolling with Tugee. A piece of cake."

"A piece of ass." Rhonda say goodbye in Sistah talk.

"A piece of pie." Brooklyn says her goodbye.

Brooklyn bumps pass Crystal with the intent to excite Crystal into a knock out in the backyard. Last time Brooklyn broke her nose. Today Brooklyn wanted to break Crystal's snooty face but would settle for giving her a mouth fill of wild and free hair. Brooklyn flings her flow of hair in Crystal's face. Crystal gave no attention to Brooklyn's subtle attack. Brooklyn hops into her brand new Maybach 62 S, 2011 model. Rhonda jumps into the passenger seat.

"Did you see Traci, snake ass?" Rhonda questions.
"Which part of her? Her hanging off De'Andre's arm or when she was hanging off Malik's dick?" Brooklyn responds.

"It's good Tay is rolling on the bus, we can find out how Traci the snake plays the scene with De'Andre and Malik both in the terrain?"

"What did Benny say?"

"Not much but I know my nephew, sommin is so wrong."

"Whatever it is we gonna fix it."

"Hold on G.I. Jane. Remember, the boys are young men with young problems. You can pack up ya auto and semi sweet weapons. The only thing you may bring out the car is your taser. Nothing more, okay killer?"

"Sounds like ya a little shell shock from earlier privet?"

"From the point when you buned ya hair with a paper clip to the shots fired into Roc's tires and windows I know your angry issues has definitely escalated since we were teenagers. You really need to get that looked into by a doctor sweetie before end up killing somebody."

"Stop frontin, you enjoyed the show?"

"Aint no frontin yes I did, especially when you shot his toe off. Just thinking about it makes me laugh. You're a fool wit it."

"Fuck Roc, I was just playing wit his ass!"

"Damn, ya joke cost a nicca a toe. What ya got for an encore?"

"Taking out an eye."

The two Sistahs filled the car's air with good deep laughter. They laugh so hard at Roc's expense. Paying the experience back with a cost of tear filled eyes and weak limbs from laughter.

"Le'Roy knows 'bout what cha did to Roc?" Rhonda questions.

"Le'Roy hinted toward the topic but I ignored it. Le'Roy don't know that side of me and I hope I don't gotta introduce him to Brooklyn Zoo."

"I hope not too. This world aint ready for ya sense of humor."

Brooklyn drives her Maybach 62 S, 2011 model into a parking spot. As her right hand turns the key in the ignition her left leg is already out the car and her left intriguing tangerine colored Christian Louboutin Bollywoody pumps hits the concrete. Rhonda is on Brooklyn's heels as the doorman greets them. In the lobby of the building there are two elevator banks. One elevator use is for the tenants of the building and the other elevator is for exclusive use of the Sistahs. Brooklyn uses her key on a red cupcake keychain to bring the elevator to the lobby. The two Sistahs enters the elevator. As the elevator start rising to the penthouse apartment, the influx of terror swells into their faces. The paleness of questions of what could be awaiting them contrasts their complexions. The two elevator doors open to the young whiz world of living young, wild and free. Brooklyn and Rhonda didn't need no introduction to this world. They vacation there often enough to recognize this type of scenery. Brooklyn's and Rhonda's eyes drink on the the new edition of work hard and play hard, the work and the play is different from the Sistah's youthful days. The Sistah's youthful party days consist of alcohol, friends, good greenery and good music. Everybody came to have a good time. They had a few drinks and a few good laughs. Then, they had a good night. The room of new edition youth partiers drug dilated pupils stares as Brooklyn and Rhonda. Every girl sucks feverishly on lollipops to satisfy the heighten sense of taste induced by the pure white sugar or brown sugar of ecstasy capsules rolling in their veins. They have chosen to drink, smoke or sniff the ten hour lasting ecstasy sugar effects of orbit stimuli to the physical sensitivity to the animate being. The ecstasy sugar consumes all your senses. The heighten sense of hearing becomes an eye-opener to music appreciation at frequencies never heard before. The sights of things are very bright to open wide eyes. Closed wide shut eyes visuals are clear as sight. The craving of tactile sensation controls the body's limbs. Ecstasy sugar makes sex simply amazing. The heighten feeling of touch and emotions to pleasured skin never discovered orbits an immortal arousal. The everlasting freakish nectarous flow of the ecstasy sugar sensation rolling in your pores rolls up, down and inside out. Ecstasy sugar of orbit mentally affects your brain. The brain has been up active for hours using up adrenaline. Energizing gratifying awareness about yourself sweetens the feeling of acceptance. The glucose luscious sweetens of ecstasy sugar has crystallized acceptances of everybody around you. Ecstasy sugar sweetens the pot with no appetite, no sign of exhaustion and no worries fueling the perspiration sweet water dripping skin. The "just at one with the world" ecstasy sugar mental feeling comes crushing down as the intoxication depression starts building up. When the sweet fantasy effects wears off, deep down sour reality awakes from peaceful dreams. Sleep doesn't strike easy but when sleep hits it's a knock out for hours. The body needs to rejuvenate the juices burned out in the endurance of partying. Benny, Calvin, Dino, Polo are the Sistahs off spring. The off springs dilated pupils are filled with concern. The new edition was live on an internet website recording their play hard as they work hard Rack and Back City productions. Rack and Back City productions present full service sexual pleasure made nasty for your ecstasy sugar entertainment. Benny, Calvin, Dino and Polo are young and get money off of the sweet bed rock films. They spontaneously filmed one of their house parties and the rest is a story best told in dollar amount. Rack and Back City productions last year net worth was three point seven million according to Forbes's under twenty five self made millionaires. Dino is the camera man directing the sexual dance. The up, down and inside out tango dance off your feet. The dance is done well. They have traveled from California hotels to Miami Beach making pit stops in Oregon, Philly, Texas and everything in between making it Christmas all over the united nation. Ecstasy sugar snow falls over the party goers in any season. They played a little game called "I'll be sure". They would spot a girl and if one of them announce, "I'll be sure to get a nut of that" the girl is asked to be a star in their movie. Every school break and every summer they went on an "I'll be sure" tour to find the perfect face and the perfect head of each state to excite viewers. To bring sexual dreams and nightmares to the viewers is the goal. Miguel, Dino's older brother, edits the footage and digitally captures the viewer's dollars and attention. The young dream chasers are the bosses of their operation. The new edition of young men has announced their present in the lucrative x-rated adult film industry. They enjoy filming the new kids on the block of nudity. They could sniff out any armatures like bloodhounds. Filming female's diamond glissade skins with Jade fire eyes was enjoyable and profitable. Females lined up to spend a night with the young new edition of money. The females sip ecstasy sugar coconut juice in the day under the sun and sniff ecstasy sugar at night under the moon light. Tonight's live **popcorn love** [52]movie is starring Mickey D's a five foot six inches fire red head with supersized double D cup breast. Popcorn love is no strings attached. Mickey D's is a sexual heart breaker. She serves up combos of all you can eat sexual delight according to the value of your dollar menu. She is the kind of young woman that can stand the flurries of ecstasy sugar. Mickey D's two infamous protégées, Hot Caramel Sundae and Sin-a-Buns. The two protégées are small fries in the industry. Mickey D's bought the two protégées along to pop their cherries into her franchise. Mickey D's co-stars are Holli Molli and Brown Bobbi. Holli Molli is the Hollywood ecstasy sugar candy girl. She rains her bougie nose with the sweetness of ecstasy sugar. The scene is set up. Mickey D's falls into humping around session with Mr. Telephone man, Brown Bobbi, under the blue moon on the balcony. Brown Bobbi's beautiful baby face sells out the gray mercy of real love in ecstasy sugar. Every little step Brown Bobbi took was a dance inside Mickey D's stomach. Mickey D's couldn't get away. Brown Bobbi is king of the stage. He headed, footed and was standing the set. He mounted his co-star with twelve plays of hard bumping and deep grinding. He didn't mean to be cruel but his masculine manly twelve inches masterpiece and thug loving technique was camera friendly and a mix of pain pleasure for his co-star. Mickey D's cries of pain over powered her creamy "I'm luvin it" tears dripping on twelve inches. Holli Molli busts in on Mickey D's creamy sexiness being

---

[52] **popcorn love** is a quick pop off sexual desire.

pounded by Brown Bobbi at a hundred twenty miles per hour on the balcony. Brown Bobbi's go for broke stoke service is a guarantee trip to the nearest salon. Holli Molli enters the scene as a jealous girl. Holli Molli proves there is a thin line between love and hate and she joins in the sexual pleasures of Brown Bobbi and Mickey D's. Ecstasy sugar inebriate bodies spills into the living room. It takes two to play the sweet game with Brown Bobbi. His over sized chocolate coated sugar cane filled with sweet nectar of ecstasy stands strong with an eye of creamy tears. Mickey D's licks out the bitterness of infidelity from Holli Molli's sweetened sexiness. Holli Molli's tongue expresses gratitude and returns the favor. Mickey D's tongue lubricates Brown Bobbi's solid twelve inches of sweet meat filled with ecstasy sugar. Brown Bobbi's twelve inches of sweet meat crawls deep up into Holli Molli's body like a panther. Brown Bobbi is known for sexual pleasures in the public eyes. His public acts at parks, pool halls; just any place eyes were viewing has made him a celebrity of the sexual fit club. Brown Bobbi wasn't sweet on Holli Molli. He pounded her with jaw breaking blow of passion in atomic positions. The cream jump shot exposed from deep within in his knee numerous times. The excess cream was definitely camera friendly. He swapped between Mickey D's and Holli Molli like a light switch without losing or skipping a beat. The second film is Polo, the stone cold gentlemen. Polo usually grabs a girl, an ecstasy sugar capsule and a camera to show how it's going down. Polo had saved up more money than a little. He is hoping to find the right girl. He learns the costly way money can't buy love. He was eyeing a no name cutie face and thin waist on the couch. He was thinking about giving her a name and a career. The no name girl arrived to the party with Holli Molli. Calvin is the extreme super lover. He wraps a body tight with quiet time of play while he rubs the body in the right way. His cute sweet love addition can get any young woman in the mood for love. Young women have bust it open in the elevator or the nearest secluded area. Calvin's cute looks and art of seduction is the perfect combination to drive any young woman half crazy. Calvin's rise of a young lasting king was up in Hot Caramel Sundae careless creamy world. Calvin swam from Hot Caramel Sundae's top to Sin-a-Buns's bottom. Benny position is to spread love of ecstasy sugar. A little bit of love is all it takes to make the films happen. With ecstasy sugar everything is done in love all the way. Tonight, Benny is recording Calvin's sweet ecstasy sugar episode. The background is of pink and red butterflies flying on white walls in the bathroom. Calvin exposes the two young ladies in the Jacuzzi hot tub. Before each filming, they all thank god for always to being able to live through their films as tigers in the woods of sexual bogies with beautiful birdies. Beautiful birdies who don't have no hard feeling after the deuces. They trip into a small stream of trouble while filming in Idaho Fall. The community natives boycotted their party. In the middle of the whole thing, Brown Bobbi was arrested and charged with a gun. He was sentence to eight months but won at trail. He still had to serve a month for his urination in the back seat of the police's cruiser. Amen to the end of that small stream of trouble. The young new edition of money never had no real bullshit in their year of production until tonight. Molli Holli prerogative was to inhale pebbles of ecstasy sugar until she passed out cold. She crushed the grove of the party. Only the regulars stayed behind, everybody else left. Benny panics, it is crucial for him to call Rhonda to save the day. His thoughts were maybe Brown Bobbi stabbed her to death with his rod of pleasure.

"Tell me the truth what happen?" Rhonda questions the wide eyed living room of young adults.

"She popped more pills than ever. She was drinking water for the sweating. I just thought she was trying to get in the mood until she fainted." Mickey D's reveals her eyewitness encounter.

"Why is she wet?" Rhonda questions

"We put her in the shower under cold water." Mickey D's responds.

"How long has she been out?" Brooklyn questions

"Only an hour. Should we call somebody?" Benny's voice trembles with panic.

Brooklyn uses her index finger and middle finger to find a pulse under the back of Holli Molli's jaw bone. Brooklyn's right hand dance around in her purse and expose her hand with an ammonia capsule at her fingertips. She breaks the capsule under Holli Molli's nose. Holli Molli show signals of life but is not fully conscious. Brooklyn's right hand dance around again in her purse this time her right hand emerges with a Taser gun. Brooklyn electrifies dynamite recovers energy into Holli Molli. The no name young woman shadows Holli Molli's right side. A sigh of relieve filled the living room of young people.

"I'm wet, why?" Holli Molli questions.

The no name young woman hands Holli Molli a towel.

"You passed out, scared the living shit outta us." Hot Caramel Sundae's reports the concern of the room.

"We put you in a cold shower trying to wake you up." Mickey D's responds to Holli Molli.

"I was gonna put it in ya butt to wake you up but they wouldn't let me." Calvin jokes.

"Nice. Only you would try to get a freebie." Holli Molli jokes back.

"How do you feel sweetie?" Rhonda questions Holli Molli.

"I feel fine. Thank you"

"You're welcome. You gotta be more careful." Brooklyn warns.

"Maybe you should take a little break." Rhonda suggests.

"I do what I gotta do to survive. Thanks, but I'll be just fine." Holli Molli responds

Brooklyn and Rhonda saves the day and leave. Benny, Calvin, Dino and Polo each took turns hugging and kissing Brooklyn and Rhonda farewell. As quickly as they arrived was a fast as they departed. Brooklyn and Rhonda had their share of action for the day and night; they are ready to retired to their homes. The young new edition of money popped more love ecstasy sugar, recording popcorn love continued as the elevator door closed with Brooklyn and Rhonda inside.

"Are you gonna hit me off?" Polo questions the no name young woman.

"Off camera?" the no name young woman questions.

"The camera is gonna give you a name. Do you wanna a name?"

"Yes, I do wanna name."

Sin-a-Buns loosen up the no name young woman for Polo with her tongue's circular sticky tastes of the no name girl's sexiness between her legs.

****

Chyenne takes a deep breath before she removes her key from her blue Ford Focus's ignition. She hasn't been home in five days straight. She fears facing Malik's disappointing glares and stares. She takes two minutes to put her game face on before she sticks her key into the lock on the wooden framed double French doors to her Staten Island home. She holds her breath as her right foot steps out of vestibule into the living room. Karol, Malik's mother, is sitting on the black leather Jennifer

Convertibles sectional in the living room watching cartoons with Capri, her nine years old daughter. Capri leaps into Chyenne's arms showering her with kisses. Capri misses her mother. Karol's eyes rolls in greeting Chyenne.

"Grandma made cupcakes. Try one. Grandma's cupcakes are better than Chef Robert's." Capri suggests.

Capri drags Chyenne into the kitchen to the smell of southern food aroma. The cupcakes mounted on the kitchen table, like a tower of sweet deliciousness. Karol follows behind Capri and Chyenne.

"Grandma, can I have another one?" Capri questions

"Sure baby. You can even eat it while you finish watching your movie. I'll be right out with your juice." Karol orders Capri.

"Mama, Can you watch the movie with me? It's a love movie, "The Little Mermaid.""

"She'll be right out baby, now go on." Karol politely demands Capri.

Capri waltz out the kitchen and went back to giving her attention to "The Little Mermaid".

"What cha doing to your marriage?" Karol questions Chyenne.

"Karol, I'm not comfortable discussing the state of my marriage with you. You are kinda bias."

"Don't cha know he's in love with you? Honey, back in the day I lived on the other side of the game. I too was out here chasing a green eye soldier when love was in my face. I want you to look at me as a common Sistah with your best interest at heart, now and in the next lifetime. I don't meddle in people's love affairs 'cus if I did, I would barge in on Dwight's love cases. Call my brother Tyrone, he'll tell you I don't get involve in matters of the heart. My brother and my sons are the love of my life. I want you to see pass the healer or a mother in-law title and just listen. I don't want you to end up like a bag lady going on and on about the past. You have the power to fix whatever is broken." Karol shines wisdom on Chyenne.

"Everybody got somin to say. Well keep your fucking opinions. I'm tired of all "I'm just look out for you" speeches. I've been looking after myself for a long fucking time. Now everybody is relationship experts. They know what's best for my life. Aint no need in chasing the green eye soldier, I got Ace soft gray eyes to stare into." Chyenne's chitachatter

Chyenne's mind drifts off into her time spent with Ace. In her vision are her fingertips roaming through Ace's soft light brown baby curls. Looking into Ace's low chief soft gray eyes is the vision clouding her judgments. She remise about her laughter when he opened his mouth, those grills gleaming out, shinning the eighty carats on his chest. Chyenne humped on Ace like a rabbit. His red candy painted 5.0 Mustang with the clean chrome feet and elegant white leather inside skin was their bed for love making.

***"I need a soldier. You know the type to carry big things if you know what I mean."** Street credibility allows him to return after 20 years and flip that money three ways. If there's one thing I do know, it's hard to find that perfect lover. Ace knows how to keep my body screamin' and know how to drop that beat in the back. **"I need a soldier"**. A soldier with built broad shoulders chiseled muscular chest and abdomen. A solider aint scared to stand up to me. Malik is reserved, play life by the rules. Ace is a wild boy, he don't give a fuck about the rules. Ace is a honey dipped rude boy that's promised to be good to me. Sometimes you gotta lose to win." Chyenne's chitachatter*

CRESHIE WRITES

"Just swing it left, swing it right. You gotta slow it down."

Slow It Down
The Dream ft. Fabolous
Four Play

The Ball player picks Sammy up from in front of her two stories, three bedrooms, and two bathroom home in White Plains area in the Bronx. Her house is on a quiet block. Her neighbors keep to themselves. The Plains is the meadows where Sammy can have a leveled head. She shines her authoritative cinnamon spice in the sexist court room jungle by day and under the stars she travels the predicted terrain of genuine advice to family, friends and the Sistahs. The Plains is her cloud on ground level. Sammy's five foot petite frame stands on four inches of glitter art designed by Jimmy Choo. Her cinnamon complexion sprinkles out from under her Yves Saint Laurent authentic snow white low cut neckline, fitting on the waist, mini sun dress. She accessorized her outfit with a multi colored glitter fitting belt, accentuating her thin waist and multi colored glitter clutch purse to set off her multi colored diamond stud earrings. Her soft ebony ear length curls flies in the spring afternoon breeze like the butterflies swimming in her stomach. The alcoholic slushy cocktails at Tay's house was kicking in, Sammy felt a little light headed. The pass seven days the Ball player has sent flowers, candy and gifts to Sammy's office. The Ball player had Sammy's receptionist and Rhonda in his court. After day three of the spring showers of gifts from the Ball Player, Benny started cheerleading for the Ball player. The Ball player broke down the walls he built around Sammy's heart. She final decided to go on a date with him. Sammy's crystalline vision through her prescribed clear contacts spots a persistent tenacious red Porsche Carrera GT sports car. Sammy hadn't seen the Ball player since his move out the guest room in Sammy's house to his own home. Sammy assumed he had moved on. The Ball player hops out the driver's side door. He slides his semi lanky, semi sweet milk chocolate six foot nine inches frame across the hood of the car, smoothly landing on his size nineteen feet on the passenger's side to open the door for Sammy. Sammy burgundy wine tint heart shaped lips giggles and wiggles away the nerviness swimming in her veins. Her memory dives in to the pool of skinny dips into intimate pleasures, doggy paddling through a friendship and heart filled breast strokes into a romantic relationship. Her heart reminds her how her arms and legs had to fight against the media drowning her with the Ball player's "new" wife. Sammy wadded her emotions inside and stood on a waft of her Sistahs with her head held high. The Ball player's butter soft lips glazed the nape of Sammy's neck as he placed his hand left hand on the small of her back. The kiss of burgundy blush on Sammy's high cheek bone concealed the flush of emotion in her face. His settle gesture nipped Sammy's taste for granting the Ball player another shot at her heart. He had to prove he was worthy of playing the game. Sammy's heart was a trophy that can't easily be won. During the drive the radio mix of nineties music transported Sammy and the Ball player down memory lane. From every boy's in nineties thinking, the LL lick of lips was cool and a guarantee panty dropper. The nineties house of pain jumped around carefree. The nineties when the end of the road to boyhood came and men were born. Every crazy, sexy and cool young lady didn't want no scrub. Young women birth to aware of the down falls of waterfalls sealed with a kiss from a rose. Young women's eyes open to that thing Mimi called a vision of love. It was time when there was a delight to have groove in the heart. Parties when you couldn't touch hammers. The Motown Philly swing was music to soul. It's around the time Sammy met the Ball player in college. From the start, Sammy knew her friendship slash lover relationship with the Ball player wasn't right but it was okay. When the Ball player had to leave school to go home to Houston, Sammy realized she would always love him. She just had trouble being with him. She can't believe how her allowances of her feeling from college boomeranged into the present. The mid nineties was a shaggy time for Sammy. She was twenty years old in her second year of a seven year term in college when she thought the Ball player was her someone to love but was proven wrong. After seven female rump shakers confessions of their personal freaking sexual escaped with the Ball player, Sammy decided until he did right by her she was gone. Sammy totally couldn't see how the Ball player found the time, they were Siamese twins. Then she gave birth to Benny giving her one more big chance at someone to love. The Ball player broke down every brownstone Sammy put up to his pleading his case, his words built reasoning that if Sammy loved him; she would allow him to prove his love. Sammy made him pay for the wrecks of his actions he just wasn't prepare for the effects of losing Sammy. The groove theory of Sammy's life is every one telling her their sugar hills of troubles from A to Z. she gave advice to Rhonda, who at the time had just received her bachelor's degree in accounting. She had a day job but like to party at night. Her mind slipped past her four year old daughter, Paris. Sammy had to keep Rhonda on track. Teddy was a fifteen year old sophomore in high school getting fondled by high school girls. His chest stood out like a man. Sammy had to pump the manly air out Teddy's chest, at least once a week. The Sistah lives were in full swing of circumstances. Chyenne was under doctor's care because Crystal keeps her head ringing. Once a month Sammy would personal retrieve the doctor's mental medical report on Chyenne's state. Brooklyn was working the deep dark brandy colored axe of pain to her broken heart and the whack to her chops. Sammy often baby sat for EPMD so that Brooklyn could enjoy the fit of her own skin and not the Carlito's designer way of living. Tay was doing what she is done back in the days now. Tay constantly immature vagina is looking for love in a sixty nine tootsie roll on the sheets. Sammy is always mending Tay's crushed emotions after a guy has smash her tasty cappuccino curves and didn't look back. The Ball player pulls up to his St. Olivette New Jersey boat home. He gives Sammy a tour of his half furnished home. The Ball player walked Sammy through his newly purchased four bedrooms, three bathrooms, day room, living room, dining room and the kitchen. The part of the house that stole Sammy's heart was the cozy patio furniture settled on the boardwalk style wooden boarded floors, the mystic colored peddles on the edge of the patio boundary fades into a hundred foot yacht. The sunset red orange glow background on clear skies made the Chianti Tuscany wine sweeter to the eyes. Behind the tinted glass windows on the yacht the Captain tips his hat at the Ball player, signaling time for sail. The Ball player extends his hand to bring Sammy aboard the yacht. At first they enjoyed the cool breeze under the fading glow of the sunset on the front deck lounge on soft cloud white pillows. Their minds soaking up the soothing tunes lingering in the air from Andre Ward's saxophone. When the air chills Sammy's bare arms and the Ball player's body heat wasn't enough to keep her warm, the Ball player led her to warm air. The Ball player leads Sammy by the hand to the back deck lounge area up the stairs on the right to a glass ceiling and glass walls. On each square of the glass ceiling and walls is big white lines made from can snow, outlining a heart shape. In the center of the room is a glass table set for two. The two tall white candles illuminate the glass room. The flicking glow from the candles tickled sexual desire within Sammy. The spotlight ray of the moon peek through the heart shape tinted windows. The yacht settles on the Hudson. Laughter is enjoyed between two of them over a gourmet meal of grilled steak, buttery combination of Yukon potatoes mashed, and steamed fava beans. They both come to the realization they have share a major portion of their life together. Over the sweet chocolate mousse cake and vanilla ice cream the Ball player candy coats his belief in their joint relationship.

"Did I say you look amazing tonite?"

"Yes, this will make it the fourth time."

"My apologizes, I can't help it you all dressed in love"

"Well , I see you went all out. So now you think you gonna get you some?" Sammy's crystalline vision questions

"I got one night only to gain your confidence. I hope by morning you are willing to give love a chance."

"Oh, so it's deeper than a one night toss in the bed?"

"Jesus promised me a home here with you. I left the D league in Atlanta to be near you. I know giving myself to you is not only heart but body and soul. I want to prove I know how to value your worth."

"You a Christian now?"

"I'm not changed, I'm changing. I'm not asking you to marry me tomorrow. But let me court you. I'm telling you I'm not going nowhere."

"To love me is to produce the actions of love. To say I love you is to feel good about commitment to show love. So do you love me?"

"Love you I do. I've lived America's ideal life, smashed the televisions dream girl but with you it's this feeling words can't describe. I know you can feel it too. If it isn't love I don't know what it is."

The Ball player's right hand reaches under the table and emerges with a Valentine's Day card dated nineteen ninety three. Sammy's love stricken hands trembles as her teary eyes reads the personalized love letter. This was the card the Ball player gave Sammy to ask her out on their first date twenty years ago. He was lost in love with Sammy during their month long tutoring sessions. After a month of tutoring, the Ball player just couldn't get an enough of Sammy's loving smile. He sent out college radio love messages through song request on the campus radio station to try to get Sammy to notice him. The Ball player couldn't figure out how to tell Sammy about the love and how he was feeling. The love letter on the Valentine's Day card was given to Sammy from the Ball player and just like that, he won her heart. Inside the love letter written by the Ball player's hands "No one is gonna love you as much as I do." These are the words burning her eyes with tears right now.

"So where you at in this, we gonna dive into love like two teenagers?" the Ball player questions through his watery eyes.

"Yes, I'm ready to take a leap on love. Don't make me sorry or you'll be the one who gets hurt this time." Sammy's cinnamon spice is sweetened on the Ball player's truthful commitment glowing eyes.

"Since you are a control freak I have one request. Can I drive sometimes?"

"Yes, I'm willing to give up the wheel from time to time."

"Promise?"

"A piece of solitude, I got this!"

The Ball player knows the Sistah's signature words. From Sammy's promising words he knows she meant it, Sammy lives by the Sistah's code. The Ball player leads Sammy by the hand downstairs. Down the stairs, pass the food pantry; pass the small room with a twin size mattress to the soft candle lighted master bed room. The Ball player sugary soft chocolate dipped lips kisses on Sammy soft spot. The chocolate dipped lips inflame the memories of how sweet it is to be under the mellow but aggressive passionate touch of the Ball player. The Ball player is fine at pleasantly harmonizing the sexual essence of a woman. He transfers the moment to the tenth world of classical soul music. His professional feelers stir tingles through the blood, senses and veins. The sound of sexual appetite streams in the air. The naked sensitivity and sexual arousal sweetens the aroma of the air. Close eyes feel the goose bumps of throbbing longing. The sweet taste of the love letter creeps into the taste buds, sweetening the tongue with the vibe of love. The closer their body gets together the deeper the emotional explosion gets. When Sammy opens her heart to love she prepares for when the love isn't felt anymore. She'll see if his love letter promises least 'til Christmas. The delicate tender twist of naked skin lasted through the night. The Ball player took his shot at Sammy's heart. Sammy found out just why the Ball player is number one shooter in the D league. The steamy passion reminded Sammy of her spontaneous episode with the Ball player in the back seat of a taxi cab previous years. Sammy has taken a bite of the forbidden fruit of the past and is willing to bask in the juices. Sammy eyes open in the Sunday morning to breakfast in bed and a boyish grin on the Ball player's face.

"I just wanna say I love you girl." The Ball player confesses his emotions.

After breakfast they worked off the waffles, sausage and fruit salad with a two hour pleasing tender twist of naked skin before taking a regenerate catnap. The Ball player awakes to the purrs of Sammy's fluffy soft lips and fuzzy warm emotions. Sammy's soft sounds are itching with desire. Sammy's murmur is silenced with strokes of the Ball player's solid thick long chocolate dipped kitty cat scratching pole. Sammy had to literally pry her skin from the Ball player's grasp. She had to leave if she didn't she would be late to Teddy's custody celebratory dinner at Lorraine's house. The ball player steals a few more kisses before he drops Sammy off to her home. Sammy showered and dressed in record time. She had to be the adult at Lorraine's house; she can only imagine what was going on over there. Sammy rummages for left shoes under her queen size bed. Sammy had to stop in her tracks and take a deep breath; her perspiration was undoing her just taken shower. The light went off in her head. The Ball player was right, Sammy fascination with control consumes her every move and thought. Sammy realized anything and everything can't be in her hands. She was willing to open her hands, spread her fingers and just let go. She took her time construing her outfit while rebuilding a new kind of free. She slowly curls her hair, curving her first step toward a piece of solitude. Sammy arrives to Lorraine's house at the same time a beautiful familiar face is walking up the four steps to the front door. The beautiful familiar face use her right index finger to silence Sammy shouts of joy. Sammy silently runs over to the beautiful face wraps her arms around the body attached to the beautiful face and plant a million sweet kisses on the beautiful face. Sammy and the beautiful familiar face knocks on the front door to the sound of a party going on. Benny opens the front door and melody of good times and laughter avalanche out on to the outside air. Once the eyes in the house recognize the beautiful familiar face, there was a landslide of human body falling onto the body of the beautiful familiar face.

"Come on in, it's a celebration." Lorraine attempts to move the party back inside the house and off the porch.

"Whatever is your pleasure a dedication celebration that will last throughout the years is only shared with family." Is the sound avalanching out of Lorraine's house onto the windows and doors of all the houses on the street.

"Oh wow, my baby is here!" Rhonda intoxicated slurs shouts.
"Hi mom, I miss you." Paris wraps her beautiful arms around Rhonda's neck. Paris's words echoes is Rhonda's ear as Paris plants a kiss on Rhonda's cheek.

"Look at uncle cool and his gang." Paris jokes as she hugs Teddy, Kira Marc and TJ

"Come in baby girl, have a drink wit cha little old ma."

"Ma, you just don't change." Paris speaks through her laughter.

The males of the family Benny, Teddy and TJ gets to greet Paris before she is whisk off into the kitchen by the woman of the family. Kira and Marc join the woman of the family in the kitchen. The cackling of the hens in the kitchen was drowned out by sounds of music in the living room. Teddy is amuses by the gossip story behind Benny's latest movie collection. Benny is entertained by competing against TJ in a video game.

In the kitchen the women are trying to fill Paris's ears with the light of new events.

"Malik has a newborn baby?" Paris questions

"Oh Hun he brought the other "baby mother" to my restaurant." Marc exposes.

"What she look like Uncletiti?" Paris questions.

"She looks like my cousin." Kira interjects.

"Wow, it's a small world. I like ya cousin's style come with one man and leave with another. She gotta teach me how to act like a hoe but walk like a lady." Rhonda comments.

"Play nice." Sammy warns Rhonda.
"Wait a minute, you all are telling me Chyenne is gonna leave Malik for Polo's father?" Paris questions.

"Oh yeah and Malik whipped Ace ass. Malik was just 'bout to finish Ace right when Dwight broke up the fight."

"When was the fight?" Sammy questions, this was new information to her. Sammy hates to interrogate an alcohol sauced Rhonda.

"They fought at the pool party that just so happen to be at his wife "Crystal's" mansion. Ace straight up told Malik to his face that for the last 4 days he has been fuckin' Chyenne and Malik hooked off. That's when Benny called my jack 'cus some chick passed out at his party at the *Pink Pussy Cat*. No worries Brooklyn Taser da little thing back to life. Brooklyn needs anger management A.S.A.P. Ya girl shot at Roc's tires and one of his toes."

The kitchen roars in laughter from the fight at the pool party to the shot off toe. Real life is the best comedy.

"Brooklyn really shot Roc's toe off?" Paris questions. Sammy had plenty of questions but the tears of laughter prevent her from being able to breathe.

"Yes, she did! I was sitting in the car I watch her do it. She almost put electricity to Crystal for talking sideways dat same night."

"Wait a minute, I'm confessed. Where was Tay while you and Brooklyn was at the *Pink Pussy Cat?*"

"Oh Miss fire crotch had her eyes on Tugee." Rhonda reveals.

"Not again, she gotta stop fuckin wit these ruffnecks!" Marc disappointment is voiced.

"Roughnecks talk dirty but their mouths are clean. They grind hard for dirty money but their hearts are pure. They live in the cloudy public eye, everyone can see their dirty laundry but their clothes are spotless. A roughneck packs tools to put in that work. Holding hammers for rumble. Lays pile to make ya stumble. I love roughnecks myself." Paris confesses.

"Refill?" Lorrianne offers to pour alcohol to flush the smooth sight of Paris's womanhood.

"So how things went wit da Ball player?" Rhonda questions.

"He went all out! I had dinner on a yacht. I had a late night and early morning."

"So I guess you guys are getting back together?" Paris questions.

"To be honesty wit ya baby girl, they never truly broke up." Rhonda interjects.

"We are dating. Since you all in my BI who's climbing ya sheets these days Ms. Rhonda?" Sammy questions.

"Well, I'm glad you asked. I've been bitten by the love bug. I spent the night with King and not once did I make a move to jump his sexy body." Rhonda reveals.

"Ace father King?" Sammy questions.

"That man is my age. Rhonda ya crazy!" Lorraine diagnoses.

"Anyway, this morning we read the Sunday's comic strip together and one of the cartoons was about a woman who tried to convince her husband that the high heel shoe in the window is different than the shoes on her feet. So the husband rips out his hair because she keeps going on and on about nonexistent difference in the shoes. That isn't Tay?" Rhonda questions.

"Ya right, I read that comic strip every day and you right, it is about Tay. What if the artist is her secret admirer? He did send a painting." Marc concludes.

"I wanna know more about you wanting to date a man your mother's age. Rhonda, I hate that you play that stupid game but I rather you do dat than date an old man." Sammy states.

"Sammy, he is sexy for his age. He looks half as good as men my age. A pure *slick dick* ass nicca."

"I guess I'm gonna have to talk to you when you are sober."

"What ruffneck are you dating?" Rhonda questions Paris.

"Ma, I am not dating any one yet. I have two years left in college, after graduation I shall be dating but right now my mind is on my studies." Paris responds.

"You and Camille are going to be staring in the "40 year old virgin". I aint knockin' ya but how ya doing it, is beyond me." Marc comments.

"You can't miss what cha never had. Auntie taught me that." Paris states.

"That right!" Lorraine agrees.

"Why can a 20 year old understand but Chyenne old ass can't grasp the meaning of the same words?" Sammy comments.

"Because Chyenne aint listening." Rhonda concludes.

"You can tell Chyenne shit stinks but she gotta smell it for herself to be a believer." Marc comments.

"That still aint enough for Chyenne. She gotta taste, chew and shallow the shit before she realized the shit stinks." Rhonda corrects Marc's statement.

The cackling ladies and Marc burst into laughter over another round of drinks.

"How long you staying? Maybe we can get our hair and nails done before you go back, for old time's sake." Rhonda questions Paris.

"I'm leaving next Saturday, after Melissa's baby shower. I wanted to stay to Sunday to help move Amber into a new apartment but I got an exam on Monday. I gonna use Sunday to refresh my memory for the exam." Paris responds.

Teddy startles the ladies and Marc by cracking the kitchen door open. He pokes his head though the kitchen's swinging door.

"Sorry to break up da chitachatter but I need ya attention in the living room for a quick second."

Marc and the ladies relocated their gathering to the living room. Kira and Marc sat on the love seat side by side, limiting TJ's leg room on the couch. Benny lays on the floor like a Persian rug with controller to video game system glued to his hand. Lorraine, Rhonda, Sammy and Paris took a seat on the sofa. All eyes are on Teddy but his eyes are on the love seat couch. Teddy bends down on his knees in front of the Kira's, Marc's and TJ's feet.

"You two are the best things that happen in my life. I can't imagine living without you two and I don't want to." Teddy declares.

Out of each pocket on his crush plush deep brown velvet blazer, Teddy's hands emerge with a ring boxes in both hands.

"If you two are up to it? Can I share the rest of my life with you two? I can't legally marry both of you but I can offer a lifetime of a committed engagement."

Kira's and Marc's eyes swell with joy. Their cheeks are wet from the unisons tears streaming down their face.

"Yes, I will have you for the rest of my life." Marc accepts.

"You can't get rid of me. I love you and I'm here to stay." Kira accepts.

Teddy seals the deal by placing the rings on Kira's and Marc's hands. The room admires the sweet diced pineapple rings of marriage.

"They are coming to live with us?" TJ questions

"We gotta get a bigger apartment but yes, Kira and Marc are going to live wit us. You okay wit dat?"

"Yes, that's okay with me. Now Kira can watch a movie with me all the time and Uncletiti can take me to the park every day."

TJ hugs Kira and Marc. He is genuinely happy. He is receiving a step mother in Kira. Marc has always been an uncle slash aunt figure in TJ's life; having his Uncletiti full time was something TJ looks forward to.

****

Brooklyn's Maybach 62 S, 2011 model pulls off Timber Lake's parking lot. Brooklyn was practicing her target shooting skills at the shooting ranch to relax her nerves. Brooklyn drives down to the city from upstate. The car radio is set to soften Brooklyn's heart. The song of 2009's Sorry to Cece's apologizing today plays in the air. Brooklyn has never said "Sorry" to anyone in her life. She does what she does and thinks nothing of it. Usually, Brooklyn is a speedy demon on the highway but today she drives like a responsible adult. She dreads facing Lewis much less apologizing to him. Thank God for Harlem. Harlem has a way of embracing the soul and freeing the mind. Brooklyn parks her car in the parking lot of *Uncletiti's* restaurant. She sits absorbing the tunes from the radio. She pours her "Hennessy" straight complexion filling up her five foot two inch hourglass figure out the car. Her shinny jet black shirked curly hair falls down her intriguing honeydew melon light green Indian tunic dress to her butt. Her strong sexy calves support the six inch Indian theme honeydew melon light green Christian Louboutin Bollywoody pumps. Brooklyn's signature bangles chime on her waist as she walks to the entrance of the restaurant. Her India feathered earrings and curly hair blows in the early spring air. Her approach is a photographer's dream. Harlem hugs Brooklyn's legs from behind. Brooklyn immediately recognized the sweet embrace of Harlem. Brooklyn turns and bends down to return the love to Harlem. Brooklyn's eyes crawls at Vanessa standing behind Harlem.

"Lewis is a bitch nicca. He sends out his snowflake to face me?"
Brooklyn's chitachatter

"Are you surprise to see me? Well since Lewis can barely walk, I had to drop Harlem off. How could you? What could he have said to upset you to the point of tasering a man?" Vanessa questions.

Brooklyn bends down to the puzzled faced Harlem. Brooklyn rambles through Harlem's back pack and emerge with Harlem's iPad. She plugged Harlem's ears with the head phones. Brooklyn stands to fire at the snowflake's questions falling on her ears.

"I am gonna tell you like I've been begging Lewis to tell you. I speak to Lewis and Lewis speaks to you. Me and Lewis share Harlem. Me and you do not share nothing. I don't have to answer none of your fucking questions. What I did to Lewis can easy happen to you. Stand ya ground before you get hurt. This is ya final warning."

"Are you threatening me?"

"No "Mama Nessa" it's a promise! Try me; ask ya husband what trying me can get you? Just stand down!"

Brooklyn secures Harlem in the back seat of the Maybach 62 S, 2011 model before she pulls out her parking spot. Brooklyn unplugs Harlem's hearing. Brooklyn drives and talks to Harlem through the rearview mirror. Brooklyn siege any moment to observe the conspicuous diverse Harlem.

"Had fun with Daddy's house?" Brooklyn questions

"Yuppy! We go party. A biggest ever ball loon house. Bunch of ball lees. The biggest ever cake." Harlem responds in childish gibberish. "Sounds like a lot of fun."

"I was a butter fly."

"Really, face painting? You were painted as a butterfly? What colors?"

"Pink and yell low."

"Wow. What you wanna eat?"

Brooklyn didn't get a response. She looks in the rearview mirror at Harlem's motionless angelic sleeping face. Brooklyn continues to drive to pick Dino up from the supermarket. Brooklyn is cooking Sunday dinner tonight as Le'Roy's introduction to her family, Dino and Harlem. Brooklyn picks Dino up on the drive to her Condo apartment. Dino carries Harlem sleeping angelic body up to her room. Brooklyn handles the grocery bags. Brooklyn settles in and begins to prepare dinner. Dino enters the kitchen offering his assistants.

"Ma, whatcha cooking?" Dino questions

"I have 'jus cooked up a Dominican cold salad, lasagna and garlic bread. Did you pick up the pie from *Uncletiti's*?" Brooklyn responds with a question.

"Yes Mama. Miguel said he might stop by to edit the footage from last night party."

"That would be nice. I haven't seen him in a while, how's he going?"

"Ma, ask him ya self."

"You know Miguel don't talk much."

"Try him, he is very talkative."

The doorman is ringing the intercom. The doorman is asking permission to grant entrance to Miguel. Brooklyn voice consents Miguel's entrances. Brooklyn hugs and kisses Miguel at the door. Dino whisk Miguel to his temporary room on the second floor in Brooklyn's condo to visual brag about presents at the party last night with Holli Molli. Brooklyn's kitchen mitten hand is pulling the lasagna's pan out the oven. The ringing of the intercom startles Brooklyn. The doorman on the other end of the intercom is asking permission to grant entrance to Le'Roy. Le'Roy greets Brooklyn at the door with flowers in one hand and a bottle of red wine in the other hand. Le'Roy sets the table in the dining room. Le'Roy takes the time to update Brooklyn of the party bus affairs.

"De'Andre was pissed Traci came with him but left with Malik. Malik confessed Traci is his Baby mother. De'Andre went from being pissed to apologetic. Then we had to consol Anthony. You remember Anthony from the art exhibit at the museum?"

"I know who your cousin is."

"Well his heart was broken 'cus Tugee left with Tay. He's been crushing on that woman since we were kids. But Tay's eyes see right pass him. He was hurt."

"Maybe Anthony is Tay secret admirer." Brooklyn's chitachatter

****

"Well, I had my share of men from Blacks to whites to pure Indians. Tugee had that I'm never scared in his cup with 24's on his truck and 24's fronts in his mouth. Tugee is different from Mr. Bryson Mitchell's, Henni complexion with a bone crushing muscular frame. Tugee's body moves like Usher up in the club. Tugee has a get crunk attitude like Jon. Sorry I was fooled by the tip of Bryson's grand hustle. Tugee was good sex but Bryson had dat Luda red carpet dick. What, you really surprise I fuck Tugee? At leaset I used protection I could be bitter about the AIDS shit and spread it like mustard but I'm not living like dat. I'm still gonna get mines off. I'm wrong for that? From VA to GA from Miami to the Lou from the Carolinas to Alabama even down in Mississippi I'm looking for a man with the southern values, willing to provide, protect and penetrate the queen of their world. I get Butterflies in my gut thinking about finding the right man. I wonder what's up wit Anthony? If looks could kill I would've died last night." Tay's chitachatter

"All I ever wanted was your love and devotion. I wasn't looking for my heart to be broken."

Love and Devotion
Faith Evans
Love and Devotion

For the past five days the Sistahs have been hard at work. Brooklyn juggles family, work and Le'Roy in the beautiful eyes of Harlem. Rhonda maneuvers around all week long at her accounting firm with King in her eyes. Sammy closed Brooklyn's custody case this week. Sammy's arrangement between Brooklyn and Lewis is solid. Lewis has been court ordered to keep a lid on his silent partner. Tay's mind, body and soul were consumed by preparation for Melisa's baby shower and the organization of Amber's moving party. The curveball of help was in the hands of Chyenne. Chyenne has been at Tay's house since she ran from Malik's mother's words of advice last Sunday. Melissa enters the rented hall holding onto Marc's right arm. Tears of joy swell up in Melissa's eyes. Melissa is mesmerized by the decoration and set up as her mind pictured and voiced her happiness to Tay. The blue room is decorated by Steven's designs. The center pieces, rafts hanging on the wall and the wishing well of gifts are made of baby boy pampers. The survivor keepsakes rattles are also made of baby boy pampers. The detail features on the five foot long and two feet tall milk chocolate frosted sleeping baby boy cake is amazing. The sleeping baby boy cake is laying on his stomach, his cutie little face has a blue pacifier. The sleeping baby boy cake has his pampered bottom sticking up in the air. The pamper reads: presenting prince Mecca. The sleeping baby boy cake is surrounded by southern food catered by *Uncletiti's* restaurant. Melissa and Omar relationship was running on pure faith. Their jobs keep them far apart for days. There's something about faith, the further apart their bodies were the closer their hearts grew together. Melissa is Omar's first lady. He was use to being a part of the single good life, until he found a faithfully love with Melissa. He decided he would never find a love like this again. Melissa and Omar will never let each other go. They are keeping the faith of their true love. There's not many to have a strong faithfully and hopefully love with someone without having the person lay with all night long. Every relationship is unique. Love is blind and if you can't see that then you gets no love. Today's baby shower is Melissa faithful Christmas. Melissa's celebrity clients pop in and drop off their gifts. Omar's brothers in NY blues also popped in with gifts and popped back out. Omar and the males devoted to attendance were closed off in a room being entertained by a basketball game. Chyenne was summoned to relay a message of a needed store run to Omar for ice. To sweeten the request, Chyenne was given a six pack of ice cold beers to carry to the room of man along with the store run request. At the entrance to the room of man Chyenne drops the six of glass bottled beer as her eyes soak up a vision from the television. During half time at basketball games people can take advantage of having the world's attention and nationally declare their love. Today halftime declaration of love is Traci marriage proposal to Malik. Malik answers with a tongue down Traci's throat. The Sistahs run to Chyenne's side. Their eyes are glued to the television.

"Aint that ya husband?" Omar questions Chyenne.

"That was her husband! She aint got him no more." Calvin comments.

The Sistahs begins to consol Chyenne's infamous eye sprinklers.

"Stop ya cryin. You don't care. You want Ace remember?" Rhonda questions.

"I remember when Malik use to love me. The embarrassment of losing my guarantee *waters my pain. I couldn't take Malik being close to me but he is now miles away. He seen too much but didn't know enough. The pain of strong wrong is starting to creep into my bones." Chyenne's chitachatter*

"I know ya type. Don't want a nicca but don't want nobody else to have him neither. Selfish!" Rhonda's chitachatter

"Sweetie, I know ya hurting but today it's about Melissa's unborn son. Can we focus? Let's get back to the showering Melissa with our love and devotion. A piece of cake." Tay suggests.

"A piece of mind." Chyenne agrees.

"A piece of pie." Brooklyn agrees.

"A piece of ass." Rhonda agrees.

"A piece of solitude." Sammy agrees.

The Sistahs return to their post as Benny and Polo fetched the ice from the store. Chyenne returns to Marc's side behind the sleeping baby boy cake, laboring over the hot southern food serving portions of food for the guest. Kira stands beside Marc serving can sodas. Food servers are wearing light blue tee shirts with "Baby Helper" written on the back. Brooklyn returns to her post next to the over flowing wish well of gifts. Brooklyn stands on cotton candy light blue Christian Louboutin Bollywoody heels. Her fairy tale custom intriguing cotton candy light blue spandex tank top and mixing colored tutu. The front of her intriguing cotton candy light blue spandex tank top reads, "Baby Helper". Brooklyn's post is guardian angel of the gifts. Rhonda's spontaneous light blue baby's whole sleeper with the words "Baby Helpers" airbrushed on the back is covering her body. Rhonda's post is being her chi chi self floating through the guest giving them a free chuckle or two. Sammy's maternal instinct is running the baby shower games by the rules. Sammy's five foot frame of pure cinnamon spice looks like an adorable cutie in the authentic light blue baby's whole sleepers with the words "Baby Helpers" airbrushed on the back. Tay's enlarged breast stretch out the airbrushed letter spelling out "Baby Helper" on her naive cotton candy light blue spandex tank top. Her voluminous bottom cheeks peeks out the end of her mini custom cotton candy light blue tutu. Tay's post at the entrance giving out acknowledgment hugs, kisses and saying "Thank You" at her discretion. Tay is all giving out custom baby shower ribbon corsages and memory keepsakes with deliberation. Tay has already pricked two people with the custom baby shower ribbon corsage's stick pin. Just when things had calm down Crystal, Lisa, and Traci falls through the door. Tay gives the three the standard hug and kiss. Crystal is the third person to be pricked by the stick pin to the custom baby shower ribbon corsage.

"I'm so sorry." Tay makes an attempts at a fake apologize.

"No worries, that's a small thing to a giant such as me. Where shall I pull my gift? It has to be somewhere safe. This is a Gucci baby bag, net value 2 gees." Crystal states.

"All gifts go in the wishing well." Tay notifies.

"Nice shoes girl, what are they and where can I get a pair?" Tay questions Lisa.

"Are you making over 7 seasons old Dior hand me downs? Step up ya fashion knowledge. You are a movie star slash model right?" Crystal's thin upper lip distinguished superior tone intercepts Lisa's response to the compliment.
Before Tay could alert the authorities like Sammy to deal with Crystal's down grading thin upper lip distinguished superior tone, Chyenne has found her way to the door first.

"Hello Traci. My name is Chyenne, you know Malik's wife. How are you going to propose to my husband?" Chyenne's hurt streams in her words.

"Sweetie, Malik stopped being your husband a long time ago, just like you stopped being a wife a long time ago." Traci responds.

Chyenne's broiling angry swings in her right fist back by the strength of betrayal of devotion from Malik. Traci fights back. She lands a hit to Chyenne's face. All Chyenne's mental and physical strength grabs on to Traci's hair. Traci grabs hands full of Chyenne's mix bred hair. They are lock together like two dogs in heat. Chyenne puts her backbone into the rapid blow to Traci's face with her right hand while her left hand had a power hold on Traci's hair. Traci continues to pull Chyenne's hair. Traci begs Cheyenne to let go but Chyenne responds with more rapid blows to Traci's face. Traci retaliates by biting into Chyenne's face. The Sistah's jump in and break up the fight. The fight has drawn the attention of the whole party. The hits Chyenne throws are hitting Traci but meant for Crystal. Melissa has had enough of grown woman behaving like teenage girls. She couldn't stand for this foolishness. She waddles out Tay's gift of a classic wooden rocking chair. As Melissa gets closer to the crowd she starts shouting her opinions of their actions.

"Ayeeeee!" Melissa shouts the sound of a woman's priceless soul falling onto the Kelly green moss of evil fungus.

Melissa has stumbled over a DJ's cable wire. She falls flat onto her stomach. The crowd stops what they're doing and rushed to Melissa's side. Her screams festers in the heart of on lookers.
"Call 9-1-1 NOW!" Marc shouts over his tears.

Omar pulls out his cell phone and obeys Marc's request. Melissa cries of agonizing pain pierces the hearts of everyone in the room. She lies in a creek of clear water with streaks ruptured red rum. The heart broken crowd cries along with Melissa. The two ambulances arrive in record time. One ambulance for Chyenne's bit wound and the other for Melissa. Melissa was taken out on the gurney with Marc at Melissa's right side and Omar on the left. They both were allowed to ride in the back with the

Melissa wails of excruciating pain. Each and every one of Melissa's screams is torturous blows to Marc's and Omar's hearts. The one EMS worker riding in the back working on Melissa has emotional droplets in her eyes. Chyenne had to walk out to the ambulance.

"Chyenne is always gonna be a bottom feeder, always fighting over dick that aint hers, what a shame! Time moves on but people stay the same." Crystal comments to Lisa as Chyenne walks pass with the EMS workers.

Chyenne cocks her right fist back and fires it into Crystal's thin upper lip distinguished superior tone. Chyenne's fist heat burns Crystal's front tooth loose from her gum. Crystal's priceless front tooth landed in front of her three thousand dollar Dior shoes covering her feet.

"Now that's a hit right there!" Rhonda comments through laughter.

A third ambulance is called for the toothless babbling Crystal. At the nearest hospital the whole party waits in the waiting area to hear anything about Melissa and the baby. Chyenne has siege the moment while everyone's attention was captivated with worry. Chyenne received a tetanus shot and breaking news that she was three months pregnant with Malik's baby. Chyenne sneaks out the back door of the hospital. She dials Ace's number. Chyenne sat forty five minutes in the diner waiting for Ace to arrive. The waitress has started to harass Chyenne. Chyenne is standing up from the table with defect in her eyes. Ace shows up to her table. Ace has three women hanging from his arms.

"Meet my lucky charms. These are my sweet frosted colored marshmallows. Meet Toni, Tony and Tori." Ace introduces.

"I must be from planet mercury feeding on Ace's pillow talk. It's my anniversary of feeling so foolish. I once accepted Ace dissemination of his body around to other woman in my face, now it's one of the things I regret. He feels comfortable with flaunting his magically delicious young pot of

gold. *Looking at Ace sitting in front of my eyes with southern California bleach blond twenty something's he must feel good in a world where it never rains tears. I can't believe this is the man I chose out of a million I gave my heart to. I know age aint nothing but a number but looking at these teenie bobbers I feel like my age is rocking the boat to senior citizen status. At my best I can be more than a woman, I can be a Sistah. I wonder if me being pregnant will grant me another try again at my marriage. Will Malik wanna give our love another chance? Or will I end up Queen of the damned?" Chyenne's chitachatter*

"It's nice to meet you all. Ace, you look like you back to your old self."

"Well I've been feeding on the 12 vitamins and mineral in this trio source of calcium. Crystal put me out so I moved on. That Crystal is a pure bitch. She is proof the Devil do wear Prada. Cum to find out the binding marriage certificate is a fake. She didn't even have a descend bone in her cosmetically altered body to tell me. Lisa broke the news."

Chyenne's mind sheds light on the dark part of her relationship with Ace. Chyenne's mind reminds her of all the nights she cried herself to sleep while Ace serenade her ears with moans and groans of sexual pleasure coming from the wall of the second bedroom. Chyenne's mind brings tears to her cheeks. Crystal hurt him with lies but he bruised Chyenne. Ace's actions broke the blood vessel of Chyenne's mental and physical compassion for him. In Chyenne opinion, stripping Ace of her mansion and money wasn't enough.

"Whatcha crying for? You belonged to 'ole dude. I couldn't belong to nobody. You are married to 'ole dude, it was wrong for me but we gonna always be best of friends. You take care of yourself. Live life not ya mental pictures of life."

Chyenne's twenty minutes of nonstop eye water sprinklers takes ten minutes for Chyenne to clear it up. She drinks like an Irish fish on the intoxication of the dullness of her mind. She is overwhelmed with the feeling of stupidity. Finally, after getting herself together Chyenne calls Malik after ducking him for twelve days. She slows down and reevaluates her circumstances. She realized that being pregnant with her destiny child her fate is in the arms of Malik.

****

Malik aids Traci with her buries and lumps. Traci jokes chop Malik up with laughter. Traci is taking the fight lightly. The sound of love in her skin has sparked jealously in her own cousin, Kira. Kira believes Traci and Malik's love is stoned walled by marriage. They only had a future in sex not in commitment. Kira words weren't going to make Traci lose her way to Malik's heart. She vows to love Malik to the end of time. Malik deservers Traci's love is her sentiment. Malik enjoying been with Traci, she brings his sexy back. Their relationship is fresh as a summer love but crisp winter love making wasn't new. Malik likes their conversations. Traci is a sexy woman that lets Malik talk to her and replies with intellect. Malik's phone vibrates. He looks at the caller identifying screen. Malik's thoughts are "What goes around comes around." He presses ignore to Chyenne's call, which was the same thing she's been doing to him for twelve days. Chyenne leaves a voice message. Malik listens to another crying song in acapella sung in Chyenne's tears. Chyenne's voices the same promises all over again being recorded on Malik's voice mail. Chyenne calls twenty more times. Traci had enough of the damn girl for one day. Malik's tongue massage relaxes Traci's mind. The sound of love making moan from Malik's and Traci's lips all night long drowned out the sound of the rings on Malik's phone.

****

Melissa wide awake lifeless body lies in the hospital bed. The view staining her vision is the light blue wishing well filled to the max with presents. On her pillow is an angry fistful of tears. She can't believe the second life that was shinny dipping in her womb is out. Melissa three pound baby boy's life hangs in a series of wires and tubes. The tubes tunnel Melissa's heart. Doctor's voice fortunate life in Melissa's being. Melissa blames her bad habits of flashing her bright spring dreams of human development with a soaring career and escalating family growth as the cause of decline into a black summer nightmare. She knows her woman's work is to smile and hide the hurt of the clipping of her pretty wings. Whenever, wherever and whatever happens, Melissa prays for a chance to get to know her baby boy. A lifetime of wondering will never vanish. Melissa's mind, body and soul are broken into pieces. She has refused all visitors including Omar. She lies resting after a screaming match with the doctors. She is not going to let the doctors play the possibility game. Melissa's mind congregate poetic words to compose her feeling into words:

Through the wire I feed nourished and watched you grow. I felt you flow. A person I beg to know.
Through the wire I heard your heartbeat the sound 'cause heat to rosey my cheeks and warm my heart 'cause I love your heart's melody so much. A melody my ears crunch into memory.
Through the wire I met you in 3d images, your hand, finger, feet and toes. God's power is a miracle and it shows. Your ears, eyes and nose perfectly grown.
Through the wire I fell and lost my maternal glow a possible fatal blow. I'm dying inside and nobody knows. Hurt so strong can't help but show. Regret fester and grew.
Through the wire your heart music rhythm faintly beeps. The sound creeps under my skin and digs deep inside my heart. The beeping music of her heart makes my heart leaps to its lyrics.
Through the wire I pray this isn't the end 'cause I look forward to being a motherly best friend.
Through the wire I tell you I'll be missing the one chance to be kissing and loving you.
Through the wire I sing my loving song praying you not already gone.

Through the wire as soon as we get home I'll never be alone.

"Freeze-framed yelling, "Please Play!" She got me up all night."

Power Trip
J. Cole Ft Miguel
Born Sinner

Chyenne's body, heart and mind are racing as she sits completely still, not even batting an eyelid. Her body, heart and mind are competing for reasoning of her recent actions.

"What imbecilic would jeopardize their whole world for Ace. Ace aint worth killing my home. Ace aint worth being alone. I'm such a fucking moron. I should've loved Malik right when I had the chance. Now I might be ass out, literally. My heart is ready, willing and able to plead the black and blues of my love to Malik." Chyenne's chitachatter

The darkness of her month long demonstration of blatant disrespect and disloyalty to her ten year marriage is the light in her mind. How will she be able to express remorse for an individual deed? Chyenne fingers herself as part of the cause of her marriage stumbling down but she fingers Traci with her pointer and middle finger. Chyenne's unfaithfulness of their verbal unison pledged before family, friends and the heavenly father can't be wiped clean with a magic sponge. Chyenne inflicted the blue bruises to her marriage. Chyenne's body, heart and mind assemble a figment of all the favorable traits complied over the years of knowing Ace. Chyenne's favorable visual memory crumbs drops on the trail of enthusiastic little boy that stole a lollipop from Pop's corner store for Chyenne's sixth birthday. The favorable enthusiastic little boy shines his growth with sympathy hands available to Chyenne when her grandmother passed onto heaven. The sympathy young boy develops into a considerate young man surprised Chyenne with an eighteenth birthday party. The favorable figment look, talks and walk just like Ace. He standing up and laying down just like Ace would. Yesterday sitting at the dinner table across from Ace with his three groupies made Chyenne finally realized that the figments of her memory are just in mind. The person she so deeply loves doesn't exist. Chyenne sits and waits. Her nerves are numb. Her physical heartache of buying into a dream nobody was selling. Her mental agony of plain stupidity is the true torture. The torment of her feelings hurting is she knows she has cause the same pain in Malik's heart. Her light at the end of the tunnel is her spiritual ruling that the unborn baby will be enough to appeal her love and sorrow and piece her and Malik back together.

"Good morning. How are you doing? Not feeling well?" Malik's chestnut syrup questions Chyenne.

Malik talk and walks as he approaches the table at the restaurant. He takes a sit across from Chyenne. He looks closer at her eyes. She appears to coming down with a flu or something is Malik's observation. Chyenne's is distress.

"I'm over here love sick and this nicca is light on his feet. All chipper. He called me here. I was gonna start off with a sorry or two but now I'm just gonna shut up and listen. Shit, Ace already shitted on me, what's the worst can happen? If he gets too crazy imma gut punch that ass with the baby." Chyenne's chitachatter

"No, I'm not sick."

"You sure?" Malik questions as his eyes take third and fourth helpings.

"Oh are you referring to the dark circle on my cheek? That bitch Traci bit me!"

"No need for name calling of an absent person."

"So what's up Malik? You ask me to come here for what?"

"You don't want to talk over breakfast?"

"Are you trying to lighten the blow by stalling? Malik what's up?"

"Nothing's up. I just wanted to disgust our future...." Malik clears his throat.

"Uhmmm, it's clear we have chosen path without one another and I think we should go with that and finalize it." Malik continues.

"Oh, so you're divorcing me to marry Traci? The truth please!"

"Would you believe me if I said I'm in love?

The words was treacherous enough for Chyenne's heart but what her eyes saw in Malik's eyes and smile turn up the torment in her mental, physical, and spiritual being.

"Please don't cry. I still love and will do anything for you but be with you. You can keep the house and the car they both are paid for. I came here to tell you, you don't have to worry. I've completely moved out. My mother is at the house waiting for you come home. I'm gonna give you a thousand dollars every two week to take care of Capri. If you need anything just call me."

"I'd didn't think it'd get this bad." Chyenne's words climbs over her tears cracking her voice.

"If one forces something to break don't be mad it's broken."

Malik's phone rings. Malik answers his phone and said maybe two words before Traci appeared in the restaurant. Traci sashayed over to the table with shades on her face concealing her black eye. Traci grabs a chair from a vacant table and has a seat between Chyenne and Malik at the square table.

"Chyenne, I wanna start of by saying I'm sorry. The fight was very immature and we are women. We should behave as such."

"She is compelling me to do this. Is this bitch up in here power trippin 'cus she got Malik on her arm? Gut punch time." Chyenne's chitachatter

"Malik, I'm pregnant."

"I'm gotta figure out in my mind what to do? I can't find the words to say." Malik's tongue is tied.

"You not happy? We were trying." Chyenne questions

"I don't know how to feel." Malik answers.

"You sure it's his?" Traci questions.

"Yes, Malik I'm sure it's yours. I'm 4 months. Traci, you are the new kid on the block. Ya are on step by step bases. Hang tough kiddo."

"Chyenne, you have to calm down all this yelling can't be good in your condition."

"Malik fuck you and this bitch!"

Chyenne stands up. Like a sweet breeze on a hot summer day Chyenne is gone. Malik is unease. His intent wasn't meant to upset Chyenne. Somehow, Chyenne has maneuvered herself sympathy to manipulate empathy in Malik's heart. Malik restored his composer but his eyes told Traci his mental emotional state has been touch by Chyenne's tears. Traci is satisfied with Malik's proof their love is at its highest. Chyenne dropped a bomb on Malik's heart. His pride stands strong off his outstanding publicly known noble fatherhood. Malik's heart wants to cuddle the wounded Chyenne back to health and dry her bleeding tears flowing from her heart but his mind reinstates Chyenne's habit of unstable flying the coup once her organs is temporary cured. Chyenne's sensitivity feathers can be ruffled at the drop of a dime. Her body, mind, and soul immediately fleet at the sight of an uncomfortable nest of thorny feeling. As soon as Chyenne's back faced Malik and Traci the sprinkles of losing a genuine black gradually showers from her eyes. Chyenne's heart is hit with the windstorm of the reality of her current circumstances. Her body fights the strong whether of cloudburst of various emotions to her car parked in the restaurant's lot. Chyenne's emotional shaking right hand fidgets the car key into the door. Once Chyenne is in the car her head falls on the staring wheel. The hurricane passionate regret and stupidity twist Chyenne's mental state. Malik's cold words thunder in Chyenne's mind. Her soul's distaste for Traci blustered in her bite wound on her cheek. Chyenne's tornado storm of her feeling spins inside, instead of showering down her face. She begins to drive the car and her mind through the highway to Tay's house. Today's Amber's moving party. Chyenne stood up last night talking with Tay. Everything she told Tay she was going to say she didn't say. Before Chyenne's right foot took the first step to the entrance to Tay's cherry stone townhouse, Tay opens the front wooden door.

"What happen?" Tay questions

Tay's words are a gusty storm of tears whirlwind into Chyenne's eyes. Tay aids Chyenne's light weight sweater off her body. Chyenne's body exhales as if the light weight sweater weights heavy on her shoulder. Chyenne words scatter the sequence of retelling of words surrounding Ace, Malik and Traci. Tay ushers Chyenne to the kitchen table. Tay hopes Chyenne's love confessions will talk her mind off Melissa. Chyenne's dark black prints around her eyes reveals she is running on two hours of sleep. Chef Robert takes a glance at Chyenne's wet cheeks and snotty nose and begins to pour two glasses of red wine. On second thought, Chef Robert retrieves a third glass for him. Chyenne's pity parties are downers, might as well intoxicate the spiral fall into her emotions. Chyenne's blunder tears squirts at random. Tay's emotional sensor is ticklish as she waits for health state news of Melissa's and the baby. At the end of Chyenne's verbal cyclone of emotions Tay's eyes were teary. Before Chyenne and Tay could shower in their tear of sorrow the door bell rings.

"Ding Dong," sounds the door bell.

Calvin heads to the front door to answer the sound of the bell. As soon as Calvin opens the front door TJ darts pass Calvin to the kitchen. T.J flashes through the kitchen out the back door into the yard waving at Chyenne and Tay.

"What's goody little homie?" Teddy questions.

Calvin claps his right hand with Teddy's right hand and wraps his left arm around Teddy's back along with brotherly love.

"Aint shit, I'm just chill. I see ya brought the girls out?
Stevie can't see ya love jay shot hop in these sets hips."

Calvin compares Teddy's lifestyle of having the best of both genders to a reality series superstar whom fail to accomplish the same lifestyle. Teddy arrives with his two fiancés. Kira and Marc arms are balancing stacks of large aluminum pans filled with southern food. Southern food leftovers from yesterday's baby shower. Chef Robert frees Kira's arms of the overload of large aluminum pans. Chef Robert and Marc head to the dining room. Chef Robert alerts Tay's ears of the beginning arrival of guest to Amber's moving party. Chef Robert returns his childish behavior back to the children enjoying the sunny day. Tay's backyard is a mini public park. A large jungle gym equipped with tire swings and tube slides. April and Harlem are dressing dolls and combing the doll's hair. Nico is building with oversized Legos. Capri is practicing her ballet moves. T.J is enjoying his hand held video game. Kira is enjoying the view of the children in the back yard over the point of view from the Sistahs in the kitchen. Calvin and Teddy migrate to the living room.

"Yo, Benny showed me ya last week's production. You young boys have ya fun now."

"A Rack and Back City production is a full service of visual sexual pleasure. The motto is to make it nasty for your ecstasy sugar entertainment. You gotta see last night's production. Polo's pops gave us three chicks named "Toni" I gotta copy of the draft. You know once Miguel put his technical stink on it will be a featured film. "

"Show me last week. You went fool wit those two chicks in the Jacuzzi."

"I would invite ya to a filming but I know 1 chick aint gonna rock with that plan but ya got ya self 2 chicks. You'll never get a live performance!"

"With them 2 I make movies every night." Teddy jokes.

Calvin pokes fun at Teddy's relationships. Teddy laughs at the humor. Calvin begins to set up the draft production on his portable DVD player.

"Ding Dong," sounds the door bell.

Calvin heads to the front door again to answer the sound of the bell. Brooklyn, Dino, and Miguel enters Tay's house. Brooklyn gives Calvin a kiss on his cheek and proceeds to find the Sistahs. Calvin claps his right hand with Dino right hand and wraps his left arm around Dino back with brotherly love. Calvin repeats the brotherly love ritual with Miguel. Miguel hands Calvin the final cut of last night's Rack and Back City production. Teddy watches the young, wild and free x-rated production with Calvin, Dino and Miguel. In the kitchen Chyenne serenade Brooklyn's ears with the heartbreak hotel song of self pity. Benny and Sammy enters Tay's house through the back door leading into the kitchen. Benny parked two blocks down from Tay's house. He couldn't find parking on Tay's street. It was just easier to enter through the back instead of walking an extra block. Benny gives hugs and kisses to the Sistahs before forcing his attention to Miguel's final cut of last night's film. Chyenne wastes no time to sing her melody of rues of depression.

"Ding Dong," sounds the door bell.

"You all gonna have to start tippin a brother if I'm gonna be da doorman, ya heard!" Calvin shouts towards the kitchen.

It's Rhonda accompanied by King and Polo. Rhonda pulls herself from King's side to join her Sistah's in the kitchen. King's attention is left to the movie playing on the portable DVD player. Polo comes into the kitchen and hands Chyenne a bag of cosmetics. He then joins the boys club in the living room. Rhonda enters the kitchen. The despairing heartbreaking sorrow blue smog in the air is stifling. Humidity slaps Rhonda's carefree luminous white chocolate skin face.

"Oh, hell no it more muggy in here than it is outside and it's 90 today. Chyenne, what happened? Why are you in here suffocating everybody?" Rhonda questions.

"Rhonda, don't be so callous. She's has been legitimately wounded. Malik went hard." Tay passive naïve tone eased the demand to Rhonda's behavior with words of facts.

"Tay let her talk. You all already know the story."

Chyenne retells her tragic cold world story started with dinner with Ace in between breakfast with Malik and ended with the sideline story of

Traci. This is Tay's fourth time hearing the same story but just like the other Sistahs, the acid rain rolled down their cheeks forming puddles on their chins. The flow of the rain drops from the Sistahs eyes is the warm up the light of the uncovering third power of a Sistah. Each Sistah has spiral into a relationship with luggage of the past. Luggage packed with shirts of "I can't get enough", pants of feeling loved and panties of "I only want to give it to". In the arms of the past a star is born. Going to bed at night with the "all I want is you" in the morning waking up with a cup up on another shot at trouble of the past. Blowing up the good forgiving and the bad forgetting that nobody's perfects. The heart pumps love and war ora from the past. Workouts with men that truly belong to the past. Friday night lights dances with "hopes" of this time being the right time in your purse. Attention deficit of present, future is a beautiful bliss of arrears riding the dead horse of the past. Chyenne practices of spending more love than is receiving love on the wrong one now she is paying the expensive price, costing her the right one. Ace's sharp cut into reality stashed the Sistahs, as well as Chyenne. Ace's sarcastic audience display gave the Sistahs a tart taste in their emotions. The harsh handle of Malik's tangy soft words in front of Traci was tingling in the Sistah's stomachs. The third power of a Sistah is to start the rebellion inside against the heart. The outside will soon show the libration of affection, nurturing, protective in the glow of the skin. Admiration of self while remaining loyal to self is a Sistah.

"This concludes this story." Rhonda announces.

"Damn Rhonda! Why are you being colder then the AC?" Chyenne questions

"It hurts me that you are hurting but I can't be sad for someone who jus' don't listen. I hate to say I told you so but..." Rhonda replies.

"Chyenne is jus hard headed sometimes. We all are." Tay defends.

"Now it time to start the heal process. No dating until you're ready." Sammy advises Chyenne.

"You can't even be mad 'cus we practically begged her not to as Sistahs but as woman. But on another note I got news." Rhonda announces.

"Spill it, 'cus I got somin to tell too." Brooklyn states

"I came here wit King. I spent the nite at his house in Jersey for the second time after I drop Paris off at the airport. Poor thing worrying her little head off about Melissa and the Baby all night." Rhonda continues.

"Tay, you heard anything yet?" Marc asks. He is being so quite the Sistahs forgot he was in the room. His tongue is tied with heavy concern for Melissa.
"He was such a gentleman but my koowie was slobbing all nite. I wanna jump his bones but we watched *"Five heartbeats"* and cuddle. I can't take it. It's be a week of no sex. I feel like a Bitch in heat! I don't wanna blow this, I really like King. He's a Slick Dick guy, plenty chick throw da koowie at his feet but I'm trying to be different. I'm dying!" Rhonda's lips is spiting as fast as her feet pace the kitchen floor.

"Focus on the things you like about him." Chyenne advises.

"I love the higher learning of relaxation we share in each other's company. Like this morning we read the newspaper's Sunday comics together. Tay, I'm telling you it's about you. It called "Over the heel". In today's comic the wife hides heels in the kitchen cabinet. The husband is having breakfast out of a pair of heels, one for cereal and one for juice. The wife pops her lid when she sees him. He says "It's not fine china, it says made in china on the bottom."

The Sistahs roar in laughter. The thought of someone disrespecting Tay's heels like that was more than humors. Tears of laughter squirt out their eyes.

"Well, I don't know if the cartoon artist is talking about Tay but I know who gave you the painting." Brooklyn reveals.

"Who?" the Sistahs asks

"Le'Roy told me it's his cousin Anthony."

"He's a geek." Tay declares.

"That's your downfall. Your gangster killer glorification with their long snap backs and tattoos. You have dated many different faces but the same person. Change your taste for happiness." Sammy advises Tay.

"Speaking of killer, Santana dropped Nico off Friday. He's been deployed. Speaking of bouncing, what's the word on you and the ball player Missy?"

"Did you fuck him?" Rhonda asks

"You gotta ask? It's Tay we talking about for crying out loud. Of course she did!" Chyenne states

"And you know this. Man are like a box of chocolate, you gotta taste everyone 'til find ya favor." Tay confirms.

"So are you wit da ball player?" Brooklyn asks.

"We've been flying together through the kitchen of hell. We even had lunch at the Devil's own red café, never stopping take in the air of each other. I'm in love all over again with the same man. Crazy aint it?" Sammy reveals.

"Did you fuck him?" Rhonda asks

"You gotta ask? Listen to how she is talking. Of course she did! " Chyenne states

"Shit, at least somebody is getting it." Rhonda comments

"Rhonda, you gotta relax. Do you know how he feels about you?" Chyenne questions

"King absolutely adores me but I'll truly know how he feels when I get it off the smooth skin muscle."

"Relax, have a talk with him." Tay suggest

"Tay, only you solve problems wit talking. Imma action kinda girl but I want him to want me as much as I want him."

"Well, I invited Anthony to help with the move. He should be here shortly wit Le'Roy." Brooklyn confesses.

"It's gonna be awkward. I already fuck one of his friends that I know of. How's thing with Le'Roy?" Tay voices her discomfort in Brooklyn's actions.

"I like him a lot and he likes me but I don't know if he can swallow Brooklyn Zoo. For his birthday next week imma dress up sexy with my 44, either he like it love it or leave it. Why ya ask?" Brooklyn asks.

"Well, you definitely know where he stands when he sees ya guns." Sammy declares.

"So I know to act chi chi for your sake." Tay announces.

"That would be nice." Brooklyn accepts Tay offer to be fake to Anthony.

"A piece a cake." Tay promise good behavior to Brooklyn.

"Ding Dong," sounds the door bell.

Le'Roy and Anthony arrive. Their presence brings in the gloominess in Tay's face. Anthony has brought an edible floral arrangement. Brooklyn greets Le'Roy with her lips.

"I heard through the grape vine the last one I sent you barely got to enjoy." Anthony voice sings into Tay's ears as his lips dance on her cheek.

The last edible floral arrangement arrived at Tay's house anonymously about a week ago. Tay's children and the Sistahs destroyed it with their taste buds.

"Thanks." Tay's wide smile says more words then cappuccino lips.

"I know its coward shit to sent anonymous flowers and gifts. But I have had a crush on you forever, fear kept me from your beauty. You're such a fascinating woman."

"Well, this has gotta be the longest crush ever." Chyenne concludes.

"If he gets to ever hit it, it's gonna be the longest bust ever." Rhonda jokes at Anthony's expense.

"Imagine the trail of chicks cryin' 'cus they know that they lost out on the chance to win his heart. He had it well kept under lock and key for Tay." Le'Roy exposes.

"I know you not talkin Le'Roy. Brooklyn gotcha ya nose wide open. The players club has kicked you out and disowned you. Your crime of wifin' in night club and cuffin in the daylight has the players looking at you with slanted eyes." Anthony fights back with words.

Tay accepts the edible floral arrangement. Anthony's thoughtful gesture knocks on Tay's wall against the sound of his love. Tay checks with her chitachatter, there is nothing on the radio. She will listen to Anthony's love song.

"Are you the cartoonist of "Over the Heel?" Rhonda asks Anthony the suspense was killing her.

"Rhonda!" Sammy shouts

"I wanna know. Well, are you?" Rhonda inquires.

"Yes, I am. Are you a fan?"

"Absolutely, so is King!" Rhonda shouts.

"You ladies need ya own reality show. You just can't make this shit up." Chef Robert verbalizes his observation of the Sistahs.

The Sistahs laugh off Chef Robert's comment. Chef Robert return to the backyard to entertain the children and Kira.

"Ding Dong," sounds the door bell.

"Ma, it's the furniture guys." Calvin announces.

Tay shuffles to the door in her six inch heels. The furniture guys are dropping off assembly required furniture. Amber's two bedrooms condo doesn't have the space for building furniture. The furniture arrival marks the beginning of production.

"*Disparos a la hermana amar.* A piece of pie." Brooklyn repeats the Sistah's toast quote: "Shots to sister love"

Brooklyn illusion of making someone a pie in the sky a violent reward but there is no one the responsible for Melissa's misfortune.

A piece of cake." Tay toasts her glass.

"A piece of solitude." Sammy toasts her glass.

"A piece of mind." Chyenne toasts her glass.

"A piece of ass." Rhonda toasts her glass.

All the Sistah's constant piece of the song they sing is the solutions of problems being drinking down with a shot to out drown the concern for Melissa. The Sistahs start repackaging new glass cups, dishes and vases in bubble wrap. Anthony and King assemble the computer desk. Le'Roy and Teddy assemble the bookcases. Benny, Calvin, Dino, Miguel and Polo are loading up the rented moving truck with furniture ready for its new home. Amber, Camille and Cayne await the furniture to be place in their reserved space. Amber is over thrilled. The move represents her emancipation into adulthood and Cayne can have salvation in daylight from his mother's night street dreams. Rhonda carries a box of ready cargo to the rented truck. Her eye of sexiness catch a glimpse of King shirtless gladiator frame drilling wood under the spring sun's spinning air. The sight brings tears to her eye of sexiness. The eye is ready to kiss the King. Omar's police cruiser pulls up on the sidewalk, snapping

Rhonda out of fantasy. Everybody flew from what held their attention and was drawn to Omar's car. Everybody holds their breath awaiting words of Melissa to spill from Omar's lips.

"I still don't know anything about the baby and Melissa. She won't see me but I'm hanging in there." Omar cried out eyes spoke height volumes then his voice.

"But what's Melissa health status?" Marc asks

"She's physically a woman that just had a baby but the problem is her mental state. I'm just praying everything worked out. But I'm here on business. Upstate trooper found a dead body shot 69 times in the groin in a parked car by Timber Lake farm. He had your address in his GPS and this in his pocket." Omar reveals his business with a picture of the victim of the shooting.

Omar hands Tay a jewelry ring box. Tay slowly opens the ring box. The box has an inscription in the top of the box, it reads: *'Til the afterlife.* The written words poked at Tay's soft spot in her heart for Bryson.

"I can't believe Bryson is dead but this ring is vital. I'll wear it in his memory."

"Yup, he's dead alright. Next time you see him he'll be in a suit and tie laying in a pine box." Omar confirms.

"I can't believe he was at Timber Lake. I was just in Timber Lake last weekend. When did it happen?" Brooklyn questions

"May 25th, that's three days ago." Sammy questions.

"I can't believe you all care."

"Rhonda, he is still a human being." Chyenne states

"Oh, cry me a river. He's lucky that's all he got." Brooklyn agrees with Rhonda's careless attitude.

"Who's Bryson?" Omar puzzled eyes scans for an answer.

"Bryson is the man in the picture."

"The truth is the name of this man is Travis Morrison. He is wanted in LA for burning down the house of the woman who infected him with AIDS."

The news of Bryson was a tough glass of water to swallow with the pill of Melissa's state. Omar drives off but his words swims in the air. The oppressive cloud lingers over Tay's house. Everybody returned to their project. Everybody packed tape and haul boxes until they were finish. They all moved in silence, even the children played at a very low frequency. In a matter of a few hours everything was out of Tay's house and into Amber's apartment. For their hard work Amber treated them to a home cook meal with a dash of Marc's spice and a surprise Mildred ingredient in her new condo apartment. Everybody ate in silence but their mind was blowing nowhere fast. Their thoughts are wrapped in Melissa's vapors. The fumes of tender passion gasses forming in the atmosphere wasn't something liquid or solid but was felt by every human's heart at the dining room table. The heavy hazy of dispirit steals the joy of the sunny spring day. Dessert artistically constructed by Chef Robert is delicious. The savory dessert sweetens the taste buds, forcing words to cause laughter to push the clouds out the way of the sun. From Amber modern design deluxe two floor condo apartment on the upper west side of Harlem everybody parted ways with an ancestral sentimental warmhearted prayer from Mildred's Christian lips. In the pure sunlight Mildred's borrowed words are rooted from heaven. The Sistahs are the last to leave. They supported their extended family with a hugs and tears of a brighter day.

"A piece of cake." Tay wishes life was just that easy.

"A piece of solitude." Is what Sammy needs. The combination of the emotional disaster and the warm day had her exhausted.

"A piece of mind." Chyenne voices as she hop her hopes in yellow cab heading home.

"A piece of pie." Brooklyn illusion of making someone a pie in the sky a violent reward but there is no one the responsible for Melissa's misfortune.

"A piece of ass." Rhonda's sexual sensitivity over powered her emotional anxiety.

****

Tay pulls her car into her parking spot in front of her cherry brick house. Anthony is at Tay's side. Tay turns her attention to sound of burning rubber. Before Tay could focus her eyes on the screeching car tires, a pot of boiling hot water becomes the center of attraction on her skin. The scorching water liquefies her cappuccino skin off the right side of her face. The tropical red flesh blistery exposed on her shoulder and arm. The sizzling feeling burns deeper than Tay's skin.

"NOW WE EVEN BITCH! YOU BURNT ME FOR LIFE AND I BURNT YOU'R ASS FOR LIFE." Roc's icy voice slings chilling words out the passenger's side window of his cranberry colored BMW X6.

Roc's frosty words have Anthony's body in a frozen stance. Anthony's shaky hands dial for assistances. Anthony stays at Tay's sizzling right side of face, shoulder and arm. The sight of fierier third degree assault of criminal bodily harm stains Anthony's heart. The Sistahs red eyes sirens greets to ambulances at the hospital's entrance.

"When the skies are grey and all the doors are closing, You'll find him next to me."

**Next to me
Emeli Sande
Our Version of Events**

Mary, Mason, Marc, Melissa, Melissa's nursing aid, Omar, Camille, Nico, Calvin, Amber, April seats in the front pew directly facing the prophet. Mildred sits with pride and honor in the prophet besides her husband, Reverend Michael Jacobs. Melissa's nursing aid stands by with bandages to heal the pieces of the broken essential essences of a woman. Melissa's bursts of verbal tears of pain cripples the bodies feeling the pews behind her. She has lost her head. Everyone watching has cast away into her visible falls to rising pressure on the heart of lost loved one. Her breathtaking sight collapses several times. Omar offers a hand to stop the tears from pouring. Melissa's sounds makes is it hard to see to everyone around the tearful ears. In the pew behind immediate family sits the extended family, the Sistahs. Chyenne, Brooklyn, Rhonda and Sammy sits with the end has come in their hearts and the buildings of understanding falls down fast. Four days ago on Sunday night at ten thirty p.m. Prince Mecca was pronounced a heavenly angel.

"I am not going to sermon your ears off; I can hear the affliction in the air. I know it's troublesome to forfeit a precious little angel. I know you can't comprehend the Act of God but he is trying to tell all of us something right now. I want everybody in here to seize this moment of silence to apprehend the message. Don't go where the rest go! You won't ever find the message in a drink under tables or in the roll of dice. You won't ever find the message staying out 'til three in the morning. You won't ever find the message in the arms of another woman by being unfaithful. When all your money is spent and all my friends have vanished and you can't afford to find help or love for free the message will be found. You won't find the message in greed of fame, money, or power. These are promises the devil offers. But you will catch the message in you. Use the silence sunshine to understanding. He is trying to tell all of us something right now. I know it feels like salt in your soil of solid understanding. I know what it feels like when pain has dried up all your sea of faith. I ask you to just listen; I promise you there's a message! I can't give it to you because each message is uniquely designed. So open up your ears to your heart and receive the message in the silence." Reverend Michael Jacobs speaks and sits as the tears rolls down his cheeks. He also sits and absorbs the silences as he has directed the full pews to do.

Chyenne's brain receives the message like he was talking and sitting next to her. She will use the wisdom from her past to proceed to her future. She shall never forget but she will lighten the load with forgiveness. She shall be given a piece of mind. Brooklyn's memo against her violence rides is alongside her. The whisper in her ear mentions her pie of motherhood. She has been eating up the piece of seeing Miguel face, not Carlito's eyes, nose and chin. She is willing to indulge in the pieces of pie love from Le'Roy, while remaining true to self and nourishing the piece of motherhood with EPMD. Rhonda's heart is the nearest voice. Rhonda's heart tells the tale of finding a soul mate. This is news to Rhonda. She was clear to herself about not having a relationship but has been dazed by design from the higher ups. She's been granted a permanent piece of ass. Sammy's solitude is reported. Her mind makes vacancies the thought of mothering others from her head. She has freed her attention to focus on the ball player. Immediately coming into the space is stirring her emotional emptiness filled with communicative demonstration of love. After everyone has endured their limit of tolerance they flee from the darkness of sorrow. The message travels to the intensive care burn unit to Tay's torturous wounds. Anthony sit at next to her assuring her beauty wasn't scalded off. Anthony's eyes sees pass Tay's promiscuous pass and her permanent health issue. His vision goes deeper than the scars on her skin to her heart. The heart of Tay holds his love. Tay is enlightened by the version of back to back life lessons. The events are many things but a piece of cake forever changing Tay naïve charm to wise charisma. At the door of the church Crystal stands with two

CRESHIE WRITES

uniform police officers pointing out Chyenne. Chyenne is arrested for crazy gluing Crystal's lips shut with her fist. Crystal's message was received from Chyenne's fist. Crystal lost a tooth but received the message of gained humbleness. Chyenne serve three months in a mental stabilizing faculty. White lies in white pills are surrounded by white wall in white clothes is an atmosphere Chyenne is no stranger too.

To be continued...

Look forward to more books from Creshie:

Brooklyn Cruz January 2014
Chitachatter II Summer 2014
Four singers, one Mic 2015

www.ingramcontent.com/pod-product-compliance
Lightning Source LLC
Chambersburg PA
CBHW051446260626
47162CB00001B/272